DOMENICA DE ROSA

One Summer in Tuscany

Quercus

First published in Great Britain as *Summer School* in 2008 by Headline Review
This edition published in 2017 by

Quercus Editions Ltd
Carmelite House
50 Victoria Embankment
London EC4Y 0DZ

An Hachette UK company

A CIP catalogue record for this book is available
from the British Library

PB ISBN 978 1 78648 437 6

10 9 8 7 6 5 4 3 2 1

Typeset by CC Book Production

Printed and bound in Great Britain by Clays Ltd, St Ives plc

For Alex and Juliet

CHAPTER 1

Preparations

31 July

Patricia O'Hara, also known as Signora O'Hara, also known as Patrizia, also known as the Englishwoman from the Castello, pushes her damp hair away from her face and tries to concentrate on her list. Although the kitchen is cool, the heat outside is so intense that it seems to be pressing against the windows. Her writing, very black against the white paper, pulsates unpleasantly on the page.

To Do
Tell Aldo re aubergines
Towels in yellow room
Swimming pool cleaning – Matt?

She pauses, sighing. The question mark next to her teenage son's name seems significant, even ominous. These days so much of her relationship with him seems to be taken up with questions: Where are you going? When will you be back? Who with? How much? Did you take precautions? As his answer to these enquiries is invariably a grunt (if she is lucky) or a torrent of surprisingly eloquent abuse, it is no wonder that the question marks themselves seem to float, phantasm-like, around the head of her sixteen-year-old son. In fact, they can be distilled fairly simply: What are you doing and who are you doing it with? She thinks she knows the answer to the second question. Matt has unerringly bonded with the only two teenage delinquents in San Severino. While most local Italian boys are having Sunday lunch with their parents and putting flowers on the graves of their *bisnonni*, Graziano and Elio are tearing around on their motorbikes, taking drugs and attending heavy metal concerts in Milan. And these two have to become Matt's closest friends! His 'posse' as he once, without a trace of irony, described it. 'Three boys don't make a posse,' she had protested. But Matt, losing patience with her utter embarrassing stupidity, had already left the room.

Even the aubergines present a different, though less agonising, problem. Aldo, her chef, is an expert at cooking aubergines, *melanzane* in Italian: drizzling them with oil and salt and cooking them on the barbecue, slicing them thinly for pasta sauce, roasting them with tomatoes and *parmigiano* for a perfect light lunch. But, this year, one of her guests, Catherine Ferris-Merry from Brighton, has announced that she is 'allergic to aubergines'. Patricia sighs again, pressing her hands against the cool marble top of the cutting board. Although seventy-five, Aldo is still known as the best chef in this part of Tuscany, but he is a man of dogmatic views, no less inflexible for being delivered with twinkling eyes and a charming, crooked smile. In particular, Aldo does not believe in allergies or food intolerances. He does not believe in veganism, no-carb diets or in keeping kosher. *Non esiste,* he will say, smiling sweetly, chopping onions with a gleaming *mezzaluna. Non esiste,* he will say, while serving pork simmered in milk for a visiting rabbi.

But Catherine Ferris-Merry most definitely does exist and she has paid 3000 euros (excluding flight) for a two-week creative writing course, set in the beautiful Tuscan countryside, eating delicious meals cooked by our charming local chef, and if she doesn't like aubergines she shouldn't bloody well have to eat them.

Next to her 'To do' list she has a printed list of this summer's residents. She studies it, although after several weeks' feverish planning, she knows it almost by heart.

Name: Catherine Ferris-Merry
Age: 39
Profession: copywriting consultant and mum
Resident in: Brighton
Allergies: aubergines, mushrooms, caffeine, non-gluten-
   free bread and I can't eat too much dairy or I swell up!
Reasons for coming on course: To release the writer I
   know is inside me!

Name: Anna Valore
Age: 38
Profession: full-time mother
Resident in: Brighton
Allergies: none
Reasons for coming on course: My friend Cat suggested
    it and I thought – why not?

Name: Sam McCluskie
Age: 44
Profession: ex-broker, now unemployed
Resident in: London
Allergies: none
Reasons for coming on course: To write a bestseller

Name: Sally Hamilton
Age: 50ish
Profession: landscape gardener
Resident in: Salisbury
Allergies: nuts
Reasons for coming on course: I've attended all Jeremy's
    courses – to me, he is Creative Writing

Name: Mary McMahon
Age: 74
Profession: ex-civil servant
Resident in: London

Allergies: none

Reasons for coming on course: To visit Tuscany and to
   try to make some progress with my writing

Name: Jean-Pierre Charbonneau

Age: 45

Profession: lawyer

Resident in: Paris

Allergies: Italian wine

Reasons for coming on course: To hone my writing skills

Name: Dorothy Van Elsten

Age: 61

Profession: home-maker

Resident in: Vermont, USA

Allergies: nuts, seafood, red meat

Reasons for coming on course: To find closure through
   writing about my childhood

Looking at Dorothy Van Elsten's admittedly impressive allergies, Patricia feels none of the irritation that she does at
Catherine Ferris-Merry's. Maybe, she thinks honestly, this is
because she has seen from their photographs that Catherine
is dark and stunningly beautiful whilst Dorothy is grey-haired
and motherly. Moreover, Catherine is only five years younger
than she is. Also, Dorothy is American and maybe she expects
Americans to have allergies and to talk about 'closure'. But,

deep down, she knows it is because Dorothy is bringing with her a husband, Rick. Dorothy only describes him, tantalisingly, as a businessman 'in the oil trade', and Patricia has secretly decided he is a benevolent multimillionaire who will invest in Castello della Luna and save her from bankruptcy. If that is the case, she tells herself, she will ignore Aldo's flat stare of disbelief and ban shellfish from the Castello for ever.

Unable to bear the list any longer, Patricia stands up and prepares to go in search of towels for the yellow room. Two young girls, Croatians, are here to help her with 'changeover day' but they are busy making beds and cleaning out shower rooms. Besides, though lovely girls, their English (and Italian) is very limited and it would probably take her half an hour to describe what she wants. She thinks she has seen the missing towels in the pool house where some recent resident must have taken them (in defiance of house rules).

As she steps outside the back door, she is temporarily blinded by white light. It is twelve o'clock and the sun is at its hottest. Although Patricia is only a wearing a light, sleeveless dress, she is immediately pouring with sweat; it trickles unpleasantly down her back as she takes the winding path down to the swimming pool.

The Castello della Luna is built into the side of the hill. From the front it looks low and squat, too small for the impressive driveway lined with umbrella pines, but from the back it cascades down the hillside, terrace after terrace overflowing with bougainvillea, ivy and wild roses. It is a genuine small castle, built in the thirteenth century, and restored in the nineteenth. The previous owners added ten of the fifteen bathrooms and built a swimming pool on the lowest terrace. Patricia and her husband Sean, falling in love at their first sight of the house ten years ago, converted it into a gracious shell of its former self, designed to accommodate up to twenty guests at a time. The effort was too much for their marriage – they divorced three years ago – but Patricia is still here, running courses which are heavy on the adjectives ('romantic', 'inspiring', 'gorgeous', 'heart-stopping', 'authentic') and light on the detail of what the guests will actually *do* when they reach their romantic, inspiring, etc. location.

The path to the swimming pool is overgrown with lavender. Mindlessly, Patricia presses a flower between thumb and forefinger and inhales the heady, spicy scent. In their bedrooms, the guests will find fresh lavender in the drawers and a single flower resting delicately on their welcome pack. She bets Catherine will be allergic to it.

In the pool house, she finds the yellow towels, thrown into a negligent pile beneath the sunloungers and, by the pool, she finds Myra Hamdi, stretched out on a sunbed.

Myra attended one of Patricia's first courses ('Finding Your Inner Artist') and has become a friend. She now comes every summer and, in return for a free holiday, teaches yoga and relaxation techniques as well as helping Patricia to entertain the guests. This last is most important as Patricia, though meticulously organised and always civil, is not good at the softer stuff: the chatting, the cosy confidences, the 'oh that happened to me, I know just how you feel'. Myra, on the other hand, is passionately interested in people and actually seems to enjoy talking about the guests' friends and family and why they have inexplicably failed to become famous. Tomorrow she will be on hand to greet, soothe and charm the aspiring writers; now, though, she lies in the sun, slim, oiled and serene.

'I hope you've got factor forty on,' says Patricia, pausing to dip a toe into the water, so shiningly blue as to appear solid, like paint.

'Sure, hon,' says Myra without opening her eyes.

'Have you seen Matt? I want him to clear the leaves out of the pool.'

Myra opens her eyes, small, shiny and dark. All her movements are clean and sharp, like a bird's.

'I think he went out on his bike.'

'In this heat!'

'Kids don't feel the heat like we do,' says Myra, who could happily lie in the sun all day like a lizard.

'He's not a kid,' says Patricia, feeling unreasonably angry. 'He's sixteen. And he promised to help.'

'Isn't the new handyman starting today?'

'He's not coming until three. And I don't know what he'll be like. The agency might send another halfwit like last year.'

'I liked last year's guy.'

'Myra, he had sex with one of the lilos.'

Myra laughs, stretching out on the sunbed. 'I'm sure they'll be very happy together. You worry too much. I'll clean the pool. No sweat.'

Which is, reflects Patricia as she stumps back up the path after gratefully accepting Myra's offer, the most inappropriate phrase for Tuscany in summer.

Matt O'Hara, also known at Matteo, or Mattino, also known as Lupo (the wolf) and sometimes known to his mother as Matthew, stretches out in the long grass at the bottom of the hill. Next to him, his motorbike lies on its side, still vibrating gently. If he keeps very still, he can just about hear, above the din of the crickets, the sounds of the Castello being prepared for tomorrow's guests. The mosquito whine of Aldo's Vespa as it negotiates the steep turn into the drive, the hiss of the water sprinklers on the lawn and, furthest away of all, his mother's voice giving orders.

She's good at giving orders. She does all the stuff he once saw in a programme about assertiveness. She says things calmly, allocates priorities, gives people the chance to think that they had the idea first, and she never, ever forgets to say thank you. It's just, it's all so *false*. He prefers Dad's way of forgetting about things until the last minute and then getting into a flap and losing his temper. At least that's real. At least it doesn't make you feel as if you've failed him in some small but no less significant way. In fact, while he's in the flap, Dad is so touchingly grateful for any help that you end up feeling pretty good about yourself. He remembers when Dad managed to lose his return plane ticket in the summer; he was so impressed with Matt ordering a new ticket online that he took them both out for an Indian meal with a bottle of wine. And, even when Dad eventually found the first ticket, in the pocket of his just-washed jeans, it didn't really matter. They had still had the meal.

Mum never loses things. She has her lists (Item 1: interfere in every aspect of Matt's life), her calendar with the days neatly crossed out, her itinerary for every second of these awful courses and her iPhone, like a shiny support blanket, always at her side. And, if she ever did lose anything, she would immediately and efficiently form a search party. 'Matt, you take upstairs. Myra, you start downstairs. Aldo, you do the kitchens.' His mother, he reflects gloomily, is very good at delegating.

It wasn't always like this. Matt likes to annoy his mother by pretending that he can't remember anything that happened before his tenth birthday. ('What was the point of me giving you all those *experiences*,' she would wail, 'if you can't remember any of them?') But in fact he can remember when they first came to Italy. He was six and he remembers living in a flat in Sinalunga: the market with live chickens in cages, the children's playground where you could get pony rides on a tiny, bad-tempered Shetland, the lift which had glass doors and a padded, velvet seat. He remembers when they first came to live at the Castello, camping out in three rooms while various impassive workmen pulled up floorboards and festooned the ceilings with multicoloured wires.

Then it had been wonderful, like paradise. He remembers finding a porcupine in the woods, as big as a small dog. He remembers Christmas, with a tree that seemed to touch the sky and funny, chestnutty cakes. He remembers the snow and sledging with Dad right down to the bottom of the hill, his mother running beside them, her laughter steaming out behind her in the cold air.

It all changed when the first guests came. Then, the Castello wasn't paradise any more. It was neat and packaged and run exclusively for others. Dad adopted a new walk, he remembers, legs slightly bent, head deferentially on one side, as he carried cases and listened to endless complaints about the air conditioning, the food, the heat (they were in Italy in August, for God's sake!), the lack of proper English tea. That was when his mother got good at orders. 'Sean, the towel rail isn't working in the Blue Room. Matt, can you run and get *The Times* for Mr Lessiter? Aldo, little less garlic in the bruschette, please.' He wasn't a fool. He could see that his father started to perfect a technique of hiding from the guests. He had a variety of hiding places: the woodshed at the end of the drive, the room next to the kitchen where Aldo kept his homemade wine, the loo that the guests didn't use, the one with the cracked wooden seat (Dad would disappear in there for ages on the day that the *Guardian* came from England). Matt could see that his mother ended up doing most of the work. He could see that his father wasn't exactly supporting her, hiding in the woodshed while she talked to some boring bastard about watercolours for hours. It was just that, when his father left, the Castello wasn't fun any more. It wasn't their home. It was just a business.

And the guests themselves! Matt likes to think of himself as fairly tolerant (whatever his mother says) but, Jesus Christ, the types who come to stay at the Castello would drive Mother Teresa to murder. What sort of person spends thousands of pounds going to some old house in the country and having *lessons*? If he had thousands of pounds, he'd buy a new motorbike and go round the world or something. He certainly wouldn't sit about on a terrace, drinking wine and talking about the light. (What is it about the light anyway? Everywhere has light. You'd think they all lived in the bottom of a mine or something the way they ponce about all the time saying, 'Ooh the light!' Get over it!)

The writers are the very worst. At least the painters are sometimes quite a laugh. There was that year when a load of them got drunk and had an orgy (at least that's what he suspects from listening to Mum and Myra talking, they wouldn't tell *him*, of course). But only last year there was that brilliant etchings guy who drank a bottle of grappa every night and kept talking about sex (everything set him off, from *prosciutto melone* to the pistons on Matt's motorbike). But the writers – all they want to do is sit around and moan about what hard work it is to write books. Hard work! It's not as if they're builders or bricklayers or WWF wrestlers. They just type words and read them aloud in stupid, pretentious voices and complain about publishers ('They only want the obvious books. They only want bestsellers.' Well – duh!). And he's noticed that not a single one is ever really interested in anyone else. They ask about each other's books but they all have this glazed look like they're just waiting for the moment to talk about themselves again. And if anyone does seem interested in their writing, they go all twitchy as if that person's trying to steal their ideas. A few of them try to talk to him but he can tell it's only because they fancy the idea of having a teenage boy in one of their novels. *The Catcher in the Rye*'s got a lot to answer for.

And the tutor, Jeremy, is a complete tosser. Mum says he's a great writer but Matt has Googled him and he's only written a few books and the last one was years ago. OK, there was lots of stuff about how this last book was amazing, life-changing, masterful and all that crap, but the fact remains that he hasn't done anything for twenty years but ponce around telling other people how to write. And, guess what, he reckons that's hard work too. 'So draining,' he says every night, hiding from the guests in Mum's office. 'They want everything from me.' Well, that may be true as Matt once caught Jeremy and a woman guest having it off in the pool room but Jeremy didn't exactly seem to be complaining at the time. And, as for the woman, she *still* didn't get published so Jeremy can't be that good a teacher.

They all think they are going to write The Book, the one

that will sell millions and make them rich and famous. Well, excuse me, but hasn't J. K. Rowling already done that? (Slagging off Harry Potter is a favourite occupation of the guests.) And, anyway, they are not going to write The Book because Matt is going to do that. He's already halfway through but he's not going to show it to anyone. Least of all Jeremy.

Patricia's study is just off the main hall. Unlike the rest of the house, with its vaulted ceilings and expertly restored stonework, this room is unapologetically modern. Steel filing cabinets line the walls, the desk is vintage IKEA circa 1981 and adorned with a gleaming laptop, a notepad and an empty pesto jar full of pens (all working). There are no photographs and no pictures, unless you count the screensaver which shows Matt, aged ten, diving into the swimming pool. The water is so impossibly blue that sometimes it makes Patricia want to lick the screen. Now, though, she sits frowning at a document entitled 'creativewritingAug17'.

Patricia scrolls with an expert finger, one ear on the sounds in the hallway (where the girls are cleaning the stone floor).

Arrival
17.00–19.00 Guests arrive and settle in
19.30 Drinks and crostini on the terrace
20.30 Dinner in the Great Hall

The Great Hall is, in fact, one of the three drawing rooms but Great Hall sounds grander and it does have a wonderful view over the valley (the lights of Siena just visible in the distance). She will have to make sure there is orange juice as well as prosecco as there is always someone who doesn't drink. Was Jean-Pierre Charbonneau joking about Italian wine? She'll have to get in some Chablis just in case. She's damned if she's going to give him champagne. Just because Italy beat France in the World Cup.

Day 1
07.30 Meditation and stretch (optional)
08.00–09.30 Breakfast
10.00 Writing session
13.00 Lunch
Afternoon: Free writing time
18.00 Trip to San Severino

She has learnt from experience that it is better to schedule trips in the morning or early evening when the weather is cooler (memories of guests fainting in the piazza at Siena). She views the day trip to Rome (Day 3) with extreme trepidation, not least because Aldo is driving.

The afternoons are politely billed as 'writing time' but, in reality, most guests will sleep or relax by the pool. This is when Patricia will be at her most twitchy. She doesn't like the guests wandering aimlessly around the place. She likes them to be safely corralled: writing, eating or stretching. Someone is sure to venture down to the kitchen and question Aldo about his cooking techniques (to no avail as Aldo will, charmingly, pretend not to understand) or invade her study complaining about the lack of hypoallergenic pillows.

Day 2
07.30 Meditation and stretch (optional)
08.00–09.00 Breakfast
9.30–11.30 Trip to neighbouring vineyard

That should finish them for the day, she thinks with grim satisfaction. Anyone who is up for the afternoon's writing session after spending all morning tasting Gennaro's Chianti deserves the Booker Prize at the very least.

She stops because someone has entered the room. Not Myra or Matt or Aldo. Not Ratka or Marija but someone else, someone infinitely more graceful and self-contained. Someone, moreover, supremely sure of their welcome.

A large ginger cat strolls into the room and sits down in a patch of sunlight. The cat looks at Patricia. Patricia stares back.

'Ratka!' she calls. The blonde Croatian girl appears in the doorway.

'*Sì?*' she says guardedly.

'Where did this cat come from?' asks Patricia, in Italian.

'*Gatto?*' repeats Ratka blankly. The cat starts to lick its hindquarters.

16

'The cat.' Patricia points. 'Did you see it come in?'

'No,' says Ratka. 'We are working very hard.'

'Could you possibly take it outside?' asks Patricia. 'I'm allergic to cats.'

As she says this she thinks, uneasily, of Catherine Ferris-Merry. Am I really allergic to cats? She wonders. Sean had a cat when they first met and it had certainly made her sneeze. But it was really the cat's habit of sitting on Sean's chest and gazing lovingly into his eyes that had made her suggest that maybe it might be kinder to think of re-homing . . .

Wordlessly, Ratka scoops up the cat (it is almost too big to fit in her arms) and backs out of the room. Patricia goes back to her itinerary.

In the kitchen, Aldo is slicing onions and parsley. His *mezzaluna*, a gleaming, scimitar-like knife, flashes to and fro across the marble chopping board. He is making *polpettine* (meatballs) for tomorrow. Nearby is a bowl containing pork and beef mince, breadcrumbs and grated cheese. He will add the onions and parsley, stir in an egg, and create the perfect meatballs, to be simmered gently in tomorrow's *sugo*. He has already made the *sugo* (it is all the better for spending a night resting in the fridge) and cooked the *peperonata* (sautéed peppers, garlic and tomatoes). He hums tunelessly as he works. The radio is on (news of a kidnapping in Modena, a forest fire in Naples and a showbiz wedding near Lake Como) but Aldo is oblivious. As long as he is cooking, he is happy.

The kitchen is Aldo's lair, although Patricia is grudgingly allowed in to make meals for herself and Matt. It is a medieval room, at the lowest level of the house: thick stone walls, giant fireplace, scrubbed wooden table, an uncomfortable high-backed settle, herbs hanging from the rafters. Although it also boasts a high-tech cooking range and an American-style fridge, the kitchen still looks as if it might have been used by cooks preparing a welcome-home feast for the lord of the manor (an impression heightened when Aldo has game hanging from the ceiling). Patricia often thinks it is a pity that the guests can't see it (this is, of course, impossible).

The door to the kitchen garden is open and Aldo, without looking up, says, '*Ciao,* Mattino.'

The light motes in the doorway rearrange themselves into Matt, very hot and sweaty, motorcycle helmet in hand.

'Where is she?' asks Matt.

'Upstairs,' says Aldo. 'You are safe.'

Matt sighs deeply and sits down. He trusts Aldo, whom he has known since he was eight. For Aldo's part, the presence of Matt is some consolation for the loss of his daughter (and grandson) who emigrated to Australia five years ago.

Matt reaches into the American-style fridge and brings out a bottle of water. He drinks deeply.

'Too much water is bad for you,' says Aldo, a superstition he clings to.

Matt grunts. 'Everything nice is bad for you.' He picks up a dried fennel flower and sniffs it.

'*Finocchio*,' he grins. 'Just right for Jeremy.'

Aldo laughs, showing surprisingly white teeth. *Finocchio*, or fennel, is Italian slang for a homosexual. Both he and Matt continue to believe, despite substantial evidence to the contrary, that Jeremy is gay.

'*Patate al finocchio*,' says Aldo. 'To go with the *polpettine*.'

Matt groans. 'If you cook them all this good stuff, they'll never go away. What's wrong with giving them a McDonald's or something?'

Aldo smiles but, deep down, he does not approve of the M word being used in his kitchen. He still has nightmares about the American guest who put ketchup (brought over in his own suitcase, naturally) on his spaghetti carbonara.

Three o'clock. Matt is in the shower, hoping his mother can't hear the water gushing out of the drainpipe. Aldo is putting labels on his wine. Patricia is doing the accounts, head in hands. Myra is asleep by the, now pristine, pool and the cat is asleep on the roof.

The Castello, too, is sleeping. The clock ticks heavily in the hallway, a solitary fly buzzes high in the rafters, Aldo's radio sounds like a voice from another world. Patricia, therefore, is thoroughly startled when her nightmare of incomings versus outgoings is interrupted by a knock on the front door.

For one lunatic minute she thinks it is the cat, come back to demand bed and breakfast. She shakes herself impatiently. It is just that, guests apart, no one really uses the front door or the heavy lion-headed knocker.

Barefooted, Patricia pads across the baronial entrance hall (complete with armour). She flings open the massive, studded door to reveal, standing in the golden afternoon sunlight, easily the most beautiful man she has ever seen.

'*Buona sera*,' says the apparition. 'I am Fabio. I have come about the handyman job.'

Cat's blog www.whatsnewpussycat.com 31.07.07

Well, folks, I've finally done it! Signed up to a creative writing course. I've been thinking about it for some time. People have very kindly said that my ramblings on this page deserve to be published. 'Better than Bridget Jones,' said someone (not a relation). 'Your Yummy Mummy diaries would be an instant bestseller,' said someone else (also not a relation – honest!). Well, I don't know about that but I do know that writing has become something I absolutely *have* to do. You know: get up, do yoga, make children's lunch boxes (because Useless Husband has no idea what they like and actually once gave cheese to my dairy-allergic daughter), do school run (often still in my pyjamas – OK, they are the silk ones from Boden, but still!), come back, get house ready for Edna (is there anyone out there who *doesn't* tidy up for their cleaning lady?), write, write, write.

Sometimes Useless Husband will come home and ask what's for dinner and I'll say, 'I've no idea, I've been writing all day.'

And he'll laugh and take me out for a meal at the new brasserie in St James's Street. Honestly! Anything to get out of cooking himself. In fact it was UH himself who suggested that I come on this course. 'You deserve it,' he said. And frankly, guys, I do and so do all you hard-working mums out there! Two weeks in Tuscany with like-minded people, learning how to make my writing better and more commercial. Seriously, I don't think that just because I read English at Cambridge I know everything there is to know about writing. Far from it! I may be more advanced than some people on the course but I am sure there will be others that I can learn from. Remember, you can learn from anybody, folks! Really, some of the things that Edna says! She's the one who should write a book (sadly, though, she's almost illiterate, finds it almost impossible to write me a note about buying more washing powder).

So, tomorrow I'm off! With my bessy mate Anna in tow, I'm off for a fortnight in the Tuscan sun, staying in a medieval castle of all things! The tutor is Jeremy Bullen, author of *Belly Flop* (which was made into a film starring the wonderful Bill Nighy), so I'm really looking forward to meeting him. I'm looking forward to all of it. Of course, I worry about leaving Sasha and Star with UH but I think the experience will be good for all three of them! And my own Yummy Mummy (seventy years young) will be on hand to help so it won't be that bad. Anyway, it's about time UH learnt what real life is like – away from that corporate womb he calls work.

Tuscany – here I come!

CHAPTER 2

Travelling

1 August

Anna Valore stands helplessly before the 'Summer Reads' shelf at W.H. Smith, Gatwick airport. What does someone buy to read on a creative writing course? Nothing too obvious – she shies away from a raft of books featuring Tuscan farmhouses, olive trees and artfully arranged Chianti bottles. Nothing too lowbrow – regretfully she puts down a book offering, in shiny silver letters, to tell her the 'true secrets of a woman's heart'. Nothing too highbrow – she wants to enjoy herself, after all. Maybe something by Anne Tyler. Didn't someone call her the best writer in the English language? And she has proper characters, not amusing types with names that mean something else, or depressing Bolivian child molesters. Cat sashays across the shop and Anna notices, without surprise, that she has made the perfect book choices. Something witty but light, something classical (she can tell by the spine) and something by someone Italian. Why didn't she think of that? Now is the time to catch up on Italian authors like . . . Her mind goes blank. Is Franco Zeffirelli an author or a film director? And isn't Lampedusa a type of wine?

Cat looks exactly right too. She is wearing black jeans, a skinny white T-shirt and has a black hoodie tied loosely round her waist. Anna, in blue jeans and trainers, feels scruffy and fat. Her jacket is far too hot but it was cold when they left Brighton that morning. Of course Cat had simply snuggled into her hot pink pashmina, now stowed away in her bag, while Anna had shivered in her coat. Not even a coat, almost an *anorak*.

'Oh, I've read that,' says Cat, pointing at the Anne Tyler book. 'It's great.'

'Honestly, Cat,' sighs Anna. 'Is there anything you haven't read? It's very dispiriting for the rest of us.'

'Sorry!' Cat gives her a quick, one-armed hug. 'I'll go and get us a cappuccino from Starbucks, shall I? We've got heaps of time before the plane.'

I'd hate Cat if she wasn't so nice, thinks Anna as she moves slowly along the bookshelves in search of *Captain Corelli's Mandolin*.

In another airport bookshop Jeremy Bullen searches grimly along the Bs. He has a particular hatred for authors who come before and after him in the alphabet. Maeve Binchy, William Boyd, Emily Brontë, Bill Bryson, Dan Brown. Bloody

Dan Brown! Two whole shelves of the sodding *Da Vinci Code*. Ah, there it is. *Belly Flop* by Jeremy Bullen. Two miserly copies! He takes out the book and strokes it lovingly. 'A masterpiece,' screams the jacket quote. 'A remarkable book,' agrees the critic on the back. Despite knowing that these glowing recommendations were written over twenty years ago, Jeremy is soothed. After all, he reasons, putting the book back, face out, on the shelf, maybe there are only two copies *left*. Maybe people have bought all the rest.

Mary McMahon made her reading choice weeks ago. She took two books out of the library (*Captain Corelli* and a history of Tuscany) and ordered another from her book club. It is a lavishly illustrated book combining a story of house-hunting, unreliable Italian workmen and gorgeous sunsets with authentic Tuscan recipes. Mary loves cooking or, to be strictly accurate, she loves eating. Living on her own, she would feel silly cooking *risotto con calamari e pomodoro*. She doesn't mind eating it if someone else cooks it, though, and as Italian chefs are rather thin on the ground in Streatham, the next best thing is reading about it.

Mary has, in fact, had everything ready for over a month. Her taxi is booked (an expense but she really wouldn't fancy the train at that hour), her bag is packed, she has even, for the first time in her life, bought suntan lotion. She worried a little about the factor, the girl in the shop said forty for fair skin but she feels as if she'd like to get a *little* tan, it always makes the young people look so healthy. So she has compromised on thirty-five. The brochure said there was a pool and she has brought two costumes, so one can be drying while she wears the other. Mary loves to swim. Twice a week, she goes to the baths at Tooting and ploughs up and down with her surprisingly muscular front crawl. A few years ago, she had a group of like-minded elderly swimming friends and they would go for a cup of coffee and a piece of cake after their swim (extraordinary how hungry swimming makes you). But, one by one, the swimmers had left London, to go into homes or bungalows by the sea. She still gets Christmas cards from Joan in Eastbourne and Shirley in Southport but now she swims alone.

To Mary, it seems unbelievable that she is over seventy ('Seventy-four.' She practises saying it to herself so that she can get used to it). Maybe if you have a family, children and grandchildren, the years get parcelled out neatly: birthdays, weddings, christenings, anniversaries. But, if you are on your own, there is so little to distinguish one year from the next that it is a shock to realise that suddenly time has caught up with you and there you are, old, but disturbingly feeling exactly the same as you did when you were eighteen.

When she cuts through the chlorine-heavy water at the pool, it feels exactly the same against her arms as it did when she was a schoolgirl, on holiday in Brighton, wearing a skirted bathing costume and trying to swim out as far as the boys. Once she'd swum between the piers for charity. She won a silver rose bowl; she's still got it somewhere. That year she kissed Bobby Preston at Sherry's and she'd thought, this is it, this is how it begins. Not that she'd wanted to marry Bobby or anything (he had a disconcertingly big Adam's apple, which wobbled as he spoke) but she'd thought this was the start of the whole cycle – kissing, courting, marriage, children, all that.

Except it hadn't been, she's not sure why. She'd always thought, maybe next year I'll meet someone, but it had just never happened. Sometimes she hears girls talking on the bus: 'Oh, I dumped him, I'm with Steve now.' 'Then I finished with Dave and went out with Tony.' 'Harry was my first husband, I'm with Terry now.' It never seems to occur to them that after Steve or Dave or Harry there might just not be anyone else. There might come a time when they just don't meet any more men, not men who are interested in them anyway.

Why had it happened to her? She had been pretty when she was young. 'A real English rose,' her dad used to say, which she didn't like because she knew it referred to her pale skin and pink cheeks. But one of Dad's workmen had once given her a rose and said that it cheered him up to look at her. Dad had been furious and had wanted to sack the man but Mum had said, 'Let him be, a girl's got to have admirers.' Admirers! If only. Here she is, seventy-four years old, unmarried and hardly ever been kissed (there had only been two after Bobby, both unsatisfactory in their own ways).

Maybe it was her job. Mary was clever, got into grammar

school and then passed the exam for the civil service. She'd risen high, too, higher than most women (but, of course, she hadn't had to interrupt her career to have children). She'd travelled, mostly in England, but once, thrillingly, to America. She'd had an office of her own, a secretary, could have had a company car but she'd never got round to learning to drive. It was just that, somehow, she'd got to the point when they were giving her three cheers and wishing her a happy retirement and she'd thought, is this it?

Oh, she'd met men: people's brothers, cousins and friends. There had been men at work too. She'd got on well with some of them; she wasn't shy and people sometimes said that she was witty. It was just that, somehow, she'd never got beyond the chat-at-the-party stage. It was as if everyone else knew the password that would turn an acquaintance into a boyfriend and she didn't. And, eventually (later than you would think, though), she'd had to accept that it wasn't going to happen to her.

She is not unhappy. She has enough money (the civil service pension is very good), she has a nice flat in a mansion block, she has friends (though they are disappearing at a rather alarming rate) and she has her writing. She has kept a diary since she was a teenager and, for years now, she's been trying to write a book. Goodness knows why, she doesn't know anyone else who writes, but it's just something she enjoys. She'd never really thought of getting it published until, one day, she'd heard her great-niece say, casually, 'After my gap

year, I might write a book.' 'Write a book?' Mary had quer-
ied. 'Do you want to be a writer then?' She'd thought Caitlin
wanted to be a doctor but she'd never been that close to her
sister's children or grandchildren. 'Oh no,' Caitlin had replied.
'But I might just write one book, about my travels, you know?'

That did it. If Caitlin, who finished every sentence with a
question mark and didn't know that, in the *book*, Mr Darcy
didn't go swimming in his frilly white shirt, if Caitlin was
going to write a book then she, Mary, who has been writing
hers since she was thirty, was going to get hers published.
She was not going to let another thing just not happen to her.

Anna and Cat sit in the departure hall, poised for take-off.
Their flight must surely be the next to be called (all the ones
above it have gate numbers next to them) and they clasp coats
and bags and books, ready to move as soon as their own magic
number appears. Anna's Steve is a real worrier about planes.
He would have insisted that Anna and the children stand
next to him in front of the departures board. As soon as their
number came up, he would have raced them down corridors
and along moving staircases so as to be the first at the gate.
'Why?' Anna always asked. 'There's no prize for being first.
We'll only have to wait again when we get there.' But now,
with no Steve scurrying ahead of her, bowed down with hand
luggage (he always carries everything himself), she feels a little
lost. She's glad Cat is there. Cat is always travelling, casually
mentioning at the school gate that she has been to New York

for the weekend, going to Paris for Christmas shopping, taking the kids to Disneyland Florida every holiday. Of course, Cat's husband, Justin, is very well off, he runs his own company and drives cars that make Steve breathe heavily and stomp off to the computer so that he can prove they are a bad investment as well as being terrible for the environment. But Cat never shows off about money. She's always talking about how good the clothes are at Asda (though she doesn't wear them herself, Anna notices) and about buying toys at jumble sales. She's just an ordinary mum, she always says, though of course looking the way she does makes her out of the ordinary for a start . . .

'There it is!' Cat grabs her arm. 'Gate thirty. Let's go.'

Even without Steve striding ahead, Anna finds herself trotting to keep up with Cat's long yoga-toned legs. Why does Cat always make her feel like a small, fat child running to keep up? She's not fat, she knows. She put on some weight after Jake but she's still a size 12 in most shops. The problem is that Cat is a size 8 and she's had two children as well. That's how they met, at a toddler group. Anna was there with Tom. He was two and she was already pregnant with Jake and feeling sick all the time. Cat had Sasha running about and Star in the baby sling. Star must have been only ten months or so but Cat's figure, in artfully ripped blue jeans, was enough to make grown women cry. Perhaps that's why none of the other women seemed to be talking to her. Cat didn't appear to mind though. She talked to Sasha all the time, just as if he was grown-up ('Shall we go to the park this afternoon, Sash?

Or would you like to go to Starbucks for a babyccino?'). And, at snack time, instead of letting Sasha have squash and a biscuit like the other children, she had whipped out a plastic box of carrot sticks. Anna had been tremendously impressed, had been ashamed of Tom, wolfing down jammy dodgers like there was no tomorrow.

Why Cat chose her as a friend, Anna will never know. But, after that first excruciating singalong ('Row, row, row your boat', sitting on a splintery floor with twenty screaming children), Cat had turned to her with a wide smile and said, 'What about tea at my place? Organic fish cakes for the kids, glass of wine for us. What do you say?' Anna had said yes almost before Cat had finished speaking. And, despite the fact that Tom had spat out the organic fish cakes and that Cat's house made her feel physically sick with envy, they have remained friends. The children are at the same school (a Catholic primary, though Cat had to fudge the church-going a bit). Sasha and Star are slightly older than Tom and Jake but light years ahead in other ways. This doesn't bother Anna; she *expects* Sasha and Star to be cleverer, which is just as well really. Sasha can say hello in ten languages and, though he often misses school because of holidays and allergies, he was reading Harry Potter when Tom was struggling with Biff, Chip and Kipper. Star is a real little princess, does ballet and all that, always wearing something pink and sparkly. Sometimes she makes Anna wish she had a girl, which is maybe why Jake is always a bit naughty with Star. Cat was really nice about the time when he locked her in the playhouse . . .

Cat's cleverer than her too. Well, that's only to be expected; Cat went to Cambridge and Anna went to Anglia Polytechnic (it's a university now). Funny, because Steve thinks of her as a real intellectual just because she has any further education at all (he left school at sixteen) and because she's had a few short stories published. Honestly! He should read Cat's book, which is just brilliant and so funny. It's not Steve's sort of thing though, he only likes books about Hitler or the *Titanic.* She hopes that not everyone on the course will be *quite* as clever as Cat.

'Are there any others here, do you think?' says Cat, when they are finally sitting by the departure gate.

'Other whats?' asks Anna stupidly, trying to stuff her jacket into her shoulder bag. She's absolutely boiling after the trek along the corridors.

'Other people from the course,' says Cat, looking round at the grim rows of plastic chairs. 'This is the only flight to Pisa today. There might be other writers here.'

Anna follows Cat's gaze around the departure lounge. There are several families, the mothers slowly losing the fight between bribery and yelling, some young Italians, making more noise than you would have thought possible, a smug-looking businessman with a laptop and a couple of elderly ladies travelling alone.

'I wouldn't have thought so,' she says.

But, in fact, two other aspiring writers are on the plane. Mary has just rechecked her handbag (passport, purse, spare glasses, crossword book, pen, details about the course, Polos) and is now reading *Captain Corelli* with unseeing eyes. Her heart is thumping so hard she is surprised it hasn't set off the security alarm. It is ten years since she went on a plane (holidays are either spent with her sister in Norfolk or on the English coast) and she has never, ever done something as daring as this. Going to Tuscany on a creative writing course. Creative writing! It's almost like being a real author. She hopes her unfinished novel won't look too feeble compared to the brilliance of everyone else's work. 'Published and unpublished authors welcome,' said the brochure. What if everyone else is a published author? She's sure it said somewhere about not to worry what standard you're at. She gets the notes out to check.

'Excuse me?'

A woman is leaning towards her. She has bright red hair and is wearing a denim jacket but she doesn't look scarily young. She could be any age really.

'Are you going to the creative writing course? At Castello della Luna?'

'Yes,' says Mary shyly.

'That's wonderful! So am I.' The woman extends her hand. 'Sally Hamilton.'

'Mary McMahon.'

'McMahon. Are you Irish?'

'Well, my father was.'

'I love Irish people. I'm sure I've got an Irish soul.'

Mary doesn't quite know how to respond to this. Fortunately Sally does not wait for an answer.

'Have you been on any of his courses before?'

'Whose?'

'Jeremy Bullen's. He's the course leader. He is utterly brilliant.'

'He wrote *Belly Flop*, didn't he?' Mary looked this up before she left.

'Have you read it?'

'No,' Mary admits.

'It's amazing. Life-changing.' Sally Hamilton looks at her very intently. She has pale blue eyes ringed with black eyeliner. Mary smiles back nervously.

'Let's sit together on the plane,' says Sally. 'I have a feeling that we're going to be soul mates.'

CHAPTER 3

Mary's diary, 1 August

I have arrived. It hardly seems possible. None of it seems
possible. When we actually saw the leaning tower of Pisa out
of the minibus window, I wanted to scream. I couldn't believe
that something I'd only seen in postcards was actually there.
Large as life against the blue, blue sky, with cars screaming
around it. No one else on the bus seemed to notice; Sally
was still talking about Jeremy Bullen and the two girls were
busy with their mobile phones, sending messages to their
husbands, I suppose. But Aldo turned and smiled at me, as if
he understood.

It was a shock to realise, at Pisa airport, that the two
glamorous girls on the plane were actually with our group.
I think they were surprised to see me too – with my old-
fashioned suitcase and sensible shoes. One girl, Cat, looks
just like a model – black, wavy hair, stunning figure. The
other, Anna, is pretty too in a quieter way – light brown hair,
friendly freckled face. They both seem really nice but I think
I like Anna better. I'm not sure why. Maybe it was because,
although Cat told very funny stories about her children Sasha

and Star (extraordinary names children have these days!),
Anna seemed to miss hers more. I suppose, because I don't
have children myself, I tend to romanticise the relationship
and the thought of a mother actually wanting time away from
her children (as Cat said she did) seems unnatural somehow.

We were met at the airport by a charming Italian man
called Aldo. He told us in broken English that he is the chef
at the Castello as well as the 'care giver'. I suppose he means
caretaker but I like 'care giver' better. Cat spoke to him in
Italian (she seems very clever) but he kept answering in his
funny English. He has a lovely strong face and very blue eyes,
surrounded by smiley lines. He must be my age at least but he
picked up the cases as if they weighed nothing. 'I am fat,' he
kept saying. I think he meant fit. He isn't fat at all.

The Castello is just wonderful. I had another 'couldn't
believe it' moment when I first saw it. You turn off the main
road and bump along an uneven track, then you see a pair of
huge ornate gates, propped open by heavy stones. The drive
seems to go on for miles, it's lined with trees and you can
see wide fields, turned yellow by the sun. Then, suddenly, the
Castello is there – very solid and grey, with actual towers and
wonderful purple flowers growing everywhere (I must find out
their name – I'm a real Londoner about these things).

My room is in one of the towers and it is very luxurious.
For the first time in my life, I've got a four-poster bed! I've
also got my own bathroom, all tiled in blue, it's like being
under the sea. Everything smells beautifully of lavender and

lemons. I spent ages just holding the towels up to my face and sniffing. Thank goodness no one was there to see me. I also have a writing desk with a laptop (what luxury – I only have a very old PC at home), a sofa covered in yellow velvet and two walk-in cupboards. My few clothes look very lost inside.

After I had washed my face and changed into a lighter dress (I felt hot and sweaty after the drive although the minibus was air-conditioned) I had a little prowl around. My room overlooks the front drive but, when I got to the back of the Castello, I had another shock. There were three balconies below me and, at the bottom, the most marvellous swimming pool, like something from a magazine. The water shimmered in the sunlight and seemed to overlap the sides as if it was about to flow down the hill. I ached to swim in it but I didn't want to mess up my hair before dinner. Tomorrow, though, I will be there first thing.

As I watched, a figure emerged from the trees at the side of the house. A man, blond, wearing swimming trunks and carrying a towel. He dived into the pool and swam a length under water. I just stood there, envying him. I could almost feel the water, the sudden shock of diving in, the sun against my face as I surfaced. The man swam a few more lengths and then got out and, without even bothering to dry himself, set off again through the silvery trees. Are they olive trees? I wonder.

Afterwards I wandered through a few more corridors. It's a huge house – stone floors, timbered ceilings, lots of little steps here and there. But all the doors were shut and I didn't want to end up somewhere I shouldn't be, somewhere private. So,

with some difficulty, I retraced my steps back to my own room.
Only an hour before 'drinks and crostini on the terrace'. What
an exciting, terrifying thought.

Patricia is not feeling excited or terrified as she arranges
glasses on the terrace. She feels tired and slightly put out, she's
not sure why. Everything is going to plan. The Van Elstens
arrived in the morning and they both seem very pleasant. Rick
Van Elsten seems particularly friendly, with a hearty Texan's
laugh. Whether he will be friendly enough to sink a million
or so into the Castello della Luna remains to be seen. After a
light brunch, the Van Elstens went to sleep off their jet lag,
leaving Patricia to prepare for the afternoon's arrivals.

What ruined everything was the Frenchman, Jean-Pierre
Charbonneau, arriving at midday, screaming up the drive in a
rented sports car, demanding coffee and sandwiches and a glass
of white wine, 'something chilled and not too sweet, definitely
not Orvieto'. He irritated her the moment she set eyes on him:
tall, balding, dressed elegantly in a blue shirt and chinos. He
looked around the (undoubtedly impressive) entrance hall and
said, with a twisted smile, 'Ah, the Great Hall. You even have a
few suits of armour around. Just to add atmosphere.' The infer-
ence was that the Castello was over-restored, inauthentic, even
kitsch. His English was infuriatingly perfect.

'There's a dungeon,' said Patricia, more sharply than she
was wont to speak to new guests. 'But we keep wine there,
I'm afraid.'

'Italian wine,' shuddered the Frenchman. 'How quaint.'

He couldn't complain about his room though, one of the best suites, with its own balcony. He even remarked on the beauty of the view, the hills ochre and yellow in the midday sun, the cypresses like sentinels on the horizon.

'Is that Siena?' he said, pointing to a distant hilltop, where towers rose into the sky like the background to a Renaissance picture of heaven.

'Yes,' said Patricia shortly.

'Beautiful city.'

'You don't mind Italian cities then?'

Jean-Pierre Charbonneau smiled, showing disconcertingly white teeth. 'Italy I love. It's the Italians I can't stand.'

Jean-Pierre Charbonneau had put her in a bad mood because, although she frequently complains about Italy, she can't bear her adopted country to be criticised by outsiders. Especially by a Frenchman who, she notices, is not above driving an Alfa Spider and dressing in Gucci.

The English women, when they arrived, were a relief. Mary McMahon was charming, delighted with everything. She is a petite elderly lady, with ash-blond hair in a pixie cut and a surprisingly girlish figure. Sally Hamilton she knows from previous courses. Sally gave her a hug and produced a battered-looking twig from the depths of her bag. 'Raspberry bush,' she declared. 'Perfect for the kitchen garden.' Sally is a professional gardener.

The younger women are friendly too. Catherine Ferris-Merry

(Cat) is not the monster of her imaginings, although she is annoyingly attractive. Anna Valore is a sweet, shy woman, already turning pink in the Italian sun.

'Valore,' said Patricia. 'Are you Italian then?'

'My father was,' said Anna, blushing. 'Well, his parents were. But I don't speak Italian, I'm afraid.'

'Nonsense,' said Aldo, who seemed to be hanging about rather. 'You talk it very well.'

Cat laughed. 'That was me, Aldo. Crazy, isn't it? Anna's the Italian one but I'm the one who speaks the blessed language.'

Aldo didn't laugh. He picked up Mary's case and started to carry it upstairs.

'I can do that,' Mary protested.

'No.' Aldo smiled, his moustache quivering. 'Is no trouble. I am fat guy.'

Now, arranging wicker chairs into sociable clusters, Patricia wonders how the group will get on. Sometimes they gel wonderfully, remaining friends for years. On other courses it has been stickier, which is much harder work for her, Myra and Jeremy. Myra is excellent at bringing the shyer guests out of themselves (she will sit her next to Anna at dinner) but Jeremy really only talks to people he finds interesting. His groupies, like Sally, he barely tolerates (not that they seem to mind). She sighs. Jeremy is due any minute, she must make sure that *Belly Flop* is face out in the library.

Sam McCluskie is also expected soon. He is driving from Lake Como, where he has been on holiday. She hopes he will be less objectionable than Jean-Pierre Charbonneau. Actually, it is quite rare to have two single men on a creative course; she hopes the women know how lucky they are. Often these are women-only events, which gives them a certain giggly friendliness but cuts down on the opportunities for an authentic Italian holiday romance. Anyway, both men will probably fall in love with Cat, who is married. What a waste.

A soft footfall interrupts her. Fabio stands in the doorway, carrying a trestle table.

'Excuse me,' he says, in his cultured Italian. 'Aldo said you might need this.'

'Oh, yes, thank you, Fabio.' Patricia can hear herself sounding flustered. Does he have to go around being so good-looking *all* the time? She hopes she gets used to it soon.

Fabio puts down the table and Patricia covers it with a white linen tablecloth. It is now ready for the plates of gleaming crostini which will appear magically later (Ratka has agreed to be waitress). Patricia looks out over the balcony. Dusk is settling, almost imperceptibly, just a faint blue tinge to the air and the scent of jasmine wafting up from the lower terrace. She must make sure that the pool lights are lit; the water looks so attractive at night.

She must have said this aloud because Fabio offers to do the lights for her. He backs out smiling and, looking, she is sorry to say, still very handsome indeed.

*

Cat is looking forward to the evening. She will wear her red halter-neck dress. Lucky she's already quite brown from that fortnight in the Dordogne. She hopes there will be some men on the course. Not that she would ever dream of being unfaithful to Justin but she just prefers men's company somehow. Women can be so bitchy and trivial. Like those cows at the toddler group, bleating on about the cost of yogurt at the supermarket. When she'd tried to talk about her experiences of eating real Greek yogurt *in Greece*, they had ignored her. Thank God for Anna.

Cat is not quite sure why she likes Anna so much. She's very quiet compared to her Cambridge friends but, somehow, those dazzling university friendships didn't last and now Anna is really her only close woman friend. Anna is kind and funny and a loyal friend. She stood up for Cat when one of those über bitches at playgroup slagged her off (Cat, heating up soya milk in the kitchen, overheard it all). And in Anna's open admiration Cat finds something very soothing to her soul. Anna looks up to her and that gives her a certain responsibility towards her. She must make sure that Anna makes something of herself. God knows, she's not going to get help from that gormless husband of hers. He doesn't appreciate her at all, probably just wants her to be another brainwashed housewife. Well, we'll see about that. It was Cat who suggested that they come on this course and it will be Cat who rescues Anna from her suburban rut.

Cat smiles as she looks at herself in the mirror.

*

Sam has still not arrived when the guests sit down to dinner. Matt, too, has not put in an appearance. Jeremy arrived late for the pre-dinner drinks. He brushed aside Sally's welcome and immediately established himself beside Cat, who was looking gorgeous in a red dress with her hair piled casually on top of her head. At intervals Patricia heard him discoursing about 'the vacuosity of modern cultural life' and 'the credibility gap in English publishing'. At least, as Cat went to Cambridge (something she has already let slip once or twice), she will be able to cope with this kind of thing. Myra, she was pleased to see, sat with Anna and Mary and talked animatedly about Tuscany. This left Patricia to chat up the Van Elstens and Sally to entertain a bored-looking Jean-Pierre.

Things are a little better at dinner. Jean-Pierre is quite amusing about French driving and Myra makes them laugh describing her attempts to ride a Vespa. There is a sticky moment when Dorothy Van Elsten wants to say grace, just as everyone else is tucking into their *rigatoni ai peperoni*, but this is swiftly skated over by an experienced Patricia, who says a brief prayer in Italian which is sufficiently ethnic not to upset the atheists at the table but Godly enough to please Dorothy. Just as she finishes, Matt slides in.

'Where have you been?' Patricia can't help saying. 'I thought you were going to help this afternoon.'

'I was busy,' says Matt evasively. 'Doing stuff.'

'My son Matthew,' says Patricia to the table at large. 'Now you see him, now you don't.'

Mary looks up and, recognising the blond swimmer, smiles. Matt smiles back, rather warily.

The *rigatoni* and the *polpettine* which follow are absolutely perfect and, for the thousandth time, Patricia thanks God (in Italian and English) for Aldo. The guests may think they come to the Castello to hone their writing skills but the abiding memory they will take away with them is of Aldo's cooking skills. All the narrative workshops in the world won't stay in the mind as long as Aldo's *pappardelle con melanzane e peperoni.* He may be infuriating sometimes but Aldo is worth his weight in gold.

It is a tradition that Aldo comes into the dining room as coffee is being served, to meet the guests and receive their congratulations. At first, Patricia felt a little awkward with this. It was a little bit too much like parading a quaint Italian character for the amusement of the paying public. Matt thinks, and frequently says, that it is demeaning for Aldo to be surrounded by women cooing, 'Isn't he an absolute darling?' But Aldo himself seems to enjoy it and, in his gleaming chef's whites, he cuts an oddly dignified figure, polite but not servile, sublimely confident in his abilities.

He is on good form today. All the guests praise his cooking, even Jean-Pierre. Dorothy Van Elsten makes a huge fuss of him, asks him to sit beside her and to give her all his recipes (Aldo goes temporarily deaf at this point).

'Have you lived in this area all your life, Aldo?' she asks. Americans are always so good at catching people's names.

'Yes,' says Aldo. 'I was born in San Severino. My father was the baker there.'

'The baker. Oh my! I bet he taught you all his secrets, hmm?'

'He teaches me some things,' says Aldo modestly.

'And I bet you know all the secrets about this place too. Tell me, is it haunted? I'm psychic and I've got the strangest feeling about it.'

Aldo looks at Patricia. 'There is a legend, yes.'

'Tell us!' say at least four voices.

Aldo takes a deep breath and begins. Surreptitiously Patricia turns off the lights and leaves only the candles burning.

'Once in this castle there live a count and contessa. The contessa is very beautiful but the count is old and not a good man. Cruel man. The contessa she falls in love with local boy. Very handsome with blond hair like an Englishman. Every night she looks for him from the North Tower and he rides through the woods on his horse. Beautiful white horse. But the count finds out. He is angry and he sends his men to catch the boy, the lover of his wife. He catches him but he does not kill him. No, he is more cruel even than this. He put the boy in a cage and he hang it from the North Tower. The contessa she must watch her love die slowly. The contessa, she cannot stand it. One night, she go to the tower and she shoots an arrow and she kills her lover herself. She does not want him more to suffer. Then she jumps from the tower. Kills herself.' Aldo takes a sip of wine, looking slowly round the room. 'And they say, when the moon is high, you can see the boy riding up to the castle, the light shining on his blond hair. And, when the light of the moon touches the North Tower, you can see the cage swinging to and fro and you can hear the contessa's screams as she falls.'

A chorus of oohs and aahs greets this story but Patricia is surprised to find herself genuinely shaken. She has heard Aldo's tale many times, of course. It is an established part of the first evening's entertainment. But this is the first time she has heard the detail about the moon and Patricia has a superstitious fear of the moon. She always shuts her curtains tightly so that no sliver of moonlight falls on her bed and if she sees a full moon she crosses herself (though she is not a Catholic). She thinks she knows why as well. It is to do with her childhood but Patricia's childhood is a place where she never, ever goes.

'Who's sleeping in the North Tower?' asks someone.

'I am,' says Mary brightly. 'I'd better watch out.'

'Don't worry, dear,' says Dorothy. 'If you're not susceptible, you won't hear or see anything. Now, if I was in that room, I'd never have a wink of sleep.'

'I slept in that room for years,' says Patricia soothingly. 'When I was . . . when my husband lived here. And we never saw a thing.'

'It's just a typical apocryphal story really, though,' says Cat, holding up her glass so that the wine gleams in the candlelight. 'It has all the traditional elements: the jealous older husband, the unfaithful wife, the young lover. Even the white horse and the tower in the moonlight.'

'So true,' murmurs Jeremy admiringly. 'Of course, there are only six archetypal story types: siege, quest, rags to riches, rebirth—'

'And they say,' says Aldo, raising his voice slightly, 'that on stormy nights you can hear the white horse galloping up to the gates, hear the door creaking open . . .'

Right on cue, the dining room door creaks open and a man appears, silhouetted in the doorway. Dorothy screams. Someone else pushes their chair back violently. One of the candles flickers and goes out.

'I'm sorry,' says the man. He is dark and thickset, carrying a suitcase. 'The maid let me in. I'm Sam McClusky.'

From: Anna Valore
Date: 1 August 2017, 23.40
To: Steve Smith
Re: Hello Sexy

Hello, love. It was lovely to find your email waiting for me when I got back to my room. It's a beautiful room with a huge double bed. I wish you were here to share it with me!

This is a really amazing place. You know you said that castello was probably Italian for prefab bungalow? Well, it really is a castle, with towers and everything. It's set in beautiful grounds with olive trees and lavender everywhere. There's a fantastic swimming

pool and tennis courts and even a gym. Not that I'll
be doing any sport obviously! The owner, Patricia, is
very nice. She's super-organised but in a good way.
She must be in her forties but she's very slim and
attractive. She's got a son called Matthew who's about
seventeen. The tutors are a lovely American woman
and a rather stuck-up Englishman called Jeremy
Bullen. Thank goodness he's ignored me so far. Too
busy chatting up Cat!

The other guests all seem nice. There's a sweet old
lady called Mary, who's writing a detective story, of all
things. There's another woman called Sally who's been
on courses here before. She seems to know Jeremy
really well. There's a nice American couple called
Dorothy and Rick. Dorothy is very New Agey and told
me that I had a lovely aura! I couldn't help thinking
what you would say about that! There's a Frenchman
called Jean-Pierre (JP). I didn't like him at first but he
was quite funny at dinner (the food! It's amazing!). The
last guest, Sam, turned up dramatically after dinner
just as Aldo (the chef) had finished a really creepy
ghost story. Poor Sam. We all jumped when we saw
him and Dorothy actually screamed. Apparently he'd
had a puncture on the motorway and was delayed.
Aldo got him some food and we all had more coffee
and liqueurs to make up for the shock. I had a grappa.
It was absolutely disgustable, as Tom would say.

Oh, I do miss you all! I must admit I had a low moment when I first got here and saw the pool and thought how much the boys would love it. And how much you would love the food – and the double bed! I feel very guilty, swanning about in luxury, and thinking of you getting up early to take Tom to football and Jake to his swimming lessons. Cat says I deserve this holiday but I don't know that I do really.

Well, you don't want to listen to me rambling on. I can hear you saying, 'Well, you're there now, just get on and enjoy it.' So I'll try. I'm sure I'll feel much more cheerful in the morning.

Give the boys big hugs and kisses from me and tell them I'll buy them lovely presents (I know you and Tom both want Italy football shirts!).

Love you

A

xxxxxxx

CHAPTER 4

Day 1

2 August

'Writers don't write about people they know. They write what they know about people.' Jeremy pauses impressively, looking around the room at the assembled guests. 'At least in my own humble experience.'

The first workshop session is held in one of the sitting rooms. Guests sit on sofas and chairs rather than behind desks. Jeremy strides to and fro in front of the open French windows. From outside comes the hum of crickets and a sense of heavy, golden heat but the room itself is air-conditioned. In fact, Anna feels rather cold in her T-shirt and cotton skirt. Cat, in a sleeveless vest and the shortest of shorts, does not seem to be bothered. As she crosses her long, brown legs, Anna sees JP, Sam and Jeremy all look at her.

'So, enough about me,' says Jeremy unconvincingly. 'Did anyone do the task I emailed to you? Write two hundred and fifty words about yourself and tell us something you've never told anyone before?'

Sally's hand shoots up but, after a pretence of looking round the room, Jeremy says, 'Cat. Why don't you start?'

'Why do I have to be first?' pouts Cat, but she is quick to pull a piece of paper out of her folder. Tossing back her hair, she begins.

'My name is Catherine but most people call me Cat. I used to hate it but now I quite like the name. Cats are beautiful and cool, but they have claws too as my husband often points out! The kids would love to have a cat but sadly I'm allergic so they just have to make do with me!

'I live in Brighton with my husband Justin and my children Sasha and Star. Our house is a real Victorian monstrosity, lots of stairs and huge, draughty rooms, but we love it. Before I got married I used to have rather a whizzy job in copywriting and I must admit that I get bored sometimes. I'm happy being a mum but sometimes it does frustrate me, being stuck with people whose mental age is about ten (in my kids' case, obviously precociously!). My musings on this theme turned into a blog which, in turn, became a book, *A Year in the Life of a Yummy Mummy*. It's not published yet but, after this course, I'm going to start a new life as a writer.

'Something I've never told anyone? Well, at Cambridge I went out with someone rather famous. No names but there is a royal connection! But whoever has heard of a Princess Cat?'

'Thank you, Cat,' says Jeremy. 'I see we will have to curtsy when we meet you from now on. Who's next?'

Before he has time to pick someone, Dorothy stands up and, clearing her throat nervously, addresses the room in a clear, high-pitched voice.

'My name is Dorothy and I was abused as a child. There were seven of us and we grew up real poor in Missouri. I was the eldest and, for some reason, my mom never loved me. She used to beat me with belts and fuse wire and even with a table leg. I had to do all the chores and I wasn't allowed to eat with the others. I had to eat out on the porch, with the chickens. Mom never beat up on the other kids. Only me. I don't know why and for years I've struggled with my self-esteem because of it. When I was sixteen, I was raped by a family friend but my mom blamed me and threw me out. I was a prostitute for a while but then I found God. He led me to San Antonio where I met my second saviour, my husband Rick. Though I've got a good life now, I've never found closure because I've never been able to forgive my mom. Or myself. So I'm writing a book. Telling the truth. Putting the record straight. Starting with you guys. That's all.'

There is complete silence in the room. Even the crickets outside seem to be still. Patricia, who arrived in time to hear the end of Dorothy's speech, stands stricken in the doorway.

Jeremy groans inwardly. How the hell is he going to follow that?

'Time for lunch,' he says at last.

*

'It was unbelievable,' Patricia says to Myra as they clear away the lunch plates. 'She just came out with it all. Like she was telling us the weather forecast or something. All this terrible, shocking stuff.'

'Maybe after all these years she just felt she had to tell someone.'

'Well, she's writing a book about it so I suppose she's decided to tell everyone.'

'Misery memoirs are hot these days,' says Myra, dipping her finger in a bowl of green olive oil. 'She'll probably clean up.'

'Don't.' Patricia doesn't laugh.

Lunch is always a buffet, laid out on the lowest balcony, overlooking the pool. Aldo surpassed himself today: bruschetta, stuffed tomatoes, wafer-thin slices of carpaccio filled with rocket, tiny crostini with pâté and olives. The guests ate heartily, obviously recovered from Dorothy's bombshell. Dorothy herself seemed serene and composed. She exclaimed loudly over the food and was very disappointed not to see Aldo again. 'I just love Aldo! He's a real wise old soul.' But Aldo never appears at weekday lunch. He has a room in the Castello where he rests before starting the dinner preparations. Aldo's siestas are sacrosanct.

Halfway through lunch the cat put in another appearance. It waited until they were all looking at it and then sat down and began, laboriously, to wash its whiskers.

'Isn't he lovely?' said Mary. 'What's his name?'

'I don't know,' said Patricia, 'he isn't mine. He's a stray.' Was it her imagination or did the cat look up and catch her eye?

'We must give him a name,' said Cat, who sat sparkling between JP and Jeremy.

'Cat,' suggested Jeremy.

'Oh, you!' Cat aimed a mock slap at him.

'What's the Italian for cat?' Mary asked.

'*Gatto*,' said Patricia. 'Although the pet name is Misha. Like pussy, I suppose.'

'Misha,' Sally called to the cat. He ignored her.

'I think he's an Irish cat,' announced Cat.

'Why?' Jeremy smiled winningly.

'I don't know, I just do. He's so contrary. He must know I'm allergic but now he's rubbing round my legs.'

Jeremy looks as if he doesn't blame the cat for this.

'Patrick?' suggested someone.

'Brendan?'

'Declan?'

'Sean,' decided Cat. 'I think he's called Sean.'

So Patricia is stuck with a cat named after her ex-husband.

After lunch Dorothy, Rick and Sally went to their rooms to rest. Cat, JP, Sam, Anna and Mary announced their intention of swimming.

'I hear you swam this morning, Mary,' said JP. 'You must be keen.'

'I love swimming.' Mary smiled.

'I'll race you,' offered JP.

'Leave Mary alone,' laughed Cat. 'Pick on someone your

own size. I'll race you. I used to be in the school team. Don't worry, Mary.' She smiled charmingly at the older woman. 'My mum swims every day. Two lengths of breaststroke and never gets her hair wet. Good on you, I say.'

Mary smiled but did not reply.

Now the sun is at its highest and the trees are shimmering in the heat. Patricia can hear the group laughing as they approach the pool. She'd love to swim herself but she never uses the pool when there are guests. They don't want her hanging about all the time. She'll have a cool shower after she's cleared away lunch. That'll be just as good.

'Shall I take these?' Fabio has appeared and is gesturing towards the plates.

'Yes. Thank you, Fabio.'

Watching his slim, departing back, Myra says, 'He is *so* sexy.'

'I hadn't noticed,' says Patricia tightly.

'Oh, come on!'

'Really. He's young enough to be my son.'

'Mine too. But a girl can dream.'

But dreams don't get you anywhere, thinks Patricia, as she descends the stairs to the kitchen, trying not to step on Sean, who is weaving annoyingly around her legs.

By the pool, Cat, in a tiny pink bikini, is teasing JP about his challenge.

'You don't know what you're taking on, JP. Us St Martha's girls are hot stuff at swimming.'

'Did you go to a convent school?' asks Sam.

'Why do you ask?' Cat looks at him over her shoulder.

'You just seem the type, that's all.' He doesn't smile as he says this. Anna finds him a rather brooding presence, with his heavy, dark face and watchful eyes.

But Cat laughs. 'What type is that? Yes, I went to a convent school. What of it?'

'I went to a convent school too,' says JP, 'but they called the police.'

Everyone laughs and Cat and JP line up for their race. Cat looks wonderful, thinks Anna. She wonders if she'll ever have the confidence to take off her T-shirt.

They dive in. Cat swims well but JP, though splashier, soon pulls ahead. They are at the halfway mark when someone else enters the water. A figure in a neat bathing cap, doing an exemplary racing crawl, catches them, overtakes and, performing a perfect racing turn, starts a second length.

It is Mary.

Jeremy is in his room looking at the seven manuscripts piled up in front of him. He has requested examples of the students' most recent work and can see immediately that they vary considerably in length and, probably, quality. Mary McMahon's must be nearly 100,000 words, neatly contained in a blue folder with 'Barclays Bank' printed on it. Sam McClusky has submitted three examples, each less than 5000 words. 'I've tried every genre you can think of,' he wrote in his covering note, 'but just can't seem to get very far with any of them.' Cat's is professionally bound, Anna's looks like it has Marmite on page 5 and Sally's — God, Sally's is as familiar to him as the reviews of *Belly Flop*.

Jeremy, naturally, has one of the best rooms, with a balcony overlooking the swimming pool. Unfortunately this now means that he is distracted by the noise of laughter and splashing. Possibly one of the most evocative sounds in the world, he thinks, the splashing of water on a hot day. One of the loneliest too, when you can't join in, every laugh underlining your status as an outsider. Then he thinks, this is quite good, shall I save it? But, as he reaches for his notebook, he thinks: when will I write a novel featuring a swimming pool? I'm not Alan bloody Hollinghurst. There's not much laughter in Jeremy's novels either, come to that.

So he turns up the air conditioning, draws the blinds and concentrates on the embryonic novels in front of him. He turns to Cat's first, for obvious reasons. Christ, she's good-looking. Got a fantastic body too. He imagines that body, sleek and wet, emerging from the pool and shifts uncomfortably in his chair. He has quite a good success rate with women on this course. Usually, all he has to do is suggest that they need some personal writing tuition (it helps if the novel in question is sexy and/or confessional) and after a few evenings sharing a bottle of wine, he's in there. He opens Cat's file eagerly. He's almost certain she will need several one-to-one sessions.

But, half an hour later, he puts down *A Year in the Life of a*

Yummy Mummy with a sigh. It's not that it's terrible. It's not badly written – there are some good jokes and shrewd observations – it's just that it has all, every word of it, been done before. The heroine, disorganised but deeply lovable. The Useless Husband, the children who come out with Universal Truths at bedtime ('If you love Daddy, why do you fight so much?'). Even the gay best friend (well, she *does* live in Brighton, after all) and the eccentric mother-in-law. Jeremy feels as if he has read about these people hundreds, if not thousands, of times before. And it's not even his genre, for God's sake! It's no good. A year's worth of evenings on the terrace won't make this book different enough to be publishable. Shit.

Next he picks up Mary McMahon's tome. He's not expecting much. Mary seems a sweet old dear, but old ladies always write about cats or romance. He's also allergic to cats and, if he ever thinks about romance, it's only as a sign fixed to a shelf in a bookshop (a shelf which won't feature his books either). His marriage was over twenty years ago and none of his frequent affairs have achieved the category Romance (few have progressed beyond Hobby).

So it is with another sigh that he opens a can of Coke and begins Mary's script. *The Case of the Streatham Hill Strangler.* What *is* this?

Fifty pages in he is still not sure but he has revised his opinion of Mary McMahon somewhat. The book is set in South London in the fifties and the era is evoked very skilfully: the corner shops, the cinema, the hand-knitted, home-cooked texture of life. The hero, Detective Inspector Frank Malone, is an interesting character, a misanthropic Irish policeman who keeps racing pigeons and broods about his dead wife. The plot is far too convoluted, Jeremy gives up trying to follow it after a while, but there is a huge cast of characters, rather Dickensian and grotesque certainly, but all written with a kind of dash which Jeremy certainly does not associate with the motherly figure in sensible shoes. Overall it's the kind of over-ambitious epic that he would expect from an intelligent undergraduate. She needs to cut and prune and to lose about five sub-plots, but it definitely has something.

He doesn't waste much time with Sally Hamilton's effort. Entitled *Castration,* it's a wildly violent thriller set in a dystopian future. There are echoes of his own work here (the obsession with torture and bodily functions and a tendency to ironical first-person narration) but it is, quite simply, boring as hell. He puts it aside with a shudder, wondering what on earth he's going to say that he hasn't said a hundred times before. Go away and get a new hobby? Find someone else to fantasise about?

Sam McClusky is equally frustrating. None of his scripts (a Dan Brownesque thriller, a Rankinesque detective story and a Nick Hornbyesque comedy) are bad exactly. He is quite good at grasping the essentials of the genre and there are nice flashes of humour but it is just that McClusky obviously loses interest very quickly. And, if the author loses interest, how on earth is the reader going to hang on in there? A cracking introduction, some interesting plot lines, a few red herrings and McClusky is off to start another book. Jeremy has met the type before. 'To be a writer,' he sometimes says to his evening class in Putney, 'you have to bloody well finish something.' Sam McClusky is obviously never going to get beyond chapter one.

He picks up JP's file with interest. Last night he had identified the Frenchman as his biggest potential rival in the group. Attractive, ironical, obviously intelligent – Jeremy had disliked him at first sight. Let's hope he's a crap writer.

He expects a thriller, or maybe a stream of consciousness oh-aren't-I-intelligent-and-sensitive type love story. What he gets is a children's story. He turns over the pages to make sure. Yes, definitely a children's story. *The Story of Louis the Lion.* Jesus.

Jeremy hates children's books. Ever since Harry bloody Potter, every wanker thinks they can write a children's story. Simply mix together a wizard, an unhappy childhood, some stupid place names and, hey presto, a million pounds in the bank. If it's so easy, he wants to say, why doesn't everyone do it? Why don't I do it? And, as any fool can tell, the next Harry Potter, whatever that mythical creature may be, is definitely not going to be a boy wizard wearing glasses.

It's not going to be *Louis the Lion* either. Jeremy gives up after a few pages. Louis is a boy, not a lion, and he is timid and afraid of everything. His favourite character is (of course) the cowardly lion in *The Wizard of Oz*. The story of how Louis finds his courage, with the help of a talking cat called Caruthers, is one that Jeremy is happy to leave for ever unread.

He spends even less time with Dorothy Van Elsten's heart-felt few pages, *Innocence Abused*. Tolstoy might have said that all happy families are alike, but in Jeremy's experience, all dysfunctional families are completely bloody identical. Absentee father? Check. Abusive mother? Check. Sensitive child shivering under bedclothes? Check. Stranger who brings a ray of hope into child's life? Check. Escape, trauma, therapy, catharsis. Check, check, check, check. Jeremy groans as he takes another Coke from the fridge. It is depressing to think that, of all the books, Dorothy's is by far the most likely to find a publisher.

It is late afternoon by the time he turns to the last script. The swimmers have left the pool and the only sounds are the clatter of plates from the kitchen and the tree frogs croaking from the olive grove. Patricia will be rounding up the guests for the evening's trip to San Severino. Jeremy is happy to give it a miss. San Severino is a charming hillside town but, when you have marvelled at the view and sat in the piazza drinking over-priced beer, there's fuck all else to do. He'll finish the scripts, have a glass of whisky and a nap before supper. If the food wasn't so good, he thinks he might have chucked this gig years ago.

The last script belongs to Anna Valore. Jeremy opens it unenthusiastically. It is called *Hi Ho Silver Lining* and is the story of an intelligent, sensitive girl from a working-class background who goes to university and meets a charming, feckless upper-class boy. So far, so clichéd and yet . . . there is something. Maybe it is in the naive but clear-sighted voice of the heroine. Maybe it is in the surprisingly biting descriptions of the upper classes at play. The story is rubbish, of course, but Anna Valore undeniably has a vestige of talent.

Jeremy closes his eyes, trying to conjure up Anna. So far she has only featured in his mind as Cat's friend. Nice face, freckles, quite a passable figure hidden under terrible clothes. A surprisingly throaty laugh. Jeremy smiles to himself. He has a feeling that he is going to get to know Anna Valore a whole lot better.

San Severino is a hill town, perched on a pinnacle of rock above fields of sunflowers and tobacco plants. From the distance it looks rather forbidding, with steep stone walls, crenellated towers and tiny arrow slit windows. But, when the minibus drives under the archway cut into the rock and begins to ascend the steep, winding streets, all marked *senso unico,* wonders begin to unfold: tiny courtyards with fantastically carved fountains, a blackbird in a cage singing from a high window, breathtaking views glimpsed through doorways, houses built, seemingly, one on top of the other, their balconies and washing lines spiralling up into the sky.

Aldo parks the bus by the main piazza, a paved semicircle at the very top of the town. One side is lined with shops, from the other you can see for miles across the valley: the sunflower fields, the lake, the hills, purple in the twilight, and the ribbon of road curling away into the distance.

'Oh my!' says Dorothy, reaching for her camera. 'The view is just to die for.'

'Many people have died for it,' says Aldo. 'Was a major battle here quite recently.'

'In the Second World War?' asks JP.

'No, I think it was in fourteen forty. A battle between Florence and Milan.'

Anna, sitting on the stone wall, still warm from the sun, thinks it is easy to imagine Renaissance armies marching across the darkening valley, the inhabitants of San Severino retreating to this hilltop, prepared to defend their town or die in the attempt.

'I must buy some postcards,' says Dorothy next to her, video whirring. Sam, too, is clicking away with a very expensive-looking camera.

'You've only just come,' laughs Cat. 'I prefer just to experience a place rather than take photos or send postcards.'

'Do you, dear?' says Dorothy mildly, still videoing. 'Well, we're all different, I suppose.'

Patricia marshals the group towards the tables arranged outside one of the cafes. She and Aldo organise drinks while the guests sit, experiencing or photographing, according to taste.

Cat and Anna find themselves sitting with Mary and JP. Dorothy, Rick, Sam and Sally make up another table.

'I wonder where Jeremy is,' says Cat, folding one of the paper napkins into a flower.

'He stayed behind to read our scripts,' says JP, grimacing.

'God, what an awful thought,' says Anna. 'I don't suppose he'll spend much time on mine though.'

'What's it about?' asks JP.

'Oh, it's just a tedious university story. Well, polytechnic story really.'

'Honestly,' says Cat. 'Who cares if it was a polytechnic? A lot of those courses are really good. Anyway, I think your book is fab. It needs work, of course, but whose doesn't? Have you still got those notes I did for you?'

'Oh yes,' says Anna. 'You made some really good suggestions. It's just . . . sometimes I feel like ripping the whole thing up and starting again.'

'I know what you mean,' says Mary. She hasn't spoken much but her eyes, as they take in the piazza, now filling up for the evening, the medieval buildings, the view over the hilltops, are wide with wonder.

'What's your book about, Mary?' asks Cat.

'It's a detective story,' says Mary. 'Set in London.'

'So, are you the next Agatha Christie?' asks Cat, smiling up at Aldo as he comes over with the drinks.

'I love Agatha Christie,' says Aldo unexpectedly, sitting down next to Mary. 'I love the Mrs Marple.'

'Oh, me too,' says Mary.

'It's *Miss* Marple,' laughs Cat. 'She's not married.'

'Another thing we've got in common,' says Mary lightly.

'I'm not a fan of Agatha Christie,' says Cat. 'I prefer P.D. James. She's more intellectually challenging somehow.'

CHAPTER 5

Day 2

3 August

Fabio offers to drive the guests to the wine tasting. Patricia is delighted.

'Do you have an HGV licence?' she asks.

'Yes,' says Fabio. 'I love driving.'

So does Aldo, but his passengers frequently do not share his enthusiasm. Aldo himself is less happy about Fabio driving his beloved bus but at least this will give him the chance to start lunch. There's no way he's going to let Fabio drive to Rome tomorrow though. Aldo loves the trip to Rome.

Cat, Anna, Mary, Sally and Sam volunteer for the wine tasting. JP stays behind ('Taste Italian wine? *Voluntarily?* Are you mad?'), Jeremy pleads pressure of work and Dorothy doesn't drink ('I've been in AA for years'). Patricia, too, stays at home. She has a lot of work to do and Myra is more than willing to go in her place. She enjoys an enthusiastically flirtatious relationship with Gennaro, the vineyard owner, who is always asking her to marry him.

Fabio skilfully negotiates the hairpin turns as they rise higher into the hills. Cat looks at his brown forearms as he swings the huge wheel round. He's really very handsome, by far the best-looking man here, although JP has possibilities, in an intellectual sort of way, and Jeremy is pleasantly attentive. She shakes out her black hair and grins at Anna.

'Enjoying it so far?'

'Oh yes,' says Anna, looking out of the window to where the Castello can still be seen, sheltering behind the umbrella pines. 'It's so beautiful here.'

'It is, isn't it? I've been to Tuscany loads of times but this is the prettiest place I've ever stayed in.'

'What do you think of the course?' asks Anna, lowering her voice slightly, although Mary and Sally are having a lively conversation about Marcello Mastroianni and couldn't possibly hear anything. Sam, though, is sitting only a few seats away, brooding and silent.

'It's OK,' says Cat. 'Jeremy seems quite bright. I'm looking forward to having a proper chat with him about my book.'

'I find him a bit standoffish,' says Anna. 'But it's great meeting all the other writers. So fascinating, to think of all these different people writing such different sorts of books, all ending up in the same place for the same two weeks. I should think we'll influence each other as much as Jeremy influences us.'

'Mmm,' says Cat. 'I'm not sure how much Sally, say, is going to influence me.'

'Maybe not,' says Anna, 'but she's very nice.'

'We're not here to make friends,' says Cat in a mock-stern voice. 'We're here to work. It's not a holiday, remember.'

It is hard to remember this, though, as they step off the air-conditioned bus into the blistering morning sunshine. Fabio parks the bus under an overgrown pergola. Opposite them are fields upon fields of vines and, on the hill, a low, stone house ringed with archways. Gennaro, a handsome middle-aged man in jeans and an Italy shirt, is waiting by the pergola. He greets them with a roar of boisterous welcome and hugs Myra, lifting her off her silver ballet pumps.

'Myra! Will you marry me?'

'One day, Gennaro. I keep telling you,' says Myra, picking up her sun hat. 'One day I will marry you. Then you'll be sorry.'

'Ha ha,' shouts Gennaro. 'Never, never will I be sorry.'

Myra introduces the guests and there are hand-shakings and extravagant compliments all round. Even Sam is told that he is a 'typical handsome Englishman'.

'I'm Scottish,' mutters Sam, but he doesn't seem too displeased.

Gennaro leads them along a stony track between the vines. Sprinklers are at work and, occasionally, they get a welcome shower of fine water. Their clothes dry again in an instant. It really is shockingly hot.

'These are Sangiovese grapes,' explains Gennaro, 'the best in the world.'

'Are they used for Chianti?' asks Sam, mopping his forehead.

'*Sì.* And Brunello. Sangiovese means the blood of Jove. It is only used for the best, richest wines.'

'I'm not sure I want to drink blood,' laughs Cat, twinkling up at Gennaro.

'Ha ha,' laughs Gennaro. 'My wine is the very nectar of the gods.'

Anna admires the way that Cat seems completely unaffected by the heat, looking as cool as a grape in her white dress and green scarf. She is sure that she, by contrast, is red-faced and sweating. She falls back beside Mary and Sally, still discussing fifties film stars. It is all very beautiful but Anna is longing for them to reach the house. The sun is pounding on her head and her feet hurt.

At last Gennaro leads them into a courtyard which is surrounded by covered terraces, rather like a cloister. There, laid out on a long table, are tea, coffee and mineral water, plus plates of olives and pecorino cheese, cut into translucent slivers.

'First we drink tea like true English people,' says Gennaro. 'Then we see the cellars, the oak barrels, then we taste the wine.'

Anna, gulping down mineral water, would be happy to stay sitting in the shade but seeing Mary, who must be at least thirty years her senior, jump up eagerly, she feels too ashamed to ask to stay behind.

'In this vineyard,' says Gennaro, 'we make the best Chianti in the world. Gallo Nero. Does anyone know what that means?'

'Well, *nero* means black,' offers Cat.

'*Brava*. Well, Gallo Nero means black cock.'

Anna catches Mary's eye and has to fight not to laugh. Behind her, Sam coughs loudly.

'Black cock,' beams Gennaro. 'The black cockerel who has his pick of the hens, yes?'

'Oh, a *cockerel*,' says Sally. Sam coughs even louder.

'Now,' says Gennaro, 'I take you to our cellars and you can see the black cock for yourselves.'

'I can hardly wait,' mutters Sam as they follow Gennaro through the low, arched doorway.

Patricia is looking forward to a morning on her own. She was slightly put out when she learnt that Dorothy, Rick and JP had opted out of the vineyard trip but, as Dorothy and Rick retreated to their room after breakfast, she comforted herself with the thought that they would probably all simply rest or even (just possibly) get on with their writing.

After helping Ratka clear away the breakfast dishes, Patricia retreats to her office to finalise the itinerary for tomorrow's trip to Rome. The restaurant where they usually stop for lunch is closed in August and so she has had to find a replacement. The new place is recommended by Aldo, which means that the food will be excellent but who knows if it will be in some grotty basement somewhere. Aldo thinks that, in a restaurant, all that matters is the food but Patricia knows that her guests will expect hanging baskets, Chianti bottles and views over the Tiber. Oh well, perhaps Aldo will overturn the minibus on the motorway and they'll never even get to Rome.

With this obscurely comforting thought in mind, she sits down to open the post. Several fliers for local restaurants, a postcard from a friend in New Zealand, a catalogue from a shop where she bought a pair of trousers five years ago and . . . a letter from her bank. Patricia stares at the envelope: the officious see-through window, the irritatingly precise spelling of her name, 'Signora P. A. O'Hara', the smug date stamp in the right-hand corner. Patricia is not a procrastinator but every fibre of her being longs to put the letter in a drawer and, preferably, nail the drawer shut for twenty-five years. Last year she took out a bridging loan and she knows it is time to pay it back. That much is simple; what is less clear-cut is how the hell she is going to find the money. It is only the memory of Sean merrily throwing bank statements on to the fire, 'Sure and why do we need them to tell us we're skint', that forces her to slit open the envelope and read its brief, deadly contents.

'Mrs O'Hara? Patricia?'

Patricia looks up to see two entirely unwelcome visitors. Sean the cat has prowled into the room and is sitting washing his paws by the window and Jean-Pierre Charbonneau is standing in the doorway, a hairdryer in his hand.

'Yes?' Patricia pushes her hair back from her face and tries to look businesslike.

'Are you all right? I just wanted to ask . . . I think the fuse has blown on this hairdryer.'

'Of course.' Patricia stands up. 'I'll change the plug for you.'

'No. It doesn't matter.' JP waves an impatient, Gallic hand. 'Not bad news, I hope?' He gestures towards the letter.

It is, of course, monumental cheek for him to comment on her private correspondence but she can hardly tell him so. Instead she attempts a light-hearted tone which comes out rather high and wavery. 'Just money troubles. It's an expensive place, the Castello.'

JP strides into the room and, uninvited, sits down opposite her desk, the hairdryer flex trailing incongruously from his hand.

'You must make a great deal out of these courses. Three thousand euros for two weeks.'

Patricia looks at him sharply. 'Have you any idea of my overheads?' she snaps. 'The food, the drink, this damn castle. I had to repair the roof in April, half the trees need to come down and the North Tower needs repointing before winter.'

JP grins. 'That'll be the ghost's fault, I expect. But seriously,' he leans forward, 'this place is half empty. I've got a massive suite all to myself.'

I didn't hear you complaining, thinks Patricia.

JP stands up and, stepping over Sean, strides to the window. For a second he stands there, blocking out the light and then he says, almost angrily, 'It's exquisite here. Really extraordinarily beautiful. You should be full all year round. You should be turning people away.'

'Well, we are busy most of the year,' says Patricia, rather defensively. 'Lots of people come for *la vendemmia*, the grape harvest. We do wine tasting tours.' She stops, expecting some caustic comment, but JP says nothing. He is still standing by the window, his face in shadow. 'And we do art courses and pottery courses. We're only shut in February and March. That's when we do all the repairs.'

'Why are there only eight people on this course then?' asks JP.

'Well,' Patricia sighs, 'writers like peace and quiet. I try not to overbook. And, well, there's not a lot of money in creative writing.'

JP snorts. 'You're right there. But what about husbands, wives, partners? Why not offer a reduced rate for them? You could offer them a second week at half price.'

'It's an idea,' says Patricia slowly. 'And I wouldn't be using any more rooms. But don't people come here to get away from husbands and wives?' She looks at JP as she says this but he just laughs.

'My ex-wife certainly won't be rushing to be at my side. But take those two lovely girls, for example, Catherine and Anna. I should think their husbands might be tempted. I certainly would be.'

What did that mean? thinks Patricia, after JP has gone. That he would be tempted if he were married to Cat or Anna or that he is already tempted by them? And then, sitting at her desk to scroll through addresses, she thinks: why would a balding man be using a hairdryer anyway?

Mary's diary, 3 August

Oh dear, I hope I haven't disgraced myself. We had a lovely morning visiting a nearby vineyard. The owner was a wonderful Italian chap called Genaro (sp?). He was full of charm and said that I looked just like Helen Mirren (not true, sadly, but a nice thought!). Anyway, it was very interesting and he showed us his cellars and we got to taste all these different types of Chianti. I usually don't like red wine but this was delicious – some really light and almost sparkly, some rich and smooth like dark chocolate.

Afterwards we sat on a long terrace, covered with vine leaves, and had a lovely lunch – salami, cheese, olives, delicious crusty bread. Then we came home on the minibus (I had a long chat with Anna, she's really a very nice girl). It was a very hot day and when I got back to my room, I just collapsed on the bed and fell straight to sleep. A couple of hours later when I woke up I had a raging thirst. All that wine, no doubt. The only problem was, in my little fridge there was fizzy mineral water, Coca-Cola and mini bottles of wine – no plain water. Fizzy water gives me indigestion and I didn't want to be suffering all through supper so I thought I would go in search of some ordinary tap water. This is where I made my big mistake.

After lots of wrong turns, I found my way down a long flight of stairs and there, at the bottom, was the kitchen – huge with a stone floor and all these herbs hanging from the ceiling. I thought it was empty so I rushed to the sink and filled my tooth glass with water. I was just gulping it down when I heard a sound behind me. I turned and there was Aldo! I was so embarrassed! I remember Patricia saying, when we arrived, that the kitchen was 'Aldo's domain'. She said it with a laugh but the implication was clear – trespassers will not be tolerated. And there I was, trespassing like anything!

He was holding some fish on a sort of pole (had obviously just been out to collect them) and didn't look at all friendly. I blurted out an apology (in English) and he smiled and said it didn't matter. Then, just as I was edging past him, he asked if I liked fish. I said I did, very much, and he showed me his catch – ten enormous flat, white fishes. Solia (sp?), he called them – I expect that means sole. He showed me how he was going to cook them, mimed dusting them in flour and frying. He also showed me a bowl where he was mixing greenish nuts (pine nuts?) with garlic, oil and anchovies. I told him that my uncle had been a fishmonger ('fish catcher' is actually what I said) and he seemed delighted with this information. He said he could tell I really liked food. I hope this doesn't mean he thinks I am fat or greedy.

He was very sweet and gave me a big bottle of cold water

and some almond biscuits but I hope I haven't committed some major solecism. It would be too awful to be in Patricia's bad books. I hope Aldo doesn't tell.

From: Anna Valore
Date: 3 August 2017, 23.34
To: Steve Smith
Re: Hello Sexy

I'm glad Tom had such a good time at Sebastian's house. They're nice people, aren't they? I loved your description of your 'father/son bonding' with Jakey. How did you get the ball down from the roof? I must admit that, despite the castle and everything, I really wished I'd been there.

I had a good day today, though. We went to a vineyard in the morning. It was a bit hot for me (we had to walk miles, and you know how much I like exercise!) but the place was beautiful and they laid on a fantastic lunch with lots of cheese and wine. The owner was a real character – chatted up Cat like mad, of course! Oh, and by the way, the best Chianti has a black cock on it – don't ask!

On the way home I had a chat with Mary, the elderly lady on the course. Turns out she is really interesting, had an important civil service job, travelled all over England, knows lots about books

and history. She says she has been writing her book
for thirty years! This made me feel really pathetic, as
I think I have been working on mine for ages but it's
only a year or so. She says her problem is she keeps
adding bits and now even she can't follow the plot (it's
a detective story, sounds really interesting).

Anyway, the good thing happened in the evening.
When I went back to my room, there was a note
from Jeremy (the course leader) asking if I'd like a
drink before supper. I feared the worst – that he'd
read my book and thought I wasn't good enough for
the course – but he was lovely. We had a drink on his
terrace and he said he thought the book was really
promising! I couldn't believe it! I mean, he is a real
author and a very experienced teacher. If he thinks I
have some talent . . . He said he thought the story was
a bit thin (all that stuff about Piers and university) but
he liked my style and he liked the heroine. He actually
said he thought I could write something much more
ambitious! Honestly, I was reeling when I came out of
his room! I mean, I know you think I can write but,
let's face it, you are biased! Jeremy is the first person
ever to talk to me as if I were a proper writer. He said
things like 'this probably isn't commercial enough
for the mass market' and 'it's a bit like Donna Tartt
without the murders'. I mean, to think of me having a
market at all or of being anything like Donna Tartt! He

has given me lots of ideas and wants to have another talk in a few days. I really have misjudged him. I thought he was shallow and conceited, only interested in himself and in chatting up the more attractive guests (Cat!) but he was so kind and helpful. Cat was really pleased for me but she did say that he probably has a session like this with all the guests. I bet it will be her turn soon and then I won't get a look in!

At dinner tonight (some amazing fish dish) Patricia said that she was doing a special offer next week for 'friends and family'. Relatives of the guests can come here and stay for half price. I know we can't afford it but I did fantasise about showing you the castle and the grounds – and my double bed! I do miss you. Cat says Justin will be too useless even to read Patricia's email. She says he has probably just sat the kids in front of the PlayStation all week (that's one thing to be said in favour of not having one!).

Rome tomorrow!

Love you

A xxxx

CHAPTER 6

Day 3, Rome

4 August

'In Roman times,' says Patricia, 'it was possible for fifty thousand people to enter the Colosseum in ten minutes.'

Sam, looking at the seemingly endless queue in front of them, asks, 'What did they know that we don't?'

'America hadn't been invented then,' says JP sourly, as a large family in plaid shorts elbows past them.

Patricia wishes JP would keep his prejudices to himself. Personally, she likes Americans; they are invariably polite and considerate guests. Also, she doesn't want Dorothy to be offended, or her husband Rick, who may or may not be a multimillionaire Texan oil baron looking for fresh investment opportunities.

'Strictly speaking,' smiles Cat, 'America was where it's always been. It's just that the Europeans hadn't found it yet.'

'Discovered by Cristoforo Colombo,' declaims Aldo from the back of the group. 'An *Italian*.' Patricia often wonders why

Aldo, another particularly vociferous critic of America, is so proud of Christopher Columbus.

'Actually, Aldo,' twinkles Cat, 'I think it was the Vikings who—'

'Look at this,' Aldo interrupts her, waving a proprietorial hand towards the towering arches of the Colosseum. 'One of the wonders of the world. Built over two thousand years ago. When Rome ruled the world.' Even dressed in a Hawaiian shirt and chinos, Aldo, with his hook nose and fierce eyes, looks as if he could have strolled in from the Senate on his way to see a good gladiator fight. He is a huge fan of the Romans and even, unthinkable in a Tuscan man, supports Roma football club. This is why he insists on coming on this trip; to harangue guests about his mate Julius Caesar.

Anna, wilting in the heat, edges towards the shade of a looming edifice. The sun-scorched grass in front of the Colosseum is a seething mass of humanity: tourists taking photos of each other, salesmen offering a bewildering range of mini Colosseums, tiny wolves and myriad pictures of the Pope, guides holding umbrellas aloft to summon their wandering flocks, even several men dressed as gladiators exhorting visitors to have their photo taken with them.

Thinking that the boys would love to see her with a real gladiator (albeit one wearing designer sunglasses), Anna asks Patricia if she has time to have her photo taken. Patricia, who is waiting for their guide to turn up, says crossly that they have all the time in the world.

'Oh, come on, Anna,' says Cat, 'you don't want to bother with all that tourist rubbish. It's a real rip-off.'

'Why the hell shouldn't she?' explodes Sam. 'If she wants to.'

There is a shocked silence. Everyone looks at Sam who scowls back, red-faced from the heat. Anna wants to dissolve with embarrassment. To think that she should be the cause of Sam speaking to Cat like that! But Cat just wrinkles her perfect nose in a mock grimace. 'Oh, don't be grumpy, Sam,' she says. 'Anna's a big girl. She can do what she likes.'

Stiff with self-consciousness, Anna walks over to the gladiators. The heat beats down on her head and her thighs are sticking together beneath her cotton skirt. 'A big girl.' What did Cat mean by that? Aldo comes with her to remind the gladiators that he is an Italian and so cannot be conned.

'*Una fotografia*,' smiles a gap-toothed gladiator engagingly. '*Sì, sì.*'

A few terse words from Aldo halves the asking price and Anna is soon cringing between the two gladiators, halfheartedly brandishing a sword.

'*Bella, bella.*' The gladiators kiss their hands to her, obviously holding no grudge about Aldo's strong-arm tactics.

'Thank you,' says Anna to Aldo, as they walk back to the group.

'No problem,' says Aldo. 'That Caterina, she is bitch in the manger.'

Anna thinks it is safest to ignore this.

*

79

The guide arrives at last and they take the fast track past the sweating queue of tourists and into the gloom of the Colosseum. Dorothy complains about having to put her bag through the airport-style X-ray machine. 'Is the law,' says Aldo impressively.

Inside they climb steep, dark steps and emerge into the glare of the arena itself. It doesn't take much, thinks Anna, peering over the railings, to imagine this place full of the roar of the crowd, the Emperor, resplendent in purple, rising to greet the gladiators on their way to death. 'We who are about to die salute you, Caesar.'

The guide is directing them towards a giant cross. 'This place was consecrated as a shrine to the Christian martyrs who perished here,' she says.

Dorothy sways dramatically. 'I feel them,' she declares. 'I feel their restless spirits.'

'If anyone feels my restless spirit,' mutters Sam to Anna, 'I'll smack 'em.'

'This place is very haunted,' says the guide obligingly. 'In fifteen thirty-four, the sculptor Benvenuto Cellini held a seance here and, it is said, he conjured fiery demons. There followed a terrible plague which did not end until a bull was sacrificed to the devil.'

Anna shivers, despite the heat of the day, but beside her Sam says, 'And now we're subjected to a plague of bullshit. Christ, I'm sick of this psychic crap.'

'Shh.' Anna looks towards Dorothy but, supported by Rick,

she is busy peering over the railings at the labyrinth of tunnels below.

'Here, below the stage,' says the guide, 'were the cages for the wild beasts and the mechanisms for the spectacles. It was possible to flood the whole arena and stage magnificent sea battles.'

'The Romans,' booms Aldo, 'were master engineers.'

'They were indeed,' smiles the guide, a pretty Italian girl with spiky hair. 'But we must not forget that this was a brutal place. The aisles between the seats were called *vomitoria* because so many people would throw up during a performance. The floor would be covered in sand to stop gladiators from slipping in the blood.'

'I smell the blood,' announces Dorothy.

'I smell a rat,' says Sam, moving aside for a crowd of Japanese tourists who swarm past, clicking their cameras like a flock of humming birds.

Matt, *il lupo,* is lounging against his bike in the piazza at San Severino. Graziano, *il leopardo,* and Elio, *il leone,* are beside him, eating ice creams. The nicknames, first invented when they were at *scuola elementare,* have now, in their own minds at least, acquired a sinister resonance. They are noms de guerre, aliases for desperate men who must leave behind their true identities, tributes to the animal spirits that lie beneath. Like animals, they are nearly always attired in leather although today it is too hot and all three wear jeans and T-shirts. Matt's proclaims that he is the son of the antichrist.

'Stupid tourists,' says Elio, indicating the lost-looking English families queuing up in the *gelateria*. 'Let's buzz them.'

'Buzzing' tourists, circling them on their motorbikes, crooning dialect curses, is a favourite summer sport of the threesome. The English ones, mostly middle-class families who have rented villas nearby, are always satisfyingly terrified. The Dutch, much to the posse's disappointment, actually seem to enjoy it.

'Too hot,' says Matt, wiping his hands on his jeans. 'Let's go to the lake and have a swim.'

'Bird at three o'clock,' says Graziano suddenly and all three swivel to watch the progress of a slim Italian girl in white jeans and a halter-neck top. She walks past very slowly, teetering on high-heeled sandals.

'Gagging for it,' says Elio.

'Desperate,' agrees Graziano.

Matt knows that Graziano will now, unless checked, embark upon a lurid description of one of his sexual adventures. Whether these stories (inevitably involving threesomes and trainee nuns) are true, Matt does not know. He only knows that they are incredibly boring.

'The Castello is empty today,' he says quickly. 'We could go up there and watch *Kerrang!*'

The other two brighten instantly. The Castello, with its sculptured grounds, its air conditioning, swimming pool and numerous widescreen TVs, is the promised land to them. Unfortunately, it is nearly always full of stupid tourists.

'No pond life?' asks Elio, using one of their milder terms for the guests.

'All gone to Rome for the day,' says Matt. He puts on an affected English accent.

'Oh, look at the Colosseum! Oh my, isn't it old? Oooh, look at the Vatican! Let's see if we can have tea with the Pope.' It is nothing like any English person on earth but it always makes the others laugh.

'What about Aldo?' asks Graziano.

Aldo, though he dotes on Matt, is no big fan of Graziano or Elio.

'He's gone too. He's driving the bus.'

'God help them,' says Elio.

Matt laughs. 'He's bought an extra-large crucifix to hang from the driving mirror. He probably won't even see the road. Come on, let's go.'

He is about to mount his bike when he sees a familiar figure coming towards them. A young man, slim and elegant, in faded jeans and a crisp white shirt. It is a few minutes before he recognises him as Fabio.

'*Ciao.*' Fabio smiles as he passes Matt.

'*Ciao*,' mutters Matt.

'Who's that?' asks Elio as Fabio disappears into the nearby clothes shop.

'The new handyman,' says Matt.

'Christ, must be paying him well if he can afford to shop

there,' says Graziano, pointing to the shop window where, designer labels are displayed in tasteful profusion.

'I don't know anything about him,' says Matt, unaccountably irritated. But his reply is lost in the explosion of sound as the motorbikes kick into life.

After the Colosseum, the writers admire the Roman Forum (the guide points out the House of the Vestal Virgins and the Temple of Julius Caesar, where Mark Antony read Caesar's will to his friends, Romans and countrymen) and cross the Campodoglio, past the statue of Marcus Aurelius and the 'wedding cake', that gleaming marble monument to Italian unification. A notice on the monument asks visitors to respect the eternal flame and not to eat, drink or sit down. Mary, sipping still mineral water, looks extremely guilty but is kindly reassured by Aldo that the notice refers only to Americans. Dorothy, who is finding the heat very trying, is mercifully absent at this point. She is sitting under a tree, fanning herself with *A Guide to Ancient Rome.*

Following Patricia, they then cut through ten lanes of traffic and make their way to the Piazza Navona, where they are to have lunch. On the way, Patricia points out the Foro del Argentina, a perfect miniature forum, below street level, which is reserved exclusively for cats. Cared for by volunteers, the cats live in a paradise of broken columns and headless statues.

'Oh, how dear!' Dorothy leans over the railing to chirrup

at a large tabby sitting under a cypress tree. A smaller black and white cat is fastidiously climbing the steps to what was once obviously a temple. A ginger cat stretches out on the very steps of the temple itself.

'It's so good they have someone to look after them,' says Dorothy.

'I don't know,' says Patricia. 'Cats are usually pretty good at looking after themselves.' She is thinking of Sean the cat who, despite her best efforts, is now an established member of the Castello household. Ratka, contrary to her name, is particularly besotted, buying the cat a beribboned basket which he has, so far, completely ignored.

Leaving the forum of the cats, they snake through the backstreets on the way to the Piazza Navona. Mary, trailing behind because her shoes hurt, sees ivy-covered churches squashed between tiny shops filled with dusty bottles, a shop selling priests' robes and another selling thousands of rosaries, hanging like spiders' webs from the doorway. Looking up, she sees dizzying steeples; once, she is sure, she sees a deer, its bronze antlers glittering in the sun, another time a square medieval tower like an illustration from a tarot card. She becomes so dazzled and disorientated that, when they turn a corner and, suddenly, the piazza is in front of them, she staggers and almost falls.

Instantly Aldo is at her side. 'Are you OK?'

'Yes.' Mary grasps his arm as she looks about her. The space in front of her seems to be filled with writhing stone: dryads, gods with flowing beards, horses with flowing manes and serpentine mermaid's tails. Around these incredible sculptures, which she now sees are fountains, teem hundreds and hundreds of tourists. Here and there human figures in gold draperies are pretending to be statutes, bowing with disconcerting suddenness whenever money falls into their collecting tins. The whole effect is wonderful, terrifying and strangely surreal.

'It's amazing,' breathes Mary.

Aldo puffs out his chest. 'In Roman times was a stadium, for chariot racing. Now is most famous piazza in Rome.'

'Amazing,' says Mary again. She realises that she is still clutching Aldo's arm and lets go, hastily.

As Patricia suspected, Aldo's restaurant is not in the main piazza, but hidden away down a dark side street. The food, though, is superb and the writers seem to enjoy the calm and the shade after the excitements of the morning. Everyone eats and drinks slightly too much and it is a sleepy, unsteady crew who stagger out into the baking sunshine of the afternoon. The plan is to do some shopping in the Via Veneto before the final stop of the tour – the Vatican. Anna and Cat, revived by designer labels, dive eagerly into the elegant boutiques. JP and Sam, too, seem drawn towards the Gucci, Versace, Dior axis of evil. Sally, Patricia, Dorothy, Rick and Aldo opt to sit in a nearby cafe drinking coffee and *digestivi*. Mary, though, feels restless. She doesn't want to shop (has never really worked out why this is supposed to be a pleasure) and she feels that she will explode if she has anything else to eat or drink. She knows that if she doesn't walk off lunch, she will soon have terrible indigestion. One of the most boring things about getting old, she decides, as she announces her intention of having a short walk, is the way that your body keeps finding new and embarrassing ways to let you down.

Mary walks through the crowds of people clutching gilt-embossed carrier bags and feels hotter and hotter. She is desperate for some water but doesn't want to stop and drink in the street. Her stomach is churning ominously and her feet are hurting worse than ever. What she wants is somewhere to sit down on her own, drink some water and recover her equilibrium. A cafe is out of the question as she doesn't speak enough Italian and she is terrified of the debonair waiters who slide between the pavement tables with such practised ease. Where can an elderly woman sit down, slip off her shoes and loosen her waistband in peace?

The answer comes to her as she reaches the end of the street – an ornate-looking church, complete with an actual monk standing at the door. Mary edges past the monk, who ignores her, and dives into the dusky interior. It is so dark that, at first, she cannot see anything. The only light comes from a few candles burning at the altar. Mary edges to a chair, sits down and takes off her shoes. Oh, the blissful cool of the stone under her feet! She takes out two Gaviscon tablets and washes them down with mineral water (she is not sure if drinking is allowed in churches but the place seems to be deserted). Feeling much better, Mary leans back and closes her eyes.

She must have fallen asleep because she wakes with a start to see a line of people, led by the monk, filing past her. Mary puts on her shoes and scrabbles for her bag. These people must be on a guided tour. Maybe you aren't allowed just to sit in the church and rest your feet. She decides to follow the line. She can always pay the monk on the way out and, at least, this way she will find the way out.

The monk leads the way to a small door and the line, with Mary at the back, descends a narrow staircase. They emerge into a long, narrow room with an earth floor. The light is very dim and it is a few minutes before Mary realises that she is in what seems to be an underground chapel, its walls covered with ornate, gothic designs in gold and what looks like ivory. Swaying chandeliers illuminate hundreds of round stones set into the walls. The monk is talking to the group in Italian but Mary edges forward to examine the stones. They are so uniform in shape, so carefully arranged, she is sure there must be some purpose that she is missing, like looking at one of those magic eye pictures in the Sunday papers. At the far end of the room, the stones are piled into archways and between the arches hang – Mary's heart stops. Between the arches hang the skeletons of three monks, wearing cowls identical to their guide's. And now, with a gasp of horror, she realises that the stones are actually skulls, hundreds, thousands of skulls, piled on top of each other to create monstrous, leering towers. Looking up, she sees that the ceiling, too, is decorated with skulls and other bones, arranged in a gruesome mosaic of circles, arches and crescent moons. Looking right up into the vault of the chapel she sees a full-size skeleton, holding a scythe made of bones. She realises now that the very chandeliers are made of bones, their shadows huge and misshapen in the dim light.

The next moment, the air is full of ghastly, spectral chanting. The guide turns to Mary and says something, pointing at her with a hand that looks bony enough to belong to one of his colleagues on the wall. Mary opens her mouth to say that she doesn't understand but no sound comes out. The monk moves towards her. In the background she can see his skeletal brothers grinning horribly from the rafters. She hears a door slam behind her. She is trapped. She is about to become a victim of a terrible cult. Her bones will shortly be decorating the ceiling, alongside the grim reaper, her sightless eyes forever looking down. Mary screams.

'It is OK, Mary,' says a blissfully familiar voice behind her.

Mary swings round and finds herself facing the gaudy blue and green of a Hawaiian shirt. She feels Aldo put his arm round her and hears him talking to the guide. With a brief laugh, the monk flicks a switch and the ghastly chanting stops. Now Aldo, too, is laughing and talking in rapid Italian. Steering Mary with one arm, he presses some money into the monk's hand. The monk makes a gesture of lofty refusal while, at the same time, mysteriously pocketing the money.

Then Aldo is guiding her up the steps, through a heavy oak door (that was the door she heard shutting), through the dark church and, at last, out into the sunlight.

On the Via Veneto, the designer-clad crowds pushing past them, Mary turns to Aldo, half laughing, half crying.

'What *was* that place?' she asks.

'It is the Capuchin cemetery,' says Aldo, smiling.

'Capuchin?' At first all that occurs to her is a coffee, sprinkled with chocolate, then she thinks of the monkeys and then she remembers that the monkeys were named after an order of monks (or was it the other way round?). Both the monkeys and the monks (and the coffee) being famous for their headgear.

'A monastery?'

'Yes.' Aldo is steering her through the crowds. She doesn't mind his being in control of their pace. In fact she finds it rather restful.

'The crypt is where the monks are buried,' says Aldo. 'Their bones are used to make the walls.'

'How horrible!'

Aldo shrugs. 'Many tourists go there. It is quite beautiful, I think. But not for me. I prefer the sunlight.'

They have now reached the Piazza di Spagna. Flower-lined steps are in front of them, full of people laughing and talking. At the foot of the steps is a marble fountain, its water reflecting the sky of brightest blue.

'So do I,' says Mary taking a deep breath. 'So do I.'

'Mary!' Patricia comes hurrying towards her, looking concerned. Mary sees Sally, JP and Sam sitting on the shallow steps by the fountain. Cat and Anna are cooling their feet in the water. Dorothy and Rick are videoing madly.

'What happened to you?'

'I got lost,' says Mary. 'Aldo found me.'

'Thank goodness,' says Patricia. 'Let's get on to the Vatican. I've just about had enough for one day, haven't you?'

Three hours later, the minibus is making its way back on the SS2 (the *ess ess due*) towards Siena. As dusk falls on Italy, there is a tangible feeling of warmth and friendliness in the little bus. Cat is plugged into her iPod and Anna is asleep but Sally and Dorothy are talking in low voices and, on the back seat, JP, Sam and Rick are playing a complicated card game taught to them by Aldo. At the front of the bus, Patricia and Aldo are talking in Italian. Once or twice Mary catches the name Matteo and realises that this must be Patricia's son Matthew, that friendly but enigmatic figure she sometimes sees swimming in the early mornings or disappearing on his motorbike in the evenings. Mary was invited to join the card game but she declined (though she loves cards and, at home, plays a mean game of whist). Now, though, she prefers to sit and stare out of the window, the images of the day rewinding in her head as the landscape changes from suburbs to hills to pine forests and mountains. She sees the arches and shadows of the Colosseum ('He conjured fiery demons . . . a bull was sacrificed to the devil . . .'), the gleaming white of the wedding cake, a ginger cat lying majestically on the steps of a temple. As the shadows turn purple and the lights shine from castles in the mountains, Mary sees statues coming to life and bowing to her. She sees walls made from human bones and robed figures moving towards her. Then, as she hovers pleasantly between sleeping and waking, she sees the bright embrace of a Hawaiian shirt, its technicolour brilliance blotting out the shadows of the day.

CHAPTER 7

Day 4

5 August

'Plot,' says Jeremy, 'is crap. Plot is not life. Plot is full of coincidence; life isn't. I have never, for example, met my ex-wife, by chance, in an all-night chemist. I wouldn't want to.' He pauses for laughter, thin on the morning air. 'But this sort of thing is always happening in plots. Dickens is the very worst. The man who betrayed Miss Havisham had to also be the man who betrayed Magwitch. *Of course* he does. Who does Oliver Twist bump into on the street? His grandfather. *Of course* he does. Now that never happens with Jane Austen. Her plots serve the characters, not the other way round. There is more truth in one of Miss Bates' monologues than in all of Dickens' work put together.'

'But if you never have any coincidences,' objects Anna, 'your story would never get anywhere. We need to have people bumping into other people, just to keep things moving.'

She wonders if Jeremy will be irritated by this interruption but he just laughs. 'Very well put, Anna. "People bumping into people" is, indeed, the very essence of fiction. I just ask that you don't make it too obvious, that's all, too nineteenth century. No hero galloping up on a white horse, no sudden legacy, no last-minute marriage proposals.' Anna can't imagine any of these things featuring in her book, which, suddenly, makes her feel rather sad. She prefers Dickens to Austen.

Jeremy's little audience is rather restless. It is Sunday and Dorothy and Rick have gone into San Severino. JP is at Mass. The others are half-heartedly participating in a writing sesssion. As the day is so beautiful, Jeremy suggested holding the session under the trees on the front lawn. This sounded attractive in theory, but in practice the trees prove an irresistible magnet for mosquitoes and the wooden seats, so pretty from a distance, are hard and uncomfortable. Anna and Cat soon sink on to the grass and, after a few minutes, Sally joins them. They look, thinks Sam sourly, like disciples before Jeremy's bearded guru.

'Dickens sold books,' he says. 'Isn't that what it's all about? The public likes a coincidence or two.'

'Should the public always get what it wants?' asks Jeremy idly, watching as Aldo's Vespa trundles up the drive. He hopes Aldo will cook something special for lunch. He is just in the mood for a good meal, a glass or two of wine and a long sleep.

'That's the law of supply and demand, isn't it?' says Sam, twisting round so the sun is out of his eyes.

'Spoken like a financier,' smiles Jeremy.

'Ex-financier,' corrects Sam.

'I read somewhere,' says Mary, who sits, very upright, on one of the uncomfortable wooden seats, 'that a writer should collect coincidences.'

'Paul Auster kept a book of coincidences,' admits Jeremy. 'He wrote about them in *The Art of Hunger*. But that's advanced stuff. What I want you all to do is try to free yourself from plot. Write something stream of consciousness, go with the flow. And, for heaven's sake, avoid happy endings.'

'What shall we write?' asks Mary, getting out her notebook.

'Write about your trip to Rome,' suggests Jeremy. 'Start with yesterday's trip and see where that takes you. Don't have a plan or a structure. Just write.'

Anna stretches out on the grass. She watches a line of ants heading towards the place where, earlier, she spilt her orange juice. The day seems too hot to bother about style or structure or work of any kind. The grass is yellow and smells of herbs; the ants march remorselessly past.

Cat, too, is uncurling in the sun. She has kicked off her sandals and flexes one brown foot, red nails twinkling. 'I quite often use stream of consciousness in my writing,' she says. 'I'm quite experimental.'

I bet you are, thinks Sam.

'Always experiment,' intones Jeremy. 'Never let yourself get stale.'

Cat smiles up at him, eyelashes fluttering. 'What are you working on at the moment?' she asks.

*

Aldo's lunch is as special as Jeremy hopes. Afterwards the guests go to rest in their rooms; the afternoon is heavy and golden, the air seems almost thick, holding in suspension the buzzing mosquitoes, the scent of lavender, the noise of the crickets. Jeremy collapses on his bed; he has drunk the best part of a bottle of Chianti and so expects to fall asleep at once but his head is full of words, bumping impotently against the sides of his brain, like butterflies shut in a box. One sentence in particular hovers for a while just out of reach and then bursts, italicised, on to his consciousness. *What are you working on at the moment?* Jeremy twists his head, trying to find a cool patch on his pillow. *What are you working on at the moment?* The air conditioning hums unpleasantly, he starts to scratch a mosquito bite on his leg and finds that he has drawn blood. *What are you working on at the moment?* He gets up and takes a bottle of Coke from the fridge, gulping so greedily that the sticky liquid runs down his chin. He undresses and goes into his bathroom. A shower will fix it. A cool shower and then a refreshing sleep. But the water drumming against the glass doors is playing the same old tune. *What are you working on at the moment? What are you working on at the moment?*

Jeremy hasn't written a word of fiction since *Belly Flop*, twenty years ago. It happened so slowly that it was many years before he said the words 'writer's block', even to himself. *Belly Flop* was a huge hit and so for a long time there were foreign rights to be sold, prizes to win, speeches to give, reviews of other, less fortunate, writers. Then there was the film script to write, in collaboration with a laconic American called Tom Bates. In dark moments, Jeremy wonders whether Tom Bates isn't actually responsible for his present inability to write fiction. He learnt a lot from Tom. Jeremy is a verbose writer. Dickensian in his flourishes, he never uses one word where he could use a paragraph and several quotations from Molière. Every morning, in their Beverly Hills hotel, Tom, pencil in hand, would score through Jeremy's best lines. 'Lose it,' he would say. 'No one talks like this.'

'Couldn't we use it in a voice-over?' Jeremy would plead.

'Voice-overs are for wimps,' Tom would reply.

And, over a year later, when Jeremy sat down at his computer, wanting to make a start on the next dazzling bestseller, that is what he'd hear in his head: 'Lose it. No one talks like this.' The screenplay for *Belly Flop* won a Golden Globe award and was nominated for an Oscar but, even so, Jeremy never quite forgave his collaborator. When he read, some years later, that renowned Hollywood scriptwriter Tom Bates had been found dead in a hotel room after taking a massive drugs overdose, part of Jeremy wanted to say, 'Serves you right, you smug American bastard,' even as his better side composed a tasteful message to Tom's widow.

It wasn't all Tom's fault, of course. Part of the problem was the universal acclaim heaped upon *Belly Flop*. Jeremy's first two books received sparse, though respectful, reviews but *Belly Flop* was lauded from the rooftops. Soon Jeremy could quote the reviews in his sleep. 'Stunning talent . . . life-changing book ... rewrites the script for twentieth-century life.' And, as he sat at his computer, as a counterpoint to Tom's voice he could hear the reactions to the new, as yet unwritten book: 'Disappointing ... suffers from comparison with ... Bullen has lost his edge.' He couldn't bear it. He couldn't bear to spoil his perfect score. He couldn't bear to use *Belly Flop* to flog its pallid sibling, 'By the author of ...' He couldn't bear to hear people say that maybe he had just the one good book in him. Better to keep them waiting, if necessary for ever, for the elusive perfect sequel.

And that's the other thing. He can't think of a plot. Oh, occasionally he has ideas. Sometimes he even writes them down (artist haunted by childhood muse – man marries sister without knowing it – Wilkie Collins meets the woman in white) but nowhere does he find the spark, that hidden element that will fuse his ideas into a whole, into a book. When he was offered a job teaching creative writing, it seemed the perfect solution. He would be earning money (*Belly Flop* still brought in royalties but Jeremy likes good living) and mixing with congenial people. He may even, said a tiny ignoble voice inside him, find some new ideas. But the would-be writers, though congenial enough, turn out not to have an original thought between them. Soon Jeremy becomes bored with turgid confessions and rip-offs of the latest bestsellers. He sticks with it for the money, the ego boost and the chance to bed young women who might not otherwise be interested in a middle-aged man with a beard and questionable clothes sense. For the author of *Belly Flop,* though, they are only too anxious to get their knickers off.

For all this he is much in demand as a tutor. He is an astute critic, with great personal charisma and still a faint dusting of stardust from the Hollywood days. He can take his pick of jobs and, when Patricia offered him the post on her creative writing course, he accepted like a shot. Tuscany was, after all, a far cry from Watford Adult Education Centre. But, after four years of talking about plot in the baking Italian heat, even this has lost its charm. He'd like to jack it in but what the hell would he do all summer?

Jeremy lies naked between the cool sheets. He thinks he would swap anything, even his treasured Golden Globe, for just one fresh idea.

Patricia is in her office. She never drinks alcohol at lunchtime but, even so, the somnolent afternoon is starting to get to her. It is cool in her office but she knows the heat is out there, waiting to strike. The fact that it is Sunday somehow makes the day seem even heavier, even more indolent, than normal. The clock ticks from the hall and Sean purrs on the visitor's chair; otherwise all is silent. What she would really like is to go to her room and sleep all afternoon (for some reason she hasn't been sleeping much at nights recently) or go to the pool for a quick swim. But, no, she has to work. All the guests are asleep, Matt is off on the rampage somewhere. A perfect chance to check the bookings for her October wine tasting course. She clicks on her computer. Still several places to fill. She'll have to send an email round to past guests and put something on the website. Sean, who was good with computers, used to run her website but now it is managed by a teenage computer whiz in San Severino. She'll write some copy and email it to Lorenzo.

Nestled in the beautiful Tuscan hills . . . Christ, what sort of a word is 'nestled'? It sounds like a cross between a chocolate drink and a mother hen. *The beautiful Tuscan hills provide an exquisite setting for* . . . Exquisite? Another chocolate box word . . . *provide the perfect setting for Il Castello della Luna, a genuine thirteenth-century castle, exquisitely* – no – *lovingly restored to include every modern luxury*

Except, thinks Patricia, that the shower in the Blue Room leaks and the central heating makes peculiar noises at night. Will they have to have the central heating on in October? Maybe; the nights can be cold. She can have a fire in the Great Hall though. People seem to enjoy that. Maybe put in a line about open fires somewhere.

She should also put something on the website about her special offer for families of guests. People are quite likely to log on to the website while their families are at the Castello. Perhaps Lorenzo can do a pop-up or something?

Patricia types away for another half hour. *Beautiful . . . exquisite . . . authentic . . . sun-kissed . . . stunning hilltop towns . . . rolling hills . . . olive groves . . . famous vineyards . . . medieval . . . full-bodied . . . magnificent*. It seems a long way from her experience of living in Tuscany but the clichés are all there, rolling, sun-kissed and magnificent, outside her window. It is beautiful and that does help. Sometimes.

Patricia stretches. Five o'clock. To hell with it, she will have a quick swim and then start preparing for supper (just a light meal on Sunday). She runs up to her room, puts on her trusty blue Speedo with a towelling dress over the top and rolls up her towel. In the corridor outside her room she listens. Silence except for one keyboard tapping. Who is working on a Sunday afternoon? Her bets are on Mary or JP. Mary is obviously very serious about her writing (has she really been writing the same book for thirty years?) and JP seems serious about everything. Tucking her towel under her arm, Patricia runs back down the stairs.

But, by the pool, she has a shock. JP is lying face down on one of the sunloungers, apparently asleep. Patricia hesitates. Part of her wants to tiptoe away without being seen but the sun is pounding down on JP's back and head. She doesn't want him to end up in hospital with sunstroke.

'JP?' She touches his shoulder gently. He turns his head sleepily towards her.

'You shouldn't sleep in the sun,' says Patricia. 'It's dangerous.'

JP blinks as if he is trying to get her in focus. He has brown eyes with surprisingly long eyelashes.

'Mrs O'Hara.'

'Yes,' says Patricia patiently. 'You should come out of the sun. Or at least put a T-shirt and hat on.'

JP sits up and touches the top of his head. He winces.

'The sun is still very strong,' says Patricia.

'Especially if you're almost bald.'

'I didn't say that.'

JP reaches for his shirt and puts it on. 'I didn't mean to fall asleep,' he says. 'Too much wine at lunchtime.'

'I thought you didn't drink Italian wine,' says Patricia waspishly.

'I forced myself.'

He looks at Patricia. In her yellow towelling dress she suddenly looks much younger, less poised. Her hair is ruffled and she isn't wearing any shoes.

'Did you come down to swim?' he asks, reaching for his water bottle.

'Well, yes,' says Patricia, rather defensively. 'I don't usually when guests are here but . . .'

JP gestures towards the still, blue water. 'Go ahead.'

Patricia doesn't like the way he says this, as if inviting her to swim in her own pool. Also he is looking at her a little too intently, his eyes narrowed. But, on the other hand, the water does look incredibly tempting. Suddenly, she can't bear it any more. She whips off her dress and, very conscious of the skimpiness of her old swimming costume, dives into the pool. Oh, the bliss of the cold water closing over head! She floats under water as long as she can and, when she surfaces, she is almost at the other end of the pool. JP is squatting at the side, looking at her.

'Is it good?' he asks, smiling.

'Wonderful.'

Patricia floats on her back. When she closes her eyes she can still see motes of light, black against the red. When she opens them, JP is still staring at her.

'Why don't you come in?' she challenges.

'I just might,' he answers, standing up.

Patricia is expecting a big, macho dive but suddenly JP looks up. Slightly disconcerted, Patricia follows his gaze and sees Matt, sweaty and filthy in jeans and a T-shirt, standing at the opposite end of the pool. He is carrying his helmet and has obviously just got off his bike.

Patricia swims to the side. She can't be properly angry with Matt while floating in the pool.

'Where have you been?' she asks.

'At Graziano's,' grunts Matt, looking down at her. 'What are you doing, Mum?'

'Swimming,' snaps Patricia. 'What does it look like?'

'But you never swim when there are guests.'

'It's hot,' says JP, who has retreated into the shade. 'Give your mother a break.'

Matt rounds on him. 'Who asked you?'

'Matt!' Patricia heaves herself out of the pool. 'Apologise!'

Matt looks at her with lowered head, saying nothing.

'Hot day to ride a motorbike,' says JP in a conciliatory tone. Matt ignores him.

Patricia wraps herself in her towel. 'Did you have lunch with Graziano?'

'Yes.'

'You might have said. I was expecting you here.'

'I'm sure you had plenty of people to amuse you,' says Matt, giving JP an unfriendly look.

Patricia stands irresolute, wondering whether to challenge Matt for his rudeness or just to let it go. Part of her is always so relieved to see him, safe and well, after he has been out on his motorbike, that she is reluctant to provoke a row. But, really, he is being unnecessarily boorish.

'Why don't you carry on with your swim?' JP asks Patricia.

'I will if you will.'

Matt looks from JP to his mother and, in three easy strides, jumps, fully dressed, into the pool.

The Seven Moons of Jaconda
by Lupo O'Hara

Chapter 10

The time has come, thinks Hengest. Now the lune is in its seventh circle, the time has come. It is his fate to rid Jaconda of this creeping menace, this serpentine stranger, this Grenouille from the land of Eye Fall. He knows this even before the portents give him the message. 'The son of Erin must fell the son of Eye Fall.' He knows it and yet he hesitates. Grenouille is cunning, he has a body servant who tastes all his food before it crosses his lips, he sleeps ever with the Sword of Power at his side. He sprinkles holy dust around his bed. Hengest knows that, if he crosses the sacred circle, he too will be dust.

On the new lune, Hengest and his household go out moon hunting. They seek the Silver Stag of Melchior. Grenouille accompanies them, mounted on his poison-green steed, Sicorax. Hengest, astride faithful Ducati, follows close at hand. The portents will show him the way. He fingers his ice-sharp sword.

'Now, by the powers, show me the way to rid Jaconda of this man. And thus my royal father will be avenged.'

CHAPTER 8

Writing

Rome

by Anna Valore

It's hard, trying to write in a new way, like trying on new shoes or changing your parting, feels wrong somehow until you get used it I keep wanting to put in full stops, can't help it, it was the way I was taught at school. Those nuns were terrifying, Sister Anthony with her strap wouldn't be allowed today, good thing too, neither Steve nor I have ever smacked the boys though I think I've got nearer to it than he has, well, I'm the one at home with them all day, it all seems so perfect when he gets home, kids in their pyjamas, 'Daddy! Daddy!' down the stairs, little woman in the kitchen, smell of shepherd's pie. The perfect marriage except we're not married.

I'm off the subject but isn't that the point of stream of consciousness? From the eternal city to shepherd's pie in three easy stages. So – Rome. The heat, that's the first thing, you can almost feel the ground bubbling beneath your feet, like walking on a volcano, dangerous and exciting too. But the heat really saps your energy; you edge along from shade to shade, like a vampire, sweat running down your neck, your clothes limp and sticky. Only Cat seemed unaffected, cool and perfect in her strappy top and shorts (pity they wouldn't let her in the Vatican, wouldn't have thought they'd be so strict in this day and age) and Aldo, in his amazing Day-Glo shirt, he didn't seem to feel the heat at all. But I felt terrible, knew I was all pink and sweaty. Sam took a picture of me and I am literally puce, looking about a hundred stone. The heat and the light, sun gleaming on marble, the sky a hard bright blue like coloured glass. Once all these ruins would have been covered in marble. What would Rome have looked like then? Unbearably bright and rather gaudy, I imagine, the Disneyland of the ancient world. Aldo wouldn't like that. For him, Rome is absolutely perfect. Funny, I can't imagine feeling like that about London, especially Wembley, where I was born. The grandeur that was Wembley. My God.

Heat and light and all these amazing buildings, coming one after the other, like a film that is speeded up. Ruin upon ruin, ancient columns rising up out of modern apartment blocks, a temple built on a forum built on a pagan burial site. Layers and layers of the past. Even the Vatican was built on the site of a pagan temple. Sister Anthony wouldn't like that at all. I lit a candle there, in front of the Pietà, such a moving sculpture, the mother cradling her dead son, how can marble be so human? Do I still believe? I certainly said so to get the boys into St James the Great. I thought then that God would punish me for that and then I thought, well, I do believe after all, so that's all right. St James the Better than Average, Steve calls it. Maybe I believe in the league tables more than I believe in God. Sobering thought.

I'm not getting on very far with Rome or maybe that's the point of the whole exercise. It feels weird being given homework like this. I was always very conscientious about homework, sat studying late into the night while Mum and Dad (who never really understood about schoolwork) kept asking me to come down and watch telly with them. I was a little prig though, said things like, 'I'm studying for my future not getting square-eyed in front of Casualty.' Now Dad is dead I wish I'd watched Casualty with him, snug on the sofa with a mug of cocoa in my hand, watching Charlie Fairhead deal with an outbreak of bubonic plague or something. I made him feel stupid, patronised him, and I'd do anything to turn the clock back. That's why I'll never do that to Steve. Never make him feel that I'm better than him because I'm not. He's twice the person I am, a better father than I'm a mother and he's very clever, he just doesn't realise it. Just like Dad.

Maybe Steve is a father substitute. After all, I did meet him just a month after Dad passed away. That has never occurred to me before. I suppose Steve is steady and reassuring, like my dad. But he's lots of other things as well. He's funny and sexy and tough. Actually, I've been thinking a lot about how sexy he is. Maybe it's the heat and the food and the wine and sleeping alone in that big empty bed.

He isn't a father figure at all.

Well, I'm certainly a long way from Rome now. If all roads lead to Rome, do all streams of consciousness lead back to the river of childhood? Discuss.

Rome
by Sally Hamilton

Blood flows from the stones of the Colosseum. Rich, scarlet blood pumping from severed limbs and decapitated bodies. The groans of a gladiator who feels his opponent's foot on his neck, ready to stamp on his face, crushing the bone to powder, gouging out an eye with a metal fist whilst the other eye looks around wildly, at the cheering crowds, the emperor's down-turned thumb.

The blood flows into the Forum where Mark Antony declaimed over Caesar's dead body. Shakespeare does not tell us about the blood but it is here, staining the white toga a rich vermilion. Friends, Romans and countrymen. Except he didn't say this. Or did he? The experts only tell us that Mark Antony read his will. Shakespeare made up the rest. No matter. His words are here along with a million stories, myths and legends. And it is Shakespeare's Caesar that I see, his fear turning to despair when he saw his favourite, his illegitimate son, advancing on him with a dagger. Et tu, Brute? Then fall, Caesar.

The vestal virgins, walled up in a temple of lust and hypocrisy. One moment, power and glory, at the emperor's side for the games, knowing the secrets of all men's hearts. The next second, betrayed by the urges of the body, and it is the slow death, buried alive, the terrible sound of the earth filling up your living grave, your screams for help, earth in your eyes and mouth, your last gasps for air, the worst moment when you know that, finally, there is no escape. The arteries popping, the heart exploding, blood filling your world.

Blood. Always more blood.

The statue of Giordano Bruno in the Campo dei Fiori. The priest who turned to the devil. Who, along with Benvenuto Cellini, conjured the devil in the ruins of the Colosseum. Bruno was burnt alive. Hearing the flames crackle below his feet, feeling the dreadful heat stealing up his body, knowing that soon it would turn his blood to liquid fire. From the crowd someone holds up a crucifix, waves the sacred cross before Bruno's contorted face. He reaches out a hand. Will he kiss the cross, confess his sins? No, with a snarl, he dashes the cross to the ground where it burns along with his own funeral pyre. And, with a dreadful shout and a smell of burning entrails, Bruno gives himself up to the devil.

A day trip to Rome. Pizza, pasta, ice cream, tourists, Versace, Prada, the Pope. Death, torture, mutilation.

Rome

by Sam McClusky

She's beautiful but she doesn't know it. Has no idea. Prefers instead to look up to her dreadful, hard-faced girlfriend, the

one with tits like tiny daggers. But she . . . she is all soft curves
and slow, shy smiles. She has beautiful hair, long and wavy like
a statue of the Madonna. When she is hot, she pushes the hair
back from her eyes. When she is bored, she plays with a strand
of it, twisting it round and round her finger. By the pool she lifts
up her hair, unselfconsciously, simply because her neck is hot, and
reveals the most amazing sweep of neck, vulnerable enough to
make a grown man cry.

Her eyes are blue, they fill with tears when she mentions her
children. She sometimes frowns and smiles at the same time, a
most heartbreaking combination. As if she can't let herself be
completely happy. I want to make her happy. To shower her with
presents and perfume and flowers. To see the dimple appear
in her creamy cheek. To see her nose wrinkle and her freckles
(oh God, those freckles!) disappear in the blush. When she leans
towards me I smell perfume and toothpaste and something else,
something sharp, like lemon. She eats the lemon in her drinks,
skin and all. Once she drops a pip and I pick it up, imagine
it growing into a tree, right there, in the humid depths of my
jeans. What's that song about the lemon tree and the fruit being
impossible to eat? Not for her.

I'm looking at a picture of her. She stands, delightfully uncertain, in front of the Vatican. She was brought up a Catholic, she
tells me. I catch her crossing herself in front of the Pietà (doesn't
do much for me, sentimental nonsense). She blushes when she sees
me watching her. She has no idea what I feel for her. I defended
her when she wanted a picture taken with those ridiculous

gladiators. I thought then that she might have guessed but she was just the same afterwards, laughing at my jokes, offering to take a picture of me in front of the Colosseum. 'I hate pictures of people,' I said. 'I only like views.' But I took a picture of her all the same. Her face is flushed, her hair loose, her eyes squinting against the sun. You can just make out the outline of her legs, Lady Di-like, through her thin skirt. Funny, although I have seen her legs in their entirety, beside the pool, the sight of their hazy outline gives me the most tremendous hard-on.

God, she is beautiful. I can't believe I have got such a crush on her after only a few days. And she is married, talks about 'Steve and the boys' all the time. Well, I'm married too or as good as. I've been with Jenny for five years now, we've had our ups and downs but we're still together. She never understood why I had to jack in the city job to be a writer though. She likes the city, likes the wheeling and dealing, the lunches, the thrill of the deal. She's still in that world, while I'm sitting at home wondering whether or not to make my narrator a poof. Anna understands though. She's a writer herself. She has even had some stories published. We were all tremendously impressed to hear this although, typically, Anna played it down, said it was only some stupid women's magazine. Bitch Queen Cat was quick to agree. 'They're better known for their knitting patterns than for their literary taste.' Cow. I hate her.

I want to protect Anna from Cat's bitchiness (a cat who's a bitch, how about that? I daresay it makes a point about derogatory animal analogies as applied to women but it's true nevertheless. She's catty as well) and from Jeremy's lechery and JP's indifference. I want to hug her and hold her and stroke her hair. I want to make love to her over and over again until she screams my name out loud and never mentions Steve again.

Christ, I can't show this to Jeremy, can I?

Postcards

Darling Tom and Jakey,
This is the Colosseum where the gladiators used to fight. I'll send you a picture of me with some real gladiators. I've even got a sword! I saw the Vatican too, where the Pope lives. Tell Dad he wasn't in though.
   I'm missing you loads, can't wait to see you again.
   All love
   Mum

Dear Stacy,
We are having a real cultural time in Italy. This is the town near where we are staying – it's real old, like something from a book. Everyone on the course is very nice and we are staying in an actual castle!
   Love to you, Harvey and the boys
   Mom and Pops

Dear Joan,

Yesterday I saw a forum (in Rome) where hundreds of wild cats lived. I thought how much Snowball would have loved it. Am having a very enjoyable stay and have been swimming every day. Hope you are managing to get some swimming this summer.

    All the best

    Mary

Darlings,

This is the Forum where the Romans used to have their markets and temples. It's incredible – like going back in time. Having a lovely time, doing lots of work (writing is very hard work!) but missing my babies!

    Lots of love

Mummy

Hi Jen babe – They call this building the wedding cake and you can see why. Rome is beautiful but too bloody hot. Hope the Greeks are treating you well.

    Love

    Sam

    X

Dear Mum,

Course going very well – Jeremy on good form as ever. Some very nice people this year. Hope your arthritis is not too bad – will drive down to see you when I get back.

    Much love

    Sally

Simon — Just look at the balls on this! Doing my usual time in Tuscany, teaching creative writing to a bunch of no-hopers. Wondered if you'd heard anything re the radio serial for Belly Flop?

    Cheers

    Jeremy

CHAPTER 9

Day 5

6 August

'So you see, you've got to trust your reader more, not apologise when you go off on a tangent. Believe that the reader wants to know what you want to tell them. Remember what I said about plot. Character is worth more than coincidence. I'm not interested in a neat plot structure. I *would* have been interested to find out more about Sister Anthony or your father.'

Jeremy smiles, leaning back in his chair. Anna smiles too, though she feels a little embarrassed at having her work discussed so minutely. She can't remember the last time when someone concentrated so intensely on her. Except Steve, of course, but he only really concentrates on her in bed, the rest of the time their relationship is casual, comradely, quick kisses on parting and hasty text messages throughout the day. The boys love her but take her for granted, as perhaps they should. Certainly no one has ever looked at her writing in this way, examining it as if it is worth examining, talking about her as if she is a set text. It is a heady and also a slightly scary experience.

They are sitting on Jeremy's balcony, drinking cold white wine. It is seven o'clock, so the drinking is forgivable, but the day is still hot and, far below, they can hear people in the pool, the laughter floating up to them, tantalising and distant. Aldo is preparing a barbecue and the tang of wood smoke mixes with the usual evening scents of lavender and lemon balm. Far up in the sky, a plane is lazily writing a white trail against the deepening blue. It makes Anna think of travelling; it makes her think of home.

She takes a sip of her wine. 'But I thought we were meant to be describing Rome.'

Jeremy sighs inwardly. Anna is being a little more obtuse than he likes. Still, beggars can't be choosers and hers was the only piece on Rome worth reading. Cat wrote a dreadful arch story from the point of view of a cat, Mary wrote well but waffled on about some stupid crypt, Sally's was terrible and JP and Sam didn't even bother to hand anything in.

Jeremy leans in towards Anna, letting his hand rest briefly on her bare arm. She's looking pretty good today, wearing a red sundress that shows off the beginning of her tan. It shows off her tits too.

'What is Rome to you?' he asks teasingly. 'As you say, if all roads lead to Rome, do all streams of consciousness lead back to the river of childhood? A clever metaphor, by the way.

A little too clever for the context perhaps. Remember, the Anna who is writing might not choose a device like this. You started the piece with domestic metaphors, women's things, shoes and hairstyles. Maybe the Anna who is writing is a more prosaic creature, not the highly intelligent woman I see sitting in front of me.'

Now Anna positively burns with self-consciousness. *Highly intelligent. Belly Flop* ('one of the most brilliant books ever written in the English language') actually thinks she is highly intelligent!

'How do I know which Anna is writing?' she asks, not too stupidly she hopes.

Jeremy laughs. 'Who knows? We are what we speak. There is nothing outside the text.'

Anna smiles politely though she hasn't a clue what he is talking about. 'But the reader doesn't want to know about me,' she says. 'They want to know what will happen next. In the story, I mean.'

'Who decides what happens next?' asks Jeremy, leaning back into the shadows.

'Well, the author, of course.'

'Really? Have you never had a character decide for themselves what they want to do, almost as if they were defying you, their creator?'

'Mmm.' Anna thinks of her novel, where Sophie, her narrator, will insist on going to bed with Hugo's best friend, no matter what this does to the structure.

'Does that happen in your books?' she asks.

'God, yes!' Jeremy laughs. 'My characters shag, fart, masturbate, die when it pleases them. They don't listen to me.'

There is a silence. The words 'shag, fart, masturbate, die' seem to linger, embarrassingly, in the still, scented air. Jeremy waves an airy hand, as if to waft them away.

'We think we are the authors,' he says, 'but we are merely conduits for language. We put pen to paper and who knows what comes out? Sometimes the text takes over. That's why you can't afford to be too anal about structure.'

'I like books where things work out neatly,' says Anna stubbornly. 'There's one of the Harry Potter books, the one with the time turner, where everything just works out so cleverly, it gave me real pleasure to read it.'

Jeremy chokes on his wine. He can't believe that Anna has just quoted a Harry Potter book as an example of literary art. Maybe she's not as attractive as he thought.

'In a children's book,' he says at last, 'perhaps things are different. I'm talking about literature.'

'The Harry Potter books aren't just for children,' protests Anna. 'I started off reading them to the boys but now I just buy them for myself. I love them.'

Jeremy reaches across the table and pats Anna's hand. 'Would you like me to draw up a reading list for you?' he says kindly. 'A list of proper, grown-up books?'

Anna hesitates. She wants to defend Harry Potter and books with neat endings but she doesn't quite know where to start.

After all, Jeremy must know best. He is the tutor and a published author, after all.

'That would be very kind,' she says at last.

Patricia has broken her rule about not socialising with the guests. True, this time she is not actually in the pool but she is sitting at a nearby table under an umbrella, to all intents and purposes relaxing. The fact that the other occupants of the table are Dorothy and Rick slightly explains the lapse but the day has been extremely hot, even by Italian standards, and Aldo is also nearby, starting the fire in the great stone barbecue. Fabio is acting as Aldo's assistant (a thankless task), carrying the wood, chopping the vegetables, crushing garlic, pouring oil and wine. In his snowy white T-shirt and jeans, he does not look hot, or flustered, simply attentive and interested. And Aldo has, so far, not thrown a saucepan at him or cast doubt on his sanity and/or parentage. A record.

Cat is lying face down on a sunlounger, her bikini strings untied so as not to leave a line. JP, sitting nearby under an umbrella (Patricia was right about the sunburn), fantasises about her jumping up suddenly and losing the bikini altogether. He is not in the least interested in Cat or in her views on literature but he is, he is obliged to admit, slightly interested in her breasts.

In the pool, Matt floats on a lilo. As the lilo drifts to the edge of the pool, he pushes against the side with one lazy foot and floats back to the centre. Strictly speaking, Matt should not be in the pool when there are guests around but there is something hypnotic about the lilo's progress, its slow drift to the sides, its sudden propulsion back into the centre, that makes Patricia reluctant to ask him to stop. And, after the way he spoke to JP yesterday, she finds herself not wanting to provoke Matt. He has never spoken to a guest like that before. Usually he just ignores them. What can have got into him?

Also, though she doesn't quite admit this, even to herself, she enjoys watching Matt, the slim brown body revolving in the blue water. Sometimes he is so close that she could almost touch him. Not that she would, of course. Earlier on, though, she had offered (quite brusquely) to rub suntan lotion into his back and was quite shocked at the pleasure it gave her, running her hands over his back, the wide shoulders, the bony spine covered with downy blond hair. Sean had the same hairs on his back, she remembers, the same rangy body. Pity that, in his case, it was spoiled by him being a feckless bastard.

Sam is also sitting at the table. He is wearing a baseball cap and does not look as if he is enjoying the heat. Patricia and the Van Elstens are drinking tea but Sam has a bottle of Peroni, which he is drinking very quickly.

Patricia and Dorothy are discussing *Ferragosto*, the Feast of the Assumption, a day of celebration throughout Italy. There is always a *festa* in San Severino and Patricia organises a special dinner at one of the restaurants. There are fire-eaters, acrobats and children dressed in motley. The evening ends with fireworks and is usually the high spot of guests' visits.

'Which day is it?' asks Dorothy.

'The fifteenth. Wednesday.'

'My birthday,' says Fabio suddenly. He is standing by the pool, watching Matt's lilo as it comes to ground against the wall nearest to him. Wordlessly, Fabio leans down and pushes the lilo back into the open water.

Dorothy twinkles at him. 'Leo. King of the jungle.'

Fabio looks modest and JP says impatiently, 'Surely you don't believe all that stuff?'

'I surely do,' says Dorothy composedly. 'I'm a typical Pisces. I'm sensitive and artistic and I don't like conflict. Also, I'm ambivalent about eating fish. When is your birthday, Jean-Pierre?'

'November the tenth.'

'Ah, Scorpio. A very strong sign. Very highly sexed.'

Patricia has to hide a smile as JP clearly struggles between satisfaction at this description and contempt for the whole concept of astrology. She has her own mixed feelings. Sean was also a Leo and she is a Virgo. Whilst she doesn't, for one minute, believe in star signs, most of the characteristics (Leo, generous, sociable, expansive; Virgo, neat, fastidious, organised) prove irritatingly true in their case.

Rick breaks the silence, asking, with his charming lopsided smile, 'What is the Assumption?'

'It's when the Virgin Mary was taken up into heaven,' says Patricia. 'It's a very important day for Catholics.'

'I don't hold with all this Mary worship,' says Dorothy. 'Catholics seem to put her above our Lord and Saviour.'

'She is the mother of God,' says JP, rather aggressively. 'That's rather important, don't you think?'

'Mothers are always important,' says Dorothy darkly, 'but not always for the right reasons.'

Patricia, who agrees, tries to think of a way to change the subject. It surprises her that JP, who dismissed astrology with such high-minded contempt, should speak of the relationship between God and His mother as if it were an established fact. As a Frenchman, she supposes he must be a Catholic, she had just always thought that Frenchmen, like Italian men, didn't take religion too seriously. He did go to Mass yesterday, she remembers.

To everyone's surprise it is Fabio who speaks next. He is now stacking logs neatly on the barbecue while Aldo coaxes the coals to light.

'Sometimes the father doesn't understand,' he says. 'Then you go to the mother for help.'

No one quite knows how to answer this. Patricia doesn't think it is the thing for Fabio to enter a conversation with the guests but doesn't want to reprove him in front of everyone. Dorothy looks as if she has a whole lot more to say on the iniquity of mothers.

It is Sam who breaks the new silence. 'What the hell is he doing up there with her?' he says suddenly, slamming his beer bottle down on the table.

There is another pause while everyone works out who 'he'

is and then JP, of all people, says soothingly, 'He's teaching her. That's what this course is all about, isn't it?'

'Is it?' says Sam sulkily. 'I don't see him teaching you. Or me.'

'Well,' says JP mildly, 'I didn't write a piece on Rome. Did you?'

'Yes. No. That isn't the point. The point is he's clearly favouring Anna over the rest of us.'

Patricia cuts in; this situation has arisen before and she knows it is imperative to stop the rumblings of dissent before they grow into a revolt.

'Jeremy is very conscientious about individual tuition,' she says firmly. 'I'm sure he will have time for private sessions with everyone. He's very professional.' She'll talk to Jeremy before supper, she thinks grimly. Tomorrow he'd bloody well better have a tutorial with Sam McClusky.

But Sam is still looking mutinous. 'It's not as if she likes him much,' he mutters.

Patricia is about to speak when Matt causes a diversion by falling off the lilo and Cat jumps up to see, holding her bikini, very inadequately, over her breasts.

Mary's diary, 6 August

Very hot today. After lunch, we had a writing session with Jeremy and then I just went to my room and slept. It felt very decadent, sleeping in the afternoon, but I woke up feeling really refreshed, as if I'd slept for days. It was seven o'clock, the others were all down by the pool, supper wasn't till nine, so I went for a stroll, planning to get up into the hills.

It was quite hard going, the ground was full of little stones, very pretty some of them, like quartz or rough marble. There were low trees and silvery bushes, but spaced far apart so you could walk between them. After about a hundred yards there was a wooden gate, fastened by a plaited wreath, rather like the crown of thorns (a funny thought to strike me, an agnostic). I pushed open the gate and found myself walking up another path, steeper, marked by shallow wooden steps. I try to keep fit with my swimming and walking everywhere but I was panting by the time I got to the top of the hill. It was worth it though, the most wonderful view: hills, purple and blue in the evening light, trees, stark and black as if they had been drawn on with an ink pen, the towers of Siena misty in the distance and the sky, streaked pink and yellow with occasional patches of deepest blue. I wished I was an artist so I could paint it or a better writer, so I could do it justice.

Aldo cooked a wonderful barbecue tonight. Nothing like an English barbecue, the sort Alan and Sue have every summer, with shrivelled beef burgers, tomato ketchup and wilting salad. Aldo cooked beef ribs, lamb chops, the thinnest slices of pork and veal. He threw great stalks of rosemary on to the fire so that it smelt heavenly and everything was marinated in garlic, lemon and wine. He grilled vegetables too – peppers, courgettes and aubergines. They were delicious, brown and salty on the outside, tender and garlicky inside. Cat said she was allergic to aubergines and Aldo said that she must be sick in her head. I think she was a bit offended though she took it quite well, she even tried a piece of aubergine when Jeremy held it out to her on his fork.

We ate the meat with green salad and great hunks of Italian bread. I'm going to be the size of a house by the time I leave Tuscany. Aldo must have realised what a pig I am because he keeps giving me new food to try – a special olive oil that comes from the next-door farmer, a cheese, very sharp and crumbly, a glass of limoncello that made me feel quite light-headed.

I sat next to Jeremy at dinner (we ate by the pool). I hadn't really taken to him before (he seemed to concentrate mainly on Anna and Cat – not that I blame him) but tonight he was really friendly. He said some very kind things about Inspector Malone and was even nice about my weird Rome piece. He offered to have a private session with me to 'winnow out the dead wood'. He's seeing Sam tomorrow but it will be my turn next. How exciting.

The pool looked so beautiful, floodlit at night, that some people wanted to swim. Aldo said they would be sure to die, swimming on a full stomach (he seems to love making these blood-curdling predictions) so Cat suggested a midnight swim, tomorrow. I would so love to swim at midnight but I am pretty sure the invitation didn't include me.

CHAPTER 10

Day 6

7 August

It is the very hottest part of the day. The guests have eaten a light lunch on the terrace and now most of them are in their rooms, glorying in the air conditioning. Sam sits in front of his laptop but he is not writing, even though he is going to have one of Jeremy's famous 'one-to-ones' in a few minutes. Instead he is staring at his photographs, an ever-changing slide show of views: the castle, the swimming pool, the hills in various lights and moods, Gennaro's vineyard, a close-up of the famous Black Cock Chianti, the Colosseum, the Forum, a ginger cat stretched out on the steps of a temple, the backstreets of Rome, thronging with tourists and dense with churches, the Piazza Navona, Aldo's restaurant, Via Veneto, the Spanish Steps and, finally, Anna, standing hot and embarrassed in front of St Peter's Basilica. Sam stops the slide show and zooms in on Anna's face. The pixels merge as he moves closer and closer, hovering over her mouth as if to catch a word from the slightly parted lips. Her lips are beautiful, soft and serene. Sam backs away again until her whole face comes into focus: the tousled hair, the anxious frown, the half-shut eyes, the freckles. Frozen on the screen, she is, for that moment, his and only his.

Sam sighs. He came on this course because, aged forty-four, he had surprised himself by becoming obsessed with thoughts of mortality. Was this really all there was? A successful career, an attractive partner, a converted warehouse apartment in Clerkenwell? Yes, would be Jenny's answer, what more is there to want? Apart from bigger apartments, better holidays, smarter clothes to draw attention away from the effects of ageing. Neither of them had ever wanted children so the most conventional route to immortality was closed to them. What does a man do if he wants to be remembered?

The answer came to Sam one evening when he was surfing the net looking for a bigger and better Caribbean holiday. He'd looked on Friends Reunited, just a routine check to reassure himself that he was still richer than anyone else in his year, when he'd come across a new entry for Tom MacDonald, a spotty boy he remembered from standard grade. According to Tom MacDonald's entry, he had just published a fourth successful thriller under the name Don Willis. A quick Google on Don Willis came up with myriad pictures of fat, shiny books with titles like *The Hitler Code*. They looked like utter rubbish but the fact remains that Tom MacDonald, a boy who was always picked last for teams and who used to collect Action Man accessories, has achieved what Sam has not. Don Willis will live on after spotty Tom MacDonald has faded from memory. Although, looking again at his Friends Reunited entry, Sam sees that Tom has somehow acquired four children. So this immortality, too, he has achieved.

Sam is a man with great belief in his own abilities. He is also a man of quick decisions. Within the month, he had given in his notice and informed a stunned Jenny that he was going to write a bestselling book, several bestselling books, and secure his place in the history books. After all, how hard can it be? If Measles MacDonald has done it, so can he.

But the code proves surprisingly hard to crack. Watched by a disbelieving Jenny (who puts it all down to mid-life crisis) Sam sat down in front of a new laptop, armed with a stack of the latest bestsellers, and prepared to make his fortune. But, although each book starts smartly enough and Sam is a fluent and witty writer, they always peter out after the first few chapters. The problem is the characters. He constructs them carefully, drawing on the profiles of the ten most successful fictional creations that year, but somehow they just never seem to come alive. He describes their appearance (the women are all blonde; the men chiselled) and gives them a brief back story but, from that moment onwards, they absolutely refuse to cooperate. They seem unable to speak naturally or even perform the smallest action without getting tangled up in each other. Just getting them in and out of rooms is a nightmare.

How is he ever going to make them fall in love, have hopes and fears, solve ingenious riddles based on Renaissance art?

This course had seemed the perfect solution. He can find out the secret to creating memorable characters, go home and write a book that would perch on the top of the bestseller lists for years. Instead of which he has fallen in love, like a character from some stupid chick-lit book. It's not even the right genre. He closes Anna's picture and opens a file called bestseller4. He'll put in a good hour's writing before his session with Jeremy. But, ten minutes later, Anna's face is once more filling the screen.

JP lies on his bed with the shutters closed but he doesn't sleep. His sunburn hurts and he has a headache. A mosquito is buzzing somewhere in the room and he is grimly certain that, as soon as he closes his eyes, it will pounce, gorging itself with fine French blood. Should he introduce a mosquito into *Louis the Lion*? You could use the Italian word, *zanzara*, a perfect, onomatopoeic name for a restless, relentless, irritating character. A paparazzo perhaps – another wonderful Italian word, perfectly capturing the snapping of camera lenses, the fleeting, hustling nature of fame. JP sighs, he hasn't experienced fame himself but, as a lawyer, he has often seen it in his clients, caught a whiff of that high-octane world. His ex-wife, Barbara, is an aspiring actress. She wants fame, lusts after it, is still chasing it assiduously after ten years of walk-on parts and lingerie advertisements. She thinks more of being famous than she does of their son, thinks JP darkly. Their son, the eponymous Louis, whose favour JP courts with as much single-minded determination as Barbara ever pursued a part in a daytime soap. It is for Louis that JP has written his book. The little boy loves stories about Louis the Lion and begs for each new instalment. JP has even recorded himself reading the Louis stories for the many, many nights when he is not there to read them in person. If Louis, a worldly, discerning child, likes the stories so much, there must, JP reasons, be something in them. It does not occur to JP, clever lawyer that he is, that Louis only loves the stories because he loves his father.

Lying on his bed, listening to the buzzing growing fainter and fainter until it seems that his fine French blood must be safe, he thinks of Patricia and her face when she looks at her son, the moody Matt. She loves him, he thinks, even though he is now a sulky adolescent with bum fluff and a bad attitude. She loves him every bit as much as he loves the perfect seven-year-old Louis. He wonders about Patricia's husband; she never mentions him, where is he now? She must have had Matt when she was quite young, he thinks. Yesterday, by the pool, she looked about eighteen in that yellow dress. He remembers her slim figure in the sporty bathing costume, cut high on the hip and criss-crossing her bony shoulders at the back. She seemed to lose her unapproachable veneer with her clothes and had looked at him with something like invitation.

Or was that his imagination? If only the biker son hadn't turned up at precisely that interesting moment. JP groans, easing his burning shoulders.

Patricia is, once more, in her office, ignoring Sean the cat who is sitting on her desk purring loudly. Patricia checks her emails. No one has yet responded to her second week offer. Oh well, it was worth a try. She wishes she hadn't mentioned her money troubles to JP but he had been surprisingly understanding. He's quite a puzzle, JP. On the face of it, every inch the aloof, sarcastic lawyer but there is some thing else too. By the pool yesterday he had seemed oddly vulnerable, not just because of the telltale pink marks on his back. He had annoyed her by being lordly about the pool but then had smiled in an oddly appealing way. And he had looked at her so intently, as if he was trying to work her out. Patricia doesn't want the guests to know her too well; a friendly distance is what she aims for. Why does she have the feeling that it is possible for Jean-Pierre to get beneath the surface, to thoroughly disturb her peace of mind? Who is he anyway? She doesn't know anything about him. She looks at the blameless blue computer screen, the temptation to Google him is suddenly very strong.

To stop herself, she clicks on the itinerary for the second week.

Day 8

07.30 Meditation and stretch (optional)

08.00–09.30 Breakfast

10.00 Writing session

13.00 Lunch

Afternoon: Free writing time.

18.00 Trip to Siena

Day 9

07.30 Meditation and stretch (optional)

08.00–09.30 Breakfast

10.00-12.00 Trip to the market at San Severino

13.00 Lunch

14.00–16.00 Writing session

16.00–20.00 Free time

20.00 Supper

After supper, a chance to see the film *Enchanted April* starring Josie Lawrence and Miranda Richardson.

Patricia doesn't care much for the film. It is a highly romantic story of a group of people holidaying in Portofino after the First World War. All the couples are paired off, thanks to the healing powers of the Italian sunshine, there are no loose ends and no inconvenient realities (like ex-husbands or teenage sons). However, the film has proved very popular with previous guests and Jeremy usually sets a slightly ironical writing task around it.

Days 10 and 11 are the weekend so things are a little more relaxed. On Day 12 there is a special session when the writers are encouraged to read their work to each other. On Day 13 there is a feast cooked by guests on a nearby cookery course. Day 14 is *Ferragosto* and on Day 15 the guests will return home. Patricia stretches, stroking Sean mechanically with one hand. At this stage in the fortnight, it seems as if the course will never end but she knows from experience that, from Day 10 onwards, the time will start to fly by and, by the end, she will genuinely miss some of the guests. She already likes Mary and Anna and she's quite fond of Sally after all these years. She's ashamed to find herself disliking Cat and she's neutral about Sam. The jury is out on JP.

She has a slight headache from staring at the screen and decides to go to the kitchen to make a cup of tea. Afternoon tea is one English habit she has never lost, even though, mysteriously, it never tastes quite the same in Italy. She crosses the hall, closely followed by Sean, who also favours afternoon snacks. As she descends the stairs to the kitchen she sees a figure at the bottom, blocking the light. It can't be Aldo, he will be having his siesta, and it is far too large and flowery to be Matt or Fabio.

'Dorothy?'

Dorothy Van Elsten turns, looking slightly flustered in her dressing gown. 'Oh my, Patricia. I hope you don't mind. I was just desperate for some tea and I've used all the tea bags in my room.'

'Great minds think alike,' says Patricia, moving towards the kettle. 'I was just about to make tea for myself. Will you join me?'

Anna and Cat are by the pool. Anna lies in the shade of an umbrella but Cat stretches out in the full glare of the sun. Her mother is half-Malaysian and she goes brown very quickly (her skin is always slightly golden, even in winter). Anna lies on her front, reading her Anne Tyler book. Anne Tyler writes so well, so effortlessly, she wishes she could write like that. Jeremy has suggested she scrap *Hi Ho Silver Lining* 'or at least put it aside for a bit' and start something new. The problem is, she can't for the life of her think of another plot. The good thing about the story of her and Piers meeting at college is that the characters are all there already, give or take a few tweaks. She has made the girl, Sophie, prettier than she is and much cleverer. She was slightly surprised at the impulse to make Hugo stupider than Piers, his real-life counterpart. How strange – there must be part of her that is still angry with Piers.

'Who do you think will come swimming tonight?' says Cat, sitting up and rubbing suncream into her long legs.

'Are we really going to do it?' Anna twists over on to her back. 'The midnight swim?'

'Why not?' Cat grins wickedly up at her. 'It should be fun.'

'JP might come,' says Anna. 'And I think we should ask Mary. She loves swimming.'

'Oh, I don't think it would be Mary's sort of thing,' says Cat. 'It's for the young people really.'

'Young people,' says Anna gloomily. 'Does that include us?'

'Anna!' Cat looks at her sternly above her outsize sunglasses. 'We're still young. We're not forty yet.'

'I will be in two years' time.'

Cat, who will be forty in six months' time, says nothing. Then she says, 'Do you think Sam will come?'

'I don't know,' says Anna. 'I don't think I've ever seen him in the pool.'

'No,' Cat giggles. 'I'd quite like to though. I bet he's got a good body.'

Anna thinks about Sam. She has never really noticed his body. He's shorter than Steve, she thinks, and a bit stockier. She can't really picture much else about him although she can hear his voice in her head. It's deep and slightly Scottish, especially about the consonants.

'He's nice, isn't he?' she says, slightly tentatively because she remembers Sam being rude to Cat about the gladiators.

'Yes,' says Cat. Then she giggles again. 'You know,' she says, 'I think he's got a bit of a crush on me.'

'Sam?'

Cat looks at her. 'Don't sound so surprised. He's been a bit short with me once or twice and that's always a sign.'

'Is it?'

Cat laughs. 'You're hopeless, Anna. I bet you'd never notice if a man fancied you.'

'Well, no one does.'

'Except Steve.'

'Yes,' says Anna doubtfully. 'Except him.'

Cat looks at her closely. 'Everything all right with Steve?'

'Yes.' Anna adjusts her sunlounger so that she, too, is sitting up, 'It's just . . . I miss him, that's all.'

'I know.' Cat reaches over and pats her hand. 'I miss Justin too but you have to . . .' She stops.

'What is it?'

Anna follows Cat's stare to the other side of the pool. Fabio is standing there with a long-handled net, obviously about to clean the pool. He is wearing faded jeans and nothing else, his chest is brown and smooth.

He looks very embarrassed to see them. 'I'm sorry,' he says. 'I didn't know there was anyone . . .'

Anna thinks how good his English is. 'I didn't know there was anyone' seems a very complex sentence. She has no idea how she would say it in Italian.

But Cat answers him in Italian. '*Non c'è problema*,' she says graciously. '*Come sta, Fabio?*'

'*Bene grazie*,' says Fabio warily.

'Do you like working here, Fabio?' says Cat, switching back into English. For my sake, thinks Anna gratefully.

'Yes,' says Fabio, carefully sinking the net into the water. 'The work is not hard and Signora O'Hara is very kind.' He lifts the net with one arm, easily. He has long, smooth muscles, like a swimmer rather than a weightlifter.

'But is this what you want to do with your life? Be a handyman?'

Fabio straightens up. He pushes the thick, dark hair back out of his face. 'Maybe not for ever,' he says at last.

'You could be a model,' says Cat, smiling. 'Or an actor.'

Fabio smiles. 'I think not. I would prefer to be a racing driver.'

Cat laughs. 'Well, I think every Italian man wants to be a racing driver.'

'I think so too,' says Fabio seriously. He seems uncertain whether to stay or go.

'Fabio,' says Cat suddenly, 'would you like to come midnight swimming tonight?'

Patricia puts cups, saucers and a plate of Aldo's almond biscuits on the table. She is conscious of the fact that this is the perfect moment to talk to Dorothy, perhaps to mention her financial difficulties, but now that they are together in the intimacy of the kitchen, it seems hard to start the conversation somehow. Not that Dorothy looks awkward. Far from it. She leans back in her chair, smiling round at the gleaming kitchen, the copper pans over the stove, the wooden settle, the ropes of garlic and herbs, the pizza oven, the chef's knives arranged neatly in order.

'This is a wonderful space,' she says.

'Yes,' agrees Patricia hovering over the kettle (it is an electric one, brought from England). 'It's one of the oldest parts of the castle. The walls are a metre thick.'

Dorothy shivers pleasurably. 'It has an ancient aura,' she says. 'So many meals, so much good energy. But there is sadness here too. Someone has been unhappy in this room.'

Patricia thinks of herself, after Sean left, sitting at the scrubbed wooden table and thinking, 'Well, this is it; I've got to spend the rest of my life without him.' She remembers how, despite Matt, despite everything, for that moment at least a life without her lazy, good-for-nothing husband did not seem worth living.

The kettle boils and she pours water into the teapot. She is annoyed to find her hands shaking slightly. The cat rubs himself against her legs and she bends to stroke him.

Straightening up, she asks, in her most professional voice, 'Are you enjoying your stay?'

'My, yes,' says Dorothy, biting enthusiastically into an almond biscuit. 'This is such a wonderful house and I just love Italy.'

'What about your writing? How is that progressing?'

'Well.' Dorothy leans forward conspiratorially. Patricia gets a disconcerting glimpse of ample, freckled bosom. 'My book is really writing itself.'

'Is it?' says Patricia, leaning back slightly. 'I've heard other authors say similar things. The story takes on a life of its—'

Dorothy shakes her head. 'No. I mean it's almost an unconscious process. You see, I saw a therapist, back in the States, a wonderful man and he taught me to explore all these buried memories. Can you believe, I'd almost blotted out the horrors of my childhood? I had to go on a journey of self-discovery. I had to go back into myself, into my past, and confront what I found there.'

'That must have been hard,' says Patricia carefully.

'Hard?' Dorothy laughs. 'It was torture. Like childbirth. And I should know. I suffered the torments of the damned giving birth to Stacy. Made damn sure I had a caesarean for the other two. No, this was like childbirth in reverse. In essence, I was giving birth to myself.' She takes another bite of biscuit.

'And the memories came back?'

'Yes. Once I'd done my memory work with Ivan, it all came back. All at once, like an avalanche. And I wrote it all down.'

'There and then?'

'Well, I recorded most of it on tape. When I came to write it out, I was worried it didn't sound too good. I haven't had much education, you see. That's why I came here. To turn it into a proper book. But Jeremy has been so kind. He said it didn't matter how badly my book was written, it would still sell by the truckload.'

Patricia can just imagine him saying this. Thanks a lot, Jeremy, she thinks. These people have paid 3000 euros each for the course and you're telling them they needn't have bothered. Couldn't you at least have worked on her spelling?

Aloud, she says, 'Do you ever see her? Your mother, I mean?'

Dorothy sighs. 'No, dear. I've forgiven her, of course. She's a deeply troubled person.'

'You've forgiven her? After everything she did?'

'Well, the good Lord tells us to forgive seventy times seven. But even though I've forgiven her, it would still be too painful to see her.'

'What about your brothers and sisters?'

'I've forgiven them too. For shutting their eyes to the abuse.'

'But do you see them?'

'No, dear.'

There is a silence and then Patricia says, mopping up biscuit crumbs with her finger, 'I never knew my mother. Or my father. I was brought up by foster parents.'

'Really?' Dorothy leans forward again and puts her hand on Patricia's. 'I knew we had a connection. I knew it!'

Patricia wishes that she hadn't spoken. She wishes she could stand up, put the cups in the dishwasher, and go back to being the perfect hostess. Just for a second she sees this room, the Castello, her whole life, shattering into a million brightly coloured fragments. She sees herself buried by the avalanche, like Alice disappearing under the playing cards when she wakes from her dream. She takes a deep breath, anchoring herself in the present.

'Yes,' she says lightly. 'My foster parents weren't ... that nice to me either.'

'Have you seen someone?' asks Dorothy eagerly. 'A therapist?'

'No.'

'My dear, you must! When I think of all the good Ivan has done for me. There was all this pain, you see, lying below the surface. And, if you'll forgive me saying so, I sense something similar with you.'

For a second, Patricia imagines herself lying on a couch in a cool, darkened room. A Nordic room, a peaceful room, far from the fevered light and colour of Italy. She imagines herself talking to a shadowy therapist, telling him about the nights when the moonlight fell across her bed. She imagines herself telling him about Sean and the way that his carefree love seemed to offer a complete escape from the past. Until he left her. His love, too, it seems, was conditional.

She looks at Dorothy, who is watching her intently, almost avidly, and forces herself to smile. 'Oh, I'm all right,' she says. 'More tea?'

Sam and Jeremy sit on Jeremy's balcony under the shade of a striped awning. Yet somehow, despite the gay green and white stripes and the open bottle of wine on the table between them, the atmosphere is strictly businesslike. Perhaps this is due to the laptop, spreadsheet and files which form a rampart in front of Sam, perhaps it is due to the red pen and edited manuscripts which sit in front of Jeremy. Perhaps it is simply down to the attitudes of the two men who sit stiffly on chairs more suited to lounging and speak hesitantly in short, clipped sentences. There is none of the teasing banter which is such a feature of Jeremy's sessions with Anna.

'So you see,' says Sam, pointing to a spreadsheet, 'thirty per cent of the books in the Book Track Top Hundred were thrillers, ten per cent were misery memoirs, another ten per cent celebrity autobiographies and the rest TV tie-ins or self-help books.'

Jeremy, who is both aghast at such an approach to publishing and deeply interested, leans in to look. As ever, his eyes skim the list for books published by his own publisher. His attitude to his publisher is that of a once-adored child who has now been supplanted by younger, more favoured siblings. He bitterly resents any author who is published by his imprint. If they are also edited by his editor (now nearing retirement), his jealousy is almost unbearable.

'So is this why you want to write a thriller?' asks Jeremy.

'Well, yes,' says Sam, folding up his spreadsheet. 'I reckoned that was my best option. I was unfortunate enough to have a happy childhood (I blame my parents for that) so I can't take dear Dorothy's route and write a wasn't-it-all-awful-but-I survived-against-the odds book. I'm not famous and I've never been on TV. So a thriller was really the only one left.'

Jeremy seems to be struggling to speak. 'But do you *want* to write a thriller?' he says at last.

'Of course I do,' says Sam. 'I gave up a really good job to be a writer.'

'In these extracts you gave me,' Jeremy sifts through the pages in front of him, 'I get the impression that you have lots of good ideas but that you somehow . . . run out of steam.'

Sam sighs and, for the first time, slumps slightly in his chair. 'That's true,' he says. 'I start off full of excitement, I can almost taste the money and then, after a few chapters, I don't know, I just lose interest in the characters.'

'I think you lose interest,' says Jeremy gently, 'because the characters aren't real.'

Sam bristles. 'Real? What do you mean, real?'

'They're not real,' says Jeremy, 'because you invented them out of expediency. They didn't develop organically, from your mind, your experience, whatever. It's funny,' he says, speaking more to himself now, 'it almost never works, writing to order. It ought to. You ought to be able to select a genre, study the characteristics and write the perfect book. And sometimes people do write books this way. But those books hardly ever sell. The real bestsellers, the surprise hits, like *Captain Corelli* or *A Short History of Tractors in Ukrainian,* they're always the books written from the heart. You couldn't predict them, you can't analyse them, they're just great books.'

Sam says nothing. From the pool he can hear Cat's and Anna's voices but they are too far away for him to distinguish what they are saying. After a pause, he looks at Jeremy, who is pouring himself a glass of wine.

'Is that how you wrote *Belly Flop?*' he asks.

Jeremy takes a gulp of wine before answering. 'Yes,' he says at last. 'My first two books were slim affairs, very stylised, trying hard to be witty. *Belly Flop* is different; it's rambling, unwieldy, strange. I'd been living in LA for a year, found it a very weird place. My wife had left me. I consoled myself with a string of plastic beauties. Even had stomach surgery myself, hence the title. I wrote like a man possessed. I had no idea that anyone would ever publish it.'

'Yet it was a huge bestseller.'

Jeremy laughs, rather humourlessly. 'It was a huge bestseller and I haven't written anything since.'

'You will,' says Sam, unconvincingly.

Jeremy smiles, perhaps the first genuine smile he has unleashed all week. 'Yes,' he says. 'All I need is an idea.'

'Join the club,' says Sam, reaching for the bottle of wine.

CHAPTER 11

Day 6, evening

It is a bit like being at boarding school, thinks Anna. Not that she went to one of those schools herself but she read enough Malory Towers books as a girl to know about midnight feasts. In fact, didn't they actually have a midnight swim in one of the Malory Towers books? In an idyllic swimming pool, hewn from Cornish rocks? Anyway, planning the midnight swim with Cat definitely seems to have made them both regress to teenagers. They giggle, drop code words into the conversation and avoid eye contact with their fellow conspirators, Sam and JP. Of course, there is no earthly reason why they shouldn't be upfront about their plans. Midnight swimming isn't forbidden, Patricia would probably be delighted that they were enjoying their stay so much, she'd arrange for Aldo to provide hot chocolate afterwards. Perhaps this is why they want to keep it secret. Everything is more enjoyable if it's forbidden. Anyone who was brought up a Catholic understands that. Also Cat is keen to keep their plans from the 'grown-ups': Mary,

Sally, Dorothy and Rick. And her conviction that they alone are young and carefree is curiously seductive.

In other ways, staying at the Castello is a bit like school. There are the same shifting social groups, for a start. Is JP in the fun gang with Anna and Cat or in a more serious club with Patricia and Sally? Mary and Dorothy should go together, considering their ages, but why does Mary spend more time talking to Anna, Matt or Aldo? Is Sam in the boys' team with JP and Jeremy or the girls' group with Anna and Cat? Clearly Cat is the coolest girl in school and Anna is her faithful shadow. Sometimes, embarrassingly, Anna is also teacher's pet. Sally has a crush on the teacher, Sam is alternately stroppy or charming, JP is becoming known for his caustic asides, Rick, with his easy-going manner and Texas drawl, is popular with everyone.

Anna just went to a normal (albeit Catholic) comprehensive but she remembers the fervid atmosphere of school, the way a brief glimpse of someone in a corridor could keep you happy all day. She remembers how, if you actually went out with the person, away from the magic circle of school, their glamour would fade instantly. That must be why, at the Castello, she finds Sam oddly fascinating. If I met him at home, she tells herself firmly as she gets ready for dinner, we would have nothing in common at all. He'd just be a taciturn Scotsman who likes golf and skiing. Steve and I would have nothing to say to him at all.

What the hell should she wear? When she packed for

the course, Anna had not bargained on changing for dinner every night. Cat has a seemingly endless supply of charming summer dresses but Anna has already worn her one smart dress and spilt tomato sauce on it. She has two long, flowery skirts but she has already worn them both. It'll have to be her white cotton trousers (a bit tight but she'll try not to breathe much) and a black T-shirt. At least she has a bit of a tan so the black won't make her look too washed out. She brushes her hair, which is very unruly from so much swimming and showering, and clips on her dangly earrings (a going-away present from Steve). Oh, she does wish he was here. Does he miss her? His emails are full of the fun he is having with the boys and *of course* she is happy that they are happy but she would like just a hint that, behind the Father of the Year exterior, Steve is missing her like hell.

The thing about Steve is, she doesn't always know what he's thinking. She knows he loves her but he doesn't say it much. In contrast, Anna sometimes feels she says it all the time, 'love you', 'love you', 'miss you', 'kiss, kiss, kiss'. She says it every time she says goodbye on the phone and Steve just laughs and sometimes (if she's lucky) says, 'me too'. 'You love you too?' she says and he just laughs again. That's Steve: laid-back, laughing, cope-with-anything Steve. When Cat suggested this holiday, Steve didn't say once that he wouldn't be able to manage looking after the boys for two weeks. No, he'd been all for it, said it would be good for her, a chance to get away from the house and the boys, to do something for herself. She knows she's lucky (when she thinks what some of her friends' husbands would have been like!). It's just . . . she can't help wishing that he had said that he couldn't cope without her.

Don't be ridiculous, she tells herself sternly, this course is a chance in a lifetime. Of course Steve loves you; he doesn't have to say it all the time. You'd hate it if he was all over you like Justin is with Cat. Anna looks at herself in the mirror. OK if she remembers to pull her stomach in. She hopes Cat isn't wearing anything too spectacular tonight.

But, when she arrives on the terrace for the ritual pre-dinner drinks, the first person she sees is Cat, sparkling in a green sleeveless dress. Immediately Anna feels masculine and drab in her trousers. She takes a glass of prosecco from a stony-faced Ratka and makes her way over to Cat.

'Gorgeous dress,' she says.

'Oh, just the Zara sale,' says Cat as if that makes it better.

Anna sits on the low terrace wall, which is still warm from the day's sun. Far below, the pool glitters enticingly.

'Are you still up for you know what?' asks Cat, her eyes gleaming.

'Our idnightmay imsway?' answers Anna, in pig Latin. 'Of course.'

'Ancay Iway oinjay ouyay?' It is Sam, resplendent in a red shirt. He, too, is tanned and, with his slicked-back hair, looks a little like a Mafia leader on holiday.

'I thought only girls knew pig Latin,' says Anna.

'Boys know these things too,' says Sam. 'Don't you worry. We even have secret societies and our own code words.'

'I don't believe it,' says Anna. 'Boys only play football. I've got two sons, so I know.'

'Ah, you're a sexist creature, Miss Valore,' says Sam, leaning over to take an olive. 'I happen to be a deeply sensitive person who enjoys baking and watching weepy films.'

'And, anyway, not all boys like football,' says Cat. 'My son Sasha prefers playing his cello or reading.'

Anna, whose son Tom once accidentally trod on Sasha's cello, feels rebuked.

Sam says, 'Your children sound perfect, Cat.' There is an odd note in his voice but Cat doesn't seem to notice.

'Oh well, I suppose it's because I've always spent lots of time with them. I've never just plonked them in front of a TV screen and left them to get on with it. Unlike my useless husband.' She laughs.

'I wish I could be plonked in front of a TV,' says Anna. 'I'm really missing *Big Brother*.'

At dinner (stuffed tomatoes followed by baked trout), the subject of husbands comes up again. Cat is describing her wedding, Justin's mother wanted her to wear the family lace but she insisted on making her own dress, and Myra makes them all laugh describing how desperate her mother is for her to be married ('she's given up on doctors and is seriously considering the garbage man'). Patricia tells them about her runaway wedding to Sean. 'A real Gretna Green job. Our witnesses were both pissed, Sean's suit still had the price tag on and our honeymoon was a bus ride to Glasgow.'

'What about your wedding, Anna?' asks Sam, tearing off a piece of Aldo's homemade bread. 'I bet you looked gorgeous.'

Anna pauses, her mouth full of trout and peppers. Across the table she sees Sam's face, his dark eyes intent, Cat, looking put out, Patricia, eyebrows slightly raised, Dorothy, smiling benignly, JP, cynical and amused.

'I'm not married,' she says.

It is Cat who speaks first. 'I never knew that,' she says, rather crossly.

'Steve and I, we've been together for fifteen years, we've just never got round to getting married. We've never discussed it.' As Anna says this, she realises that it isn't quite true.

'Why should you?' says Patricia lightly. 'If it ain't broke . . .'

'But you've never said anything.' Cat still sounds slightly aggrieved.

'Well, I don't use Steve's name . . .'

'I thought that was because of your writing.'

'God, no.' Anna laughs. 'Though I suppose Valore is a more memorable name than Smith.'

'If his name is Smith,' says JP decisively, 'you should never, never marry him.'

Everyone laughs, although Cat still looks strangely at Anna, almost as if she has edged ahead in some unspoken race.

*

The guests usually take their time after supper. They drink coffee and liqueurs, they chat, sometimes they play cards. But, tonight, everyone seems anxious to get to bed. Cat starts yawning at about ten o'clock. Patricia knows what this is about, of course. She has heard them planning the night swim and also knows that, for reasons of their own, Cat and Anna want to keep it a secret. Patricia thinks this is rather hard on Mary, who is easily the best swimmer amongst the guests, but she too keeps silent. And, anyhow, she is not displeased to have an earlyish night for a change. It means she'll be able to do a couple of hours' work before bed.

As the last guest (Sally) goes upstairs, Patricia takes a glass of brandy down to her study. She'll have a really good look at the accounts, she decides, and think of some more ways to make savings this year.

But, as she sits in front of her laptop, she is not surprised to see her fingers take another route across the keyboard. They tap-dance on to her photos file and click on a little-opened document called photospast. There, filling the screen, is the Castello when they first saw it, magnificent and overgrown, an actual tree growing out of one of the towers. There is Matt, six years old, with a toy hammer. And there is Sean, laughing as he pulls Matt through the snow on a sledge. There is Sean up a ladder doing some very inexpert house painting. And there she is with Sean, sitting by the edge of the empty swimming pool, holding cans of Coke and smiling widely into the camera. Who took this picture? she wonders. Maybe Matt, judging by the slightly wonky angle and his parents' doting smiles. And here is the picture she has (subconsciously anyhow) been looking for. Her and Sean on their wedding day. Sean in his new suit and painfully bright tie, herself in a cream dress with a rose in her hair. Twenty years ago. She had been twenty-four, Sean twenty-two. A younger man, he was fond of pointing out, a toy boy. And, in this picture, he looks barely more than a boy, smiling anxiously in his wedding suit, his arm round his new bride. How young they were, how little they knew.

Patricia met Sean when she was finishing university in London. Sean was at art college and, to prove it, usually had paint in his hair. It was at a party in a friend's grotty South London flat. Patricia remembers the paint flaking on the walls, the smell of damp, the light from the single bare bulb gleaming on Sean's hair as he leant over to catch her name. The smell of turpentine and soap, the glint in his bold blue eyes.

'Patricia. Does anyone ever call you Pat?'

'No, never.'

'People call me Pat all the time,' he said, in a voice that still retained the rhythms of his native Dublin. 'But, sure, I'm used to it.'

And that was the start of it. They sat together all through the party, sharing a bottle of sweet white wine. Afterwards they went home on the bus and Sean sang the whole of 'American Pie' and the other passengers applauded. Back at Patricia's digs, she discovered that she had forgotten her keys and her flatmates were still at the party. She remembers Sean climbing on the roof and squeezing in through an open casement. She remembers seeing him, silhouetted against the skyline and wondering why she wasn't more worried. Sean was drunk, the roof was high and unstable. But, even then, somehow Patricia knew that Sean was a man who wouldn't fall.

They made love that night. A revelation to Patricia, who had hitherto had sex only because it seemed to be expected of her. But now she discovered the joy of being in bed with the person you loved, lying tangled together so that, by the morning, you were not quite sure whose legs were whose. Sean made love like he did everything, joyously and generously, with his whole heart and soul. Patricia was in love with him before that first night was over.

They got married two years later, as soon as Sean graduated. Sean's parents, though friendly enough, thought it was too soon and, of course, Patricia had no parents to speak off. 'An orphan,' said Sean happily, when he found out. 'How exciting.' When Sean's parents suggested that they wait a year, Sean and Patricia took the bus to Scotland, intending to go to Gretna Green. Instead they were married in a small town outside Glasgow, with two local winos as witnesses. Patricia remembers how the grey streets were transformed when she kissed Sean outside the registry office. My husband.

Except he's not her husband any more. She remembers the day, four years ago, when they had stood in this very room, both vibrating with rage. She had been accusing him of not helping enough with the courses, a tedious, well-known refrain. Just because she said it all the time, Patricia had shouted, didn't mean it wasn't true. She had seen Sean's eyebrows rise at the beginning of her diatribe and knew he would dismiss the whole thing, with a humorous shrug, as 'nagging'. Extraordinary how a woman's complaints, if they go on long enough, are always demoted to nagging. That raised eyebrow had been the final straw.

'What do you want from me?' Sean had asked, with familiar weary charm.

'I don't want you at all,' Patricia had yelled. 'I'd be better off without you. Get out!'

And he had gone. She still can't quite believe it. After years of never taking anything she said seriously, it seemed that Sean had chosen this moment to take her at her word. He had packed a bag and left the Castello that night. And, apart from a couple of stilted meetings when handing over Matt, she has not seen him since. They divorced three years ago and now that Matt is old enough to visit his father on his own, she wonders if she will ever see Sean again. She knows he is back in London, that he is working as an art teacher, that he has girlfriends ('Just a woman,' says Matt. 'I dunno. Yes, of course they shared a room.'). You wouldn't have thought, thinks Patricia, remembering the glowing bride in her cheap cream dress, that love could ever come to this.

She is better off without him, she tells herself, he always treated everything as a joke and she, of all people, knows that life is serious. She clicks open her accounts file.

*

As Patricia frowns at her rows of figures, Cat and Anna creep down the steps to the pool. They move in silence, keeping up the secrecy game, until Cat turns to Anna and whispers, 'Why didn't you tell me that you and Steve aren't married?'

'You didn't ask,' Anna whispers back.

'I thought I was your friend,' says Cat, sounding about twelve. Indeed, in her white T-shirt and shorts, she looks scarcely more than that.

Anna is struck with remorse. 'You *are*!' She reaches out to clasp Cat's hand. 'You're my best friend. It's just . . . we've never talked much about our husbands . . . partners. It's always been about us or the kids.'

They've never talked much about their partners, she realises, because there isn't much to say. Justin obviously worships the ground Cat walks on and Steve . . . well, Steve is Steve. He's steady, reliable, great with the kids and just once, when they found out that she was pregnant with Tom, he did say, 'Perhaps we should get married or something.' *Or something?* And she had said (idiot!), 'Why bother, we're great as we are.' And he (idiot!) had never mentioned it again. Has she, subconsciously, been waiting all these years for him to propose? It's not quite as bad as that but, if he were to propose, it would be such a big thing, would prove once and for all that he did love her and only her . . .

They have reached the bottom of the steps. The pool lies, floodlit and mysterious, in the moonlight. The surrounding trees, too, are lit with an unearthly brilliance. Somewhere nearby, an owl hoots.

Cat squeezes Anna's hand. 'Isn't it beautiful?'

'Yes,' breathes Anna but, despite herself, she also feels that there is something slightly spooky about the silent pool and the dark castle rising up in the background. The moon shifts and she sees the battlements etched against the sky. She sees something else too, something that makes her gasp aloud. A figure, a man's figure, walking steadily along the roof, just inside the ramparts. Just for a second, the moonlight gleams on his blond hair.

'What is it?' Cat pauses at the edge of the pool where she is feeling the temperature with her toe.

Anna looks back. The castle is in shadow once more. 'Nothing,' she says.

Muffled sounds are coming from the opposite side of the pool. JP and Sam appear. JP in a white dressing gown, Sam in what looks like football kit. They place towels on the edge of the pool (the sunloungers have been tidied away) and talk in hushed voices.

'Who's going to be the first to dive in?' says Sam.

'Me,' says Cat. She pulls off her T-shirt and shorts, revealing a tight, black swimming costume. She stands on the edge of the pool and flexes her legs. JP moves forward to push her but she is too quick for him. A perfect dive and Cat's slim body dissects the water like a knife.

Sam is looking at Anna. 'Are you going to swim?'

Anna laughs nervously. 'I thought that was the idea.' She is embarrassed about taking off her T-shirt in front of Sam but he doesn't seem about to look away so she steels herself. À fuzzy faceful of cotton and she emerges, shivering slightly.

Sam moves towards her and stops. Anna walks to the water's edge and bends down to touch the water.

'It's freezing!' she says.

Sam still says nothing but Anna can sense him, very close behind her. Suddenly it seems very important to get into the pool as fast as possible. She stands up and performs a clumsy dive, smacking her stomach against the water. The cold shocks her and she surfaces, spluttering.

'Are you OK?' Sam is beside her, treading water.

'Yes. Just did a bit of a belly flop.'

Sam laughs. 'Like Jeremy's famous book.'

It takes Anna a few moments to get it but then she laughs too. She doesn't know why but it suddenly seems the best joke in the world, to be swimming in moonlight with two men she hardly knows, the Tuscan stars high above them. JP swims over and jumps on Sam's back. The two men wrestle, splashing in the shallow end. Cat sits on the side, wringing water out of her hair, until JP grabs her leg and pulls her in. Anna goes to save Cat and is ducked by Sam. She surfaces and splashes him, her embarrassment forgotten. He goes to grab her and she swims away. At the deep end, Sam catches her and clasps her round the waist. She can feel his body, slippery yet solid, pressed against her.

Suddenly she is aware that Sam has let go. He is looking at a figure emerging from the woods. A man, wearing only swimming trunks, as perfect and unselfconscious as a wood-land spirit. It is Fabio.

'Fabio!' Cat swims over, grinning up at him from the water.

'I came,' says Fabio. 'Is that all right?'

'Of course,' says Cat.

Fabio dives. He swims brilliantly, hardly surfacing for length after length. Cat sits on the edge of the pool, watching. JP and Sam climb out and wrap themselves in their towels. Anna slides out of the pool and she, too, reaches for her towel. It suddenly seems much colder and she wishes she had brought a jumper.

Eventually Fabio pauses and calls to Cat, 'Are you coming in?' With a half-laugh, Cat jumps to her feet and throws her-self into the pool. She and Fabio swim together, in perfect time, their arms stretching, their heads turning towards each other as they breathe. Anna is mesmerised, she hardly notices when JP wraps his dressing gown around her shoulders.

Cat and Fabio swim on, stretching and turning in the moon-light. Eventually they stop and cling to the side of the pool, where the water laps over the blue and green tiles. Cat pushes her hair back from her face. Anna sees her smile at Fabio, her face radiant. JP steps forward, seems about to speak but another voice cuts across the night air.

'Hi! Can I join in?'

It is Matt. Instinctively, Anna looks up to the ramparts. She had thought the blond man might be Matt but could he have got down to the pool so quickly? Cat climbs out of the pool and wraps her towel around her hair. Her body is uncovered, gleaming with water. Anna proffers her towel. Wordlessly, Cat accepts it. Matt and Fabio are splashing through the water like a couple of playful dolphins. Matt has found a ball and he calls to JP and Sam to join in a game of water polo.

'Shall we go back?' suggests Anna. Cat nods.

Regretfully, Anna takes off JP's robe and pulls her T-shirt and shorts on over her wet swimming costume. Cat picks up her clothes and follows, an Egyptian princess with her turbaned hair and towel toga. They climb the stairs, the shouts and laughter from the pool dying away behind them, and push open the door at the side of the house.

Dripping gently, they cross the castle hall. The suits of armour stare disapprovingly at them. As they climb the main staircase, they see Sean the cat running past them, intent on night business of his own. At the first landing, they pause.

'That was fun,' says Cat flatly.

'Yes,' says Anna. 'Cat?' She doesn't know quite what she's going to say but she is saved the trouble by another voice. A commanding, distinctly unwelcome, voice.

'Anna? Catherine?' It is Patricia, fully dressed, emerging from her study on the floor below. Sean stands next to her, purring against her legs. Was it him who gave them away?

But Patricia is smiling. Indeed she looks happier than either of them have ever seen her.

'Great news, Cat,' she says. 'Your husband and children are coming. They arrive tomorrow.'

CHAPTER 12

Writing

My Earliest Memory
by Catherine Ferris-Merry

When I was three, I fell in love. His name was Cuddles and he came at Christmas so, to me, he was always Christmas Cuddles. A tiny Shetland pony, barely ten hands high, shaggy and black with a rope of tinsel round his neck. I remember Daddy bringing him into the house, right into our sitting room, and my squeals of delight when I realised that this gorgeous little animal was all mine.

Cuddles lived in the orchard at the end of our garden. This was the house in Wiltshire where we lived until Daddy left. It was quite a big house, I suppose, though as a child I only remember parts of it: my bedroom with its pink, flowered wallpaper, the garden with the rope swing and tree house, my brothers' bedroom where they played loud music at all hours of the day. My brothers were (are!) a lot older than me so I don't really remember much about them in those days. They both played rugby and I do remember standing on the touchline with Daddy while Robert dived over the line, covered in mud, to score a try.

I didn't like rugby. I was a real little princess. Loved pink and ballet and ponies, of course. I remember, that first day, Daddy lifting me on to Cuddles' back and leading me round the garden. It was the best fun in the world. I even remember the little red hat and mittens that I wore and Daddy's big fisherman's jumper. Unfortunately, after that, we couldn't catch Cuddles. Neither Mummy nor Daddy knew much about horses and, in the end, we had to get a local farmer, called Stanley, to catch him. Stanley's daughter, Susan, tried to teach me to ride but I didn't like her much. She used to shout at me ('Legs! Legs! Who's in charge here? Show him you mean it. Kick, girl, kick!') and I told Daddy that I didn't want any more lessons. Then, one day, Cuddles bit me and he had to be sold. I wasn't that sad, to be honest. He wasn't really a suitable horse for me. Shetlands are very bad-tempered and stubborn. Anyway, by the end of that year we had moved away from the house in Wiltshire and Daddy went to live in Cornwall with his nice, shiny new family. They had horses, well-behaved ones that did everything you said, but no one ever offered me a ride on them. I wouldn't have wanted to anyhow. I don't think riding was really my thing, somehow.

My Earliest Memory
by Mary McMahon

My Uncle Maurice had a car. That was quite unusual for those days. My dad had a van for work (he was a builder) but he remembered the days when deliveries were made by horse and cart, the days when most businesses had a stable at the back.

Uncle Maurice wasn't really an uncle but we children called all our parents' friends Aunt and Uncle. It was considered polite, in those days. Uncle Maurice was a tailor. He made my Auntie Betty's wedding dress and I remember going to see it in his shop, hanging all mystic and wonderful on one of those scary dummies without a head. This was before clothes rationing, of course. It was never mentioned but I think Uncle Maurice was Jewish. He closed his shop early on Fridays and I remember his wife, Auntie Marie, telling my mum that she had to have a different larder for meat and for milk. Auntie Marie wasn't Jewish, she was a South London girl with bright ginger hair and the loudest laugh of anyone I've ever met. She could do impressions of all the actresses at the cinema and sing funny songs about my old man following the van. My dad used to say that she 'liked a drop'. I never knew quite what that meant, but if it was the drops that made Auntie Marie so jolly and funny and so unlike other grown-ups, I remember wishing she would give my parents some.

Uncle Maurice had a funny accent, which I loved.

He would sing too, songs in some strange, sighing language. They always seemed to be sad songs and Auntie Marie would say, 'Give over Mo, do. You'll have us all sticking our heads in the oven.' And he'd laugh and teach me a new card game or sew some clothes for my doll. Once he made her a whole outfit, just like one worn by Princess Margaret Rose.

I don't know what sort of car he had. It was square, black and snub-nosed and had red leather seats. There was a hole in one of the seats and, on one journey, I couldn't stop myself putting my finger inside and pulling out some of the stuffing. More and more of it came out until I had a whole pile of it on my lap. I still remember how mortified I felt when Uncle Maurice turned round and saw me with all this white, fluffy stuff around me. But he just laughed. My mother was furious, though.

So, on the day that I remember Uncle Maurice took me, my mother and my sister for 'a drive'. This, too, was unusual. People hardly ever went for 'a drive'; they went to visit friends and family or they went to the seaside, never just for a drive. I loved the randomness of it, the thought that a journey which started outside our little house in Camberwell could end up . . . well, anywhere. This particular journey ended up in Richmond Park. It was a beautiful day and we had ice creams and sat on the grass, watching the squirrels. Maybe that's why I remember it so well, I really can't remember another time when I saw my mother sitting down. But, on this day, she sat, almost lay, on the grass, eating a strawberry ice cream and laughing at some joke of Maurice's. It's the laughter I remember most. That and the fact that my sister was sick behind a holly bush.

That must have been in the summer of 1938. The next year

the war started and Uncle Maurice was taken away, interned as an enemy alien. That strange, sighing language turned out to be German. I never saw him again.

My Earliest Memory
by Dorothy Van Elsten

Dark. That's what I remember. The dark of the cupboard where my mom used to shut me, for days sometimes. I remember writing my name in the dust, knowing that I had to retain my sense of identity, to tell myself that I existed. That I was worthy of love. Dark, that's what my life was in those days. Dark, because even when I wasn't shut in the cupboard, I was shut out of the light, neglected, abused, shunned. I remember my mom used to . . .

CHAPTER 13

Day 7

8 August

It is Mary's turn to sit on Jeremy's balcony. It is early afternoon and a tray containing teapot, milk jug, cups and a plate of biscuits sits on the table under the awning. Jeremy normally has a glass or two of wine during these sessions but he knows that old ladies like tea and is proud of himself for being so thoughtful, of going to the trouble of asking Ratka to make the tea and bring it up to his room.

It has been a strange, subdued day. The news that Cat's husband and children are coming seems to have cast a shadow over the group, to have disturbed the camaraderie that they have developed over the past week. Fabio has been seen by the pool, blowing up inflatable toys. Aldo has reacted with stunned disbelief to the notion that the children might not appreciate *pollo alla diavola* and is flatly refusing to cook an alternative. After lunch, Cat left with Fabio to pick up her family and Dorothy said, delicately, as the group sat finishing their coffee on the terrace, 'Of course, I love children but it does seem a little inappropriate . . .'

Jeremy couldn't agree more. He loathes children and Cat's husband is sure to be some muscle-bound hunk who swims fifty lengths every morning and talks about his biceps. Still, this might mean that he has more time with Anna, who has been valiantly telling everyone that Cat's family are 'really lovely'. Jeremy has his own ideas of lovely and they do not include some brainless yuppie and his hideous children, thank you very much.

Mary, looking cool in a loose blue dress, thanks Jeremy politely, but unenthusiastically, for the tea. She really prefers black coffee. Jeremy gives her his most charming smile and compliments her on her Earliest Memories piece.

'Very well constructed, quite moving. Was it true?'

'Of course!' Mary sounds shocked.

Jeremy laughs. 'Don't be offended. The best writers make things up or, at the very least, tailor their memories. Did you tailor your memories of Maurice the tailor?' He laughs again.

'I don't know,' says Mary slowly. 'I thought it was all true, but of course you can't tell. My memories of Maurice and Marie will have been clouded by time, by the knowledge of what came after. I suppose now I think of him as quite a tragic character but, at the time, he was anything but. He was fun, he was colourful. We all loved him.'

Jeremy looks hard at Mary. This intelligent, considered

answer is not what he expected. When he speaks again, his voice is almost devoid of the auto-charm.

'Have you ever thought about writing about your childhood?' he asks. 'The descriptions are really very vivid.'

'Well,' says Mary, 'Inspector Malone is set in the past. In the fifties, of course, not the thirties, but there are a lot of my memories there. I thought it was best to work them into a fictional plot, though. I mean, who'd be interested in my life? I've never married, I haven't got children, I've hardly ever been out of the country.'

'I see what you mean,' says Jeremy. 'And the descriptions in Inspector Malone are excellent. He's an interesting character. I just wondered why you were drawn to the detective genre.'

Mary grins. 'I like mysteries,' she says. 'I like crosswords, clues, things like that. And, I thought, if I like them, maybe other people will too.'

'But, forgive me, will younger people like them?'

'I've no idea,' says Mary sharply. 'But, statistically, old ladies like me buy a lot of books.'

'Touché,' smiles Jeremy, thinking, Christ, another one quoting statistics at me. He takes a gulp of cold tea.

'I found the plot too complicated,' he says, in a businesslike tone. 'I couldn't work out how the pawnbroker came to know about the body at the railway station or whether that meant he was in league with the strangler. There are also far too many characters.'

'I know,' says Mary. 'I know it needs cutting down. Even I get lost sometimes.'

'Have you ever thought about putting it to one side,' says Jeremy, 'and starting something quite new?' This is his standard advice. Since most of the scripts he reads are unmitigated rubbish, starting again can only be an improvement.

'I couldn't,' says Mary. 'I've been writing this for thirty years.'

'Well then,' says Jeremy, 'I suggest cutting the first chapter, for a start. Most books are better without their first chapters. Do you know how *The Iliad* starts?'

Mary doesn't.

'It starts *in medias res*, in the middle of things. Homer could have started at the beginning of the Trojan War but he doesn't. When the book starts, the war has been going on seven years. Homer plunges the reader right into his world. That's what you have to do. Don't introduce things; throw the reader in at the deep end. Maybe cut the second chapter as well. Then go through, concentrating on Inspector Malone. Cut anything that is not seen through his eyes. And only give him one case at a time. You've got enough material here for ten books.'

Mary, he is astounded (but not displeased) to see, is taking notes. 'Anything else?' she asks briskly.

'Not at present. I'll read through again and give you some more detailed notes, if you like.'

'Thank you,' says Mary. 'Now, do you think we could have a glass of wine?'

Mary's diary, 8 August

Cat's husband and children arrived this afternoon. Her husband was rather a surprise. Cat is so gorgeous that I had expected her husband to be strikingly good-looking but Justin is quite ordinary, sandy-haired, bespectacled and, unmistakably, shorter than her. He has a nice voice though (rather posh) and seems friendly and unassuming. He greeted Anna with a kiss and shook hands with the rest of us (we were on the terrace before supper). I thought that the men (JP, Sam and Jeremy) all glowered at him rather but then I think they were all rather sweet on Cat. Sally seemed to take to Justin at once and immediately started chatting to him about Salisbury (it turns out he was brought up near where she lives) and about Tuscany. He was polite to me too, said he knows Streatham well but actually he was talking about Clapham, which, of course, is much posher.

The children seemed shy at first or maybe I was shy of them. I never know quite what to say to children. The boy is called Sasha but he has very long hair and this, combined with his androgynous name, at first made me think that he was the girl. A bad start. The little girl, Star, is strikingly pretty, Cat in miniature, but she seemed overwhelmed by all the new people and started to cry. Poor Cat, it can't have been easy, with one child clinging to her skirt and the other screaming. I must say, Justin was very good with the children. He picked up Star, got her to stop crying, and distracted Sasha by showing him the pool. I can't ever remember my father having much to do with us when we were children. He went out of the house in the morning and came back at night. Sometimes we were allowed, as a treat, to visit him on one of his building sites but we had to be very quiet and not get in the way. Children today are never told such things. Quite right too.

Showing Sasha the pool turned out to be a mistake because then he started screaming, saying that he wanted to go swimming. Cat tried to reason with him, talked to him just as if he were an adult, saying it was too late, they'd go tomorrow, etc., etc., but he kept on yelling, his face went quite purple. It was Matt who saved the day. He turned up with Fabio and the two of them took the children on piggyback rides around the garden. We adults sat on the terrace (I saw Cat gratefully grabbing a glass of wine) and watched the children, because Matt and Fabio are little more than children, leaping over the bushes and running in and out of the trees. It was lovely to hear their laughter. Perhaps, at my age, children are really better as background noise.

I had quite a good session with Jeremy earlier. I found him patronising at first but later he said some interesting things. For example, he said that most books would be better without their first chapter. Afterwards, I wondered, is this true? What about the famous opening lines in Pride and Prejudice or David Copperfield? But then I thought, maybe those arresting words were really originally the start of chapter two before

Austen or Dickens scrapped their dull first chapters. Certainly, my own first chapter, a rather dreary description of South London, could safely be discarded.

The children surprised everyone at supper by eating all of Aldo's food without a murmur. Cat had been rather worried, saying that Sasha had all sorts of allergies and that Star really only ate Marmite sandwiches, but Aldo brought the food in himself and, unlike me, he knows exactly how to talk to children. He told them that he had made the food specially, just for them, and let them use his special machine for grinding parmigiano. After that, they ate the pasta and even the rather spicy (delicious) chicken, as good as gold. 'Can I take you home with us, Aldo?' asked Cat, rather plaintively.

After supper I was surprised that Cat didn't take the little ones straight to bed. After all, it was ten o'clock, surely way past their bedtime, and they had been travelling all day. But maybe she thought they were happy, playing Scrabble with Matt, or maybe she just wanted a chance to relax with a liqueur. Eventually, Star fell asleep on the floor and Justin picked her up and they all went off to bed.

The rest of us chatted for a bit and Matt, Fabio, JP and Anna started a multilingual Scrabble game. When I went to bed they were still playing, with Sam peering over Anna's shoulder, though she hardly needed help; she was winning by miles when I last looked.

CHAPTER 14

Day 8, Siena

9 August

Fabio drives the bus to Siena because Aldo, who so adores Rome, has no time for his neighbouring town. This is quite common amongst Tuscans, explains Patricia to JP; rivalry amongst these hilltop towns is very strong, many have a long history of war and bloodshed. 'All around here there were battles between Sienese and Florentine armies. It was at Montalcino, quite near here, that the Sienese army made their last stand. They still fly banners in Siena saying "The Republic of Siena in Montalcino".'

'What were they fighting about?' asks JP.

'Oh, land, money, religion,' says Patricia. 'All the usual things.'

Remembering Aldo and his mention of the recent battle of 1440, Anna thinks that Patricia has a point about Tuscans. Yet, driving through Tuscany at twilight, it is hard to think of bloodshed. Siena is only a few miles away but, up here in the hills, it is impossible to travel in a straight line. The minibus takes a laborious, serpentine route that at each turn reveals a fresh delight: a farmhouse with white horses grazing, a roadside shrine where flowers are laid before a serene ceramic Mary, three cypresses silhouetted against the sky, another hill-side town seeming to rise straight out of the mountain itself.

Even the place names are magical. Anna, gazing out of the window, finds herself repeating them in her head, so that they form a kind of mantra: Montalcino, Montepulciano, Buonconvento, Monte Oliveto Maggiore. Behind her Cat is playing a very educational game of I-Spy ('You know what a deciduous tree is, Sasha. We read a book about them last year) and Justin is trying to stop Star kicking Anna's seat. Patricia and JP are now talking about the Palio and Dorothy is telling Sally about skiing in Vermont. 'We have proper-sized mountains at home, not these fiddly little things. I can't for the life of me see how they manage to build towns on top of them.' Mary is not with them. For the first time this holiday, she has pleaded tiredness and has stayed behind at the Castello. (Actually, she wants to spend time working on her book, to see if the first chapter trick actually works.) On the other hand, Matt has accompanied them, to Patricia's obvious pleasure. True, he has spent all journey plugged into his iPod but he is, at least, there.

'Are you all right?' Sam asks Anna, who is sitting next to him. A particularly violent kick from Star has just shot her into the air.

'Fine.' Anna smiles.

Sam turns round and glares at Star, which, of course, makes her cry. The words 'Don't like that man' can be heard through her sobs. Neither Cat nor Justin disagrees with this assessment.

'Don't worry, sweetheart,' says Cat, 'we'll buy you a treat in Siena.' Now Sasha cries because he, too, wants a treat. Matt turns up the volume on his iPod.

'Christ,' whispers Sam to Anna. 'Why do we have to put up with this? Isn't it past their bedtime?'

Anna had wondered if Cat would think the trip too late for the children. They left the Castello at six but, as they are dining in Siena, it will be after ten o'clock by the time they get back. But Cat explained that she did not want Sasha and Star to miss the chance of seeing Siena. 'The Duomo,' she said earnestly, 'is absolutely fascinating.' Judging from the conversation behind her, though, it looks as if Cat and Justin's first trip will be to an ice cream parlour. 'Not horrible Italian ice cream,' warns Sasha. 'Proper Calypsos and things.'

Fabio parks by the Porto Romano and the group walks up the hill towards Il Campo, the famous piazza at the centre of the city. It is now nearly seven and the shops are opening again for the evening, little treasure troves full of jewellery, silk scarves and expensive-looking handbags. Cat exclaims with delight and, a few seconds later, Justin emerges from one of the shops bearing a bag in the softest red leather. Cat squeals and embraces him in the street.

'Now I understand what she sees in him,' mutters Sam

behind Anna. He would like to be able to buy Anna a present. He'd choose something better than that vulgar-looking scarlet thing too. But Anna says nothing. She is looking at her guide-book. 'It says here that Saint Bernardino used to preach in the Campo.'

'Siena is also the birthplace of Santa Caterina. Saint Catherine,' says Patricia. 'Your namesake, Cat.'

Cat smirks.

'Santa Caterina,' says Justin, kissing her.

'She was very clever,' says Patricia. 'A doctor of the church. But her besetting sin was vanity. She used to bleach her hair by drying it in the sun.'

'How do you know all this stuff?' laughs JP.

'We have a trip to Siena every year,' says Patricia, 'and some of it has stuck. I'm good at remembering useless things.'

'Depends what you mean by useless,' says JP.

'Well, I can never remember my mobile phone number.'

'Nor can Dad,' says Matt unexpectedly. 'Once he lost his car in a multi-storey car park. He couldn't remember what colour it was.'

The guidebook described Il Campo as the most beautiful square in the world but, even so, Anna gasps as they round the corner and the golden fan-shaped space spreads out in front of them. The square is really a semicircle, an uneven raked stage full of people walking, talking and marvelling. On one side of the Campo a massive bell tower rises into the sky, on the other the restaurants are setting out their tables for the evening. Couples walk hand in hand, children run around chasing pigeons and, at the far end of the Campo, beside an elaborate fountain, a band is playing.

Anna turns to Patricia, her face glowing. 'It's beautiful,' she says.

'I'm glad you like it,' says Patricia. 'For me, it's the most perfect town in Italy. Perhaps the world.'

'What about Paris?' teases JP.

'I've never been to Paris.'

'Really? We must remedy that.'

There is a slightly embarrassed pause. Anna moves away slightly, thinking that JP might want to be alone with Patricia. Really, he seems to be very keen on her. But Matt has other ideas. He takes Patricia's arm. 'What about an ice cream, Mum?'

'Honestly,' says Patricia, 'how old are you? Six?' But she smiles and allows Matt to drag her over to one of the cafes. Away from JP.

The group sits at tables overlooking the square. The children (including Matt and Fabio) eat ice creams and the adults drink coffee. Sam has a beer. Most of the party want to explore the famous black-and-white cathedral but JP wants to climb the tower.

'All those steps,' says Dorothy. 'You must be mad, Jean-Pierre.'

Anna is torn. She'd like to see the view from the tower (and take a picture for the boys) but, once again, she wonders if JP is manoeuvring to be left alone with Patricia. Sure enough,

Patricia says, 'I don't mind going up the tower. The view's worth the climb.' Matt says he will go with them but Fabio volunteers that he knows a bar where they play heavy metal music so the young men slouch off westwards.

'I'd like to see the cathedral,' says Anna.

'Me too,' says Sam.

Mary is hard at work. She has cut the first chapter and the book now starts with Inspector Malone talking to his pigeons. It is better, she thinks. Without telling the reader that Malone is a misanthropic widower with no one to talk to, this becomes evident from the way that he is telling the birds about the latest developments in the strangler case. His world – the dreary terraced house, the pub, the corner shop – opens itself out without too much intervention from her. So far, so good.

She is still working an hour later, cutting out unnecessary descriptions or plot twists, when there is a knock at the door.

'Come in,' says Mary.

Aldo enters, carrying a tray containing a covered dish.

'I bring you supper,' he says. 'Bean soup. A local speciality. I think you rather eat here so as not to disturb your work.'

'That's so kind,' says Mary. 'You shouldn't have gone to so much trouble.'

'Is no trouble,' says Aldo. He puts the tray on a small table by the window. The soup smells delicious and there are freshly baked rolls alongside a carafe of wine.

'How is your book?' asks Aldo.

Mary is not sure if he means how is the book going or what is it about. She decides to answer both questions.

'It's about a murder,' she says. 'In London, where I live, but in the past. It's going quite well. Jeremy has given me some good advice.'

Aldo snorts, presumably at the mention of Jeremy. 'I would like to read it one day,' he says.

'I'd like you to,' says Mary. 'I've never shown it to anyone before.'

'No one?'

'No.' Thinking about it, Mary wonders if this is very odd. Unlike a lot of the other writers, she has never sent her book out to publishers. This has undoubtedly saved her a lot of rejections but it has left her with the uncomfortable feeling that her novel doesn't really exist. Can a book exist if nobody reads it?

'I like to read,' says Aldo. 'I sit on my balcony sometimes and read for hours.'

After he has gone, Mary finds herself thinking about Aldo and about what happens in his life after he leaves the Castello every evening. She somehow can't imagine him sitting alone on his balcony reading a book. Patricia has told her that Aldo is a widower. Like Inspector Malone. Mary smiles as she imagines replacing Inspector Malone with Aldo (what is his surname?). That would certainly liven the book up. The meals would improve too. Eating soup with one hand, she goes back to the laptop.

*

Patricia and JP have reached the top of the tower, 503 steps (according to the guidebook). Patricia is panting, she can't be as fit as she thought she was, but JP seems hardly out of breath. He leans enthusiastically over the parapet. 'This is incredible. I can see the Castello.'

Patricia follows his pointing finger. Beyond the city walls, amongst the darkening hills, she can just make out the towers of the Castello.

'I've never realised that before,' she says.

'It's extraordinary.'

The view is making Patricia feel slightly faint. The tower seems almost to lean out over the square and she can see the little people scurrying around below. Will she be able to see Matt and Fabio, emerging from their sweaty heavy metal club? She's glad that Matt has become friends with Fabio. He's a far better influence than Graziano and Elio. She realises that JP is asking her a question.

'How long have you been on your own?'

'On my own?'

'Without your husband.'

'Oh.' Patricia is taken aback but manages to answer in an even voice. 'Four years. He left when Matt was twelve. We divorced a year later.'

'Tough.'

She doesn't know whether he means for Matt or for her. 'Yes,' she agrees.

'I've been divorced two years,' says JP. 'It's my son I miss most.'

'I didn't know you had a son.'

'Louis. He's seven.' JP produces a wallet and shows Patricia a picture of a handsome, dark-haired child clutching a balloon.

'He's lovely,' says Patricia dutifully.

'Yes,' says JP moodily. He is silent for a moment, looking out over the rooftops of Siena. Then he says, 'Have you ever thought of marrying again?'

'No,' says Patricia, with perfect truth. 'Have you?'

'No,' says JP. 'Once is enough.' Suddenly he smiles, which seems to change his face completely. 'You're a very beautiful woman,' he says.

Patricia says nothing. They ought to be going back down, she thinks, the tower will close soon and they should be meeting the others at the restaurant. But, when JP moves closer and bends his lips to hers, she does nothing except tilt up her head and shut her eyes.

The drive home is very quiet. Dorothy and Rick are asleep, leaning on each other very sweetly. Even Star, who had a tantrum in the restaurant because they didn't serve chips, is asleep in Justin's arms, her dark curls ruffled, her lips pursed. Sasha is playing on his Nintendo DS and the electronic bleeps of intergalactic warfare are oddly soothing.

Anna shuts her eyes and Sam wonders if he dares put his arm round her. It has been a strange evening. Patricia and JP arrived late at the restaurant and Patricia seemed flustered, unlike her normal composed self. She failed to translate the menu and, when Matt and Fabio arrived, even later, she hardly seemed to notice. It was Fabio who took over, translated the menu, negotiated with the waiter, entertained the children, chatted with Dorothy about the frescoes in the cathedral ('Hardly decent, to my mind'). Now he is driving them home, his dark face intent as he looks at the road. He's a good man, thinks Sam. Patricia is lucky to have him.

Anna's head bumps against the window and Sam longs to cushion it with his arm. He feels each impact as if it is happening to his own body. Christ, what's the matter with me? he thinks. He doesn't remember feeling like this about any of his previous girlfriends. With Jenny everything had been so simple. They worked together, got on well, spent several evenings drinking together in city wine bars. Then Jenny left the bank and Sam found he missed her. He rang her up and she seemed to understand that this meeting would be different from the previous casual after-work encounters. They went out for a meal and, on the way home, Sam kissed her. They both enjoyed this so much that they went straight back to Jenny's flat and made love. They moved in together six months later.

Now Jenny is in Greece with a girlfriend and Sam is in Italy, becoming more obsessed with a woman who hardly knows he exists. What will happen when Jenny returns? He knows that she hopes that he will give up this ridiculous writing idea and go back to the city. But, despite his conspicuous failure to write anything approaching a bestseller, Sam knows that this just won't happen. Something has changed inside him, he doesn't know what. He could no sooner squeeze back into that pinstriped suit than he could fly to the moon. It is as if, having stepped off the commuting, money-making treadmill, he just can't step back on again. Becoming an author had seemed the perfect answer. A high-status, portable profession that he could combine with travelling around exciting parts of the world, looking for plots. He had never bargained on not being able to do the writing bit.

Maybe this is why he likes Anna so much. She understands. She, too, is someone struggling to escape from a mundane life (that Steve sounds a real boor). She understands those sleepless nights when you review your life and you realise that you have done nothing, nothing at all. He does not want his obituary to read: 'Sam McClusky worked in a bank. He was not married and had no children.' But if he can't write a book, what the hell can he do?

As the minibus turns into the Castello drive, Sam wonders if he shouldn't just forget the book idea altogether. Whether he should go home, get some sort of job (not in a bank) and propose to Jenny. Then, as Anna wakes up, shakes out her hair and smiles sleepily at him, he thinks that the book is probably the least of his problems.

CHAPTER 15

Day 8, night

It is eleven o'clock by the time the guests return to the Castello. Patricia makes cocoa which they drink in the small sitting room and then people drift off to their rooms. Patricia, though, doesn't want to go to bed. She feels keyed-up, excited, though not in an altogether pleasurable sense. Her skin feels hypersensitive, as if she is starting a fever, and she can feel her heart beating unevenly in her chest. Was it JP's kiss that has made her feel like this? He is not the first man she has kissed since Sean (last year she had a brief affair with a Sienese businessman) but he is, she realises, the first person who has gone a little way towards making her forget Sean. She had grown so used to living with the ghost of her ex-husband that she had really thought she would never be free of him. But this difficult, attractive Frenchman has given her a tiny glimpse of a Sean-free life. Maybe this is why she feels so ambivalent, she thinks as she washes the last of the cocoa cups (she feels, somehow, that she needs to do this by hand rather than just putting them in the dishwasher). If she loses her residual love for Sean, what has she got left?

JP is attractive, he's intelligent and he seems surprisingly kind. After their kiss at the top of the tower, he had taken her hand and they had walked down all 503 steps, neither of them speaking. In the restaurant, she had found it hard to concentrate on the guests, to check that they all understood the menu, to ask the waiter for special food for the children. Fabio had done all that; she must remember to thank him in the morning. She had been all too conscious of JP sitting next to her, the hairs on his forearm, his long fingers curling themselves round his wine glass. When she had turned to look at him, the gleam in his black eyes had made her blush. How many years is it since she has blushed?

Patricia puts the cups in the draining cupboard and looks around the spotless kitchen. On the table, Aldo has left his menu for tomorrow. She scans it quickly: *zuppa di funghi, ravioli di spinaci, scaloppine*. It sounds delicious, as ever. She is just about to write a jokey note on the menu when she sees something half hidden under the paper. She pulls it out. It is an Agatha Christie book, in English. She recognises it from her own library. There is no reason why Aldo should not borrow her books, of course, it is just that he has never done so before. She pushes the book back under the menu.

Walking slowly up the stone stairs, she thinks she will call in on Matt before bed. It was nice of him to come on the Siena trip and he was quite like his old self: funny, enthusiastic, entertaining. And he has been so good with those awful children. She'll pop in and thank him.

She knocks on Matt's door and receives a grunt in acknowledgement. Opening the door, she sees that Matt is at his computer. He switches screens as soon as he hears the door open.

'Hello, darling,' says Patricia, sitting on his bed. It is covered with a striped black-and-white Juventus duvet. Posters of Juventus players and heavy metal bands fight for space on the walls. On the cork board over the desk, though, she can see a framed picture of Sean and Matt, taken on a roller-coaster ride at Thorpe Park. Both are grinning widely, though Matt, she notices, is gripping the safety bar very tightly indeed. Sean, as ever, is completely oblivious to danger.

'Are you working?' she asks, casually she hopes. She knows he won't be doing any of his holiday assignments. Matt's attitude to school work is careless in the extreme, which does not seem to stop him getting high marks.

'I was on MSN. Talking to Graziano and Elio.'

Somehow she knows this isn't true but she doesn't pursue it.

'I just wanted to say thank you for coming tonight,' she says. 'It was lovely to have you and you've been a real help with Cat's kids.'

Matt grunts but then turns with something of his old grin. 'I don't think she's too happy that they've turned up, do you?'

Patricia hesitates. She makes it a rule never to gossip about the guests and, besides, she feels rather guilty that it was her special offer which has delivered Justin and the children and, quite clearly, ruined Cat's holiday.

But she can't resist Matt's grin. 'No,' she says. 'I don't think she's too happy.'

'We hear a bit less about how wonderful, special and talented her children are now, don't we?'

This time Patricia laughs. 'Or how useless her husband is. It's quite clear he does most of the childcare.'

'And most of the housework, I bet. Not like Dad.'

Patricia looks at Matt; his blond head is bent over his computer so she can't see his face.

'No,' she says. 'Sean never did much housework but he was good with children. Just like you.'

'Why didn't you have any other kids then?' asks Matt.

Patricia is completely stymied. Matt has never asked this question before and, over the years, she has even stopped asking it of herself.

'I don't know,' she says at last. 'We thought we'd wait a few years and then . . . well, it didn't happen.'

Sean had wanted to adopt. A child from China, Africa, the slums of Naples. His altruism was boundless. She, on the other hand, had been afraid that she could never love an adopted child as much as her own.

'Would you have liked a brother or a sister?' she asks.

Matt shrugs. 'I dunno. Would have been company, I suppose.'

Maybe that is why he is so drawn to his unsuitable posse, thinks Patricia. At least now he has Fabio for company.

She is about to speak when the air is filled with a terrible high-pitched screaming. She and Matt look at each other and then leap to their feet. Out in the corridor, Patricia hears the scream again. It is coming from the North Tower. She sets off at a run, Matt following her.

In the North Tower, Mary's door is open. Patricia knocks perfunctorily and enters to find Mary comforting a sobbing Dorothy.

'I saw him,' howls Dorothy. 'I saw him.'

'Who?' asks Patricia, coming closer. Dorothy, wearing her flowered dressing gown, is half sitting, half lying on Mary's bed. Mary, who is fully dressed, hovers beside her, looking awkward.

'The ghost!' shrieks Dorothy. 'I came to borrow an aspirin from Mary. Coach travel always gives me a headache. And, as soon as I entered the room, I heard this awful unearthly whistling sound. I went to the window and . . . oh! . . . I saw him!' Dorothy collapses once more. Patricia, patting her shoulder, is very relieved to see Rick approaching, carrying a glass of water and a bottle of pills.

'Here, honey,' he says. 'Have some of your Valium.'

Dorothy reaches out a shaking hand and manages to swallow two pills. In the background, Patricia sees JP, Sam and Anna hovering.

'It's OK,' she says, trying to keep her voice light. 'Dorothy just thought she saw something.'

'I did see him.' Dorothy raises a tear-stained face. 'I saw him as plain as I'm seeing you. I looked out of the window and there he was, hanging there.'

Despite herself, Patricia shivers. 'Hanging there?'

'Yes. I looked out of the window and there he was, blond hair and all, just hanging in mid-air. And . . . he was smiling.'

'Smiling?'

'Yes, an awful, evil smile.'

Patricia gets up and goes to the window. On the floor below Mary's room is a narrow ledge where, she supposes, a man could stand but he would hardly be hanging in mid-air. She looks up. An old flag pole is silhouetted against the sky. Above, a half-moon sits balefully in the cloudless sky.

'Patricia,' says JP from the doorway. 'Would you like Sam and me to go outside, just to check that no one is hanging around?'

'I'll come too,' says Matt.

'And I.' Fabio has appeared in the hallway. He, too, is fully dressed.

Patricia doesn't want Matt to go but she can hardly say so. She thanks JP gratefully and the men depart, rather importantly, their feet clattering on the stairs.

'Come on,' she says to Dorothy, 'I'll get us all a glass of brandy.'

'I shouldn't drink on top of those pills,' says Dorothy. But she gets up and meekly follows Patricia out of the room.

From: Anna Valore
Date: 10 August 2017, 00.15
To: Steve Smith
Re: Hello Sexy

Hi, love! Sorry to send this so late but I was halfway through writing it when there was a tremendous disturbance nearby. Someone screaming like they were being murdered. I was a bit scared but I went to investigate and it turned out that it was Dorothy (the American lady I told you about), who thought that she'd seen a ghost. Remember I told you that Aldo (the chef) had told this really creepy ghost story on our first night? It was about this countess who used to live at the castle. She had a lover, a young boy, and he used to visit her at night. Her jealous husband caught him and hung him in a cage outside the countess's window, to starve to death. Unable to bear it, the countess shot him and killed herself. Pretty gruesome, eh? And now there was Dorothy screaming that she saw this body hanging outside Mary's window. Mary's room is in the North Tower, where all this is supposed to have happened.

I don't believe in ghosts, as you know, but I must admit I was a bit spooked. Especially when Dorothy described the 'awful evil smile' on the man's face. I wasn't so much scared of a ghost than of an awful evil prowler hanging around (ha!) outside. But JP and Sam (the French chap and the ex-banker) offered to go and check outside and Dorothy has got rather a vivid imagination so I'm sure it was nothing to worry about. Mary, whose room it was after all, didn't seem worried at all. She said she was going back to work on her book. She's very dedicated. The best of all of us.

We had a lovely evening in Siena. It is such a beautiful town. We must go there together one day. It is built of golden houses all clustered, higgledy-piggledy, around this wonderful shell-shaped piazza. We went to see the cathedral – it's very striking, built of black and white bricks – and had a wonderful meal in a little restaurant near the tower. Cat didn't seem to enjoy it much (poor Star was tired and made a bit of a fuss). She doesn't seem that pleased that Justin has turned up. I hope everything is OK between them.

Well, I'd better get to bed. Jeremy (the tutor) has asked us to keep a dream diary. I should have some good material tonight!

Miss you loads and can't wait to see you all. Hugs and kisses to the boys.

Love you

A

The Seven Moons of Jaconda
by Lupo O'Hara

Chapter 12

Since the fourth ide was now in session, the council met at first moon fall. The horsemen had come early, riding their black steeds across the red sands of Sommerslath. Their Chieftain was fell and dangerous, a man cloaked always in black. The Westermen were next, marching behind their leader, Wode. They wore green and carried staffs, to signify that they wished to parley not fight. Hengest was not deceived. He had seen the battle light in Wode's three green eyes and knew him to be a warrior as fearsome as the Chief Horseman. The Brotherhood sailed across the white seas in their five-masted boat. No one knew who led them. The Brotherhood elected their leader in secret and told no one the results of the election. Five Brotherhood representatives sat at council, cloaked in white.

'So,' said Hengest to his battle brother Fabian. 'We begin.'

CHAPTER 16

Day 9

10 August

After the excitements of the night before, everyone is a little subdued at breakfast. They eat breakfast on the terrace and it is normally a sociable time, with people relaxing over coffee before the first writing session starts. Mary always starts the day with a swim and Cat usually joins Myra for the daily meditation and stretch.

Today, though, everyone seems quieter than normal. Only Mary seems her old self. Her wet hair advertises the fact that, despite being right at the centre of the great ghost sighting, she is continuing with her usual routine. Cat, on the other hand, has not been seen stretching and meditating since her husband and children arrived. Today she looks heavy-eyed and tired. Despite once telling Anna that having children is no excuse to dress badly, she does not quite look her normal glamorous self. Star has spilt orange juice down her white T-shirt and her denim skirt is crumpled.

JP also looks tired. He came to breakfast in his white dressing gown but only drank a cup of black coffee before disappearing again. Sam seems very quiet, hiding behind yesterday's *Times*, and Anna, too, seems rather dreamy although, in her red sundress, she looks beautiful enough to make Sam feel quite faint.

Patricia, although she has had less sleep than anyone, is as efficient as ever. She tells the guests that if they want to see the market at San Severino, they should leave by nine thirty, otherwise there will be nowhere to park.

'Why is it so popular?' asks Dorothy who, although she had the most exciting night of all, seems remarkably calm and rested.

'Well, it's the weekly market,' says Patricia. 'Everyone from San Severino, and the neighbouring towns too, will be there. It's where they get all their food for the weekend.'

'Will Aldo be driving us?' asks Mary.

'No,' says Patricia. 'It's his morning off. Fabio will be taking us.'

Cat and family are keen to see the market (anything to get away from the Castello for a while). JP, who emerges fully dressed just as they are finishing breakfast, also wants to go. Anna, Mary and Sam hurry upstairs to get ready. Dorothy and Rick say they will stay behind. 'It's a little hot for us,' explains Rick apologetically. 'I guess we'll take a little downtime by the pool.' Looking over at the pool, Patricia sees Matt just diving in. She'll have to tell him to get out so the Van Elstens can have the place to themselves.

It is only just after ten when they arrive in the town square but it is already very hot. The market fills the whole of the square and spills out into the surrounding streets. Anna, threading her way through the crowds of elderly women with giant shopping baskets, sees fish stalls, cheese stalls and meat stalls but also stalls selling lurid clothes covered with sequins, animals made from real rabbit fur and a plethora of tiny Japanese toys.

She buys Italy shirts for Steve and the boys as well as a cotton dress for herself (she is rapidly running out of clothes). Just as she is holding the dress up against herself, she is embarrassed to see Sam appearing at her side.

'It suits you,' he says, gesturing towards the dress, which is white and very simple.

'Thanks.' Anna hastily hands over the money for the dress.

'What about this to go with it?' He picks up a coral necklace from the next stall.

'Bit expensive,' mumbles Anna.

'Let me buy it for you.'

'No! I couldn't!' Anna sounds so horrified that he gives in, much to the stall holder's disappointment.

Patricia and JP are also strolling through the stalls. Many of the stallholders greet Patricia enthusiastically (they are sure

195

that the Castello owner must be extremely rich) and she is constantly being told how young/beautiful/elegant she looks.

'Does the constant flattery get you down?' murmurs JP.

'No.' Patricia grins.

'I'm sure I could get used to it,' JP admits. They stop at a stall glistening with olives. Green and black, filled with chillies, anchovies, peppers and lemons, they lie in front of them like the hundred eyes of Argos.

'I can't resist them,' says Patricia, 'although I know Aldo will already have bought some.'

'Why resist?' says JP.

Patricia shoots him a sharp look before choosing fifty grams of green olives filled with anchovies. She places the olives in her wicker basket and they continue their slow progress.

'Do you think Dorothy really saw anything last night?' JP asks.

'No!' says Patricia sharply. 'It was all in her imagination. You didn't see anything when you went outside, did you?'

'No,' says JP slowly. Patricia looks at him.

'You don't believe in ghosts, do you?' she asks incredulously.

'Well, my aunt once saw Marie Antoinette at Versailles.'

'Everyone sees Marie Antoinette at Versailles. It's compulsory.'

JP laughs. 'Quite so. But I don't know about ghosts. If you believe in an afterlife, as I do, well, it seems obvious that there must be some overlap between the worlds.'

'Do you really believe in an afterlife?' asks Patricia curiously.

'Yes. Is that so strange? I am a Catholic, after all.'

'A practising Catholic?'

'Well, I'm divorced,' says JP, 'which isn't a good start. I can't partake of the sacraments. Unless I get an annulment, of course.'

'Is that possible?'

'Well, it seems possible if you have enough money,' says JP drily. 'But I'm not sure I would get one even if I could. It would be like saying to Louis that my marriage to his mother didn't exist and I don't want to do that.'

Everything comes back to Louis, thinks Patricia. Aloud, she says, 'My husband was a Catholic. But I can't remember it affecting his everyday life much.'

'What sort of man was he, your husband?'

Patricia pauses. They have reached the end of the market. She can see Cat and Justin sitting at a cafe with their children. For some reason, she wants very much to avoid them.

'This way.' She propels JP down another street lined with rather more exclusive stalls. 'My husband,' she says. 'Well, he was charming, handsome, useless with money.' She smiles, rather bitterly. 'He was good at all sort of stupid things. He could walk on his hands. He even did a circus skills course. He could whistle any tune. He could ride a horse bareback. He could draw brilliant cartoons. But he couldn't change a light bulb.'

'So he wasn't much help with the business?'

'You could say that, yes.'

They stop by a shop selling postcards. JP buys several tasteful views of Tuscany. As he pays, he says casually, 'When can I be alone with you, Mrs O'Hara?'

Patricia's heart is once more beating bumpily. 'What do you mean?'

'Away from all these people. Away from Cat's screaming kids and Dorothy seeing ghosts and Aldo needing to discuss tomorrow's pasta recipes.'

Smarting slightly at the slur on Aldo's cooking, Patricia, says, 'Well, on Wednesday, the festival for *Ferragosto*, after the meal people usually just slope off and do their own thing.'

'So I'll have to wait until then?'

Patricia shrugs. JP laughs, steering her towards Gennaro's wine stall. 'Well then, I must wait to do my own thing. Come on, let's go and have a laugh at the Chianti.'

Mary, her bag clasped tightly in front of her, is finding the market rather bewildering. So many stalls, so many people, so much noise and colour and confusion. She stops to admire a crate of adorable white rabbits. Then she looks up and realises that she is in front of the butcher's stall. A whole pig's head leers horribly at her and a string of blood-red sausages forms a grisly garland overhead. Every one of those fluffy rabbits, she realises, must be destined for the pot. Mary hurries away. If only she didn't like meat so much, she'd be a vegetarian like a shot.

Another stall sells equally terrifying fish: squid, octopus, giant prawns with horrible hairy faces. The stallholder handles the slippery fish with confident ease, handing them over to gimlet-eyed women with a stream of what is obviously highly amusing banter. Mary, who has been secretly working on her Italian, is disappointed to discover that she does not understand one word of it.

'Mary!'

Hearing a word that she actually recognises, Mary swings round. Aldo is grinning at her from the bread stall. Mary makes her way over. This stall, at least, does not look scary.

Aldo introduces her to the stallholder, a cheerful-looking man with a shock of white hair.

'Mary, I present my brother, Massimo.'

'Your brother?'

'Yes. Remember I say that my father was the baker? Well, Massimo is the eldest son. He inherit the business.'

Massimo kisses Mary's hand with a flourish and presents her with a bag of star-shaped rolls. Aldo says something to Massimo in Italian and Massimo laughs.

'I tell my brother about you,' says Aldo, taking Mary's arm. 'I tell him about the lovely English lady who likes my food.'

'You make me sound so greedy,' says Mary. 'Fat.'

Aldo looks horrified. 'Fat? You are never fat. You have perfect body.'

Never, in all Mary's seventy-four years, has anyone described her body as perfect. Indeed, apart from (occasionally) doctors, no one has ever passed an opinion on her body at all. She stands in the middle of the crowded market, her bag of rolls in her hand, and feels great waves of pleasure and embarrassment flow over her.

'Now I make you go red,' says Aldo remorsefully. 'Come, we go and have a *cappuccio* somewhere.'

And Mary lets herself be led away, feeling as if her body, though far from perfect, temporarily belongs to someone else.

Cat and Justin have chosen their cafe because, although it is not the most prepossessing in the street, it does have a rusty mechanical horse which, if fed with euros, will rock gently to and fro. Star has already used up ten euros' worth and looks set for a good few more. Sasha, playing morosely on his DS, sits opposite his parents on the single outside table. Inside the cafe a widescreen TV is on full blast. The news is still the same: the same youth is missing, presumed kidnapped, in Modena, the same forest fires are raging through Naples, celebrities are still getting married beside Italian lakes.

Justin drinks a cappuccino while Cat toys with a mineral water. They both watch Star as she beats the mechanical horse with an imaginary riding crop.

'I had a pony once,' says Cat dreamily. 'He was called Cuddles.'

Justin doesn't seem to have heard. 'I shouldn't have come here,' he says abruptly.

'Why do you say that?' asks Cat.

'Well, it obviously hasn't made you happy.' says Justin,

mechanically passing Star another euro. 'When I got Patricia's email, I thought it would be a nice surprise for you, us turning up. But having the kids here has been a complete disaster.'

'No it hasn't,' protests Cat.

'Yes it has,' says Justin. 'The other guests obviously find them really annoying. It's too hot for them, there's nothing much to do and you were having a better time before we came.'

Cat says nothing. She is thinking of the evenings on the terrace, of the midnight swim, of Fabio's slim brown body in the water.

'Steve warned me,' says Justin. 'He said not to come. He said you and Anna deserved some time on your own. Away from us and away from the kids.'

'Steve!' says Cat scornfully. 'What does he know?'

'He's a bright bloke,' says Justin. 'And he was right, wasn't he?'

Cat thinks about her writing. She thinks about the fact that Jeremy has not once suggested a private session with her. She thinks about the fact that Sam, quite obviously, has the hots for Anna and not for her.

'No,' she says. 'It was going wrong before you came.'

Sam and Anna are in a rather more upmarket cafe at the other end of the market. There are tables with red umbrellas and little bowls of olives (for which they will be charged a quite frightening premium). Anna is drinking a delicious drink of squeezed lemon and sparkling water. She loves lemons, a taste which has often made Steve speculate that she must be an alien. Sam, on the other hand, seems to think that it is charming. Sam is drinking beer.

Anna and Sam are also discussing Dorothy's ghost.

'There was nothing outside,' says Sam. 'Not even a footprint.'

Anna shivers. 'That makes it worse.'

Sam edges slightly nearer. 'You're not scared, are you?'

'No,' says Anna. 'I think Dorothy was, though.'

'Dorothy!' Sam snorts. 'With all the pills she takes, I'm surprised she isn't seeing little green men by now.'

'Well, she has had an awful life.'

'What, married to a rich Texan with more money than he knows what to do with?'

'You know what I mean. Her childhood.'

'So she had a bad childhood. Get over it.' Sam is still rather aggrieved that his own childhood has not provided better material.

'I don't think it's quite that simple,' says Anna.

They sit under their red umbrella and watch as people wander back from the market. There are a few tourists (identifiable by their clothes – Italian men only wear shorts to play football) but San Severino does not feature in many guidebooks and so most of the passers-by are Tuscans carrying bread, cheese and wine and, once, disturbingly, a live chicken. Sam and Anna, watching and chatting in a desultory way, are therefore startled to see Aldo and Mary, he carrying

several large loaves and she a small paper bag, thread their
way through the crowds and disappear into a neighbouring
cafe, one they had not dared enter because it is clearly for the
locals only (there are no outside tables, only little old men
sitting on kitchen chairs, playing cards).

Sam and Anna look at each other.

'What are they doing?' wonders Sam.

'Same as us,' suggests Anna. 'Having a drink.'

'I think something's going on,' says Sam. Can Aldo really
be doing the same as him? 'I bet old Aldo's a bit of a lad
underneath.'

Mary is finding Aldo's cafe rather terrifying. It is a dark, smoky
place full of Italians yelling at each other. The clientele, nearly
all men, are watching a football match on the TV. Half of the
men are yelling at the players and the other half seem to be
just yelling. Mary assumes that they are in the middle of some
massive sports-related row. She hopes it won't become violent.

Aldo returns from the bar, holding two small cups.

'*Un cappuccio.*' He puts one cup in front of her.

'What's the difference between a *cappuccio* and a *cappuccino*?'

Aldo grins. '*Cappuccino* is for tourists.'

A monstrous roar from the crowd around the TV.

'Is there going to be a fight?' asks Mary nervously.

'A fight?' repeats Aldo astounded. 'Why would there be a
fight?'

'Well, they're all shouting at each other.'

Aldo laughs, as loudly as the men are shouting. 'Tuscans,' he says proudly, 'have the loudest voices in the world.' He gestures towards the men at the bar who are now, mysteriously, exchanging back-slaps and even embraces. 'These boys are the best of friends. They are happy, watching Juventus play. When they are happy, they shout. We do not whisper like you English.' He puts on a feeble, high-pitched English voice. 'Oh, excuse me, pardon me . . .'

Mary laughs. 'At school I was always told my voice was too loud.'

'Never,' says Aldo. 'You have a wonderful voice. Like Miss Marple.'

Mary is not sure how to take this. She sips her (delicious) coffee and looks at Aldo, who is sitting, very relaxed, leaning back in his chair. He is wearing a pink shirt no Englishman of his age would be seen dead wearing. He is quite a dandy, she decides, his white hair is well cut and his nails look manicured. His hands, though, are peasant's hands, wide and strong.

'So, Mary,' says Aldo. 'You like Italy?'

'Oh,' says Mary. 'I love it! It's everything I dreamed and more.'

Aldo beams and is about to reply when one of the shouting men comes over and engages him in friendly, ear-splitting conversation.

Aldo introduces Mary, refusing to allow her to be ignored.

The shouting man bows. 'English lady? I speak very OK English. You like Aldo?'

Mary blushes but manages to say boldly, 'I like him very much.'

'Very much!' the man yells, clearly delighted. 'Aldo, she like you very much! Lady, you eat Aldo's food?'

'Yes, he's a wonderful chef.'

'Yes! Yes! Wonderful! The best. You hear him sing?'

'No.'

'You think he's a good chef, you wait till you hear him sing.'

'Massimo's the singer,' says Aldo, 'not me.'

Other loud voices come over and begin a thunderous debate about Aldo's cooking versus his brother Massimo's baking and vocal skills. Mary can understand about one word in fifty. There is obviously much badinage and humour, accompanied by tremendous hand-waving and multi-decibel laughter. Aldo says little, smiling almost apologetically at Mary and attempting to translate, although sometimes he gives up with a shrug and a laugh. Then the original shouting man starts to sing, encouraging Aldo to join in. The noise in the bar, already deafening, reaches new heights. Mary tries to see the time on Aldo's wristwatch. What if she misses the bus back? She tugs timidly at Aldo's sleeve. 'I have to go.'

Aldo disengages himself from his bellowing friends. 'Don't worry. I give you lift home. I tell Patricia.' He gets out his mobile phone.

*

Outside the cafe, Mary looks around for Aldo's car. He sees her look and makes a theatrical gesture towards a small red moped leaning against the kerb.

'Here is trusty Vespa.'

'That?'

'Yes. You mind travelling by motorbike?'

So Mary, who has never before even ridden a bicycle, ends up flying home through the dusty mountain roads, her arms round the pink shirt of a man she hardly knows, the sun in her face and the wind roaring in her ears like a thousand Tuscans watching a football match.

CHAPTER 17

Day 9, afternoon

After lunch, which was slightly late, Jeremy holds a writing session. The subject is 'Description of place' and Jeremy talks about the difficulty of writing about scenery, of making the reader see a place through fresh eyes.

'The worst descriptions,' says Jeremy, 'simply describe things. Item: a white-walled house. Item: a hill. Item: the setting sun. Description: "The sun sets behind the white-walled house on the hill." So far, so nothing. You could get that from a photograph. The best descriptions use the things to reflect on the mood or the themes of the book. Think of Wilkie Collins writing about the Shivering Sand in *The Moonstone*. The lonely, fatal stretch of sand reflects the state of mind of Rosanna Spearman, who dies there, and the description is seen through the eyes of Gabriel Betteredge, who hates the place.' He reads:

The last of the evening light was fading away; and all over the desolate place there hung a still and awful calm . . .

The inner sea lay lost and dim, without a breath of wind
to stir it. Patches of nasty ooze floated, yellow-white, on
the dead surface of the water.

'It's all there. The words "dead", "still", "lost" that tell us what
will happen, even "fading away". The voice of Betteredge. Who
else would use the phrase "nasty ooze"? You can even, if you
are a bit fanciful, see the "inner sea" as reflecting the works
of the inner mind and the ooze floating on the surface as
being the unpleasant emotions brought to the surface in the
course of the book.

'This is not just description. This is description for a purpose. I'm not talking about pathetic fallacy here but something
far deeper. So, if we take our original sentence, it would better,
though still not that interesting, to say, "The setting sun
turned the distant white-walled house a dull red." At least then
you get some suggestion of what may be happening inside
the house. There's a sense of transition, of things happening.
White turning to red. The red could suggest bloodshed, menstruation or even just embarrassment. The distance suggests
isolation, rather than just positioning. The sentence is now
weighted with meaning.'

Sam shifts uncomfortably in his chair. He has little
patience with all this literary stuff and the reference to
menstruation is just over the top. 'How do we know that
Wilkie Collins meant all this stuff when he wrote it?' he
asks, rather belligerently.

'Oh, he meant it,' says Jeremy, with a small smile, 'whether consciously or unconsciously. After all, he was on opium most of his life. Never underestimate the influence of the unconscious. That's why your dream diaries are so important.'

Sam looks sullen. His recent dreams are definitely not fit for public scrutiny. 'Can't we ever just describe things because they're there?' he asks.

Jeremy smiles again. 'If you are writing a guidebook, perhaps. But, in a novel, description has to have a purpose. Tonight you'll see the film *Enchanted April* and we'll think about how the Italian setting is used in that film to highlight events and emotions. It's not that successful, to my mind. Italy often brings out the worst in writers. And film-makers.'

Anna chews her pencil. She thinks the original white-walled house sentence is actually better but she couldn't say why. She is also slightly worried about Cat, who hasn't turned up for this session. Justin has taken the children to a nearby water park, theoretically giving Cat the time to work, but, as soon as he left, Cat announced her intention of sleeping all afternoon. She said she had a terrible headache. Anna worries that she hasn't been paying Cat enough attention. She has been trying to leave her alone with Justin; maybe Cat feels neglected. It's funny, in all the times they have been friends, Anna has never once thought that Cat might need something from her, Anna. Cat has always had everything, known all the answers, been so supremely sure of herself. Anna doesn't quite know what has changed, but something has. Maybe it all started the evening when Cat found out that she and Steve weren't married. Cat had seemed so hurt that she had never told her. It had surprised Anna, who hadn't realised that she had the power to hurt Cat's feelings, which, up to now, had seemed as serene and perfect as the rest of her. And then, when Justin and the children arrived, Cat seemed rather at a loss. Anna is used to seeing Cat with the children, of course, but usually in her own house, where there are a plethora of consumer durables to entertain them. Here, in Tuscany, it is obviously far more difficult.

I've been a bad friend, she thinks. She should have offered to help with the kids instead of swanning around with Sam. She'll go and see Cat after the session, take her some tea and have a chat.

Mary speaks from the back of the room. 'Surely not every sentence can be weighted with meaning,' she objects. 'Wouldn't that make a book rather indigestible? Don't you need flatter passages to contrast with the more dramatic parts?'

Anna admires the way she puts this. Mary, who has not been to university ('Girls didn't in my day. Not girls like me anyway'), is often far more concise and eloquent than the people who have.

'No part of a book should be flat,' says Jeremy, rather sharply. 'I agree that you should vary the emotional tone but that doesn't mean that any sentence should be mean-ingless. It's perfectly allowable to describe things in a flat,

unemotional way, for example if you want to reflect an unemotional narrator.'

Mary looks unconvinced.

Sam says, 'What about if, for example in *The Da Vinci Code* –'
Jeremy winces – 'you need to describe a place just for the
purposes of the plot?'

'Style should never be subservient to plot,' says Jeremy
pompously. He looks at his watch. 'That's all for now, I think.
After tonight's film, I'd like you to write a brief description of
a Tuscan scene, trying to avoid all the usual clichés. Tell me
something new about Tuscany and about how you feel about
Tuscany. And don't forget your dream diary.'

The guests file out. Sally approaches Jeremy with an elaborate query about personification but Jeremy, seeing Anna
squeezing past, says, 'Excuse me . . .'

He stops Anna in the corridor. 'You were very quiet today,'
he says. 'Is anything wrong?'

'No,' says Anna apologetically. 'I'm just a bit tired, I think.'

'Why don't we have a one-to-one tonight? After supper.'

'But isn't that when the film's on?'

'Oh, you don't want to worry about that,' says Jeremy lightly.
'Load of tosh. Lots of luvvies poncing about in crinolines.'

'But I won't be able to do the assignment.'

'You will if I give you some personal coaching,' says Jeremy

Patricia provides a tray with tea and biscuits and Anna carries
it up to Cat's room. She knocks gently. 'It's me. Anna.'

After a brief pause, Cat's voice says, 'Come in.'

Cat is fully dressed but she has obviously been in bed because the covers are crumpled. Anna has never seen this room (Cat moved to a 'family room' when Justin and the children arrived); it is long and narrow with a view to the side of the house, over the trees and the tennis court.

'Are you feeling better?' asks Anna.

'Yes. No. I don't know.' Cat runs her fingers through her hair. She looks distracted, as if she has just woken up.

'Did I disturb you?'

To Anna's consternation, Cat's eyes fill with tears. 'No. It's lovely to see you.'

Anna sits on the bed. 'Cat! What's the matter?'

'Nothing.' Cat wipes her eyes with the back of her hand. 'Oh, I don't know. I'm just stupid.'

'You're not.' Anna strokes her arm. She doesn't think she has ever seen Cat cry before.

'It's just . . .' Cat fumbles for a tissue. 'It's lovely to see Justin and the kids, of course it is. It's just, before they came, I was able to fool myself.'

'Fool yourself?'

'Oh, you know, that I was young and . . . and pretty . . . and that I could be a writer one day.'

'You are young and you're beautiful and you will be a writer.'

Cat smiles damply. 'You're so sweet, Anna, but I'm nearly forty and I'll never be more than an ex-copywriter.'

'What about your Yummy Mummy book?'

Cat laughs, rather wildly. 'It's crap, Anna. It's crap from beginning to end.'

'It's not!'

'It is,' says Cat wearily. 'I reread it last night. It's not a book at all, it's just a collection of ideas I took from other places. Jeremy knows it's crap. That's why he hasn't suggested a one-to-one with me.'

Anna blushes. 'He's taking everyone in turn.'

Cat looks at her narrowly. 'How many times have you seen him? Three? Four? He knows you've got potential, you see. Even Mary and her funny little detective book. He thinks that's better than mine.'

'You don't know that.'

'I can tell. He talks to her differently. Respectfully. He respects you and Mary. The rest of us can go hang.'

'Well, he's wrong,' says Anna stoutly. 'He's a bit of an idiot.'

'He's a wanker but he's not wrong about this. The best thing I can do is go home and go back to being just a housewife.' Her eyes fill with tears again.

Anna pats her shoulder, wondering what to say. She can't help thinking that Cat's existence at home, with unlimited funds and a full-time cleaner, is hardly what most people would consider that of a typical housewife. But she does understand, she more than anyone, the urge to do something different – to get away from being your children's mother and the house's wife.

'You're not just a housewife,' she says at last. 'No one is. And, if you don't do this, you can do something else. You could go back to work part-time. Do voluntary work. Be a school governor. There are loads of things.'

'Yes and all of them boring,' says Cat bitterly but she stops crying. She sits up and blows her nose. A slightly more cheerful expression comes over her face. 'One good thing,' she says. 'Justin says he'll take me to the Caribbean for Christmas to make up for this holiday being a washout. Let's have that tea, shall we?'

CHAPTER 18

Day 9, night

Sally is surprised to find herself enjoying the film. She has seen it several times before (this is her third time on this particular course, after all) but previously she has watched through the haze of Jeremy's scorn. This time she allows herself to be carried away by the story. She finds herself glorying in the beauty of the Italian Riviera as the gloomy old house opens up in the sunshine. She finds herself willing Miranda Richardson to get back with her husband. Polly, the beautiful socialite, reminds her of Cat but even that does not spoil her pleasure. By the end, she is wiping away tears.

Sally is shocked. She does not think of herself as a sentimental woman *at all*. She never reads love stories, prefers thrillers with a healthy side order of gore, and does not own any pets. She doesn't send soppy cards, doesn't buy herself Hello Kitty accessories and never watches Richard Curtis films. She thinks that her marriage to David effectively destroyed any finer feelings she might have possessed.

She and David met at university (Cardiff) and got married in their early twenties. They were blissfully happy until David's mental health problems, hitherto suppressed by drugs and by the natural high of student life, came violently to the fore. The next twenty years were a nightmare of psychiatrists, high-dosage drugs, brief respites and increasingly terrifying mood swings. When she finally signed the committal papers she remembers feeling only a great weariness. At least now, she thought, she would be able to get some sleep. But there must have been guilt too because when David broke out of the secure institution and hanged himself in a nearby children's playground, her first instinct, indeed her first words, blurted out to a sympathetic policewoman were: It's all my fault.

She started writing as a way of escaping. She got a grim satisfaction from making sure that, however violent David was, far worse things happened in her novels. She sent a few manuscripts to publishers and received brusque rejection letters. When, two years after David had died, she read that the well-known author Jeremy Bullen was holding a creative writing master class as part of the Marlborough festival, it seemed like providence. She attended the class and, as soon as she set eyes on Jeremy, tall, bearded, effortlessly serious, she knew that here, at last, was her perfect man. She has stalked him ever since. She would be horrified to hear it described in this way, of course. True, she Googles him every day and checks the position of *Belly Flop* in the Amazon ratings (*why* hasn't he written another great book?). She attends all his courses and feels quietly confident that she has read every word that he has ever written.

In all this time she has rarely been alone with Jeremy. He has only ever been lukewarm about her writing. Once he praised a short story (about a night nurse on a psychiatric ward) but usually he advises her to rip up the current book and start again. Even this does not discourage her. She is amazed to discover her own capacity for persistence. At home she rebuilt her life, started a fairly successful gardening business and is known to her friends as a cheerful, slightly eccentric, presence. A trooper. The few people who know about David also understand that she wants to forget the past. The others wonder why she has never married again. After all, she is still attractive (even with the lurid hair) and she is both lively and entertaining. She has noticed, though, that people are starting to say this less and less. She will be sixty in five years' time.

So why is a fifty-five-year-old gardener with scarlet hair sitting weeping in the dark over a feeble costume drama? It's the heat, she tells herself. Too much wine, too little sleep. And she has been having trouble sleeping this holiday, even when the night is not rent apart by Dorothy screaming that she has seen a ghost. Her herbal sleeping pills seem to have little effect and she finds herself regularly waking at 3 a.m, running through the events of her life and finding herself guilty. This is not healthy, she knows. Guilt, as she remembers from David, is a wholly self-indulgent emotion.

She looks around the room. Cat, too, looks rather tearful

but Mary looks as calm and placid as ever. Dorothy is sniffing pleasurably, dabbing her eyes with a lace handkerchief. Rick is asleep and Sam looks rather sick. There is no sign of Jeremy or Anna. Sally gets up. She needs some air, she thinks.

At the door, she meets Sam. He still looks rather grim; she supposes it was very much a woman's film.

'I'm just going out for a little walk,' she says.

'Good idea.' Unsmiling, Sam falls into step beside her. Sally is rather flattered. She has not spoken much to Sam but she does find him rather attractive in a saturnine way.

They walk down the shallow steps at the side of the house, towards the swimming pool. Sam does not respond to Sally's attempts at conversation and does not seem to want to be told the Latin names for plants. Eventually they walk in silence. The night is still warm, with the scent of lavender in the air. The woods are pulsating with the noise of crickets.

They reach the pool, still and floodlit in the darkness. Two terraces above, the light is on in Jeremy's room. From the open doors comes the swooning music of an operatic aria.

'They're listening to music,' says Sam to Sally. They both know who they are talking about.

But then another noise joins the thrilling vibrato of Maria Callas. A woman's voice, raised in anger or fear. 'No!'

'Anna!' Sam looks around wildly. The terrace is high above them but, because of the hill, the walls are low at the side of the house. Sam sprints up the steps. The wall of Jeremy's balcony is only about six feet from the ground. Getting a toe-hold in the crumbling brick, Sam heaves himself up easily.

Sally stands, irresolute, on the steps. But then her curiosity overcomes her and she, too, climbs up over the wall.

When Sally enters Jeremy's room, the first thing she sees is Jeremy sprawled on the floor with Sam standing over him. Anna is sitting on the bed looking horrified. Maria Callas sings on unnoticed, telling the world that she lives for art.

'What have you done?' gasps Sally. She is not entirely sure which man she is addressing.

'He's a madman,' says Jeremy from the floor. 'Call the police.'

'You were molesting her,' growls Sam, who still has his fists clenched. 'You can't deny it.'

'I wasn't molesting her,' protests Jeremy. 'I was just kissing her.'

'Kissing her?' Sally does not expect her voice to come out quite so sharply. Momentarily, they all turn and look at her.

'But she didn't want to be kissed,' says Sam threateningly. 'Did she?'

Jeremy raises himself to a sitting position. 'It seems not,' he says sulkily.

Anna speaks for the first time. 'Look,' she says. 'It was all a misunderstanding. Jeremy and I were talking and he must have misread the signals or something.'

Jeremy accepts this eagerly. 'You gave me the wrong signals,' he says.

'That's not what I said,' snaps Anna. There is a pause.

'When I came in,' says Sam, 'she was struggling. You were forcing yourself on her.'

'Rubbish,' says Jeremy, now getting to his feet. 'When you *burst,* uninvited, into my room, I was just giving her a hug.'

'You were practically raping her.'

'Bollocks!'

'Stop!' Anna now stands up too. All four stand facing each other as if they are actors in some drawing-room farce. The music ends and the room seems suddenly full of silence. 'Stop this,' says Anna. 'Jeremy and I just got our wires crossed, that's all. It's ridiculous to use words like rape. Thank you for trying to help, Sam, but I really think it would be best if we all went away and agreed never to talk about this again.'

Both Jeremy and Sam look as if they want to say more but Anna's face is so surprisingly fierce that they both relapse into silence.

'Goodnight,' says Anna and she sweeps regally from the room. Sam takes a half step towards Jeremy (who retreats) and then turns abruptly and follows her.

Sally and Jeremy are left staring at each other.

'Well,' says Sally, 'that was exciting.' She feels oddly exhilarated, as if she has been watching a particularly thrilling play. The melancholy mood of *Enchanted April* has completely disappeared.

Jeremy is standing backed up against the wall. Now he turns and goes to his fridge. He gets out a bottle and, after some hesitation, two glasses.

'That Sam McClusky is a nutter,' he says. 'I was just giving the girl a hug. D'you want a drink?'

'I don't mind if I do,' says Sally.

CHAPTER 19

Day 10, Saturday

11 August

> From: Anna Valore
> Date: 11 August 2017, 08.30
> To: Steve Smith
> Re: Hello Sexy
>
> Hi, love! How are you and how are the boys? Are
> Jakey's ears better? I forgot to say that he should really
> wear earplugs for swimming . . .

Anna stops. The sun is streaming in through her open window
and, outside, she can hear Aldo's raucous Tuscan shout alter-
nating with Fabio's calmer, more even tones. She hears the
word 'Firenze'. Of course, today is the trip to Florence. She
won't go, she decides. It's too hot and she dreads the thought
of being trapped in the minibus with Jeremy – or Sam. It's

funny. She feels as cross with Sam as she does with Jeremy. Left to herself, she could have coped with Jeremy. It was Sam bursting in like that, turning everything into a drama, that made it all so embarrassing. Even now she feels her cheeks burning at the memory of Sam standing over Jeremy's prone body, Sally watching everything avidly.

Yesterday we went to the local market, which was really picturesque. People were buying chickens and rabbits to take home and cook. Don't tell the boys! In the afternoon we had a writing session and, in the evening . . .

In the evening, I went to Jeremy's room and he put on some music, which I thought was strange at the time. I should have known something was up when we sat on the sofa and not at the table. He started talking about my writing, saying that it lacked passion but that he could tell that I was passionate underneath. I was flattered, I suppose, but I also felt really awkward. He was sitting too close to me and I could smell his aftershave. I was just wondering why he was wearing so much aftershave when he grabbed me and kissed me.

No, she can't tell Steve. It would only upset him for nothing. After all, he's at home in Brighton, there's nothing he can do. But, more than that, Anna shrinks from the idea of another man rising up in protest on her behalf. Because Steve can get jealous. Last year one of Tom's football coaches had flirted gently with her and Steve got really cross. At the time she hadn't minded too much, though it had been embarrassing to have him looming beside her on the touchline, grinding his teeth whenever Wayne looked in her direction. But now . . . Now she really feels that she can deal with Jeremy better on her own.

Anna presses delete and goes down to breakfast.

Jeremy is feeling unusually subdued as he helps himself to watermelon from the long table on the terrace. Bloody frigid little bitch, who would have thought she would react like that? Normally it never fails: the summer night, the opera, the compliments on the writing. But not only had Anna pushed him away with something like revulsion on her face, that Scottish goon had come crashing in through the French windows and actually hit him. Bastard. He could sue for assault. Just because Sam McClusky fancies Anna himself but hasn't got the nerve to do anything about it. He hasn't got a hope, though. Last night Anna had looked at him, too, with complete contempt. Stuck-up little cow. But then, as Sally said last night, Anna comes from a sheltered lower middle-class background and hasn't had much experience of real men. It's a good point. Jeremy massages his bruised jaw. He hadn't expected Sally to be quite so perspicacious.

Here comes Anna now. She's wearing shorts and a T-shirt.

Not very suitable for going to Florence. Her legs are a bit fat too, now that he thinks about it. Still, better get it over with. He sidles up to Anna as she pours herself orange juice.

'About last night,' he says in a low voice.

Anna raises her hand. 'It's OK,' she says. 'Let's not talk about it any more.'

Jeremy would like to talk about it a whole lot more. He would like to make Anna see that it is, in fact, all her fault, that she gave him the wrong signals and he, as a red-blooded man, had no option but to respond. But something in Anna's raised chin and cool glance makes him subside. She looks oddly like one of his old primary school teachers. For a second, he feels six again; in the wrong and babbling about dragons in the shrubbery to divert attention from the spilt paint on his desk. Maybe she's right, he tells himself, better say nothing. Anything he said would probably be misinterpreted anyhow.

Anna sits down with her orange juice at the opposite end of the table from Jeremy. She is shaking slightly but hopes he doesn't notice. Thank goodness that's over. Now all she has to do is avoid Jeremy for the rest of the course. No more one-to-one sessions. And she'll rip up his stupid reading list. Looking across the table, she sees Jeremy deep in conversation with Sally. She wonders if they are talking about her.

Mary appears in the doorway, her hair wet from her swim. Anna smiles and waves but, before Mary can cross the terrace, Sam slides into the seat beside her. God, not another one.

'About last night . . .' begins Sam.

'Look,' says Anna, more sharply than she intends, 'I don't want to talk about it.'

'But you've got to tell Patricia,' he hisses. 'Get Bullen kicked off the course.'

'It's got nothing to do with you,' Anna hisses back.

'But I saved you . . .'

'No, you didn't,' says Anna, standing up. 'You interfered. I know you were trying to help but, please, the matter's closed. Just stop going on about it.'

And she walks off, leaving Sam scowling into his cappuccino.

An hour later, Matt watches from his bedroom as the minibus squeals down the drive. He had been counting on having the house to himself but he can see two shapes by the pool. Mary (he can tell by her swimming) and he thinks the other one is Anna. Why couldn't they have gone to Florence with everyone else and left the pool to him? Not that he has anything against these particular guests. Mary has always been very nice to him and Anna seems OK, though not as pretty as her friend. At least they're better than Jeremy or that awful Frenchman. But, really, what on earth are they doing lounging by the pool? Haven't they got any writing to do?

Matt watches moodily, picking at the peeling paint on his shutter. Mary has just swum twenty lengths (she's a brilliant swimmer for an old lady) and now they're just lying about talking. Typical women, says Matt to himself in Aldo's voice, although his own mother has never really been one for chatting. Dad, yes. Dad will talk to anyone: drunks on the street corner, mad old ladies surrounded by bin bags, even traffic wardens. Dad loves a chat. 'The blarney' he calls it, laying on the Irish accent with a trowel. Matt remembers that Dad used to chat with the guests, something which, for all her charm, his mother seems unable to do. That's why she has Myra, thinks Matt, to do the chatting for her. Myra is meant to be somewhere around today. Matt plans to avoid her. He doesn't want to be chatted at.

He takes a shower and dresses in baggy shorts and a T-shirt. On his phone is a message from Graziano suggesting they go to the lake for the day. Matt had been planning to meet the posse to discuss his brilliant plan for disrupting *Ferragosto* but he doesn't think he can stand Graziano's tales of improbable womanising or Elio's deferential agreements. Suddenly Matt feels a violent antipathy towards his oldest friends. They make him sick, he tells himself, rather surprised by his own vehemence. He simply can't face seeing them. Not today anyway.

He slouches down to the kitchen and eats some bread and prosciutto. He can tell by the light streaming in through the kitchen door that it's going to be a scorching day. He eats some more bread and two peaches, throwing the stones out through the window. Should he check his Facebook account or have a look at the Dungeons and Dragons website (Matt, under the name Hengest, is a regular player of online swords-and-sorcery games)? No, it's just too hot. Maybe he should just go back to bed.

'*Ciao*, Matt.'

Matt looks up. Fabio's face is framed in the window.

'*Ciao*,' says Matt.

Fabio is now in the doorway, carrying a parcel wrapped carefully in greaseproof paper. 'Meat,' he explains. 'For tonight.' He puts the package in the fridge.

'Aldo's got you running about for him, has he?' grins Matt. They both speak in Italian, which, for Matt, now comes as naturally as English. The one benefit of emigration, says Patricia.

'Well, he's driving to Florence.'

'At two hundred miles an hour on the wrong side of the road.'

Fabio laughs.

'Ferrari missed a trick when they passed on Aldo,' continues Matt. Then he sees Fabio's face and realises that he has stopped smiling. In fact he looks rather sad. Matt suddenly feels an urge to cheer him up.

'Do you want to see something?' he says. 'A secret.'

'OK,' says Fabio, although he looks rather wary.

'Come on, then. It's in the woods.'

They walk down, past the pool and the olive grove, to the woods at the end of the drive. The trees are mostly pines and their needles crunch aromatically underfoot, reminding Matt of his mother's bubble bath. At least there is some shade here. Matt is already sweating after the short walk from the castle. Fabio looks as cool as ever.

At the end of the wood, by the castle's outer wall, is a low shed with a tiled roof. Chopped wood is neatly stacked against its walls. 'It's behind here,' says Matt. He scrabbles about in the undergrowth for a few seconds and pulls out a chaotic-looking metal device, rather like a giant bicycle pump.

'*Dio*,' says Fabio. 'What's that?'

'It's a rocket launcher,' grins Matt.

'A what?'

Matt glances around. They are alone apart from a bird of prey, a buzzard perhaps, circling high above the pine trees.

'My friend Graziano, his father works in the firework factory at Poggibonsi. He's going to get us a seriously big rocket. He doesn't know what it's for, of course.'

'What *is* it for?'

Matt climbs up on top of the woodpile. He points at the nearest hilltop, where the faint outline of a cross can be seen. 'At *Ferragosto*,' he says, 'there will be a procession to the grotto on top of the hill. I'm going to fire the rocket. Give them the fright of their lives.'

'Matteo!' Fabio looks at him, his dark eyes wide and serious. 'You'll kill someone!'

'No I won't. The rocket won't get that far. It'll probably explode in the woods. But it should still give them a hell of a fright. Imagine old Don Tonnino swinging his incense and then — bang! He'll think it's the end of the world.'

Fabio is shaking his head. 'I still think it's dangerous.'

Matt looks at him uncertainly. Fabio suddenly sounds very much like a grown-up. 'You won't tell?' he says.

Fabio smiles at Matt's anxious face. 'I won't tell. Just do one thing for me, let me know when you are going to do this thing, so I can be there.'

Matt leaps joyfully off the woodpile, landing in a heap amongst the pine needles. 'I'll tell you,' he says. 'You won't want to miss out on the fun.'

He has another secret too but he's not going to tell that one to Fabio. Not yet.

Mary and Anna lie by the pool. Mary has been swimming and is drying off in the sun. Anna is sitting in the shade. Cat and Justin have taken the children to Lago di Bolsena, a lake where you can swim or hire boats. Everyone else has gone to Florence. Anna has just told Mary about Jeremy making a pass at her. She badly wanted to tell *somebody* and is surprised how easy it is to talk to Mary. The older woman is not over-excited by the story (as Cat would have been) nor does she seem unduly shocked. She recognises the situation for what it was – embarrassing rather than traumatic.

'Have you spoken to Jeremy this morning?' asks Mary, rubbing her hair vigorously with a towel.

'Yes. He sidled up to me at breakfast and said he was sorry about last night. I said it was OK.'

'Then maybe that'll be the end of it.'

'I hope so. It's just that Sam came over at breakfast and wanted to go over the whole thing again. I told him to please stop going on about it. As far as I was concerned, the matter was over.'

'How did he take that?'

'I think he was a bit offended but at least he's gone for the day. He had said that he wasn't going to Florence; he'd been talking about the two of us having lunch together in San Severino. But, after this morning, he must have changed his mind. Thank God.'

'It is nice to have the place to ourselves,' says Mary, looking up at the silent castle.

Anna gives her a sideways look. 'I think Aldo was disappointed you weren't going,' she says slyly.

Mary blushes. She turns her head away but the blush extends even to her narrow shoulders. 'It's too hot for sightseeing,' she mutters.

Anna looks up at the bright blue sky, which seems heavy with the promise of heat yet to come. Although it is only ten o'clock, the paving stones around the pool are already red-hot. The white retaining wall, with its cascading purple flowers, is actually painful to look at. A lizard pauses to sun itself, emerald-green against the white.

'It's too hot for anything,' says Anna.

Cat is sitting by the lake. The sand is volcanic; it runs through her fingers like coarse black pepper, a curiously soothing effect. The water is wonderfully clear. Apparently Lago di Bolsena is known locally as 'the lake that can be drunk' because of its clean, pure water. In front of her she can see Justin and the kids on their boat, it has a slide at one end and looks like some prehistoric creature rising from the depths, but the lake is so big that the opposite shore is misty and indistinct.

Cat lies on the black sand and lets the sun beat down on her face. She feels better than she has for days. Maybe it was talking to Anna, saying what she really felt, or maybe it was just that she got a good night's sleep last night without either child ending up in their bed or Justin pestering her for sex. She likes sex in its place (after a romantic meal and preceded by a tsunami of compliments) but every night is really too much. Maybe this is why Justin has come all this way, just to have sex with her. An expensive shag, thinks Cat wryly.

She knows people wonder why she married Justin. Surely someone as beautiful as she is could have any man she wanted. But, in reality, Justin is really the only man who has ever offered (marriage, that is). She has always attracted men easily but holding on to them has proved a different matter. Previous boyfriends have faded away under the furious onslaught of Cat's insecurity and vanity. Justin is the first man since her father who has taken her at her own estimation. 'We've got a lot in common,' is what Cat usually says, defensively, about Justin. And the main thing they have in common is that they both think that Cat is perfect.

Except she doesn't, not really. Oh, some days she is just bursting with self-satisfaction, looking at her glowing brown face in the mirror gives her a real frisson of delight, catching sight of herself in shop windows, glossy hair swinging, long legs striding, she is sorry for almost every other woman in the world. The trouble is that there are days, and recently there have been more of them, when being beautiful doesn't seem to be enough. Even more terrifying, there have been times when she looks in the mirror and doesn't see a beautiful young girl. She sees a middle-aged woman with lines around her eyes and once, shockingly, a white hair shining amongst the black.

The thing is, old age is all right for someone like Mary who has probably never been that pretty anyway, but for Cat it's the *end*. If she doesn't see admiration in men's eyes, who is she? Does she even exist? Once, recently, she walked past a building site and there was silence. Total silence. She even looked back, wondering if they were saving the wolf-whistles and catcalls until she was safely past, but no, there they were, calmly getting on with their bricklaying and hod-carrying. She might have been invisible. Perhaps she was invisible.

Cat knows she's intelligent (she went to Cambridge, didn't she?) but somehow that's never been as important as being pretty. She has always assumed, without much thinking about it, that she's cleverer than someone like Anna. But now, here is Anna emerging as the star of the course. Anna, who sometimes seems oddly like a real writer and who, in some mysterious way, has become more attractive because of it. Men like Sam and Jeremy wouldn't have looked at the old Brighton Anna, with her ill-fitting jeans and permanently harassed expression.

But somehow, here in Italy, Anna has managed to reinvent herself as a fascinating, intelligent creature. It can't just be the tan and a new white dress. There has to be something else to it.

The trouble is, when Cat thinks about the possibilities outlined yesterday by Anna, part-time work, voluntary stuff, etc., they all seem so incredibly boring. And, if she's honest, her old whizzy copywriting job was really just glorified secretarial work. She's not going back to sitting in some open-plan office, making coffee for some jerk with a third in marketing studies. She just can't do it. She needs something special. Something as special as she is.

Cat squints as she watches her children playing on the boat. In their bright life jackets they look so absorbed and happy. She feels a sudden rush of love for them and, though she can't know it, her face becomes quite stunningly beautiful. At that moment, Justin turns and waves from the boat. Cat waves back, blowing kisses. She has thought of something else that she can do. It may involve a little unpleasantness at first but, ultimately, it has to be better than becoming a school governor.

Sally and Jeremy are in the Uffizi Gallery. Neither of them are particularly fond of painting, but the day is so hot that the idea of walking along cool corridors looking at gloomy Renaissance portraits suddenly becomes irresistibly attractive. Jeremy walks silently through the rooms dedicated to

Fra Lippo Lippi. He can't stand all this religious crap, all these upturned eyes and unpleasantly adult-looking babies. He was brought up a Catholic (his mother was Polish) but sees that purely as a useful guide to understanding T.S. Eliot or Evelyn Waugh. Jeremy is really only able to appreciate one art form: the written word. Even now, it is the names of the portraits which resonate: *Madonna and Child with Two Angels*, *Coronation of the Virgin*, *Adoration of the Child with Saints*. He begins to play with modern alternatives: *Madonna and Child with Accompanying Social Workers*, *Adoration of Big Brother with Z-List Celebrities*, *Coronation of the Far-from Virgin*. Is there something there? An article perhaps?

Sally, too, is silent. Lippo Lippi does not do much for her either. She prefers Caravaggio. In a previous room they saw *The Sacrifice of Isaac*: the naked blade, the face forced to the ground, the stormy, portentous sky. How could you describe a scene like that? There are just so many times that you can use the trigger words: cut, flesh, slice, blood, agony. Caravaggio gives you everything in the one spine-tingling package. Christ, her feet hurt.

All day, Jeremy and Sally have felt themselves drifting together. Neither of them really wanted to talk to Sam, who seemed in a very bad mood, and Patricia was taken up with Dorothy and Rick. JP hovered around Patricia and Aldo disappeared almost immediately on business of his own. That left Sally and Jeremy to wander over the Ponte Vecchio, to marvel at the Piazza della Signoria and now to tramp the long corridors of the Uffizi Gallery. Sally isn't complaining though. Last night, she and Jeremy shared a bottle of wine and agreed that Sam was seriously unhinged. Now they are, if not deep in conversation, at least agreed on the basics.

'Jesus,' says Jeremy, 'this place is doing me in. Shall we go and have a drink somewhere?'

'Yes, let's,' says Sally, rather daringly allowing her hand just to brush against his.

The Seven Moons of Jaconda
by Lupo O'Hara

Chapter 15

Hengest and Fabian have crossed the sands of Sommerslath and are now on the shores of the Lake of Blood. The crossing has been hard. They parted from their steeds and body servants at the edge of the Astrogath. From now on the journey must be theirs alone – their bodies against the heat of the desert and the chill of the Ice Mountains, their courage against the countless enemies of the House of Erin.

Hengest looks at Fabian. He knew he was right to choose him from the band of brothers. Leopardo is valiant in a fight but he failed the Test of the Heart, not once but many times. Leone is true enough but he lacks the cunning to face Grenouille and the League of Eye Fall. No, Fabian, who is fair and true, is the only companion for this quest. And, as they stand on the shores of the red lake, they both know that only friendship forged in fire will endure.

Until death.

Dreams

Uncle Maurice is driving me up the hill in his car. The hill gets steeper and steeper and I know the car can't make it. Then the car turns into the minibus and we are driving into Rome, right through the Colosseum itself, in and out of the arches! And now Aldo is driving the bus. I shout to him to be careful but he says that I am safe with him. He drives right through the centre of Rome, down steps, through fountains, scattering tourists. And I'm laughing as if it's a fairground ride.

I'm watching television and Jenny is reading the news. She reads all these facts and figures and I don't understand any of them. I'm worried because it's finance and I used to understand all this stuff. But then she's doing the weather forecast and she looks straight at me and says, 'Stormy weather ahead.' And then I wake up.

I'm swimming, just floating in the blue, all the lights and colours around me like some sort of laser display. And then Fabio is there, swimming underneath me like a seal or something. He's naked. We're both naked. We swim together and I see each drop of water shining on his body. He smiles at me and we dive into the water, deeper and deeper until the world is full of blue.

I'm at home, sitting on the swing in the porch. It's summer and we're sleeping out there. I'm hot and my dress sticks to me. My little sister Alisha is there too. She's trying to give me something, a package. I don't want to open it. I know there's bad news inside. But Alisha keeps coming nearer, smiling her cute little smile with all her braces showing.

'No,' I say.

'It's from Mom,' says Alisha. And she smiles wider and wider.

I'm playing football with Tom and Jakey. It's hard because the ball is really big, like a beach ball. Then the ball rolls right over Jakey and he's trapped, I'm thinking, clear as anything, 'Imagine this happening! Imagine a terrible accident like this happening with an innocent beach ball.' Steve lifts the ball off Jakey and he's flat, like Flat Stanley in those books I used to read to the boys. I scream but Steve says, 'It's all right, love, we're all just characters in a book.' And we are. We're all flat 2D illustrations in some children's book. Then Steve reaches over and holds my hand and I'm breathing properly again, I can see my lungs going up and down. And the boys are all right again too, I can see them playing football in the distance, happy as anything.

He's on the roof and I'm shouting at him to be careful but he just laughs and waves. The roof is so high, far higher than the Castello. It's the Eiffel Tower, it's the Torre in Siena. But he just smiles and waves. 'Look at me!' he says and he jumps.

I'm packing to go home. I pack all my shirts so neatly, folding them into little squares. Then I hear a voice, a tiny little voice, calling from inside my case. I pull out a little piece of paper, folded and refolded. I open it out and it's a photograph of my boy. 'You forgot me,' he says.

I'm in the garden, the Enchanted April garden. I'm talking to the Joan Plowright character and she says, 'Go for it, girl. Do you think it was easy, being married to Lawrence Olivier?'

'No,' I say, 'but I bet the money helped.'

And she gives me an orchid, a rather ugly one but then the flower opens and there are all these colours – red, blue, orange and pink. And I lean right into the flower and it's swallowing me whole but I'm not scared somehow. When I emerge I'm at the opera and Joan is singing La Bohème.

'I didn't know you could sing,' I say.

'You didn't ask,' she says.

CHAPTER 20

Day 11, Sunday

12 August

Patricia is rather surprised to find quite a group setting off for Sunday Mass. Last week only JP had gone, this week Fabio is driving JP, Anna, Sam and Dorothy to the square thirteenth-century church in San Severino. Considering her earlier comments about the Virgin Mary, Patricia is particularly surprised to see Dorothy, magnificently attired in a flowered dress, straw hat and white gloves, preparing to attend a service in a place of worship called Santa Maria della Spina (Saint Mary of the Thorns). However, as Dorothy graciously points out, 'I'm a guest in this country and when in Rome . . .'

'When in Rome,' mutters JP, 'get crucified.'

Anna isn't quite sure why she has decided to go to church. Apart from some ostentatious church-going required to get Tom and Jake into St James the Great, she's not what you might call a devout Catholic. Her father, the son of Italian immigrants, used to take her and her sister to Mass when they were children. She remembers making her first Holy Communion, in a white dress and starched veil, and she remembers seemingly endless Masses, making shapes with a rosary on the wooden pews, watching as the swaying line of people approached the altar rails for Communion. When she went back to church, when the boys were little, she was amazed at how short the service seemed. Barely had she sat down after Communion than the priest was giving his blessing and saying he'd see them all in the parish hall for coffee after Mass. Coffee after Mass? Surely something had changed in the holy, Catholic and apostolic Church? Or was it just her?

The boys' school, too, has little in common (thank God!) with her own education at the hands of Sister Anthony and friends. They learn about Judaism and Islam and sing jolly songs about being children of God in one family. True, only a handful of the children's families actually go to Mass. Cat, who got in by dazzling the elderly priest and because Justin had been baptised a Catholic, is fairly typical. She caused rather a scandal by dressing Sasha in jeans for his first Communion. 'I didn't know,' she wailed afterwards. 'You should have told me about the suits and the Saint Christophers and everything.'

But today, she doesn't know why, Anna feels like going to Mass. It will be a link with home, in a funny way, maybe even a link with her father, whose parents may have attended a church very like this one. At any rate it will give her a space, a time to think, away from the ever-present attentions of Sam.

She is, therefore, extremely discomfited to see Sam, dressed in a smart blue shirt, waiting in the main hall.

'Are you going to Mass?' she asks, trying to keep the disappointment out of her voice.

'Yes,' says Sam. 'I thought it might be interesting.'

In the background, JP snorts contemptuously.

The church, a solid white building with a square tower very like the one at the Castello, is on the far side of the town. It is built on a hill and the only approach is by steep stone steps. Dorothy is panting and fanning herself by the time they reach the top and even Anna is breathing heavily. 'You have to go up on your knees on Good Friday,' says JP. Anna isn't sure whether he is joking or not.

Inside, the church is surprisingly sparse. A huge wooden cross hangs behind the altar and there are none of the lurid frescoes which made Dorothy so uneasy in Siena. In fact, Dorothy sits with a pleased smile throughout, fanning herself gently with a Mass sheet. Why, she could almost be home in Vermont at the Church of Christ the King. Pity about the fancy clothes the preacher is wearing, but at least there's no incense. Dorothy closes her eyes (the better to hear the Word of God).

Anna is surprised to find herself following the service with very little difficulty. The Italian is so like the Latin she remembers as a child and there is something universal about the priest's homily – his expressions of, variously, disappointment, anger, resignation and, finally, forgiveness. She finds herself standing, sitting and kneeling with the rest of the congregation. JP looks at her approvingly. Sam stays seated, his arms crossed. Once he gets out his camera but a glare from JP makes him put it away again. Fabio stands up in all the right places but he doesn't join in with the responses. Anna sneaks a look at him. His face is serious, even a little sad in repose. His eyelashes are ridiculously long.

None of the group gets up for Communion. Anna, who shifted aside to let JP past, is disconcerted when he stays in his seat, staring fiercely ahead of him. Of course, JP is divorced. He is not able to take Communion. Anna feels terribly guilty as if, by slightly moving her feet, she has held up a banner saying, 'Excommunicated Sinner Sitting Here.' Anna herself hasn't had Communion (or been to confession) for years. What would she say if she went to confession now? 'I went to a man's bedroom and he made a pass at me'? Was that a sin? Probably. Most things are, as she remembers it.

After the service the congregation shuffles out into the sunshine. Mostly women and children, Anna notices; there are very few men, young or old, in church. At the door Fabio says a few words to the priest, an elderly man who looks a little like Aldo. The priest smiles delightedly and shakes their hands. He seems particularly pleased with Anna and holds her hands for what seems like hours, grinning and talking animatedly. Anna smiles and nods furiously, feeling stupid.

'What was he saying?' she asks Fabio as they walk down the steps.

Fabio smiles. 'He was saying that it is good to see such a beautiful woman in church.'

Anna blushes, trying and failing to imagine an English priest saying something similar.

'He looks a bit like Aldo,' she says. 'The priest.'

'Aldo says he is his cousin,' says Fabio.

At Sam's suggestion they don't go straight back to the car. Instead they go for a drink in a shady cafe near the church. It is a very different place from the livelier bars in the main piazza. Little old men sit at rickety tables reading newspapers and playing cards (perhaps this is what they do instead of going to Mass), a dog lies panting in the sunshine and the owner shells peas at a low table by the door. The writers sit under a wooden canopy, overhung with vines. A cluster of grapes blossoms from behind Sam's head and the leaves trail on to Anna's hair.

Fabio brings coffee, Coke, mineral water and a beer for Sam. He moves smoothly through the tables, holding the tray aloft like a waiter.

'You're a doll, Fabio,' says Dorothy.

'A doll?' repeats Fabio smiling. 'Thank you.'

'It's a compliment,' says Sam.

'Thank you,' says Fabio again.

'Don't mention it.' Dorothy waves one gloved hand. 'Isn't this a darling place? I just love Tuscany. I'll be so sad to leave on Thursday.'

This remark takes the other members of the writers' group

by surprise. None of them have really thought about leaving. Anna feels a dart of pure happiness at the thought of seeing the boys again. And Steve too, of course. He must be missing her by now, surely. JP thinks first of Louis and then of Patricia. What will happen on *Ferragosto*, he thinks, when they finally have some time alone together? Sam thinks grimly that he now has only three days to make Anna fall in love with him.

'Have you enjoyed the course?' Anna asks Dorothy, really wanting to know.

'Oh yes, dear. Jeremy's been very encouraging about my book.'

Sam growls under his breath. Anna doesn't look at him. 'Has he?' she manages.

'Yes, he says it doesn't matter how it's written because it will still sell millions of copies.' She beams at the stony faces of the other writers. 'And it has really helped me, the whole process of writing.'

'Helped you come to terms with what happened when you were a child?' asks JP.

'Well, yes. I'm working through the process I started with my therapist. I've been through SARAH.' She laughs.

'Sarah?' Anna feels she's missing something.

'Shock, Anger, Rage, Acceptance and Hope. It's all part of the recovery process. I've relived my childhood and the terrible things my mother did to me. I've been angry, the tears flowed over my laptop as I wrote. I grieved for that little girl. For myself. And now I'm ready to let go.' She beams around the group once more, holding her coffee cup daintily to her lips.

'Have you finished your book then?' asks Sam after a pause. He envies anyone who finishes anything.

'Nearly, dear.'

The group are silent once more. They are all thinking of the diminishing time left to them, of the thousands of words yet to be written, of the impossibility of ever producing anything that looks remotely like a book.

Fabio leans back in his chair, taking the car keys from his jeans pocket. 'We had better go,' he says. 'We do not want to be late for Aldo's Sunday lunch.'

Mary's diary, 12 August

Oh dear, I wish I'd never come here. No I don't. I've had the best two weeks of my life. I simply can't bring myself to wish that it never happened, no matter how stupid I've been.

Dear diary, it's time to admit, between these pages at least, that I've got a silly crush on Aldo. I know, I know I'm seventy-four. Seventy-four (old! old! old!). I should be long past the age of falling in love. I thought I was. I honestly thought I was happy with my little life – my flat, my swimming, my writing. When I came on this course, I imagined myself eating a few nice meals and learning a bit more about being a writer. I certainly never imagined that I would fall for the person

246

cooking the meals or that I would feel so . . . so churned up about it.

What makes it worse is that I've never felt like this before. I've never been in love or anything near it. The closest I've ever come are crushes on Cary Grant or Frank Sinatra. No real-life male has ever come close to measuring up. Sad, I know. But true. Not that Aldo is a Cary Grant or a Frank Sinatra (though he sings very well, the man at the cafe said). When I first met Aldo I thought he was just a jolly, funny Italian. Oh, I thought he was charming but somehow quaint, with his broken English and big, white moustache. Now I don't think he's quaint, not at all. In fact, when I think about him, I want to cry. I did cry yesterday, when they'd all gone to Florence. I cried because I'm a seventy-four-year-old spinster who has fallen in love with a man she'll never see again.

I think it all started in Rome. When he appeared in that awful crypt, I was so pleased to see him but somehow it was more than that. The closest I can come to it is that when I saw Aldo, I stopped being homesick. I know this is ridiculous, I'm miles away from home and, anyway, what's an old lady like me doing talking about homesickness, like a silly schoolgirl. But when I saw Aldo, in his Hawaiian shirt, it was as if I'd come home. Not home to my flat but home home, maybe back to when I was a child and still living with my parents. I knew that when I was with Aldo, nothing bad could happen to me. Driving back here that night with the dark outside and Aldo behind the wheel of the minibus, I suddenly felt happier than

I'd ever felt in my life. I didn't analyse it then, just thought I'd had a good day out and was tired but, really, that was the moment when it all started.

How does he feel about me? Well, he's always been very nice to me, talking to me about food and giving me special things to try. He did come and find me in Rome and cooked me that wonderful soup the other night. But, really, he could just have been being polite to me because I'm a guest. Then, in the market, he said I had a perfect body. I know it was probably a mistranslation, he just meant I wasn't fat, but that didn't stop my stupid body from responding of its own accord. I felt as if I was blushing all over (and I mean all over). I've never felt like that in my life.

Then, when we went for a coffee, he was so nice to me, introducing me to those scary shouting men. Someone asked was I his girlfriend and he said, 'I wish she was.' Now, I know he was just being polite. I'm not stupid. Probably on every course there's some lonely elderly lady and it's Aldo's job to take her under his wing and be nice to her, flatter her, give her a few compliments. I know all this. It's just that, sadly, it doesn't seem to make any difference to how I feel.

Then he took me home on his motorbike. What must I have looked like, at my age, on the back of a Vespa? But at the time it felt wonderful, the wind in my hair, the feeling of speed and excitement. But afterwards I thought, how embarrassing, clinging on to Aldo like that. What must he have thought?

It's Italy, I know. Goodness me, it's hardly original. It's the heat and the light and the sheer beauty of everything. Look at that film Enchanted April – people pairing up all over the place. Look at us, here on the course. There's Sam mooning over Anna, JP following Patricia around like a shadow. There's Cat looking at Fabio all the time (not that I blame her – he's very attractive, like a young Cary Grant) and me having these ridiculous feelings about Aldo. All very silly and very predictable.

So I've come to the conclusion that I must keep out of Aldo's way. I didn't go to Florence as I didn't think I could bear a whole day in his company, thinking that it would be like Rome all over again. After I said I wouldn't be going, I headed back to my room and Aldo came after me and said wouldn't I change my mind. He said he'd take me to a place, high up on a hill, where you could see all of Florence spread out below you. He said he'd take me to a restaurant where they made special black risotto. He said we could get away from the others and just wander about, looking at the shops and staring at the statues. And I had to say no thank you, I wanted to get on with my writing. And he said, with a sort of half smile, 'Will you write about me?' and I said, 'Well, my novel's set in England,' and he said, 'I could come to England.' And that's the problem, isn't it? He would never come to England and I could hardly stay here in Italy. It's ridiculous even to think about it. On Thursday I'll be gone, and if Aldo ever thinks about me again, it'll be of that funny little Englishwoman who was writing a murder mystery and who liked my food. That's why I cried.

After my cry, I washed my face and went down for a swim.
Swimming always cheers me up. Anna was by the pool and we
had a good talk. That creepy Jeremy made a pass at her! Like
women always do, she blames herself but, personally, I think
he should be sacked. He has totally abused his position. Anna
says that almost the worst thing is thinking that he never really
liked her writing, he was just flattering her so that she would
sleep with him. I said that I didn't think that was true. His
admiration for her writing was probably genuine. The pass was
opportunistic, because she was there and because she's a pretty
girl. For all his faults, I don't think Jeremy's a complete idiot.

We had a nice, quiet day. I did get some writing done and,
in the afternoon, I went for a walk with Anna and Myra. We
went through the gate with the crown of thorns and higher
up into the hills. There's a stream, wonderfully cold and clear,
that flows right down into the valley until it meets the lake.
Myra said the water was the purest you will ever taste so I
drank some and she was right. It was like drinking liquid light.
There's a derelict farmhouse on the top of the next hill. Myra
says people are leaving the area because there isn't enough
work. She says the only people who will buy the dilapidated
old buildings are foreigners, like Patricia. The Castello is
bleeding her dry, says Myra, but she'll never leave it because
she loves it so much. Looking down at the Castello, all golden
in the afternoon sun, I thought I knew how Patricia felt. If you
manage, against the odds, to buy a piece of paradise, how can
you ever bear to give it up?

One Summer in Tuscany

We were hot after our walk so we went back via the pool. But Matt and Fabio were there, playing in the water like a couple of otters. We didn't want to disturb them so we went back to the Castello and drank tea on the terrace. Then Cat and the children came back and they went down to the pool and played water polo with the boys. I didn't join them; I'm too old for that sort of thing. Later that evening, Myra made us a simple supper and we played cards in the small sitting room. The others came home about nine o'clock. I thought Aldo might tell me about Florence but he didn't. After he parked the minibus, he got straight on his Vespa and went home. I was stupid enough to cry again before I went to sleep.

CHAPTER 21

Views of Tuscany

The Sacrifice of Isaac
by Sally Hutchinson

The father pushes his son's head against the ground. The son writhes in agony, his mouth open in a silent scream. The knife fills the foreground, its blade glinting wickedly in the half-light. Can Isaac imagine its metal teeth cutting into his flesh, its wicked kiss as it eviscerates his young body? Does the father, Abraham, his high, bald head seeming to exemplify pomposity and unthinking adherence to the rules, does he anticipate his son's death throes, the blood spattered over his tunic, the hot smell of his insides?

But the angel is there, staying Abraham's hand. The light shines on the angel's foream as it reaches across the painting. Abraham's hand is brown, a worker's hand, but the angel is white, like a being who has never seen the sun. Isaac is still screaming. Is he screaming because he knows that, without the angel, his father would have killed him? What must that be

252

like? To know that your father was ready to sacrifice you for this unknown God, this voice from the heavens. To know that you were only saved by this effete creature with the soft white arm. No wonder he screams.

Yet in the background there is a castle, soft yellow against the sky. In the castle, you feel, there is warmth, wine, feasting and the press of warm bodies. The castle is our refuge, our protection against the cruelties of the flesh.

Evening

by Mary McMahon

Sunset comes quickly after the slow evening. First the trees become infinitesimally darker, their shadows inkier, then the light changes from white to gold and everything becomes sharper: each leaf, each flower; each crumbling stone wall, each insect suspended in intricate webs against the rafters. The scents become sharper too. In the day, everything is subsumed into one overwhelming sensation – heat. Now you can smell each individual plant: rosemary, jasmine, lavender and a thousand others that I cannot name. The birds start to sing, shrill against the steady background of the crickets, and bees hum, swollen and replete with honey.

The sky, which has been a bright, almost unbearable blue, becomes gentler, tinged with violet and turquoise. You are aware of birds flying, very high up, and, as the evening draws on, the faint cartoon shapes of bats darting in and out of the barns.

Frogs croak from the trees and dogs bark from the farms in the valley. When evening comes, Italy wakes. In the towns the shops start to open. Restaurant owners arrange their tables on the pavements and young people begin to prepare for the evening's ritual of walking, flirting and chatting. Older people too – you see elderly men and women sitting outside their houses, just watching. Their faces are contented, amused. They are not excluded from the ritual, as they would be in England, but an essential part of it, with their card games, raucous greetings and ironical commentary.

If you are in the evening of your days, then surely Italy is paradise. Here is a land that does not just celebrate the morning or the showy splendour of the day. Here is a country that loves the evening, the slow pleasures of eating and conversation, the subtle scent of lavender on the night air and the sounds of the young and the old together, revelling in the twilight.

Torre del Mangia
by Jean-Pierre Charbonneau

503 steps. It seems more as you toil up the spiral staircase, occasionally flattening yourself against the wall as some overweight goon from Oregon pushes past you. But, when you reach the top and see the rooftops of Siena, magnificently chaotic, and the surrounding hills, deepest blue against the sky, then it is worth it, every back-breaking step.

The Torre del Mangia takes its name from its first watchman, who was apparently a mangiaguadagni, *a spendthrift. I like this. I like to imagine the workman, a florid man in middle age, gambling his last pennies on the Palio, perhaps, or buying himself a particularly magnificent doublet, with seed pearls strung across purple velvet. The watchman was called Giovanni del Balduccio and there is a statue of him in the courtyard. But the tower is not called the Torre di Balduccio. No, it is named after his most salient characteristic. I like that.*

The Torre is a bell tower and they used to ring the bell before they closed the city gates at sunset. I imagine its sonorous notes ringing out and people urging their horses on so as to be inside the great city before nightfall. Then the gates would be shut against intruders and the Sienese could sleep peacefully in their beds. Now the city's main square, the Campo, is heaving with intruders, barbarians shooting wildly, right, left and centre. True, their shots are made not with guns but with tiny cameras from the Far East, but the intention is the same. They want to capture Siena, to imprison her within the pages of their photo album, to boast of having defeated the most beautiful city (excluding Paris) in the world. 'We did Tuscany in three days. Siena only took an hour.'

If only we could shut the gates against them.

CHAPTER 22

Day 12

13 August

There is a heavy, expectant feeling in the air on Monday. The weather is very hot, even for Italy in August, and Aldo says that there might be a thunderstorm soon. In the morning, the guests stay in their rooms, writing. In the afternoon, there is going to be a Grand Reading, where everyone reads from their work in progress. The rules are strict: no interruptions and no criticism, only applause. But, even so, the writers are nervous and there is nobody by the pool this morning.

Anna, sitting despairingly in front of her laptop, wonders how on earth she can expect anyone to be interested in the feeble story of Anna/Sophie at university/polytechnic. Inspired by Jeremy's lecture, she has been reading *The Moonstone* (Patricia has the complete works of Wilkie Collins in the library) and she is awed by its sheer brilliance, the ease with which Collins switches authorial voices, his effortless descriptions of people and places and, almost above all, the book's colossal weight of words. Her book is about 60,000 words long and, to be honest, that sometimes involves stretching out descriptions of London at night, Sophie's first kiss, etc. 60,000 words, Collins has barely got into his stride and yet the book never feels too long, every word is absolutely right and necessary. And, according to Jeremy, he was out of his head on opium when he wrote it. Of course, that's why he is a great writer and she is an unpublished mother-of-two. Either way, it's rather depressing.

Anna also feels nervous about seeing Jeremy again. Sunday was all right because it was such a communal day. She escaped to church in the morning and then Aldo cooked a huge Sunday lunch which went on until past six o'clock. Afterwards the guests (apart from Mary, who had a headache) stayed on the terrace chatting and drinking wine. When evening came, some people went into San Severino and the others stayed behind, playing cards and eating yet more food. Anna waited until Sam and Jeremy opted for San Severino and then voted to stay behind. It was a good evening, playing contract whist with Dorothy, Rick and JP (Dorothy won easily). Cat and the children played Snap with Matt and Fabio and everyone went to bed fairly early.

But, today, Anna has to face Jeremy. She has to read aloud from her stupid coming-of-age novel (full of descriptions of fumbling teenage sex) in front of two men with whom she never wants to exchange another word, much less one about sex.

Anna sighs and starts to leaf through her manuscript, searching for the least suggestive pages. Surely there must be something here about growing up in Wembley? That should bore them all into good behaviour.

In her bedroom, Cat is trying to stop Sasha and Star killing each other and read her Yummy Mummy book at the same time. She has stupidly (in her opinion) agreed to Justin going out for a run. She views Justin's new enthusiasm for running with extreme disfavour. What's the point of him running along Brighton seafront listening to his iPod when he should be in the office making money? She blames Steve, who has recently taken up long-distance running. He plans to run the London marathon next year, Justin told her excitedly. So what? thinks Cat. Every year eighty-year-olds dressed as Wombles run the marathon. What's the big deal? But Justin thinks it's wonderful, so now he has to squeeze his skinny legs into running shorts and set off into the hills just when she could do with a bit of support for once.

Tears come to Cat's eyes as she contemplates how utterly alone she is, stuck here with two whingeing kids in a hotel room. She wishes to God that she could just go running off listening to Coldplay but no, she is tied to the kids, as women always are. Jesus, she's little better than a single mother stuck in a bed-and-breakfast . . .

'Mum, Star's sitting on my DS.'

'Star,' says Cat wearily, 'get off his GameBoy.'

'It's not a GameBoy,' shouts Sasha. 'It's a Nintendo DS Lite, stupid!'

'Stupid!' yells Star, suddenly joining in with this new game. 'Stupid! Stupid! Stupid!'

Cat bursts into tears.

JP is at his laptop, grimly deleting. Why does *Louis the Lion*, which sounds so charming read aloud to the real Louis, seem so utterly leaden on the page? How hard can it be to write a light-hearted children's book with playful allusions to modern culture? He's read all the right books, seen the right films, been to the right places. He's bilingual (thanks to an English nanny) and he's enough of a new man to have been to Disneyland and watched *The Wizard of Oz*. He was hoping to mix an old-fashioned European fable with a sprinkling of Hollywood glitz. What he's got, he realises, is the worst of both worlds: a book full of twee Disneyesque characters that he is too cynical and French to believe in. JP presses delete.

Sam is wondering which of his abortive scripts to read. Which is best (or least worst); the thriller, the detective story or the comedy? He settles for the thriller. There's nothing worse than reading aloud something that's meant to be funny, to be met with complete silence. Also, he's aware that his dour Scots accent makes everything sound like an episode of *Taggart* anyway. Sam scrolls through his thriller, *The Cortona Codex,* aware that he has not written one word this holiday.

He had expected to come back after two weeks with his novel written and a publishing deal almost in the bag. Instead he has mooned around over a married (or as good as married) woman, punched his tutor in the face and almost completely lost confidence in his writing. Good going, Sam, he thinks wryly.

The trouble is that, while he no longer thinks that he's a writer, he's still no nearer to solving the mortality problem. He is forty-four with no job and in a relationship that has somehow reached a stalemate. He hasn't even got children to disappoint him. For the first week in Tuscany he had been buoyed up by the prospect of having an affair with Anna. She was his project, his work in progress. And he still fancies her, he just doubts now that she will ever return his feelings. After he had (in his own eyes) rescued her from Jeremy, he fully expected Anna to fall sobbing into his arms. He imagined himself wiping away her tears, telling her that she was safe now and, after a suitably sensitive pause, removing all her clothes and making passionate love to her. Instead, Anna had looked at him with real irritation and implied that he had only made matters worse. She has obviously been avoiding him ever since.

Sam gets up, stretches, and walks to the window. His room overlooks the front of the house and he can see the sweeping driveway with its crumbling stone lions guarding the entrance. Sean the cat is stretched out beside one of the lions in unconscious imitation. God, it must be great to be a cat. No worrying about leaving your mark on the world, just eating, sleeping and shagging as many lady cats as you can find. Christ, they even have their own forum in Rome. If there is anything in this past lives bollocks Dorothy was talking about last night, he, Sam, is going to come back as a cat.

Sam goes back to his computer. He's going to read his script in his thickest, most impenetrable Glasgow accent. That'll fix them.

Patricia is arranging chairs for the Grand Reading. She knows from previous years that, for most people, this will be the highlight of the course. She has been running this particular course for four years and none of the guests has ever got close to being published. Nevertheless, reading their work aloud seems somehow to validate it and the Reading often ends emotionally with tears, group hugs and prophecies of Booker Prize nominations. What makes you a writer anyway? Is it being published or can anyone who writes consider themselves a writer? Patricia knows from Jeremy that, while many people start to write a book, very few will actually finish one. Maybe just finishing a book entitles you to call yourself an author. Patricia has never felt any inclination to write or paint or make sculptures out of old coat hangers. Sean was the creative one in their marriage (although, once they bought the Castello, the only things he painted were walls). Even so, he was talented. Patricia still has a charcoal drawing he did of Matt as a baby; tenderness is in every sooty line. But Sean never, to her knowledge, actually sold a painting and someone had to earn the money, didn't they?

Myra comes into the room carrying a vase of sunflowers. She places them on the main table so that they glow like little suns in the dark room.

'Lovely,' says Patricia.

'A bit of light relief,' says Myra. 'I hope it isn't all doom and gloom this afternoon.'

Patricia thinks of Dorothy. She's planning to slip out during Dorothy's reading. She really doesn't think she can bear to hear any more about Dorothy's childhood traumas. In fact, the thought makes her feel physically sick.

'Well, JP is writing a children's book,' she says. 'That should be a laugh.'

Myra looks at her curiously. 'You like him, don't you?'

Patricia turns away to tweak a curtain. 'He's all right.'

Myra laughs. 'Well, he likes you, honey.'

'Do you think so?' Patricia can't help saying.

'Of course! He follows you about all the time. He's always looking at you. I think he's got a serious crush on you.'

'Don't be silly,' says Patricia, fiddling with the tassel on the curtains.

'You're blushing,' laughs Myra. 'Go for it, I say. I think he's gorgeous. I'm quite jealous. All I've got is Gennaro.'

'Well, Gennaro's gorgeous too,' says Patricia, trying to match the light tone. 'And he's got his own vineyard. What more could a girl want?'

'What indeed,' answers Myra, swinging on the door handle. 'I'm seriously considering it. Just as you should consider Monsieur Charbonneau.'

Consider him as what? thinks Patricia, after Myra has gone. A replacement for Sean? Nobody could be that. A diversion for what's left of the summer? A casual fling? The trouble is that Patricia is not a casual person. Never has been.

The Reading starts at three. Jeremy sits at the table, behind the sunflowers, and the writers sit facing him. They will take turns to come to the front and read their work, either standing or sitting, whichever they prefer. They pick numbers from a hat to establish the order in which they will read. Anna is first.

As she sits beside Jeremy (standing would just feel too much like a performance) Anna thinks that the room looks scarily full. As well as the seven writers, there are also Patricia and Myra (both wearing encouraging smiles), Rick, looking as sleepily benign as ever, and Justin, holding tightly on to his struggling children. Then, just as she is about to start reading, the door opens and Aldo sidles in. Anna goggles for a moment, Aldo has never before appeared at any of the writing sessions, then takes a deep breath and begins.

It is not as bad as she feared. Her audience surprises her by laughing heartily at what she considers very feeble witticisms and she relaxes, allowing some expression to come into her voice. She slows down and even attempts what might be considered a dramatic pause or two. When she finishes, everyone applauds enthusiastically.

'Thank you, Anna,' says Jeremy. 'Who's next?'

'Me,' says JP unsmiling. 'But I deleted my book.'

Everyone laughs, but as JP sits stony-faced, the laughter falters and dies.

Jeremy looks questioningly at JP and, receiving no help, ploughs on. 'OK. Who's next?'

It is Sally, who reads, with smiling composure, an extract of almost incredible brutality. The audience, rather stunned, claps vigorously.

Next is Cat, who reads with great animation, standing, using her hands, sometimes almost dancing on the spot. She looks so pretty in her red polka-dot dress that it is almost impossible not to smile. She receives generous applause. Justin gives her a one-man standing ovation.

Sam, coming next, makes the discovery that people find Scottish accents funny. His grim thriller is met with waves of laughter. It is actually rather pleasant. Maybe he should write a comedy after all.

Mary stands up slowly and, once at the front, takes some time reordering her papers.

'Are you all right?' asks Jeremy solicitously. Mary nods but seems disinclined to start. Eventually she takes a sip of water, clears her throat and begins.

'Inspector Frank Malone is talking to his pigeons. Nothing wrong with that, you might say, but what is worrying him is that the pigeons are starting to answer back . . .'

Mary reads on in her soft voice and there is not a person in the room who is not transported from the heat of a Tuscan afternoon to the grey streets of South London. Mary's writing has something that is lacking in all the other extracts – utter conviction. Jeremy watches her narrowly, tapping his pen against his teeth. The rest of the audience are absolutely still. Only Anna, twisting round slightly, catches sight of Aldo and wonders at the expression on his face.

Mary's reading is met with a genuine storm of applause. 'Bravo!' shouts Aldo as if he is at the opera. Mary smiles uncertainly; it is clear that their reaction has taken her entirely by surprise. She looks questioningly at Jeremy.

'They liked it,' says Jeremy drily. He is fighting two very conflicting emotions – personal envy and professional pleasure at finally discovering someone who can write.

I wouldn't like to follow that, thinks Anna, but Dorothy does not seem to mind. She stands up, regal in a flowered two-piece, and proceeds majestically to the front of the room, stopping on the way to pat Mary kindly on the shoulder.

'Well, wasn't that just darling?' she says, beaming around the room. 'I'm afraid the piece I'm going to share with you will seem a little dark after what has gone before – Sam's charming Scottish comedy and Mary's lovely policeman. I'm going to tell you about things that happen in the very darkest places of the human heart.' And she smiles brightly as she puts on her glasses.

Patricia leans back in her chair. She deliberately sat near the door so that she could escape when Dorothy began reading but Aldo has plonked himself next to her, which means that she would have to squeeze past him, with all the disruption that would entail. The door is right opposite the speaker's table and Dorothy would not be able to miss her hostess making a quick getaway. Patricia is trapped.

Dorothy begins. 'I first knew my mom hated me when she branded me with a red-hot iron. Up till that point it had been the usual things, beatings with belts and sticks and garden hoses, being locked in my room without food or water, being told that I was useless and stupid and would never amount to anything. Mom was hard on all of us but, for some reason, I always got it hardest. But the day she burnt me, deliberately, for answering back, that was the day I knew—'

Dorothy stops. Her face goes white and she covers her mouth with one shaking hand. The audience, who have been shifting uncomfortably throughout her reading, assume at first that she is overcome with emotion. But then they see that Jeremy, too, is staring ahead of him, his mouth slightly open. One by one, they turn in their chairs to see what he is staring at.

An elderly woman is standing in the doorway. She is wearing plaid shorts and is pulling a little suitcase on wheels. She smiles delightedly at the astounded faces.

'Well, hello, you-all,' she says in a pleasant Midwest drawl. 'Pleased to meet you. I'm Betsy. Dorothy's mom.'

CHAPTER 23

Day 12

'Dorothy's *mother*? echoes Patricia, who has stood up to face the intruder. Her face is very white and she grips Aldo's shoulder tightly.

'Well, yes,' says the apparition. 'I looked on your website and saw your special offer, reduced rates for friends and family for the second week. So I thought I'd come and surprise my little girl. I got a taxi from the airport and this charming girl let me in.' She gestures towards the grim-faced Ratka at her side.

Patricia looks back at Dorothy, who is still standing at the table as if turned to stone. She has dropped her manuscript and the pages are lying scattered on the floor.

'What were you reading, dear?' enquires Betsy. 'It sounded real good.'

Dorothy gives a strangled gasp and rushes from the room, pushing past her mother in the doorway. Betsy staggers and almost falls. Aldo, ever chivalrous, comes to her aid.

'Sit down,' he says. 'You must be tired.'

'I am . . . a bit . . .' Betsy is faltering now. She sits in Aldo's vacated chair and rubs her eyes. She is older than she first appeared, thinks Patricia. Eighty at least.

Now Rick comes magnificently to the rescue. Apparently delighted at this turn of events, he bustles over to give the old lady a hug. 'Betsy!'

'Richard.' Betsy looks up at him. 'Is Dorothy all right?'

'Fine, fine,' booms Rick, kneeling in front of his mother-in-law. 'It's just the surprise, you know. Now let's get you to your room. Patricia, do you know . . . ?'

Patricia pulls herself together with an effort. She is, after all, still the hostess.

'Of course. Mrs . . . er . . . Betsy. I'll show you to your room. The Blue Room I think, Ratka. Aldo, could you see to Betsy's case?'

'*Certo, certo*,' Aldo nods reassuringly to Patricia, who smiles gratefully back.

With Rick on one side and Patricia on the other, Dorothy's mother is guided from the room.

The Blue Room is dark and somehow sad, with an unmade-up bed and the door swinging open onto an empty wardrobe. When Patricia opens the shutters, the sudden bolt of sunshine is almost shocking. Ratka brings clean sheets and she and Patricia make the bed while Betsy sits in the chair by the window, looking out over the silvery olive trees.

'This surely is a beautiful place,' she says.

'It surely is,' agrees Rick heartily. He is standing in the middle of the room, rather at a loss, his arms hanging loosely at his sides. Patricia realises that she has rarely seen him without Dorothy.

Ratka arranges soap and towels in the bathroom and Patricia plumps up the cushions on the small sofa.

'Can I get you anything?' she asks. 'Tea? Coffee?'

'No thank you, dear,' says Betsy. 'I guess I'll just have a little rest.'

'Dinner's at eight thirty,' says Patricia. 'We usually have drinks on the terrace beforehand. Shall I give you a call?'

'That would be very kind,' says Betsy. 'I think I'll sleep now.'

Patricia turns down the covers on the bed and says she'll see Betsy later. Rick gives Betsy a quick kiss and he, too, hurries from the room. In the corridor, Patricia and Rick look at each other.

'I don't understand,' says Patricia, as soon as they are out of earshot. 'After everything Dorothy said about her mother, how can she just turn up like this?'

'I don't quite understand either,' admits Rick, rubbing his forehead with a large, white handkerchief. They are standing next to a rustic cartwheel which hangs, polished and gleaming, on the white wall. The juxtaposition makes Rick look a little like a farm animal, an ox maybe.

'But was it true? All that stuff about her mother?'

'Well now,' says Rick slowly, 'I'm not sure. I know Dorothy had a tough childhood. They were dirt poor and the kids never had much schooling. But Dorothy never mentioned any actual abuse, not when we first met. She seemed friendly enough with Betsy back then. When we had the kids, Betsy even used to come and look after them sometimes. But then Dorothy got . . . depressed. She went to see this man, this therapist, and he told her to look into her childhood. Next thing I know, she's remembered all this terrible stuff about Betsy.'

'Do you think it really happened?'

'I don't know,' says Rick again. 'But I do know that Dorothy believes it. That's not an act. She really believes that she has buried the memory of the abuse because it's too painful. Every since she saw that therapist, she's refused to contact her mom or her brothers and sisters. My guess is that's why Betsy's come. She's desperate to see Dorothy. She's got no idea why Dorothy won't see her, of course.'

'She doesn't know that Dorothy planned to write a book about it all?'

Rick shakes his head slowly, more ox-like than ever. 'No. I said to Dorothy, if that book gets published, then your mom will know, for sure. But I don't think Dorothy ever thought it would get published. She knows she's no writer. But then Jeremy said all that stuff about it not mattering how the book was written and I think that got Dorothy thinking.'

I bet it did, thinks Patricia, wishing, not for the first time, that Jeremy knew when to keep his mouth shut.

'What's Dorothy going to think about Betsy turning up?' she asks.

'I don't know,' says Rick miserably. 'I guess I'd better find out.' And he slopes off, a mournful grey ox with his head down.

The guests are in the kitchen. This has never happened before on any other course and Aldo is still not sure how it happened this time. After Patricia and Rick led Betsy away, the other writers sat in stunned silence for a good minute before Sam said, still in his comedy Scots accent, 'I'm not entirely sure Dorothy was expecting that.' Everyone laughed. In fact, people laughed until tears ran down their faces. Anna was surprised how hysterical it all felt. Of course, it wasn't funny really. If Dorothy's story was true, then Betsy was a monster. If it wasn't true, then Dorothy had planned to tell a terrible lie about her own mother. It wasn't funny but, somehow, Betsy's dramatic appearance seemed so film-like that no one could take the human implications seriously. When the laughter died down, they talked and talked. Was Dorothy's book a complete fabrication? Did Rick know? Betsy certainly seemed nice enough but how could you tell? But, if Betsy really hated her daughter, why did she come halfway round the world to surprise her?

Eventually, Aldo got up, announcing his intention to start supper. Myra said that she would make tea for everyone (it was now five o'clock) and she followed Aldo out of the room. It was only when she was halfway down the stone stairs to the kitchen that she realised all the guests were following her. Somehow, the group bonding was now so strong that, whatever they did, they did it together. Ignoring Aldo's shocked expression, they filed into the kitchen and are now seated, some at the table, some perched on working surfaces, some leaning against walls, all chatting intensely about the Dorothy situation. Aldo has bowed to the inevitable and poured, not tea, but homemade wine, palest red and slightly fizzy. This has helped the chatting no end.

Maybe it's the informal setting but suddenly the guests look more like a large family than a group of strangers on a course. Aldo is the grandfather, calmly slicing tomatoes. Mary, helping Aldo by chopping the garlic (she is the only one so honoured), is the grandmother, grey-haired and serene. Jeremy, leaning back and offering everyone the benefit of his wisdom, is the father. Sally, agreeing with Jeremy yet keeping peace with the others, is the mother. Cat and Anna are the teenage daughters, giggling together over the idea that Dorothy may now rewrite her book as a childcare manual. JP, graciously complimenting Aldo on the wine, is the worldly, slightly aloof uncle. Sam is the sulky, disruptive son, alternately making everyone laugh with his Betsy impressions and saying that it's none of their business. Justin and the children have gone to the pool but when Matt and Fabio appear, in the guise of the playful youngest sons, the family is complete.

'I can't believe she made it up,' says Anna, for the hundredth time. 'It all seemed so real and there was so much detail.'

'Build-up of external detail,' says Jeremy. 'Vital for any work of fiction.'

'Do you think she was lying then?' asks JP, frowning into his glass.

'Think?' says Jeremy loftily. 'I'm sure of it. Dorothy Van Elsten wanted to write a bestseller. Which genre has had the most bestsellers in recent times? The misery memoir. Dorothy knew that her book wouldn't sell as fiction but it would as autobiography.'

'I don't think she's that calculating,' protests Anna. 'She's genuine, I'm sure of it. So's Rick.'

'So you think Betsy is Mommy Dearest?' grins Sam.

'I don't know,' says Anna. 'I only saw her for a second but she just seemed like a little old lady.'

'Many years ago,' cuts in Aldo from the stove, 'there was a trial in Italy of Nazi war criminals. They were accused of committing terrible atrocities, one quite near here. A whole town slaughtered for helping the partisans. I went to the trial. I remember the war very well, the fear, the hunger, the partisans hiding in the hills. I went to the trial, full of hate, and what did I see? Little old men. Grey-haired grandfathers. But old people can be monsters too.' He nods impressively before turning back to his *sugo*.

'Dorothy often talks about her therapist,' says Cat. 'Maybe he put it all into her head. False memory syndrome.'

'But can you really make up something so dreadful?' asks Anna.

'Of course,' says Sally. 'Writers do it all the time.' She looks at Jeremy for approval.

He nods. 'Certainly. The subconscious is capable of terrible things.'

'So maybe the abuse happened in Dorothy's subconscious,' argues Cat, 'but not in real life.'

'Ah.' Jeremy smiles irritatingly. 'What is real life?'

Aldo drops a floured chicken breast into his pan of hot oil. It sizzles enticingly, filling the room with the scent of garlic and rosemary.

'Food,' says Aldo, 'is real life.'

'Yes,' says Sam. 'Let's see what happens at supper.'

But the group are disappointed when neither Dorothy nor Betsy appears for dinner. Betsy is tired after her journey, explains Rick, and Dorothy has a headache. Has Dorothy seen her mother? asks Sally. They've had a chat, says Rick guardedly. They'll both be up and about tomorrow. And, with that, the dysfunctional family has to be content.

CHAPTER 24

Day 13

14 August

Much to everyone's interest, Dorothy and Betsy appear together for breakfast on Tuesday morning. Dorothy, though slightly pale and heavy-eyed, is her usual gracious self. She wafts around the table introducing Betsy, 'This is my mom, all the way from Poplar Bluff, Missouri,' just as if she hadn't previously described her female parent as a cold-hearted abusive monster who had made her childhood a hell on earth. Betsy, wearing another pair of amazing shorts, smiles at everyone and says isn't this a darling place, imagine, she's never been to Italy before and she just can't wait to swim in that lovely pool.

'Mary's the swimmer here,' says JP. 'She swims twenty lengths every morning, don't you, Mary?'

Mary, whose hair is, as always in the morning, slightly wet, smiles modestly and says, 'Fifty.'

'Fifty!' groans Sam. 'That would kill me. I'm getting so unfit. I must have put on a stone from eating Aldo's cooking.'

'Impossible,' says Aldo, putting a plate of honey cakes on the table. 'None of my food is fattening.' Aldo is of the firm belief that Italian food does not contain any calories.

'I bet you cook wonderful pizza pie, Aldo,' says Betsy shyly. 'I just love pizza pie.'

'Pizza is from the south,' says Aldo damningly but, relenting slightly, 'I do make pizzas, yes. We have a special oven here.'

'And, strictly speaking,' twinkles Cat, 'pizza means pie so pizza pie is tautological.'

'My,' says Betsy, not seeming to notice the words, only the speaker. 'Aren't you pretty! Are you a model?'

'No,' says Cat, tossing her hair. 'I'm a copywriter.'

'She went to Cambridge,' says Sam. 'Hasn't she mentioned it?'

'Cambridge, Massachusetts?' says Betsy with interest. 'Did you like it there? I've never been to Boston.'

After breakfast, Dorothy announces that she is going to take her mother into San Severino. Fabio offers to drive and Cat says she'll come as she wants to buy presents. Sasha and Star, alerted by the p-word, clamour to come too but Justin says he will take them to the lake. The rest of the guests stay at the Castello. After yesterday's flurry of literary activity, no one feels much like writing. It's clear that most people plan to spend the day lying by the pool.

Mary heads off to her bedroom to put on her second swimming costume and to get her book and suncream. She is surprised to see Aldo loitering outside her door. He rarely comes upstairs.

'Hello, Aldo,' says Mary, trying to keep her voice steady.

'Mary,' says Aldo, smiling. He manages to squeeze four syllables into the name Mary. For a few seconds he just stands there, smiling, as if just looking at her makes him feel sublimely happy. Mary feels acutely conscious of her flat, wet hair and her ill-fitting trousers.

'I liked your book,' says Aldo. 'That Inspector Malone, he is like a real person. He remind me of my Uncle Peppino, who is a pastry chef in Milan.'

'Oh,' says Mary. 'Thank you.' She loves the way he pronounces Malone, with the emphasis on the Mal. Mal-one.

'So,' says Aldo, coming slightly nearer. His eyes are very blue, she notices, emphasised by his brown face. 'Tonight we have a meal cooked by the students at the Villa Stella, yes?'

'I think so.'

'Will be very good. I am one of the tutors,' he puffs out his chest slightly, 'on the course.'

'Goodness. I didn't know that.'

'Yes, I am man of many talents.' He laughs self-deprecatingly 'But tomorrow is *Ferragosto* and Patrizia organises a meal at La Taverna.'

'Yes, I think so.'

'Is a good restaurant. Chef used to be my apprentice when I worked in a restaurant. But, Mary, I have another idea.'

'Yes?' Mary's throat has suddenly become stupidly dry.

'Why don't I take you to my home and cook you a meal there?'

'To your home?'

'Yes. I have a nice apartment in San Severino. I will cook you a feast, just you and me. What do you say?'

What can she say? Mary sees, all too clearly, what she *should* say. She should say that she couldn't possibly abandon the group on their last night. She should be careful, given the ridiculous state of her emotions, never to be in the same room as Aldo, much less go to his house, alone, and eat a meal with him. She should thank him, with cool politeness, but say that it is quite impossible for her to accept his kind offer. Then she should go into her room, start her packing and never think of him again.

'Thank you,' she says. 'I'd love to come.'

Patricia is in her office, looking through the accounts. Even with the extra money from Justin and Betsy, she is not going to have enough to repay her loan. The North Tower really does need work before the November rains. If they have a bad winter, the guttering might need to be replaced. She has bookings throughout September and October but one of the November courses only has three applicants. If they don't get more, she will have to cancel. How can she save money?

Aldo's food bills are huge but she cannot contemplate the Castello without Aldo. He is as much a part of the place as the square towers and the cascading terraces. And he was born only a few miles away; he has more right to be here than she does. Besides, the wonderful food plays a major part in the Castello's success (the website is full of rave reviews about the food — there are very few about the actual courses). Maybe she could get rid of Ratka and Marija and do all the housework herself? Her heart shrinks at the prospect. She doesn't mind hard work, in fact she would almost rather do the cleaning than be the gracious hostess all the time, it's just that someone has to do all the meeting and greeting, all the soothing and flattering, all the bloody *nice* stuff. Artistic people need to be fussed over. She knows that to her cost.

Patricia goes to the window and rests her head on the cool glass. She feels trapped and panicky and she knows that this is only partly due to the prospect of impending bankruptcy. She has had this stifling feeling before, as if her own heart is going to leap into her throat and throttle her, and it is always when somehow, somewhere, she has allowed the past to creep up on her. Sean used to be able to dispel this feeling, she remembers. Even in the worst times, his presence was enough to chase away the shadows. He was so *immediate,* so free from any doubts or fears (or any business sense, she adds sourly to herself), that the demons could not reach him, or anyone around him. But now he is gone and the demons are getting closer.

'Patricia?' JP is standing in the doorway. Patricia is reminded of that first conversation she had with him, about the broken hairdryer, when he had the idea about the special offer. Was that really only eleven days ago?

Patricia whirls round, embarrassed at being caught staring out of the window like a guest.

'You look tired,' says JP.

Patricia is irritated, as one usually is by this remark. 'I'm fine,' she says, with a hint of a snap.

'These courses must be a big strain on you,' says JP, coming to stand beside her at the window. On the lawn, the sprinklers are criss-crossing in a haze of multicoloured water, like a mini Versailles.

'Not really,' says Patricia. 'Besides, we don't normally have abusive mothers turning up out of the blue.'

'No,' agrees JP, grinning. 'That was quite something, wasn't it? But Dorothy seems to be putting a good face on things.'

She certainly is, thinks Patricia. Last night, Dorothy had seemed close to cracking up but this morning it's as if Betsy is her dearest friend. This has left Patricia feeling oddly uneasy, almost frightened. She had believed Dorothy but, if it wasn't true, where did that leave the analyst and the buried memories?

'I never believed Dorothy's story,' JP is saying. 'It always seemed too outlandish. Too Dickensian. Life isn't like that.'

'You'd be surprised,' says Patricia darkly.

There is a brief pause, during which Sean the cat enters the room and leaps jointlessly on to the window ledge. Patricia strokes him; his fur is warm from the sun. She realises that JP is asking her about tonight. She really must pull herself together.

'Oh, it's always fun at the Villa Stella,' she says. 'The food is always good, awfully rich though, and everyone dresses up. There's champagne, sometimes dancing after dinner.'

'Where is this Villa Stella?' asks JP.

'Quite near, just over the next hill. It's a big house with gorgeous grounds. Modern, not like Castello, but beautifully done. It's run by an Englishman called Tony Pearce. He's very nice.'

'So he's not competition for you?'

'No, we do different sorts of courses and sometimes we even do combined things. Wine tasting and sketching, that sort of thing. He does sports holidays too. He's really fit, always cycles everywhere. And he keeps horses. Sean used to help with them sometimes.'

'This Tony sounds a paragon,' says JP, rather sulkily.

Patricia laughs. 'Sometimes it's nice to have another English person to talk to. To talk about *The Archers* or Wimbledon or how much longer the Queen can keep going.'

'Who are the Archers?'

'See what I mean?'

JP is silent for a minute, then he says, 'Tomorrow is the great feast day?'

'*Ferragosto,* yes.'

'And tomorrow we will have some time alone, after the meal?'

Patricia looks at him. He looks so big, standing there in her room. He has an impressive, almost brooding, presence but his smile is surprisingly sweet.

'Yes,' she promises. 'We'll have some time alone.'

By the evening, a tangible feeling of excitement pervades the Castello. After a day spent in the sun, the guests retire to shower, change and prepare themselves for dinner at Villa Stella. After nearly two weeks spent in each other's company, it is both exciting and rather terrifying to think of meeting new people.

Anna, luxuriating under the shower, wonders why sun-bathing can make you feel so tired. She has done nothing all day and yet she feels replete and satisfied, as if she has just run a long race. Not that she ever would, of course. Steve is the runner in the family, Anna is quite content to hold the water bottles and dish out the praise. Maybe that is what has been so relaxing about today – she has had no one to please but herself. She has swum, read *The Moonstone* and chatted lazily to Mary and Sally. Even Sam seemed to go out of his way to be pleasant, there were none of the weighty asides which he has been directing at her in recent days. The group relaxed in the scorching sun, secure in the knowledge that, if they got too hot, they could swim in the pool or retire under the umbrella to drink cold mineral water. Heat is really quite bearable, thinks Anna, as long as you don't have to do anything.

She gets out of the shower, clears the steam from the mirror and looks at herself. She is amazed by how brown she looks. She has been careful with the sun, lathering on suncream and sitting in the shade during the hottest parts of the day, yet she is golden – brown all over, her hair bleached and her eyes seemingly darker and more alive than before. Anna is almost completely free of narcissism yet she takes a particular pleasure in putting on her make-up and in arranging her hair into an artful knot on top of her head. It is almost as if she is looking at a stranger.

She puts on her only smart dress, a black sleeveless shift. Previously she has thought this dress too plain and rather frumpy but, as worn by the new sun-kissed Anna, it has become mysteriously sexy yet sophisticated. She blows a kiss at her reflection in the mirror, thinking, what *am* I doing?

The rest of the group, waiting in the hall, also look unusually smart. Even Matt is wearing a clean, though crumpled, linen jacket over his jeans. Cat, in a sparkling silver dress, looks so gorgeous that Anna's mood of self-satisfaction is completely blown away. She could never be as beautiful as that in a million years. Justin looks as if he is about to burst with pride. Ratka has offered to babysit so Cat and Justin are finally enjoying an evening together. Mary looks elegant in a leaf-green two-piece and Sally is glowing in a multicoloured sequined jacket that shimmers under the chandeliers. The men, in open-neck shirts, look dowdy by comparison until Aldo arrives, very splendid in a black dinner jacket and bow tie. Although older and shorter than the other men, he has a definite masculine presence as he bows politely to the women and offers Mary his arm.

'Blimey, Aldo,' says Sam. 'You look like a film star.'

'No,' says Aldo. 'Mary is the star.'

Anna and Cat exchange looks.

Dorothy, Rick and Betsy are the last to arrive. Rick, wearing a string tie and carrying a Stetson, gains some points for the men's team and Dorothy's poppy-printed dress is much admired. Betsy is wearing what are obviously her best shorts (pink) and a T-shirt saying '100% American Beef'.

'Hope they don't put her on the barbecue,' mutters Sam to Anna.

When they arrive at Villa Stella, driven in the minibus by Fabio, it is obvious, however, that barbecuing will not be a feature of the evening. They are met at the door by Tony Pearce, a tall, elegant man in a dinner jacket, and introduced to the other guests including Gennaro, Don Tonnino the priest, and the mayor of San Severino. Champagne circulates and circulates again. Little trays of crostini are brought out and washed down with more champagne. Anna starts to see the room in glittering fragments, revolving like colours in a kaleidoscope. The waiters in their white jackets, the shocking reds and golds of the flowers, the black night seen through white arched windows, the flickering candles, the gleaming trays of food.

'I feel quite drunk,' she says to Cat.

'Me too,' says Cat, holding out her glass for more champagne. 'It's brilliant, isn't it?'

Anna is about to answer when Tony Pearce comes over and Cat greets him with much hair flicking and eyelash fluttering. Anna thinks there is a brittle edge to Cat tonight, she seems as shiny and metallic as her silver dress. But Tony does not seem to mind and nor do two other men who hastily cross the room to join them. Anna sees Justin watching narrowly as he sits trapped on a sofa between Mary and Dorothy. Anna is wondering whether to join them when a voice behind her says, 'You look beautiful.'

It is Sam.

'Thank you,' says Anna politely, moving away slightly.

'I mean it,' says Sam, his dark eyes intense. 'You look stunning.'

'I'm looking forward to the food,' says Anna brightly. 'Did you know that Aldo was one of the tutors?'

'Anna,' says Sam in an odd, tight voice, 'why won't you let me say what I want to say?'

'Because I don't think it would be a good idea, that's why,' says Anna nervously.

'But you must know how I feel about you.'

Anna feels the room spinning again and clings on to a solid fact to steady herself. 'I'm married,' she says.

'You're not.'

'As good as,' says Anna. 'And I've got two children.'

'I'm in love with you,' says Sam.

'You're not.'

'Don't tell me that I'm not,' says Sam fiercely. 'I know how I feel.'

'Shh.' Anna looks round but the buzz of talk in the room is so loud that no one seems to have noticed Sam's raised voice.

'Sorry.' Sam lowers his voice but grasps Anna's arm tightly. 'I'm going mad here, Anna.'

'Look,' Anna pulls her arm away, 'it's just being cooped up together so much. It's the place, Italy, the heat . . .'

'Don't patronise me,' explodes Sam and this time people do look round. 'I know how I feel.'

Anna sees Patricia looking over, eyebrows raised. Jeremy says something to Sally, looking rather smug as if his worst fears about Anna and Sam are being realised. But it is Aldo who comes over, a guardian angel in a dinner jacket.

'Anna,' he says, bowing slightly, 'we are about to eat. Will you accompany me?' He offers her his arm, which she accepts gratefully. Behind her she hears Sam give a loud sigh, his arms slapping theatrically against his sides.

In the long dining room the table is laid with what looks like every piece of cutlery in Tuscany (the Florentines, according to Aldo, invented the fork). The light gleams off decanters, spindly wine glasses and sparkling silver. Anna sits next to Aldo and spreads the thick linen napkin on her lap. She is relieved when Gennaro comes to sit on her other side. Sam is safely on the opposite side of the table, between Cat and Patricia. She must talk to Sam, explain that she would never be unfaithful to Steve. But not tonight. Tonight she just wants to avoid him. If only they hadn't all drunk so much. It feels as if the whole evening is getting out of control, as if there is a giant hand spinning them all round, just for the fun of seeing where they end up. There is Mary, on Aldo's other side, her eyes sparkling. There is Sally, looking adoringly at Jeremy. There is Cat (oh dear), giggling up at a rather discomfited Fabio. There is Myra laughingly, but not that convincingly, declaring to Gennaro that she is just not the marrying kind. There is Betsy, calmly spreading butter on her roll, and Dorothy, nervously patting her lips with her napkin. There is JP, glowering over to where Patricia is talking intently to Tony Pearce. What is going to happen to them all?

The cookery students make a grand entrance with the first course and the guests all stand up to applaud them. The cooks, mostly middle-aged women, look flushed and happy. Maybe I should have done a cookery course instead, thinks Anna. Food is safer somehow. Words are dangerous.

Food may be safe but the cookery students' menu is rich to the point of heart attack. *Prosciutto* with figs, pears with gorgonzola and honey, *melanzane alla parmigiana,* fried *zucchini* flowers. This is followed by stuffed pasta, veal escalopes and rabbit in a sweet-and-sour sauce (Aldo tells Anna that it is called '*agrodolce*'and is a rare delicacy but she can't help thinking about Bunny and Flossie in their hutch at home). By the time the puddings make their triumphal progress into the room, the guests are lolling in their chairs. Anna knows with certainty that if she takes one mouthful of zabaglione or pear with chocolate sauce, she will be sick. She sips her water, trying to persuade her food to stay in her stomach.

At the end of the table, Dorothy is talking about Thanksgiving. 'To my mind it's a shame you don't have it in Europe. It's such a heart-warming, family-orientated feast day. Roast turkey and pumpkin pie. Do you remember the pumpkin pie you used to make, Mom?'

Cat, leaning across the table, says in a loud, carrying voice, 'I thought your childhood was sheer, unmitigated hell, Dorothy.' She has trouble saying 'unmitigated'; Anna realises that she is very drunk.

Dorothy looks across at her, apparently not understanding. 'What did you say, dear?'

'Well, excuse me,' Cat makes a wide, expansive gesture that knocks over a wine glass, 'but aren't you writing a book about your awful abused childhood. About how your mother used to starve you and beat you up. Or have I missed something?'

There is a terrible silence. Everyone looks at Betsy, who stares at her daughter, a piece of zabaglione dangling from her spoon.

'Dotty?' says Betsy uncertainly.

The diminutive seems to undo Dorothy. She looks defiantly at her mother. 'It's true. I am writing about my childhood. I'd repressed it for years but it all came back to me. All the terrible things you used to do to me.'

'I did terrible things to you?'

'Yes! You did! You never loved me. You used to beat me. I kept it hidden inside me but my therapist helped me to remember. You abused me!' The last comes out as a kind of suppressed shriek.

Rick puts his hand on Dorothy's shoulder. 'There now, honey.'

Betsy is also at Dorothy's side, her voice suddenly calm and tender. 'Dotty,' she says, 'we had a tough time back then. Maybe I was hard on you but I always loved you. And I never abused you. As God is my witness.'

Dorothy looks wildly at her mother for a few minutes and then collapses sobbing on her shoulder. Rick gets up and steers them both gently out of the room.

In the stunned silence that follows, Cat starts to laugh and then starts to cry. Justin, who is sitting several places away, gets to his feet but Fabio is too quick for him. 'You need some air,' he says. 'It is very hot in here.' He leads Cat from the room. Anna, thinking that she might be able to help, gets up too. She collides with Justin in the doorway.

'What is that fellow playing at?' he growls. 'Going off with my wife.'

'He's just looking after her,' bleats Anna.

'He'd better bloody not look after her,' retorts Justin. Voices can be heard coming from the terrace. Justin heads off in their direction, his fists clenched.

Anna follows, fearing the worst.

Cat and Fabio are in the darkness. Cat is sitting on a low

sofa, her head in her hands. Fabio is standing slightly behind her. When Anna reaches the door to the terrace, Justin has already squared up to Fabio, his voice thick with anger.

'What the hell are you doing with my wife?'

Fabio backs away slightly. 'Nothing. Nothing. I was helping her . . .'

'I'll thank you not to help her.' Justin pokes Fabio in the chest. Anna is astonished at Justin's aggression. Where is the mild-mannered accountant now? What is he doing picking a fight with a man so much younger and fitter than him?

'I've seen how you look at her,' shouts Justin. 'You fancy her, don't you? You Italians are all alike.'

'I don't . . .' Fabio looks round helplessly and help does come, from an unexpected direction. Matt's head appears over the terrace wall. He has come from the garden and has obviously set off the security lights because they are suddenly spot-lit, lending a surreal, theatrical air to the proceedings. Matt swings his legs over the wall and walks up to Justin, standing between him and Fabio.

'You've got it wrong,' he says calmly to Justin. 'Fabio has never even looked in Cat's direction. She fancies *him* though, that's obvious. You'd better take her home now, she doesn't look too well.'

And Cat promptly fulfils Matt's prediction by being violently and copiously sick over the wicker sofa.

CHAPTER 25

Day 13, night

Back at the Castello, Cat and Justin go straight to bed. Cat looks very pale but she has, at least, stopped being sick. Dorothy and Betsy also go upstairs, holding hands tightly. When the guests had come out of the dining room at the Villa Stella, rather light-headed from so much food and so much emotion, they found Dorothy and Betsy talking intently in the sitting room. Dorothy was holding her mother's hand and Betsy was gently stroking Dorothy's hair. No one had liked to disturb them. Matt had walked in from the terrace to announce breezily that Cat wasn't feeling well. The Castello party had been only too happy to call it a day and be driven home in the minibus by a silent Fabio.

Now, though, there is a curious reluctance to go to bed. Rick sinks into a chair by the massive fireplace in the hall and JP and Sam go to sit with him. It is only a matter of minutes before Aldo joins them, carrying a bottle of brandy. French brandy, JP notices approvingly. One of the very few things the French do better than the Italians, returns Aldo. Patricia makes coffee and she, Mary and Sally join the group around the manorial fireplace.

Anna takes the opportunity to sneak off to bed. She is still feeling slightly sick and the champagne has given her a splitting headache. All she wants to do is collapse into bed and pretend that this evening has never happened. She cringes for Cat and Justin. Cat will be mortified when she wakes up. It is unthinkable that the beautiful, sophisticated Cat ended up vomiting all over Tony Pearce's patio furniture or that the cool, intelligent Justin threatened an Italian youth half his age. What *has* got into everyone?

Her room, with its calm, restful elegance, is a relief. Anna kicks off her high heels and goes to the window. The moon is shining high above the dark hills. It is almost full, just a sliver less than a perfect circle. Anna looks down on to the terrace below where the bougainvillea stirs in the slight breeze. Below that, the pool shines like a rectangle full of light. Is it her imagination, or is there a figure moving beyond the pool, amongst the olive trees? She steps out on to her balcony, breathing in the scented night air. The trees move restlessly and a dog barks somewhere down in the valley. Did she really see someone or was it just the moonlight? Nevertheless, Anna locks the balcony doors before she goes to bed.

Patricia, too, feels strangely unsteady when she finally goes upstairs to bed. She had meant to stick to coffee but had been persuaded to have a glass of brandy, which had swiftly been followed by another. How long is it since she has drunk brandy? Since you drank it with Sean, says a voice in her head. She usually avoids drinking with the guests. A glass or two at dinner is fine, staying up drinking brandy after midnight is something quite different. But tonight has been unlike any other night. She has taken guests to Tony's showpiece dinner for four years now and never before has anyone been accused of child abuse over the *zabaglione* or vomited all over the furniture. Anna and Sam were obviously having a scene before dinner and she hasn't missed the hot looks between Sally and Jeremy and even (heavens) between Aldo and Mary. And when she popped to the loo at Villa Stella, she had surprised Myra and Gennaro snogging in the passageway. Just a bit of fun, Myra said lightly afterwards. But Myra has never felt the need for that sort of fun before.

Patricia has a shower and puts on her silk kimono. She'll never sleep after all that coffee, not to mention the brandy. Should she go and make herself some tea? She knows that tea is a stimulant too but never quite believes it. Tea is comfort, coffee is excitement. Wine is sociable, brandy is dangerous.

She is just considering this when there is a knock at her door. She gets up, holding the skimpy kimono together. She is shocked, but not entirely surprised, to see JP standing in the doorway. He is holding the bottle of brandy.

'I thought you might like another drink,' he says.

'I think I've had enough,' says Patricia primly.

It is at this point that JP is meant to blush, apologise for troubling her and back out of the room. Instead he comes into the room, shuts the door behind him, puts the brandy down on a table and puts his arms round her. When she opens her mouth to point out this breach of etiquette, he kisses her, one hand feeling for her breast under the thin silk of her kimono. She knows all too well that her nipple has reacted to his touch. In fact, she seems to have lost the use of most of her limbs. He bends his head to kiss her neck, at the same time propelling her towards the bed. By now, she is kissing him back. Why not? says her body. I've been waiting a long time for this. It doesn't mean anything, he knows the rules. You can't possibly sleep with a guest, protests her mind. Besides, you like him too much, it'll all end in tears. But now, JP is on top of her and her body is definitely in charge. She reaches for him, pulling at his shirt, feeling the taut muscles in his back.

A terrible, earth-shattering scream fills the night.

'What the . . . ?' JP sits up, stupefied. Patricia rolls off the bed and, belting her kimono tightly, runs out into the passageway. The screaming is coming from Sally's room on the next floor. By the time Patricia gets there, Jeremy, Sam and Fabio have arrived. Or was Jeremy there already? Patricia hopes that JP will have the sense to go back to his own room.

Sally, wearing surprisingly girlish pink pyjamas, is on the landing. 'It's in my room!' she screams.

'The ghost?' asks Patricia stupidly.

One Summer in Tuscany

'No!' howls Sally. 'A scorpion!'

They all peer through the door. There, on the white wall, looking quite incredibly evil, is a black scorpion, its tail raised ready to strike.

'Jesus,' says Sam. 'It's a scorpion all right. I didn't know you had them in Italy.'

'They're very rare,' says Patricia, although in fact scorpions are quite often seen at the Castello. They are usually small, though, and fairly harmless. This one looks like an illustration in a book of deadly insects.

'Get it out, please!' howls Sally, clinging to Jeremy's arm.

Sam and Patricia look at each other. Sam knows he should offer but he's just a Glasgow boy, tropical insects aren't really his line.

'Let me,' says Fabio. He is carrying a newspaper which he folds into a square. He approaches the scorpion and lets it run on to the paper. He then walks quietly to the window and shakes the scorpion out into the night.

'My hero!' says Sally, moving tearfully towards Fabio. He backs out into the corridor.

'Is nothing,' he says, smiling nervously. His teeth are very white in the darkness.

'You are a hero all right, son,' says Sam, slapping Fabio on the back.

'Yes,' says Jeremy with less enthusiasm.

'I'll make us all a cup of tea,' says Patricia.

As she goes downstairs she sees that Rick is still sitting in

295

his chair by the fire. His eyes are closed and she thinks he may be asleep.

'Rick?'

Rick opens his eyes and smiles up at her. 'Sorry, honey, I must have dropped off. Did I hear a scream just now?'

'That was Sally. There was a scorpion in her room.'

'Land sakes, hasn't she ever seen a scorpion before?'

'Do you know,' says Patricia, 'you're the first person I've ever heard say "land sakes".'

'Well, I hope I won't be the last,' says Rick courteously.

Patricia thinks how much she likes Rick, with his slow-moving charm and gentle good manners. Dorothy is lucky to have him, she thinks.

'Is Dorothy all right?' she asks.

'I think so,' says Rick slowly. 'That's why I stayed down here awhile, to give her and Betsy time to talk. I really think they cleared the air tonight.'

'I'm so sorry about Cat at dinner. She had far too much to drink.'

'Oh, that's OK,' says Rick. 'Fact is, I think it helped, everything coming out in the open like that. When Betsy confronted Dorothy head on, it really shook Dorothy's belief in her so-called memories.'

'So you don't think it happened, the abuse?'

Rick pauses before answering, swirling the last of the brandy round in his glass. 'I think she had a tough childhood,' he says at last. 'Maybe Betsy was a bit heavy-handed with her kids. It must have been hard, having seven kids with no husband and no money. But actual, systematic abuse? No, I don't think it happened. I think Dorothy got ideas from other books about abusive childhoods and convinced herself it all happened to her. She does like to be centre stage, you know.' He smiles lovingly as he says this.

'So she's not going to write the book?'

'I don't think so, no. But it's been worth it, this holiday, if it patches things up with Dorothy and her mom. Cost all our savings but it's worth it.'

Slowly, the meaning of his words sinks in. 'Cost all your savings?' Patricia looks blankly at Rick. 'But I thought you were rich. I thought you were an oil tycoon.'

'You thought I was a . . . ?' Rick starts to laugh, bending forward in his seat, slapping his thigh. 'You thought I was an oil tycoon?'

'But you said . . . you said you were in the oil business.'

'I am,' says Rick. 'I own a gas station. 'And he laughs until the tears run down his face.

CHAPTER 26

Day 14

15 August

The morning of *Ferragosto,* the Feast of the Assumption, is one of the most perfect Patricia can remember. The sky is a clear, azure blue, like Mary's robes, and every leaf, every flower, every crumbling stone of the Castello is washed in golden sunshine. How ironical, thinks Patricia, leaning out of her window and breathing in the dewy air, that the Castello should look its most beautiful just when she thinks she might lose it forever. Without the fantasy of Rick's money, she cannot see how she is ever going to repay her loan. The bank will foreclose and she will lose the castle with its towers and terraces, its wooded grounds, its lordly views over the countryside. She will lose it and what will she do? Teach English in Siena? Go back to England and live on a grim housing estate in Luton? It doesn't bear thinking about and yet, as Patricia leans her head against the cool stone of the window, she can't quite bring herself to feel sad. Not on a morning like this. There is optimism in every blade of grass this morning, in the ecstatic singing of the birds, in the sound of the church bells ringing across the valley. Surely, surely, something will turn up.

She watches as Mary appears around the side of the house, carrying her towel. She walks purposefully to the pool, shrugs off her robe and dives neatly into the water. Patricia admires her smooth stroke as she swims length after length. She's quite a woman, Mary. Swims better than any man and writes like a dream. What does Aldo really feel about her? wonders Patricia. He has never paid so much attention to any guest before. She had been amazed to hear this morning, from Matt, that Aldo had invited Mary to his apartment for dinner. *She* has never been to his apartment, thinks Patricia, fighting down a quite unreasonable wave of jealousy. It must be serious. Aldo, for all his outgoing charm, is a very private man. She thinks of herself as his friend as well as his employer but the idea of asking him how he feels about Mary is literally unthinkable.

And how does she feel about JP? Again, quite impossible. She has no doubt that, last night, if Sally hadn't screamed, she would have gone to bed with him. Her body had made its own decision on that one. But how does she *feel*? She doesn't know. She is definitely attracted to JP, she thinks he is intelligent and good company but can she imagine having a relationship with him? Dully, she thinks that JP would be such a *sensible* choice. He has a good job, is reasonably well-off, cosmopolitan and good-looking. He would even be a good stepfather for Matt. It is about time she made a sensible decision about a man, she tells herself sternly. She sighs. She'd better get downstairs and start organising breakfast.

Anna, too, feels the magic of the morning. As she stands on her balcony, she feels miraculously free from a hangover. In fact, she feels more than usually alert, every nerve tingling. The air is like a magic potion, she feels as if she could gulp it down and live forever. She watches as Mary makes her way down to the pool. If she were serious about getting fit, she would run down and join her. She can almost feel the cool water against her body. But Anna, who is averse to almost all forms of exercise, is quite happy to stay on her balcony drinking in the air and watching someone else swim.

On her way down to breakfast she meets Cat on the stairs, hand in hand with Star. Anna feels nervous, she wants to spare Cat any embarrassment but how can she avoid mentioning last night? Cat, gorgeous as ever in shorts and a halter-neck, grins engagingly.

'Some night last night!'

'Er . . . yes,' says Anna.

'Do you feel OK this morning? I remember thinking you'd had a drop too much.'

'I'm OK,' says Anna.

'Can you believe, I got food poisoning from their rotten food? Justin says I should sue them but I reckon, why bother? They're only amateurs. The food was inedible, Justin says.'

Anna stares at her friend, at her smooth, glowing face, as if she is seeing her for the first time. Have Cat and Justin really convinced themselves that they are completely blameless? Have they forgotten that Cat almost precipitated Dorothy into a major breakdown or that Justin accused Fabio of fancying his wife? Have they forgotten the almost-fight on the terrace or the vomiting on the sofa cushions? Evidently they have. Cat only remembers that Anna got slightly drunk and that she was the innocent victim of a bunch of amateur Borgias. Anna opens her mouth to protest and then thinks better of it. After all, isn't it better that Cat and Justin both share the same delusional world view? It would be terrible if one of them saw last night in a different light. At least this way they are happy, secure in their continued superiority.

'Come on,' says Anna to Star. 'I'll race you downstairs. I bet there's watermelon for breakfast.'

At breakfast Patricia outlines the plans for the evening. They will leave the Castello at five, driven by Aldo in the minibus, and wander round San Severino enjoying the *festa*. At seven thirty they will meet for a meal at La Taverna. Aldo will drive them home at eleven but anyone who wants to stay later is welcome.

'I think I'll take my car,' says JP, looking at Patricia. 'Then I can please myself.'

'That's fine,' says Patricia, 'but parking may be a bit difficult.'

'You'd better come with me then,' says JP.

'We'll take our hire car,' says Justin. 'The kids may need an early night.'

This is the first time that Justin or Cat has ever acknowledged that their children even go to bed. The guests exchange glances but Cat is oblivious. 'Anyway, we've been to Brazil for the carnival so we're not all that bothered, to be honest.'

'*Carnevale*,' says Aldo scathingly as he puts a plate of cold meat on the table, 'is not *Ferragosto*.'

'What is this ferry gusto anyway?' asks Betsy brightly. She is sitting very close to Dorothy and they occasionally exchange loving smiles. 'Dotty tells me that it's about the Virgin Mary.'

'Well, it's the Feast of the Assumption,' says Patricia. 'When Mary was taken up into heaven.'

'Goodness me,' says Betsy. 'Do people really believe that here?'

'Of course,' says Aldo.

'Actually,' says Patricia hurriedly, 'the day has Roman origins.' She knows this will please Aldo. 'The Emperor Augustus initiated a series of festivals in August and they were called the *feriae Augusti*, the August fairs. The most important fair was on the thirteenth. It was dedicated to Diana, the goddess of hunting, to the moon and to maternity. Diana is the goddess of women in labour.'

'Is that something else you've memorised?' murmurs JP.

'You need more than a goddess when you're in labour,' laughs Cat. The childless women, Mary and Sally, look at her stonily.

'The August feast days also celebrated the seasons and the crops,' says Patricia, smiling at JP. 'And nowadays people pray to Mary for help in childbirth.'

'Well,' says Betsy mildly, 'I can't see that she'd be much help. She only had one baby. I've had seven. And you don't get many goddesses in Poplar Bluff, Missouri, let me tell you.'

By the woodstore at the end of the drive, Fabio and Matt are looking at a large box from the firework factory in Poggibonsi.

'So if I just fix one to my launcher . . .' Matt is saying.

Fabio is kneeling down to examine the fireworks. 'Matteo, these have their own launchers.'

'But I made my own,' says Matt, sounding disappointed.

Fabio smiles. 'Your launcher is phenomenal. If you use it, your rocket will end up in Iraq.'

Matt laughs. 'Wish I could aim it at Donald Trump instead.'

Fabio laughs too but looks slightly troubled. 'Are you still going to fire it?'

'Yes. The procession's at nine. I'm going to be in position at twenty-one hundred hours.' He puts on a terrible American accent.

'I'll meet you here,' says Fabio.

Matt grins. 'Great. I'll give you a lift into town later, if you want. On my bike.'

'*Va bene*,' says Fabio. 'If we are both still alive.'

They walk back to the house, Matt loping along, whistling and kicking pine cones, Fabio quieter, hands in pockets, frowning down at the sun-parched grass. When they are in sight of the house, he says suddenly, 'Matteo?'

'Yes?'

'Thank you for last night. For standing up for me.'

'That's OK,' says Matt. 'I can't stand that Justin Ferris-Wanker. He thinks he's so clever.'

Fabio persists, still frowning, 'I never did make a pass at Mrs Ferris-Merry.'

'I don't blame you,' says Matt cheerfully. 'She's pretty but she's so up herself.' He looks at Fabio, expecting him to laugh, but the older boy still looks serious.

'She does fancy you, though,' says Matt. 'I've seen her looking at you.'

'I'm sure she doesn't,' says Fabio flatly.

'Why not?' says Matt. 'You're ugly but you're not *that* ugly.'

And now Fabio does laugh, picking up a pine cone to throw at a fleeing Matt.

Aldo is in his kitchen. Ratka has finished washing up the breakfast things and he has the place to himself, which is how he likes it. He has already prepared lunch (very simple today – bruschette and cold meats) and is pondering a much more serious issue – what to give Mary to eat tonight. There are several traditional *Ferragosto* dishes such as quail with rice, *zucchini* tart or fried meat *alla romana*, but none of these quite hits the mark for some reason. He wants to cook Mary a dish that is perfect, simply and exquisitely perfect. It must be something traditionally Tuscan but nothing too complicated. He wants to show Mary, who has such instinctive understanding of food, that Italian cooking is not just tomatoes and garlic. He wants to show her subtlety, delicacy, a perfect marriage of ingredients and flavours. In fact, he admits to himself, standing in the sun-filled kitchen, he wants to woo her with food.

He liked Mary as soon as he saw her. He liked her neat figure, her short ash-blond hair and the way she put her head on one side when she asked a question. Above all, he liked the fact that she had come to Italy prepared to love it. So many guests are engaged in what seems to be an unspoken competition with Italy. They want to prove that they know more about Italian food and customs than the locals do, they are determined not to be impressed by Italian culture, Italian food or, especially, the Italians themselves. There are the complaints: summer is too hot, winter is too cold, the bread is all crust and the butter isn't salty enough, the pizzas are too thin, there are no electric kettles, the coffee is too bitter, the cappuccino is too cold, why isn't it more like the cappuccino at Starbucks, why don't drivers stop at zebra crossings and why are the hot taps marked C? Even visitors who know a little about Italy use their knowledge to show off rather than allowing the country to work its magic on them.

Like that dreadful Cat, with her over-accented Italian and her disparaging comments about Christopher Columbus. But Mary had gasped when she saw the leaning tower of Pisa, she had almost fainted at her first sight of the Piazza Navona and, when she first bit into his *torta di limone,* she looked as if she had seen heaven.

He doesn't just like her because she appreciates his food, though. Plenty of other guests have done that. Put simply, Mary is the first woman of his own age that he has wanted to go to bed with. When his wife died ten years ago, Aldo had been mildly surprised that the urges of the body did not die with her. It seemed faintly ridiculous for a respectable widower with white hair to be having lustful feelings for the presenters on television, even for women he saw in the piazza in the evenings, but the feelings were there nonetheless. Nobody would have objected, he knows, if he had struck up a friendship with one of the many widows in San Severino, a comfortable *nonna* who would mend his socks and cook him *pasta e fagioli.* How nice, people would say, they'll be company for each other. But the trouble is that Aldo does not fancy any of the widows. His tastes turn more to slimmer, blonder women. Five years ago, he did indeed have a clandestine affair with a slim, blonde woman twenty years his junior. His daughter had found out and was furious. It had seemed easier to end the relationship, not least because the slim, blonde lady turned out to be both demanding and rather boring. But now his daughter has emigrated to Australia and he is on his own. He had begun to wonder whether he should just admit defeat and start considering one of the widows when Mary turned up. There she was: slim, blonde, in love with Italy and with his food, intelligent, classy (i.e. English) and a good writer into the bargain. Aldo, who reads English rather well, has been rereading Miss Marple in an attempt to understand the English murder mystery but it is the moustachioed Poirot with whom he identifies. He, Aldo, will exercise his little grey cells with the aim of seducing Miss McMahon. He is in love with her too, of course.

Aldo smiles as he moves about his kitchen. He will cook her spinach ravioli with butter and sage followed by salmon *in carpaccio.* Her uncle was a fishmonger, he remembers. Also, salmon is meant to be an aphrodisiac.

CHAPTER 27

Ferragosto

At five o'clock, the guests are once more assembled in the hall. Cat and family have already left for San Severino, they don't want to miss the children's funfair. Matt has said that he and Fabio will be coming into town later, on his motorbike. Patricia is pleased, she approves of Fabio as a friend. He is a couple of years older than Matt and she thinks he is a steadying influence. It has been nice, this summer, not to have seen so much of Elio and Graziano. Patricia herself is travelling with JP in his hired Alfa. She doesn't know if this is wise but she can't resist the open-top car and the chance to forget her responsibilities for a few minutes. The guests will be gone tomorrow, she tells herself, and she can get down to some really serious housework. This thought is so depressing that she banishes it from her mind. Tonight, at least, she'll have fun.

Mary finds her legs shaking as she climbs into the bus. Tomorrow, intones a sonorous voice in her head, tomorrow you will be gone, back to Streatham and red buses and ready-made meals for one. But, somehow, she can't take in the voice's doleful message. All she can think about is that tonight she will be alone with Aldo, in his apartment. As she takes her seat in the bus, looking at the sunburnt back of Aldo's head, she seriously wonders whether, before this moment, she was ever alive at all.

Anna, watching the Castello disappear behind the umbrella pines, wonders whether she will ever come back to Tuscany again. It would be nice to come for a weekend with Steve, just the two of them, maybe to Siena. For a honeymoon, says a voice in her head. Now where did that come from? Steve is bound to ask her to marry him one day and, until then, she's very happy. *They're* very happy. She's lucky to have Steve. He's worth ten of Jeremy or Sam. This holiday has taught her that, even if it hasn't taught her to be a writer. She sees Sam looking at her intently as if he can read her mind. She *must* speak to Sam tonight. Anna watches as the Alfa overtakes them, looking like something from *The Great Gatsby*, Patricia's red scarf streaming out behind her. What does Patricia think about saying goodbye to JP? she wonders. Or perhaps it won't be goodbye. They are both free agents, there is no reason why they shouldn't go on seeing each other. It would be good if one of the relationships forged this week survived.

San Severino is transformed. The narrow streets are criss-crossed with bunting and huge medieval flags hang limply in the heat (it is still stiflingly hot and Aldo is predicting thunder before midnight). There is a big wheel and a bouncy castle where Star Ferris-Merry is, at this very moment, having a spectacular tantrum. Long tables are laid out in the main piazza and pork steaks are being grilled on a giant barbecue. Morose local boys, dressed as medieval pages, prowl the streets offering free glasses of wine. On a makeshift stage, Aldo's brother Massimo, backed by an elderly but enthusiastic band, is singing *finiculi, finicula, la la la la.*

Anna is not surprised to find Sam at her side as they stroll through the streets. They walk in silence past the stalls selling wine and cheese and frighteningly expensive jewellery until Anna says, 'Sam?'

Sam sighs. 'I know. I know. You like me for my happy-go-lucky Scottish charm but your heart belongs to Steve.'

Anna can't help laughing, partly from relief. 'Well . . . yes.'

'And there's no chance I can persuade you otherwise?'

'I'm afraid not.'

'And a sympathy fuck's out of the question?'

'Yes.'

'Oh well.' Sam tucks his arm through Anna's and they walk on in much more companionable silence until, by a display of elaborately carved watermelons, Sam says suddenly, 'Anna? What's your book about?'

Anna is taken aback. It is the first time that Sam has shown any interest in her writing. She hesitates a few minutes before replying. Her novel now seems incredibly shallow and uninteresting. 'Well, it's about a girl, Sophie, who's from a rather poor working-class family. She goes to university, the first person in her family to go, and she meets a rich law student called Hugo. They fall in love but she feels very uncomfortable with his friends and with his family. And eventually he dumps her for some posh Sloane. That's it really.'

'Is it autobiographical?'

Anna laughs uncomfortably. 'In essence, yes. I did have an affair with a rich boy at university. I loved him but he had all these public school friends who made my life a misery. They took the mickey out of the way I spoke, the way I ate, dressed, everything. His family were even worse. When I said "pardon" to his mother, I thought she was going to have a coronary. They were desperate for him to find someone else, someone "more our sort of person" and, in the end, he did.'

'Are you still angry with him, this Hugo?' asks Sam.

'Piers, that was his real name. No, I don't think I'm angry but obviously I must want to get my own back in some way, otherwise I wouldn't have written the book. I'm surprised how raw it still is, actually. I thought I'd put it all behind me when I met Steve.'

'How did you meet Steve?'

'He's a plumber and he did some work for my mum. It was just after Dad died and she was feeling very vulnerable.

'He was so nice to her, chatted to her, went out of his way to make everything as easy as possible. And he was really gorgeous as well. I found I was timing my visits to Mum to coincide with times when Steve would be there. Eventually, my mum said to Steve, "Why don't you ask Anna out? I know she likes you." I was mortified when I found out but Steve did ask me out. That first evening, he took me out for a meal and we stayed talking until the waiters put the chairs on the tables. And that was it really.'

They start to walk back to the piazza, where Massimo is now singing about saying goodbye to Rome.

'You know what I think, Anna?' says Sam. 'I think you should forget about Piers the posh bastard and write about your husband.'

'He's not my husband.'

'Well, you can do something about that, can't you?'

Aldo's apartment is in a modern block near the church. It is a plain white building made beautiful by the window boxes and balconies which overflow with a profusion of flowers and greenery. Aldo's balcony contains a lemon tree, a vine as thick as Mary's wrist and a glorious array of herbs in terracotta pots.

'This is amazing,' says Mary. 'It's as big as another room.'

'I spend a lot of time here,' says Aldo, busily watering. 'Sitting reading my paper or listening to the football on the radio.'

'I can't imagine you having any free time. You always seem so busy.'

'That's when there are courses. When there are no courses, I have too much time to myself. Especially Sundays. Sundays are the worst.'

'Yes,' says Mary, remembering. 'Sunday can be terrible.'

There is a short silence during which they can hear the faint sounds of music and laughter drifting up from the piazza. A red balloon, trailing streamers, rises silently past them. Mary watches as it floats higher and higher, a faint red dot against the blue. She imagines a child, Star perhaps, wailing inconsolably as their treasured balloon disappears into the heavens.

'Tell me about your apartment in London,' says Aldo, picking herbs with great care.

'Well, it's in Streatham, which is in South London. It's not a very smart area but it does have a nice common . . . a park . . . and there are lots of shops and a cinema and an ice rink.' She pauses. How can she make Aldo, who seems the very essence of Italy, standing on his verdant balcony with the blue sky behind him, how can she make Aldo see Streatham, the launderettes and the pubs, the corner shops covered by metal grilles, the dog crap on the streets, the children playing on the common in summer, the buses lumbering past on their way to Crystal Palace. It's a world, a lifetime, away.

'My flat . . . my apartment . . . is quite nice,' she says at last. 'It's on the second floor so I have a good view.' Of what? she wonders. 'It's in a twenties block, lots of glass and curving walls, rather attractive if you like that sort of thing.'

'Do you have a balcony?' asks Aldo.

'A small one. I used to grow geraniums but they died.' She had watered them too much, killing them with kindness. She can't imagine plants ever dying in Italy.

'I must make the ravioli,' says Aldo. 'I prepare the filling already but the ravioli must be fresh. You don't mind?'

'No,' says Mary. Watching Aldo cook is close to her idea of heaven.

She follows Aldo into the small kitchen and he pours them both a glass of red wine. Then he gets out his wicker basket which contains a covered casserole dish and a tightly wrapped plastic bag. 'The dough,' he explains.

He works quickly but without hurry, flouring the surface, rolling out the dough and dividing it into two. Then he takes a plastic box from his basket and, at careful intervals, spoons the mixture into the centre of the pasta.

'Smells lovely,' says Mary, her mouth watering. 'What's in it?'

'*Zucca*,' says Aldo, clicking his fingers to come up with the English word. 'Pumpkin. Pumpkin and sausage with nutmeg and a little amaretto biscuit.'

He takes a brush and paints water round the edge of the pasta square. Then he takes his second sheet of pasta and places it on top of the first. He presses the edges down carefully with his broad, clever fingers and, taking a knife, cuts the pasta into squares. He uses a fork to seal the edges and then he places the finished ravioli on to a floured tray and puts a saucepan of water on the stove, adding salt liberally. Then he smiles at Mary, takes the wine glass from her hand and kisses her.

*

The rest of the group are sitting down to eat at La Taverna, a charming ivy-covered restaurant just off the main piazza. The mood is lively, even euphoric. It is their last evening together and everyone suddenly feels very close. Even Jeremy exchanges email addresses with Anna and Sam and says that he will certainly come and stay with Dorothy and Rick if he is ever in Vermont. Dorothy invites Anna and Cat too, telling Anna that she thinks of her just like a daughter. Anna, though touched, finds this slightly worrying.

Before the meal, Myra makes a witty little speech about the course. This is one of her specialities, teasing the guests with a few of their more flattering peculiarities. It's a pity Aldo isn't here, he is always good for a few jokes. But Myra does her best; she mentions Mary's swimming (where is Mary?), Cat's glamour, Sally's changing hair colour, Sam's Scottishness and Rick's Stetson. Anna is teased for her constant calls and emails home and JP for his defiant jingoism. She mentions Sean the cat, Aldo's driving and Fabio's body beautiful. She sits down to wild applause.

'Thank you,' mouths Patricia. She couldn't have made that speech to save her life.

All too quickly, the last supper is over and they are trailing out into the night. It is still fairly early (nearly nine) and the sky is only just going dark. The mood in the town is wilder though. Massimo's Italian folk songs have given way to a thumping rock band and the young people are starting to come out, shouting greetings at each other across the street.

Lights are strung in the trees and across the piazza. Looking up, Patricia sees that there is a perfect full moon. She shivers.

'What happens now?' Dorothy asks.

'Well, there's a procession up to the grotto,' says Patricia, pointing to a corner of the square where Don Tonnino, surrounded by acolytes, is holding a cross high over the heads of the revellers. 'Then there's fireworks and dancing.'

'I might join the procession,' says Jeremy. 'Primitive ritual is always fascinating.'

'I'll come too,' says Sally.

'We'll get the kids an ice cream before going home,' says Cat.

The Americans also opt for the gelateria, leaving Sam and Anna to wander around the stalls. Myra has been snatched by a passing Gennaro.

Patricia feels a warm hand on her back. 'I've had enough of primitive ritual,' murmurs JP. 'Let's go back to the Castello.'

'But we're all meant to be meeting up at eleven.'

'That's hours away,' says JP. 'We can be there and back by then.'

Patricia looks at the busy lighted street and thinks of the Castello, lying dark and deserted in its wooded grounds. Suddenly she feels unaccountably scared.

'Come on,' says JP. 'What have you got to lose?'

What indeed, thinks Patricia, following him to the car.

CHAPTER 28

Ferragosto continued

Mary is rather proud. She doesn't scream or faint or otherwise disgrace herself. Considering that it is quite forty years since she has been kissed (kissed *in this way*), she thinks she does rather well. In fact, she is amazed at her own behaviour. It is the work of a moment for her hands to snake round Aldo's neck and then she is kissing him back, kissing him as she hasn't kissed anyone since Bobby Preston, that far-off summer in Brighton.

It is Aldo who breaks off and this is because the water is boiling. For Aldo, nothing, not even passion, interferes with food. He tips the ravioli into the water, takes a herb-encrusted salmon from his casserole dish, tips it on to an oval plate, squeezes a lemon over it, scatters it with chopped capers and tosses together a salad in a green glass bowl. All this time, Mary stares at him, feeling her heart pounding beneath her thin, cotton dress. She feels as if she has lost all willpower, all she can do is watch Aldo and, as he seems in perfect control of the situation, that is what she does.

317

They sit down to eat at a wrought-iron table on the balcony. The lemon tree smells sweet in the evening air and a bird sings from a neighbouring terrace. The food is exquisite. The ravioli, just four perfect pieces each, are rich yet subtle, the sweet pumpkin and the salty sausage blending meltingly together. The salmon, with which they drink a crisp white wine, is ambrosial. How can I be eating after what has happened? thinks Mary. And yet she has a second and a third helping of salmon and even has figs and a nectarine to follow. Only when the last fleshy segment of fig has disappeared does Aldo say, 'Now.'

He stands up, holding out his hand to Mary. She goes towards him, knowing that she is trembling. Aldo strokes her arm.

'What are you afraid of?'

'Nothing.'

'Well then.' He kisses her again. Again she kisses him back, twisting her fingers in his thick hair.

Aldo holds her at arm's length, smiling. 'I have wanted to do this for a very long time.'

'You haven't known me for a very long time,' Mary objects.

'Time,' says Aldo magnificently, 'is nothing. Come.'

He takes her by the hand and leads her through the kitchen towards a closed door. She knows, as she has never known anything in her life, that this is the door to his bedroom. It suddenly becomes a monstrous portal, impossible to cross. How will she do it? Will she be turned to stone? But then, somehow, she is through the door. Aldo's bed, neatly covered by a white duvet, looms before her. He kisses her again. This is how it happens, thinks Mary. Somehow she has crossed the line from one sort of woman to another. Now she is going to become the sort of woman who goes into men's bedrooms. The sort who . . . She breaks away because she is crying.

'What is it, Mary?' Aldo strokes her hair.

'I can't.'

'Why not?'

'Because,' Mary almost shrieks, 'I'm going home tomorrow and I'll never see you again.' And she collapses on to the bed and cries in earnest.

Aldo kneels in front of her. 'Is that all? Don't go home then. Stay here and marry me.'

The lights go on as the Alfa crunches up the Castello's drive but the house is in darkness, the heavy oak doors bolted. The sky is black now and the moon shines balefully above the North Tower.

'Do you think the ghost will walk tonight?' asks JP playfully. 'Will he gallop up the drive on his headless steed?'

'Don't,' says Patricia.

The door creaks like an extra in a horror movie. She has walked across this hall in the dark many times, barely noticing the armour and the arched windows and the spectral shadows except to think what clichés they were, how divorced from her knowledge of what the Castello was really like. But tonight is different. Her flesh creeps. It literally creeps as if a cold finger is running up her spine. The moonlight lies in great regular bars on the stone floor. It is all she can do to step through its doom-laden light on her way to the kitchen. Because she is damned if she is going to do this thing without a brandy.

The kitchen is deserted but there are signs of recent occupation. Several bottles of beer are standing by the back door and dirty plates lie in the sink. Olives and cheese and bread are still on the table and a newspaper, neatly folded, lies beside them. Automatically, Patricia starts to tidy up. Matt and Fabio have obviously been here but where are they now? The last thing she wants is for them to walk in on her and JP.

'*Mon dieu.* What are you doing?'

JP stands in the doorway, half amused, half irritated.

'Tidying,' says Patricia through gritted teeth.

'Come on.' JP wraps his arms round her from behind, burying his face in her neck. 'Forget about being in charge, just for tonight. Tonight I'm in charge.'

Fabio and Matt are not far away. They are by the wood store at the end of the drive, both slightly hysterical from the beer and from the whole situation. They feel like commandos on a night operation, like bandits skulking in the hills, like schoolboys playing cowboys and Indians. Matt giggles as he unwraps the firework. Fabio holds a torch as he struggles to read the instructions.

'Not to be used within one hundred metres of human habit-ation,' he spells out.

'That's all right then,' says Matt airily, fixing a stake into the ground.

'What if it hits someone?' says Fabio but he says it dreamily, as if he does not expect Matt to listen.

'It won't,' says Matt. 'Twenty-one hundred hours and counting.'

The procession wends its way up the steep hill to the north of San Severino. Jeremy, full of wine and food, is feeling breath-less before they are halfway up. At his side, Sally skips along like a mountain goat. In front, Don Tonnino swings his incense and chants in a clear, surprisingly strong voice, '*Ave Maria, gratia plena, Dominus tecum, benedicta tu.*'

'*Ave Maria,*' echo his followers, none of them seeming at all out of breath. The priest's young acolyte, holding the cross, stumbles once or twice on the stony ground.

'*Ave Maria, gratia plena, Dominus tecum, benedicta tu.*'

'*Ave Maria.*'

'Jesus,' pants Jeremy. 'It's worse than being back at school.'

'Did you go to a Catholic school?' asks Sally, alight with interest.

'I was brought up a Catholic. Absolute bonus for a writer.'

They have reached the top of the hill now. The statue of the Virgin Mary, lit by hundreds of candles, glows eerily in front of them. Below they can see the lights of San Severino and hear the distant thud of the rock band. It is as if they are looking down on Sodom and Gomorrah. Sally slides her hand into Jeremy's.

'*Ave Maria.*' Don Tonnino is circling the statue, sprinkling holy water. Another acolyte is now holding the incense, swinging it carelessly so the acrid smoke blows right in Jeremy's face. He coughs violently. A large Italian woman standing behind him offers her handkerchief. Jeremy shakes his head, eyes streaming.

'*Dominus vobiscum.*' Don Tonnino is facing his audience.

'*Et cum spiritu tuo,*' they answer.

This seems to be the signal for the little procession to set off again down the hill. Jeremy hears the priest beginning his chant of, '*Ave Maria, gratia plena . . .*' The thought of starting the long trek back, choking all the while on incense, is suddenly very unappealing.

'Let's stay behind for a few minutes,' he says to Sally. 'Admire the view.'

Sally looks delighted.

Matt struggles with the giant firework. 'Can't get it into the ground,' he grunts. 'Bring the torch, Fabio.' Fabio comes over, standing close to Matt so that he can shine the torch on to the luridly coloured paper. Together they push the rocket launcher into the hard earth. Matt is sweating and even the cool Fabio is breathing heavily.

'Nearly there,' says Matt.

Glancing at the illuminated numbers on his watch, Fabio prays that the procession has finished.

Patricia and JP are in her bedroom. She goes to close the shutters but he stops her. 'Leave them.' She obeys.

JP looks at her for a long moment, smoothing the skin around her eyes. 'You look sad,' he says.

'I'm not,' she protests.

'You often look sad.' He kisses her in the corner of each eye. 'Beautiful but sad.'

She stands still, eyes closed. He can see the shadows on her cheekbones, the droop of her mouth. To him, she is all the more desirable for her sadness, for her detachment. You may be able to have her, says a voice in his head, but you will never really know her.

He leans forward to kiss her mouth.

'The Virgin Mary,' says Jeremy, lighting a cigar, 'is a construct of oppressed peoples everywhere. Why is she most beloved by ignorant peasants, like Bernadette of Lourdes or those people in Croatia? Because she offers them an escape from the everyday drudgery of their existence. She ascended *directly into heaven.* She escaped, literally, from this benighted Earth.'

'You understand all this so well,' says Sally, wondering if she dares hold his hand again. 'It's all a mystery to me.'

Jeremy laughs. 'It's a mystery to you, dear Sally, because they want it to be. The Catholic Church with its incense and holy water and chanting. They've made it a mystery because that way they are in control. But I can see through it. I can see through the holy smoke to the pure light of reason.'

And then he is hit by a thunderbolt.

The explosion sends Patricia running to the window. 'What was that?'

'Just a firework,' says JP. 'You said there would be fireworks.'

As if in agreement, other, fainter, explosions echo from the direction of San Severino. The sky is briefly lit by red and gold stars.

'I like fireworks,' says Patricia. They remind her of Clapham Common, of Guy Fawkes Night, of Sean.

'I'll light you up,' says JP coarsely.

He kisses her fiercely now and she responds. They fall on to the bed, his hand is on her breast, the other burrowing under her skirt. She lies back, surrendering, thinking of other nights, other dark bodies looming over hers, of nameless, faceless scufflings and fumblings.

A yellow bolt of moonlight shoots over the bed. At the same time, the first crack of thunder echoes in the hills.

Patricia screams.

CHAPTER 29

What happened next . . .

Patricia screams and finds that she cannot stop screaming. JP sits up, alarmed.

'What's the matter?'

But Patricia just stares at him with wide, unseeing eyes, her mouth open in a seemingly endless scream. Outside, the thunder crashes and the sky is ripped open by lightning. The shutters swing crazily to and fro.

'Patricia, for God's sake!'

He touches her shoulder and, as if this is some kind of trigger, she leaps up and dives for the door. She runs in a hunched, odd way as if she is trying to make herself invisible. Her blouse is still open and she has lost one of her shoes.

JP tries to stop her but she is through the door and he can hear her running down the corridor. Mystified and slightly scared, he follows her. He hears footsteps descending the stairs but, when he goes to follow, Sean the cat is barring his way.

'Out of the way,' says JP, not ungently.

The cat bristles, he swells to twice his size and spits angrily. Another flash of lightning illuminates his narrow yellow eyes.

JP would not have thought it possible to be so spooked by a cat. He actually backs away. It is just the contrast between the normally placid Sean and this spitting, evil-eyed monster. It is as if the world has suddenly turned into some Grand Guignol horror movie. Come on, JP tells himself, think of Napoleon. But Napoleon was scared of cats, he remembers. Gritting his teeth, JP steps over the cat and runs down the stairs.

The front door is open. Rain is falling in solid sheets. Patricia's other shoe is on the doorstep but of Patricia herself there is no sign.

Patricia is running. She doesn't know where and she hardly knows why. She barely even knows who is running. Patricia the efficient forty-year-old hostess or Patricia the terrified ten-year-old, desperate to escape but knowing with a sick certainty that there is nowhere to escape to. She ran away once, she remembers, but the social workers found her and took her straight back to her foster parents. A wonderful couple, people said, all those children they look after. They must be saints. But the moonlight through the window has cut through the years of forgetting, the years of coping and not looking back. Patricia remembers and the memory is enough to make her sob aloud as she runs headlong through the night. Patricia has no idea if Vicky and Bob Hawkins abused all their charges, there was a sullen air of secrecy about the house that made questions or friendships impossible, she only knows that they abused her, nightly, for almost four years.

If she runs now, she will escape. She doesn't notice the rain or the fact that she is barefoot. She hardly notices the thunder; she isn't scared of thunder. She is scared of the moonlight on the bed and the face in the dark. She is scared of waking up and finding that she doesn't exist. So she runs, slipping in the sudden mudslide that has formed alongside the drive, flailing through the trees, twisting, turning (she must be careful, they are cunning), looking back over her shoulder. She runs doubled over, arms across her chest, and the sound of her ragged breathing frightens her. She sees the gates, the stone lions, the road beyond. An owl hoots above her, she sees its glowing, ill-omened eyes. She must get away. She crashes through the trees and finds herself in front of the little wood store at the end of the drive.

Without knowing why, she opens the door. And finds Matt and Fabio kissing passionately, locked in each other's arms.

And, some ten kilometres away, in an apartment block on the outskirts of San Severino, Aldo and Mary lie under the white duvet and smile at each other as the rain drums against the roof.

'Now you have to marry me,' says Aldo.

'Why?' says Mary tartly. 'It's not as if I could be pregnant, after all.'

Aldo strokes her hair. 'You have to marry me because I love you.'

Jeremy lies on the ground, arms over his head. The rocket landed just behind the statue, causing Mary to shudder on her pedestal, extending her arms towards the terrified English couple. The blast knocked them both off their feet and, the next second, the sky exploded in light. Then all was still.

Slowly Sally crawls over to Jeremy and gently lifts one of his hands.

'Jeremy?' she whispers. 'Are you all right?'

Jeremy holds her hand tightly. He can't speak. He wants to tell her that he is all right, he is more than all right, he is joyously, amazingly all right. The world seems suddenly both wonderfully simple and mesmerisingly intricate. It is as if great tectonic plates have shifted in his head and everything negative has faded into nothingness, leaving him with just a blazing sense of certainty and rightness. It isn't just that he believes he has had a vision from heaven and will reclaim his faith and gain great comfort from it; it isn't just that he will stop chasing young girls and realise that he has, for the asking, a kind, intelligent woman who adores him. No, it is better than that.

Jeremy has an idea for his next book.

'I can't marry you,' says Mary sadly. 'I've got to go home tomorrow'.

Aldo sits up. He has a scar on his chest from an old army injury and a tattoo of a Roman eagle on his shoulder. To Mary he looks utterly magnificent. 'Why must you go back?' he asks. 'Have you family that need you?'

Mary considers. Her sister lives in Norfolk and is, in any case, completely absorbed in her own family. She thinks of Joan in Eastbourne and Shirley in Southport. There is no one who will really miss her. Oh, the girl in the library and the man who collects her Kleeneze catalogue may wonder where she has got to. The attendants at the pool might ask what's happened to the old lady who used to swim all those lengths. But there is no one who would really care, no one for whom her absence would be in any way troubling.

'No,' she says. 'I don't have family who need me.'

Aldo gets up and wraps a towel round his waist. He comes to sit next to her, tilting her head so that she looks into his face.

'I have land,' he says. 'Not far from here, near the lake. We could build a summer house. San Severino is too hot in summer. We could build a pool for you. My brother has a boat. At weekends we could sail on Lago di Bolsena. In the winter we could go to the mountains. The mountains of the moon. We could go skiing. I could bake you a *castagnaccio* at Christmas. You should see San Severino at Christmas, Mary. There is a tree in the piazza lit by hundreds of little candles and, on Christmas night, the children sing in front of the crib. They are like angels, Mary.'

'But I can't,' says Mary. 'I can't.'

*

Fabio sees her first. His eyes widen and he breaks away. Matt, hair tousled, eyes unfocused, goes to grab him again but Patricia says, loudly, 'Matt!'

He spins round, an awful look of fear and shame on his face. Patricia wants to tell him that it's all right, that nothing is worth a look like that, but she can't speak. She backs out, her hand in front of her mouth.

'Mum!' shouts Matt. But Patricia has gone. She starts to run back to the house but then she remembers JP and she heads for the trees. She staggers, helter-skelter, through the pine wood. The thunder, which has been still for a few minutes, explodes above her head. Branches crash to the ground and the wind howls in the treetops. Then, just as suddenly, everything is silent. It seems as if even the rain has stopped.

Then she hears it.

Horses' hooves.

JP is seriously worried now. He has searched around the house, has run down to the pool, where the rain is splashing into the lighted water, he has looked in the outhouses, he has called Patricia's name again and again. Now he is back in the house, dripping wet, wondering if he should call the police. When the phone rings, he jumps. Then he has a frantic few seconds trying to find the phone. Finally he remembers Patricia's office and dives inside, grabbing the receiver just in time.

It is Aldo. He is on the bus with the others. Has JP seen Patricia? 'No', says JP, 'she was here but now she's gone.'

'Gone?' repeats Aldo.

'She ran out of the house', says JP, 'I don't know where she is.'

'I'm coming back,' says Aldo.

JP stands still, his hand on the telephone. This was the room where he first really looked at Patricia, saw her neat head bent over her accounts and thought, she's lonely, I might have a chance there. Well, Patricia is clearly not the poised, collected person he thought her. In fact, she is obviously deranged. JP shivers. He feels suddenly very aggrieved. What did he do? Tried to bed a completely willing partner only to have her leap up like a woman possessed and run screaming into the night. And his technique used to be considered quite good in the old days.

He shivers again. He is sure he has caught pneumonia. He should go and have a hot bath and change his clothes. But JP finds himself curiously reluctant to go upstairs. Will the mad cat still be guarding the stairs? The house suddenly seems very big and very old. Room after stone room, miles and miles of echoing corridor, arched windows looking into nothingness, doors opening and shutting, footsteps echoing on deserted landings. He listens. The clock ticks sonorously from the hall. The thunder seems to have stopped. He can hear the wind in the trees and the rain cascading from the gutters.

JP goes to the window. The full moon is like a searchlight and, by its light, he sees, as clearly as, a second ago, he saw the desk and the telephone, the ghost horse, white in the moonlight, and its golden-haired rider, eyes staring, galloping past through the whispering trees.

Patricia stumbles and falls heavily on to the sodden ground. She gets up, sobbing. The hoofbeats are getting nearer. This is it; she is going to die. The Castello is going to get her in the end. She loved it but, all along, it hated her, saw her as an outsider, wants to punish her for her presumption, for trying to escape from her past, for pretending to be so cool and rational, for asking Aldo to entertain the guests with his charming ghost story, for sitting smiling as Dorothy told her story of abuse and buried memory. Patricia's memories have risen from the dead all right and now they are going to kill her.

She has reached the end of the wood. She stumbles out into the open and sees the pool, still floodlit, the water steaming. The thunder rumbles, further away now. Patricia looks back towards the sighing trees and hears the hooves again, drumming steadily on the soft ground. Then, with a tremendous crash of branches, the horse appears, pearly white in the lights from the pool. It wheels on its hind legs and then canters slowly towards her, its rider hatless, blond hair gleaming.

Patricia's legs can no longer hold her. She sinks to the ground. The horse halts, its sides heaving, the rider leans down to her, stretches out a hand.

'Sean?' she says. And faints.

CHAPTER 30

Day 15/16

Sean leaps off the horse which, out of the moonlight, is an ordinary dapple-grey, wild-eyed from its gallop through the storm. He lifts Patricia into his arms. Her eyes open and she stares up at him.

'Sean?'

'Who else?'

'I thought you were the ghost.' And she closes her eyes again.

Leading the horse, he carries her into the house, heading for the kitchen, which is nearest. At the door, he meets Matt and another boy, both very pale and shaken.

'Matt.'

'Dad.'

Even with her eyes shut, Patricia can hear that there is no real surprise in Matt's voice. He must have known all along that his father was nearby.

'Matt, can you take the horse? Put him in the old barn,

where the table-tennis table is. There's some hay in there. He'll be all right.'

'What about Mum?'

'She'll be fine. She's just had a shock.'

Matt disappears, leading the now placid horse. The other boy follows.

Sean carries Patricia into the kitchen and lays her on the wooden settle, covering her with Aldo's apron, which is hanging nearby. Patricia opens her eyes again. Sean looks exactly the same, perhaps with just a few more lines around the eyes. He is wearing a white shirt and jeans, both absolutely dripping, but he seems amazingly relaxed, humming as he moves around the kitchen, putting on the kettle, hunting for biscuits. Without knowing it, she relaxes too.

'What are you doing here?' she asks.

Sean turns, teapot in hand. He smiles. The same old Sean grin, reckless and slightly embarrassed, but now with a hint of something else in it. Sadness perhaps?

'I've been here for a while. I've been staying with Tony.'

'With Tony? We were there the other night.'

'I know. You walked so close by me that I could have touched you. I was on the terrace when you went into supper.'

'Tony didn't say anything. We even talked about you!'

'I know. I made him promise. Don't be angry with him.'

'Did Matt know?'

'Yes. We've been meeting up. I saw him that night at Tony's, in the garden. I've been here too, at the Castello.'

'When?'

He grins again. 'I looked in at your window one night. I thought you were still sleeping in the North Tower. Then I saw some old lady in a flowery dressing gown. Gave me a hell of a shock.'

'Imagine what it did to her.'

'I know. I heard.'

'But where did you go? We looked; there was no trace of anyone.'

Sean looks smug. 'Hey, you're talking to a man who did a circus skills course. I swung down on the rope from the flagpole. When I heard the commotion, I swung myself back up again. Waited on the roof until everyone had stopped flat-footing through the grounds and trotted off back to Tony's.'

'But why?' says Patricia. 'Why have you come back?'

The door opens and Matt and Fabio come in. Matt goes to hug his father. Patricia notices that they are now almost the same height. Fabio stands awkwardly by the door.

In the distance, they hear the distinctive screech of the minibus brakes. The guests have returned.

'I can't face them,' says Patricia, suddenly frantic again. 'Sean, I can't face them.'

'I will go, Mrs O'Hara,' says Fabio. 'I will explain that you have been taken ill. Leave it to me.'

'Who's he?' asks Sean as Fabio goes out.

'The new handyman.'

'Seems like a nice boy.'

You don't know the half of it, thinks Patricia. Aloud she says, 'He's very efficient. He even drives the minibus.'

'Christ! What does Aldo think of that?'

'Aldo likes him.'

'Jesus, he must be good.'

Matt sneezes. Sean turns to him. 'Go and have a hot bath. You're soaked to the skin. What the hell were you all doing wandering in the grounds during a thunderstorm?'

Neither his ex-wife nor his son answers him. Matt mumbles, 'I'll go and have a bath then.' He slinks out, not looking at his mother.

The kettle boils and Sean goes calmly back to his tea-making. Suddenly Patricia feels violently angry towards him. This feeling is so familiar from their marriage that it is like going back in time.

'Sean!' she shouts. 'What the hell are you doing here?'

He turns, wide-eyed and innocent. This look, too, is achingly familiar. He is trying to wrong-foot her, to make her look unreasonable. She steels herself not to smile back.

'I came to see you,' he says.

'But *why*?'

He is silent for a moment, taking his time pouring the tea. Then he says, 'I came to see you but then I lost my nerve. I stayed at Tony's place instead.'

'You lost your nerve?' says Patricia, hearing her voice sounding bitter and sarcastic, another echo from the past. 'When did *you* ever lose your nerve?'

Sean looks at her sadly. The sadness is new. 'I know you think I'm just a lightweight but I have feelings too, you know. That time when you said I was useless . . .'

'I never said that!'

'That's what you meant. Well, I thought you'd be better off without me. It broke my heart to go, though.'

'Well, why did you?' asks Patricia sulkily.

'You told me to.'

'Jesus, when did you ever do what I told you?'

Sean laughs and, surprising herself, Patricia laughs too. It feels as if she hasn't laughed properly for years. Sean passes her a mug of tea. A casual, homely gesture, almost unnoticed by both of them.

'So why did you come back?' Patricia asks again.

'I know we got divorced,' says Sean slowly, 'but I never really felt divorced. I always still felt married to you. Do you know what I mean?'

Patricia nods. She sips the hot tea gratefully. It tastes of England.

The returning guests gather in the hall, shivering and talking in whispers. They all feel, variously, shaken and oddly disturbed. The thunder and lightning, coming in the middle of the festivities, was more frightening than they could have imagined. Then, when Patricia was not at the bus to meet them, they felt abandoned, as if the captain had deserted the ship in the middle of a storm. Aldo, arriving with Mary, huddled under a huge umbrella, immediately took charge. He opened the bus, turned on the heating and rang Patricia. Obviously getting no answer, he rang the Castello. The guests listened to the exchange. They had all assumed that Patricia was with JP but, when they gathered that he had somehow lost her, they were more at a loss than ever. There was a palpable sense of relief as Aldo started the minibus and headed for home. Home, that is, for one more night.

Some of the guests were less troubled than others. Jeremy, for example, sat looking out of the window with a beatific expression on his face, holding tightly to Sally's hand. His mind was whirring, he could almost feel the rusty cogs turning and grinding once more, his fingers itched for a keyboard. Anna, too, felt tense, keyed up. She knew what she had to do. She would do it by email as soon as they got back. She leant forward, willing the bus to go faster. Beside her, Mary, clutching the wet umbrella, prayed that the bus would go slower and slower, that time itself would stop. She hated every minute of the journey; she never wanted it to end.

At the Castello, they were met by a disgruntled and crumpled-looking JP. He had no idea where Patricia was, had been searching the grounds for her, had probably caught his death of cold. Cat and Justin had arrived five minutes earlier and had gone straight to their room. He hasn't seen anyone else at all.

They are all still looking at each other, wondering what to do, when Fabio appears from the direction of the kitchen. He, too, is soaked, his thin shirt clinging, Darcy-like, to his body. But he is as calm and polite as ever. Patricia has been taken ill, a sudden stomach bug, she sends her apologies. She will be fine tomorrow. Can he get the guests anything before they retire to bed? Tea? Coffee? Brandy?

Everyone declines. There is no inclination, tonight, to stay chatting in front of the fireplace. They all drift, more or less silently, upstairs to bed. Only Aldo looks as if he wants to say something but, eventually, just kisses Mary's hand and bids everyone goodnight. He will go home on his Vespa, he says. It has stopped raining.

'Will we see you tomorrow?' blurts out Mary.

'I will drive you to the airport,' replies Aldo. And he is gone.

'But why did you come tonight?' asks Patricia, more calmly. 'And why the horse?' They are sitting at the table. Sean has found old coats for them, hanging in the downstairs closet. They sit huddled up, drinking their tea, like tramps on a park bench.

Sean traces a pattern in the wood of the table. 'Sounds stupid, I know. But I thought I heard you scream.'

'All the way from Villa Stella?'

'I don't know. Sound travels a long way in the hills. Anyway, I heard a woman screaming and I was sure it was you. Tony and all the guests were in San Severino for *Ferragosto*. There were no cars so I just saddled old Dobbin and set off. I'd forgotten what hard-going it was, over all those stony paths.

I'm lucky he didn't break a leg. He did brilliantly, went like a Derby winner.'

'I thought you were the ghost rider on the white horse.'

'Is Aldo still telling that old story? Nothing changes.'

'Some things do,' says Patricia in a different voice.

'Yes,' agrees Sean. 'Some things do.' They are silent for a few minutes and then he says, 'So why were you screaming?'

Patricia sighs. 'Well, I was in my bedroom with . . . with a man . . .'

'The Frenchman? Matt's told me about him.'

'What's it got to do with you?' Patricia flares up. 'You've had plenty of girlfriends since we split up.'

'I haven't . . . that's different.'

'No it isn't.'

'Anyway, what did he do to you, this French bastard?'

'It wasn't him. The moonlight was on the bed and it reminded me of when I was a child.'

'What about when you were a child?'

Patricia takes a deep breath. She sees her bedroom at Bob and Vicky's house ('Aren't they kind to give you a bedroom of your own?'), the curtainless window, the wallpaper with its pattern of overblown roses. For years she has believed that if she thinks of what happened, much less speaks of it, she will somehow cease to exist. Sean leans across to put his hand on hers. 'Patricia, what happened when you were a child?'

Now she speaks in a dull, flat voice, pulling her coat tighter around her. 'My foster parents, Bob and Vicky, they abused me. He sexually abused me. She used to watch. It went on for years. Started when I was ten, only stopped when I got strong enough to fight him off.' She is dimly aware of Sean putting his arm round her, the warmth from his body.

'Jesus, sweetheart,' he murmurs into her hair. 'Why didn't you tell me this before?'

'I don't know,' she says. 'I . . . I didn't want to think about it. I never wanted to think about it. I thought I would go mad if I thought about it.'

'It's OK,' says Sean. 'It's OK now.'

And she finds that she is crying, messy ten-year-old's tears, snotty and unbecoming, all the tears, it seems, that she wanted to shed for herself, for Sean, for the break-up of their marriage, for what happened to her in the bedroom with the flowery wallpaper. She sobs and sobs and Sean cradles her in his arms.

Mary's diary, 15 August, midnight

Today was the best and worst day of my life. The best because now I know that Aldo loves me. The worst because tomorrow I have to leave him for ever. He says I could stay here, marry him, we could build a house by the lake, go skiing in winter all sorts of wonderful, lunatic things. I'm seventy-four, I can't just go and emigrate to Italy and live with a man I've only known two weeks. I can't do it. Everyone would think that I'd gone

mad and, really, they would be right. Seventy-four-year-old
ladies don't do things like that. They do things like going to the
library, using their free bus passes to go to the sales, having tea
in the M&S cafe, playing bingo, doing old-time dancing. They
don't go to bed with Italian men they hardly know. But I did. I
did. I can hardly believe it myself. Not that I did it but that it
was so easy. To think that, all these years, I have thought that
love (well, sex) was some great mystery, some complex puzzle
that I would never be able to decipher, the ultimate cryptic
crossword. But, in the end, what is it? It is something you do
with someone you love. And I do love him and he says he loves
me. He said all sorts of things, wonderful things that I will
remember all my life. I asked for a picture of him so I could
look at it and remember him (I even thought that I would be
buried with it) and he said no, he didn't want me to have a
picture, he wanted me to have the real thing. But I can't have
the real thing, can I? That's ridiculous. Like something that
would happen in a book, not in real life.

For Aldo it is all very simple. I'm seventy-five, he said, I may
live another ten, fifteen years, if I'm lucky. God willing. Do I
want to spend those years on my own or with the woman I
love? He actually said that. The woman I love. There's no time,
he said, no time to get to know each other. At our age we have
to take our pleasures when we can. Why are young people in
a hurry? he said. They've got all the time in the world. But we
haven't.

He got quite angry in the end. He said I was breaking his

*heart. Mine is broken already, smashed, ground into dust.
He has at least been married and had a child but Aldo is
the only man I have ever loved and, after tomorrow, I will
never see him again. We could keep in touch, I said. Keep in
touch, he mocked, a postcard every summer and a card every
Christmas? I'm offering you everything and you want to 'keep
in touch?'*

I cried then. I honestly think that I will cry forever.

In the kitchen, Patricia, too, feels as if she has been crying forever. But, instead of feeling angry with herself as she usually
does on the rare occasions when she cries, she feels dreamy
and relaxed, as if she never has to make another decision as
long as she lives. Sean has made her a second cup of tea and
she wraps her fingers gratefully round the comforting mug.
Sean's arm round her shoulders is comforting too. She can't
remember the last time they sat like this, peaceful, entwined.

'I can't believe you kept it all a secret for so long,' Sean is
saying.

Patricia sighs. 'Bob and Vicky told me that no one would
believe me.'

'Bastards!' Sean's voice is rough, the sleepy Irish accent has
vanished. 'I'll find them and kill them.'

'Vicky's dead,' says Patricia. 'I read it in the papers. "Big-
hearted foster Mum dies".'

'Big-hearted!'

Patricia says nothing, enjoying Sean's rage on her behalf

and surprised to find that her own anger seems mysteriously to have vanished. In its place is only this dreamy sense of relief and a vague pity for the little girl she had been. Jesus, is this the process described by Dorothy? What had Dorothy said? 'I had to go back into myself, into my past and confront what I found there.' Is this what she has done? Has she followed the process described by Dorothy, even if Dorothy's own memories turned out to be false? Could she have been on her own voyage of discovery? Cheaper than an analyst, she thinks wryly.

The door opens soundlessly and Sean the cat enters, checks out his bowl and jumps on the table to do some heavy-duty nagging.

'Where did that cat come from?' asks Sean.

'He's mine,' says Patricia, rubbing the cat's ear. 'Well, he lives here, at any rate.'

'But you're allergic to cats.'

'Not this one.'

'He's very handsome,' says Sean, rubbing the amber fur. 'What's he called?'

'Sean.'

'What?'

'The cat is called Sean. Sean is the cat's name.' And Patricia starts to laugh helplessly.

Sean looks at his namesake, who stares back at him with half-closed eyes. Then he, too, starts to laugh.

'A cat called Sean. Everyone running about the grounds in

a thunderstorm. Aldo letting someone else drive his minibus. What's going on around here?'

'I think Aldo's in love actually.'

'Jesus.'

They are silent for a few minutes. Patricia gets up to feed the cat. Sean puts on the kettle. 'More tea? Or do we dare open a bottle of Aldo's wine?'

'No.'

'He hasn't changed that much then.'

'Everything has changed,' says Patricia, shaking biscuits into Sean's bowl. 'Matt's changed. I've changed. I'm about to go bankrupt.'

'Really?'

'I took out a loan a year ago,' says Patricia wearily, 'and I haven't got the money to pay it back. If the bank forecloses, I could lose the Castello. I've messed everything up.'

Sean comes over to her. 'You haven't messed everything up,' he says gently. 'You've done wonderfully. You've brought up a fantastic son, you've run a successful business. So what if we need money? We'll get it somehow.'

Patricia laughs. 'I've missed hearing you say stupid things like that.'

They stand staring at each other. Patricia notices the grey around the edges of the bright hair. Her demon lover on horseback is turning into a middle-aged man.

'Do you want your stupid husband back?' whispers Sean.

'Yes,' says Patricia. 'Yes, I do.'

Their lips touch. For Patricia it is as if all the years of hurt and anger and secrecy dissolve with that one kiss.

Much later, Patricia comes back down to the kitchen. She can't sleep. Even after everything that has happened, even after the quietly joyous love-making with Sean, she still can't sleep. Upstairs Sean is lying diagonally across the mattress, as immediately relaxed as he was earlier in the kitchen. Patricia felt herself getting pushed closer and closer to the edge of the bed. Eventually she gave up and padded downstairs in search of tea. How many cups of tea has she drunk over the past two weeks? She must cut down a bit. Harder now that Sean is back, he is an even more inveterate tea-drinker than she is. *Is* Sean back? She is sure that he is. The ease with which he moved about the kitchen, the comfortable way that he hugged Matt, the way that he closed her shutters before pulling her down next to him on the bed – they all point to one thing: Sean belongs here. It is his home as much as hers. Didn't they restore it together, peeling away wallpaper to uncover the stone below, pulling up floorboards, knocking down plaster-board walls, cutting away the travesties of the years to expose the castle in all its glory? Renovated, that's the word the estate agents use. Made new again. Can the same thing happen to their marriage? She doesn't know. She only knows that she will be different now, less judgemental. After all, someone who has run out screaming into the night because of a patch of moonlight is not in a position to lecture about restraint and rationality.

Patricia puts on the kettle. The milk is still out from earlier and there are cups and a folded newspaper still on the table. God, she *must* have been carried away to leave the kitchen looking like this. She puts away the cups and gets out her favourite mug, the one with the Rolling Stones lips on it.

'Mrs O'Hara?'

She swings round, nearly dropping her mug.

It is Fabio.

He has changed out of his wet clothes into a T-shirt and cotton trousers. The rain has made his hair fluffier than normal. He looks nervous and extremely young.

'What are you doing up?' asks Patricia. 'It's nearly three o'clock.'

'I wanted to talk to you. I heard you come downstairs.' Fabio's room is on the ground floor.

'What do you want to say to me?' asks Patricia, suddenly feeling hostile. Before Fabio arrived, Matt was just a normal irritating teenager and now . . . Fabio is older than Matt, sure to go away and leave him feeling confused and hurt. And she feels sad, knowing that she would do anything to stop Matt being hurt and knowing, too, that this is impossible.

To Patricia's surprise, Fabio does not answer. Instead he picks up the newspaper and holds it out to her. It is the same newspaper, she notices, with which he dispatched the scorpion yesterday.

'What . . . ?'

'Read it. Please.'

Bemused, she looks down at the thin lines of newsprint. Her written Italian is sometimes a little slow. It seems the same old news: forest fires, celebrity weddings, the same boy missing in Modena, heir to some automobile fortune. The same boy missing . . .

She looks at Fabio.

He gestures towards the paper. 'Car Heir Still Missing' screams the headline.

She looks from the paper to Fabio's handsome face. She thinks of his cultured Italian, his ease around any sort of vehicle, the sadness that somehow never leaves him.

'You?' she says at last.

'Me,' he says, sitting down at the table.

Patricia sits opposite, wondering if this night will ever end.

'I ran away,' says Fabio in Italian. 'My father found out that I am . . . gay. He didn't understand so I ran away. My mother knew, she loved me for what I am, but she died last year. My father, he has great hopes for me. I am the heir, the only son, he wants me to marry and have lots of children, more heirs. He wouldn't mind if I was a womaniser, in fact he'd be quite pleased, but gay? No. Impossible. So I ran away. I thought I would go to some remote village, get a job, try and live a normal life. I have always been so spoilt. Designer clothes, cars, private jets. I just wanted to live like an ordinary person.

So I got on my bike and I rode away. I had no idea where I was going. I stopped at San Severino and I saw the agency's advertisement in the *tabaccheria*. I thought, why not? So.' He spreads out his hands.

'And Matt?'

He sighs. 'I am sorry about tonight. It won't happen again.'

'I don't mind him being gay you know,' says Patricia fiercely. She is not going to let him cast her in the role of another uncaring parent.

Fabio smiles. 'Matt is young. I don't think he quite knows what he is. Tonight, with the storm and the rocket, everything was a little crazy. It won't happen again. Tomorrow I will go back to Modena. Talk to my father. I will make him see that I can still be an asset to him. I learnt that here. I have been a good handyman, haven't I?'

'The best.'

'Well then, I might be of use in a car factory.'

'Why are you telling me all this?' asks Patricia.

Fabio looks at her. He really is extraordinarily handsome, she thinks. 'I am very rich,' he says simply. 'I am my father's heir but I am rich in my own right, from my grandfather's money. Today . . . yesterday was my birthday. I am twenty-one.'

'Congratulations.'

'Thank you.' He smiles. 'Now I am twenty-one I can do what I like with my money. I want to give some to you. I want to invest in the Castello.'

From: Anna Valore
Date: 16 August 2017, 02.55
To: Steve Smith
Re: Hello Sexy

Will you marry me?

From: Steve Smith
Date: 16 August 2017, 02.56
To: Anna Valore
Re: Hello Sexy

You bet!

CHAPTER 31

Departures

It is a beautiful morning. The sky is a clear pale blue, washed clean by last night's rain and in the air there is a faint, a very faint, tang of autumn. Patricia and Matt sit on the edge of the pool, dangling their legs in the water.

'Maybe it was the summer,' he is saying. 'It was so hot, hotter even than normal. And I was bored. I'd lost interest in Elio and Graziano. Suddenly they made me sick with all their talk about the girls they'd screwed ... made love to. I just kept thinking about Fabio. He was like one of the heroes in my book, cool and sure of himself. I kept thinking about the way he looked. Does that make me gay?'

'I don't know,' says Patricia. 'I think there are different rules for people who look like Fabio. I mean, I couldn't take my eyes off him either but that doesn't mean I want to sleep with him. He's young enough to be my son.'

'Would you mind?' asks Matt, kicking his legs so that the water churns up. 'If I was gay, I mean.'

Patricia looks at him. 'Darling,' she says, 'of course I wouldn't mind. It's not anything to do with me, anyway. You know I'll always love you, no matter what.'

'Then why did you run off screaming when you saw us?'

'It was the shock. Not you and Fabio so much. I'd had a fright before that. Then there was the storm and everything. I think I went a bit mad.'

'Maybe I did too.'

'Maybe.'

'Are you going to tell Dad?'

'Not if you don't want me to. It won't make any difference to him either, though.'

Matt kicks his feet some more. There are leaves and insects in the pool, blown there by last night's storm. Normally, Fabio would have cleared them away but Fabio has gone. He left for Modena at first light, leaving a letter for Matt and a large cheque for Patricia.

'Is Dad back for good?' asks Matt.

'For good?' echoes Patricia. Sean is back; that much was decided last night with that first kiss in the kitchen. But is everything going to be perfect from now on? Despite Fabio's money, making the Castello pay its way is going to be hard work. Is the new Sean going to embrace the hard work and stop sliding off to read the *Guardian* in the woodshed? Patricia smiles to herself. Maybe not. But then she looks at her son's face, so open and trusting, despite the shadow of beard on his chin and the new adult look in his eyes.

'Yes,' she says. 'Dad's back for good. Does that make you happy?'

'Yes.'

Patricia smiles at him. The morning sun is warm on her face and, in a few hours, they will have the house to themselves. 'Me too,' she says. 'Come on. I'd better go and make the Last Breakfast.'

Breakfast is a subdued affair. It is as if the guests did all their talking last night. Now, mentally, they are already on their way home. In fact, Dorothy, Rick and Betsy have already left. Rick hired a car and they have driven to the lakes. 'Spending the last of our savings,' said Rick, giving Patricia a bone-crushing hug. 'We'll never forget you or the Castello.' Patricia kisses them both affectionately. She is not sure what she thinks about Dorothy but, in some strange way, she will always be grateful to her. And, no, she will never forget her.

Aldo arrives late. He does not look his usual dapper self. He is wearing a faded T-shirt and his face looks heavy, the lines deep. Patricia supposes that he had a late night last night. Losing sleep is harder when you get older. Look at Mary, she looks positively haggard.

Sam sits silently over his coffee. As he, too, has a hired car, he can leave when he likes but he thinks he will go when the bus sets off for the airport. Then he can wave Anna goodbye and close the door on that chapter in his life. Chapter? Paragraph? Sentence? Life sentence? He supposes he'd better stop thinking in terms of literary metaphors. The course has taught him one thing: he'll never be a writer. It has taught him other things too or, rather, feelings and emotions are slowly sliding into place. He's going to leave London, for one thing. Being a professional Scotsman on this course has reminded him how much he misses his native land. He'll go back to Scotland, to Edinburgh perhaps. Maybe he'll start his own business; he never much liked being a company man. And he'll ask Jenny to marry him. Suddenly he feels a real need to see her again, to sit down and talk to her (something which he realises they haven't done for months, years even). Maybe she won't be opposed to the idea of marriage and, even, children. There are easier ways of being immortal, after all, than writing a book.

JP, too, is quiet. He feels slightly ashamed of how frightened he was last night. To think that he, a cool, intelligent Frenchman, became so traumatised by a bit of thunder and a woman's hysteria that he was scared to go upstairs. Don't forget the mad cat, he tells himself, and the ghost. He is not sure what he thinks about the ghost. On the one hand, he saw it with his own eyes, the wild, white horse, the ghostly rider; on the other, there must surely be some rational explanation. He saw Patricia this morning. She was walking up the path from the pool and Matt was with her. JP waved from his window and came down to meet her. Matt had gone and Patricia greeted him with a smile. She looked pale and tired but somehow translucent, glowing with something he could not identify. She told him that she was sorry about last night, she has always had a thing about storms. To JP's mind, that didn't explain anything – the screaming, the running away, anything. But he had the sense to keep quiet. An extraordinary thing has happened, said Patricia, not looking at him. Her husband has come back. Come back? echoed JP. He thought they were divorced. They were, said Patricia, but they are going to try again. 'Wish me luck?' she said, lifting her chin with a look, half defiant and half ironical, which he found wholly charming. Of course he did. He wishes her all the luck in the world.

JP will go back to Paris, the most beautiful city in the world, and go back to being an indifferent lawyer and the best father he can possibly be. He does not regret his deleted book or, really, his unsuccessful wooing of Patricia. It has taught him one thing: he does need a woman. One who isn't Barbara. Oh, and he's never going to have a cat.

Almost before the guests know it, Aldo is bringing the bus round to the front door and Matt is helping them downstairs with their cases. No, Fabio has gone. He had to go home, a family crisis, he sends his love. Cat is particularly sorry to hear this but she finds the older man who comes to help with the luggage utterly *charming*. My dad, explains Matt. It is not until they are on their way to the airport that Cat realises that this must be Patricia's ex-husband. Where has he suddenly appeared from? she wonders, moisturising her face (air travel is so bad for the skin). Attractive though, quite a twinkle. Cat closes her eyes, consigning the Castello to history.

Mary sits hunched forward, convinced that she is going to be sick. Aldo hasn't spoken a word to her all morning. Last night must have been a dream except that her body feels odd, as if it belongs to someone else. And she still has Aldo's umbrella, buried in her suitcase under three layers of clothes. Soon, it will be all she has to remember him by. She looks back to catch a last glimpse of the Castello before the road turns and it is lost from sight. She knows that she can never come back. How can she ever bear to come back to Italy without Aldo?

'*Arrivederci!*' cry Jeremy and Sally. '*Ciao,* Castello! *Ciao,* Patricia!'

'*Ciao, ciao,*' echo the children, thoroughly over-excited.

Anna, sitting beside Mary, gives her hand a squeeze. 'Sad, isn't it? Saying goodbye.' Mary nods, biting her lip. 'Still, it will be good to get home, won't it?' continues Anna, who, Mary suddenly notices, is positively alight with happiness. Mary agrees dully. How can she compare Anna's homecoming, children flying into her arms, with her own: piles of unopened post, mostly advertisements for stairlifts, and the sour smell her flat gets after a week with unopened windows. She suddenly thinks of Aldo's balcony with the lemon tree. She has a vision of herself and Aldo sitting there, eating Sunday lunch while, below them, San Severino bustles with life.

'Are you all right?' asks Anna. 'You've gone awfully pale.'

They are at the airport. Aldo fetches trolleys and they pile on their luggage: Cat's matching Louis Vuitton, Anna's blue sports bag, Sally's backpack. Aldo carries Mary's old leather case himself. He places it carefully on top of the pile.

'Goodbye, Mary,' he says.

Mary's eyes fill with tears. 'Goodbye, Aldo.'

'I'll never forget you,' Aldo whispers.

The airport car park swims with Mary's tears. She can only nod and, timidly, touch Aldo's hand. She wants to fling herself into his arms, to bury herself in the square chest with the soldier's scar, to cling to him, to never let him go. But she can only smile and turn away, carrying her small Gladstone bag, following Jeremy and Justin and the trolleys. When she does look back, Aldo is gone. She will never see him again.

Patricia is stripping the beds when Myra comes bouncing in to tell her that she is going to marry Gennaro.

'What?' Patricia lets the sheets fall to the floor.

Myra swings on the door (Patricia is always telling Matt not to do this), her eyes shining. She is still wearing her dress from last night and she is holding her shoes in her hand.

'You know how he's always asking me? And I used to laugh and say, one day? Well, last night, at *Ferragosto,* we were talking and he said, "Come to bed with me and see if you change your mind." And I did and I have.'

'Was it that good?'

'Honey, it was better than good. I thought, if I marry him I can have sex like this every night, so I said yes.'

'There's more to marriage than sex,' says Patricia primly.

'Sure,' says Myra, dancing around the room. 'There's a vineyard and a gorgeous Italian man and living in Tuscany and not getting to forty without being married.'

'Well, if you put it like that . . .'

Patricia looks at Myra, whom she has known now for three years. In that time she has seen Myra depressed because of faithless boyfriends, she has seen her elated when her aerobics business first took off and downcast when it finally folded, she has seen her serious, animated, anxious and (twice) drunk. She has never seen her dancing around the room, high heels in hand, giddy, almost crazy, with excitement. Can one night with Gennaro really have wrought such a miracle? Or is it all part of the strangeness of last night, secrets exposed, lovers reunited, identities revealed? If Puck himself, vine leaves in hair, had burst into the room, playing on his pipes and exclaiming about the foolishness of mortals, Patricia feels that she would not really be too surprised.

Instead the door swings open and Matt explodes into the room. His hair is wet; he has been taking advantage of having the pool to himself. 'Mum! Aldo says he's leaving.'

In the kitchen, Aldo is quietly packing away his apron and his special knives. His radio and his *mezzaluna* are already in his bag and his poster of Roma football club has been taken down from the wall.

'Aldo!' Patricia almost sobs. 'What are you doing?'

Aldo spreads out his hands. 'I am sorry. I have to leave.' And he goes on packing the knives, wrapping each one carefully in newspaper.

'But why?'

'I cannot stay here. My heart is broken.' He says it in a matter-of-fact way as if he is reporting a broken piece of crockery.

'Is it Mary?' asks Patricia timidly.

'Yes,' says Aldo and he continues his packing.

'But, Aldo, you can see her again. Invite her back here for a holiday. Invite her for Christmas. This doesn't mean you'll never see her again.'

Aldo turns to her and his face is so tragic that Patricia's bracing words seem to shrivel in the air.

'I will never see her again. So I must go. Everything here reminds me.'

'Call her,' urges Myra. 'Tell her how you feel.'

'I have told her. I asked her to marry me.'

'Take her to bed,' says Myra. 'It worked for me.'

'That too,' says Aldo with great dignity. 'That too I have tried.'

Patricia, Myra and Matt look at each other. Aldo starts to fold his apron into a perfect square. 'It is over,' he says. 'I loved Mary and I asked her to marry me. But she went away. I shall never cook again.'

'Mary?' says Sean, wandering vaguely into the room. He has just come back from returning the horse to Tony Pearce. 'There's a lady called Mary by the front door. A taxi just dropped her off. She's asking for Aldo.'

Aldo drops the knives with a clatter and races out of the door. As one, Patricia, Myra, Matt and Sean follow him. Aldo races up the steps at the side of the house like a twenty-year-old. At the top of the steps Mary is standing, holding her Gladstone bag.

'I'm here,' she says, half laughing and half crying. 'But my luggage has gone to Gatwick.'

'No matter,' says Aldo, sweeping her into his arms. 'I buy you a whole new wardrobe.'

'And your umbrella,' comes Mary's muffled voice. 'I packed your umbrella.'

'When we are married,' says Aldo, kissing her, 'the sun will shine always.'

Patricia and Sean look at each other.

'A happy ending,' says Sean.

'The only kind,' agrees Patricia.

Publishing News

Jeremy Bullen, best-selling author of *Belly Flop,* is publishing a new book in the spring, his first for twenty years. *The Virgin on the Mountain* is the story of a man's religious conversion while staying in a remote Italian mountain village. Bullen says, 'It's very different from my previous work but then I'm a very different person.' Film rights have been sold.

Seventy-five-year-old first-time author Mary McMahon

says of her fictional inspector, Frank Malone, 'He's a cross between Sherlock Holmes and Eeyore.' Three Inspector Malone books are being published and TV rights have been sold. Graham Norton, Ardal O'Hanlon and Robbie Coltrane have all reportedly expressed interest in playing the misanthropic policeman. Ms McMahon, who has recently married and emigrated to Italy, says that living in a Tuscan idyll will not stop her writing about life in 1950s London. 'If I wrote about my real life,' she says, 'no one would believe it.'

It's Different for Girls looks, at first sight, to be another slice of chick-lit. But there is one important difference in the debut novel by Brighton mother-of-two Anna Valore. This book is written from the man's point of view and details the struggle of house husband Dave to look after his children and cope with the demands of his high-flying partner Sue. Witty, tender and surprisingly shrewd.

Announcements

BIRTHS

To Justin Ferris and Catherine Ferris-Merry a daughter, Siena Caterina. A precious sister for Sasha and Star.

Acknowledgements

Special thanks must go to my niece Elly Whitehead who, during the course of one long Tuscan afternoon, helped me come up with almost the entire plot for *One Summer in Tuscany*. Thanks also to Alex, Juliet and Charlotte for their suggestions. Hope Charlotte approves of the love scenes.

Thanks also to my nephew William Lewington for telling me about the cats' forum and for being the perfect guide to Rome. Thanks must also go to Roberta Battman for checking my Italian.

Thanks to my agent Tif Loehnis and my editor Mary-Anne Harrington for their continued faith in me. Thanks to everyone at Janklow & Nesbit and Headline Review for all their hard work on my behalf.

Love and thanks always to my husband Andrew and to our children Alex and Juliet. This book is for them.